Trillion is the New Billion:
Better Than Even
By Jim Flynn

I can't complain but sometimes I still do,
Life's Been Good to Me So Far

Joe Walsh 1978

Other books by Jim Flynn

Trillion is the New Billion Series:

Book One: Losing Lola

Book Two: The Bitcoin Gambit

Humor Books

Be Sincere Even When You Don't
Mean It

Hit Your Second Shot First

See all books and formats at:
Jimflynnsix.com

Below are the Main Characters.
One Main Character will be introduced
toward the end of the book but is not listed here.

Austin, Texas

JR Johnson	Main Character
Barbara Jean Parker	His wife
Cletus and June Parker	Barb's parents
Tommy and Alice	Hands at Barbara Jean's Ranch

Fort Meade, Maryland

Toni Anne Laudano	Head Civilian Cyber Command
General Goldstein	Commander, U.S. Cyber Command
Gabrielle McHugh	U.S. Army officer
Admiral Stockbridge	Goldstein's replacement

Washington, DC

President	President of the United States
Chan Wheeler	President's Chief of Staff
Congressman Safi	Chairman of House Intelligence Committee
John Alteiri	Media Consultant to Fasi

Moscow

The Lider	President of Russia
Colonel Nihisky	Chief of Staff to Lider
Oleg Turgenev	Oligarch
General Kuznetsov	Head of FSB

<u>U.S.</u>

Sierra Quinn   Assassin, former NYC
                                Detective
Debbie and Nancy   Russian sleeper agents

<u>Minsk, Belarus</u>

Sergey Kravanesko   CEO, Network Designs
Boris Kravanesko   Son of Sergey
Andrey Schmoltz   Head Programmer, Network
                                Designs

<u>NYC</u>
John "Wishbone" Ives   Independent IT Contractor

Yesterday

That got their attention. Even over an airplane radio there's a certain timbre in people's voices when they think you are flying a plane that is carrying an unstable atomic bomb with the intention of landing at their airport, you have no experience as a pilot, and you're arriving in the middle of a hurricane.

Chapter One
Spicewood, TX
Barbara Jean Parker's Ranch
A month ago

Did you ever lose $1.5 *billion*?

I don't mean some rogue trader losing a billion or so of his investment firm's money. I mean $1.5 billion of your own money.

And I'm not talking about some super-rich high tech company founder having his stock go down one day so his theoretical net worth goes from $150 billion to $148.5 billion. I mean your personal investment account being worth $1.5 billion and having it go to $0. That's not accurate. Due to some transaction fees with the brokerage firms I dealt with, I owed a few dollars. I had to pay them so my accounts would be $0.

Professional interviewers, Oprah, Mike Wallace, Larry King always asked, "So, how does it feel to win the Academy Award, or how does it feel to be sentenced to death for a crime you didn't commit?" Bob Dylan sang, "How does it fee-eel?..."

It's a great question. So how *does* it feel to lose $1.5 billion?

I know what it feels like to lose $1.5 billion, but nobody ever asked me what it felt like, because not many people knew I lost that money. The people who did know: the President of the United States, and some who work for U.S. Cyber Command, and the Russian President and his security lapdogs, the FSB. Most Americans still think of the FSB by their old name, KGB. The U.S. President and Cyber Command didn't seem to care, and the Russians were happy. Then again, the Russian government lost $14 trillion, that's trillion with a "T", that same exact second, and that made *me* happy. But not one and a half billion of my own personal money happy.

My new wife didn't know that I had that much money, or that I'd lost it. But she thought I had a lot more than my current balance. I'll explain as we go along.

That wasn't the worst of it. I made the money over a few days and was going to donate the profits to a charitable trust, minus my initial investment. But the $1.5 billion included my initial investment, so now I was broke.

8

Broke is relative. I still lived in comfortable circumstances, had substantial real estate that I could sell, and I recently married a beautiful and wealthy woman, Barbara Jean Parker. But I never had to worry about money. And now I did. I thought things would improve from here, but Mr. Prep School/ Wall Street/Charitable Trust endower was going to find out a few things.

So, how *does* it feel to lose $1.5 billion? It feels bad. Did you ever lose your wallet? Imagine the wallet had $1.5 billion in it. Let's start at that point. But how bad could things get?

My new wife is Barbara Jean Parker. I often call her "Sweetie", but she says I call all females that I like, including her horse, and her dog "Sweetie", just so I won't have to remember their names. She might have a point there. I do use it as a sincere term of endearment.

As Barb and I were preparing for our recent marriage, the offices of JR Johnson moved from Austin to Spicewood, Texas. By the offices, I mean one person with a laptop and a cellphone. I was the sole employee of JR Johnson Money Management, so named because that happened to be me.

The two towns are 35 miles apart. That's around 400 in Light Years. Austin is a lively city. On Barbara Jean's ranch in Texas Hill Country, it was so quiet you could hear the heat rising off the sunbaked earth, interrupted once in a while by the whining of the wheels of a farm truck going down the highway in the distance.

Out the window of my home office I could see a long way into the 100 or so acres of rolling semi-arid property. Barb raised some Black Angus cattle with the help of husband-and-wife team Tommy and Alice, who had a cozy living space attached to the barn which was about 100 yards from the house.

Barbara Jean and I lived in the main house, an adobe mansion. The one-story home had thick masonry walls; a pair of hand carved walnut front doors with big black cast iron hardware suitable for a castle behind an overhang that let you sit outside shielded from the sun. The terra cotta tiled living room with a two-sided fireplace was big enough to comfortably host a party of 100.

The place was built by Barbara Jean's foolish first husband, who after making a fortune in the oil business ditched Barb for

9

a younger woman with fake boobs, fake hair, fake eyelashes, fake teeth, fake skin. Who knows what other parts might have been refurbished? I never examined her closely and didn't want to. Barb was 100% genuine real woman. I have checked *her* out extensively. The former hubby had to give Barb half his money and the house and ranch.

Barb had some quarter horses in the barn. Raised on a ranch and on a horse's back before she could walk, Barbara Jean raced around like a trick riding cowboy in the old western movies and was trying to teach me. As I now understand it, when you're riding and the horse starts to go fast, your butt is supposed to go up when the horse goes up, and down when the horse goes down. I had the timing a teeth-rattling reversed. Because of my riding style I was disrespected by Barb, Tommy, Alice, and the horses. The long, gaunt, taciturn Tommy spit a lot when he watched me ride.

Being petrified and stiff is not a good approach to horseback riding. Horses can sense your fear and it makes them nervous.

"Relax," people tell you.

It feels like I'm high enough to be on the back of an elephant, and the horse could kill me if he wants to, and there's no steering wheel or brakes. But these moments of terror did help me to temporarily forget all the money I had lost.

With the exceptions of the moments of terror on horseback, and wonderful intimate time with Barbara Jean, the lost money hung over me like an evil, corrosive fog. I knew I had to clear the fog but wasn't brave enough yet to face the pain of doing so.

Barbara Jean had initially wanted us to get married on horseback. She asked Tommy his opinion. He did speak that time, a major outpouring for him. "You'd have to drug him. And drug the horse."

Barb didn't want to drug the horse, so we got married with our feet on solid ground. My wife's favorite horse Molly attended the nuptials, even though her two grown children didn't. It was a casual event. Barb wore custom tailored blue jeans and her cowboy hat. Barbara Jean's parents were there, along with Tommy and Alice and a Justice of the Peace, and Molly the Horse. When the three-minute wedding ceremony concluded the people adjourned to the house and Barb's father

10

Cletus drank vast quantities of Jack Daniels, making it a normal day for him.

After the first few blasts of bourbon the old man went into his standard political rant.

"I'm telling y'all, this country is going to Hell in a Handbasket! Why every damn Democrat President and most of the recent Republican Presidents have been nothing short of card-carrying Communists! Even Reagan was leaning pinko by the time he left."

He went on from there. I'd heard this speech before, but not as many times as Barb and her wonderful mother.

Cletus thinks I'm a sissy boy because I can't ride a horse worth a damn and don't know my way around firearms. His family came to Texas in the mid 1800s and scratched out a meager living ranching before someone discovered their property happened to have a few million barrels of oil percolating beneath the ground.

I'm convinced that Cletus Parker thinks that the Good Lord put his family on that property that turned out to have all that oil as part of the Grand Scheme. I wanted to point out to Cletus that he was worth more money than most people would ever dream about, because his family lucked out to buy property sitting on vast oil reserves 50 years before anybody ever thought oil might be useful, or even suspected it was there. This country and its oil depletion allowance tax laws had allowed his family to get rich, and what he described as working hard was pretty much getting drunk every day.

He continued his diatribe at our tiny wedding reception. "I'm telling you this country is going to Hell! How much dadgum foreign aid do you think we paid to socialist European countries last year?' he said to no one in particular.

"I don't know. Exactly how dadgum much was it?" I asked. Barbara Jean and her mother glared at me. They knew to never speak to Cletus during one of his monologues; it only provoked him to go on longer. He was three quarters drunk and wound up enough, so he didn't realize I was making fun of the way he spoke.

"Well, goldang it, exactly I don't know… but it was a hell of a lot. Billions. Those pissants should be paying us, for keeping them safe." Cletus said. June and Barbara Jean ignored him.

11

June is a smaller, older version of her beautiful daughter. That's a good omen for me, assuming Barb and I stayed married. I felt sorry for the long-suffering June, having to put up with her blowhard husband every day. I guessed that the last time June and Cletus had sex was a few Presidents ago, but you never know what people do behind closed doors.

"Honey, you look so lovely today," June said to Barbara Jean, reaching out to hold her hand. "And such a handsome husband."

She was right. I mean about Barbara Jean.

Barbara Jean was the sole surviving child, and she was going to inherit. Her brother died young. It's nice being married to a gal who's already rich and in line to own a bunch of oil wells. Cars aren't going all electric just yet. But I don't want to be some hanger on, I want to have my own money.

Just a while ago I had $1.5 billion. About $50 million of it was initially mine; what I started with. The profits I was going to give away. One day a few weeks back, that big number was flashing at me on my computer. I was about to sell. Then I had to hurry out and save Barbara Jean from getting murdered, and almost got murdered myself, so it wasn't your standard financial transaction.

When it was time for Cletus and June to leave, the old man handed his car keys to June and let her drive. Cletus sat in the passenger seat of the big old Cadillac Escalade and fully reclined so he could sleep it off while June drove from Spicewood back to their ranch outside of Crawford, Texas. The petite June looked comical behind the wheel of the massive SUV, like she was a kid driving an eighteen-wheeler.

Barbara Jean had explained to me that Cletus had too many DWIs for even his buddy the County Judge to fix for him, and he'd better not get caught behind the wheel with the Escalade in another ditch after he'd been at the Jack Daniels, so he had surrendered to the inevitable of letting someone else drive him when he was hitting the sauce. Cletus was stubborn, but this solution was a lot better than not drinking, gosh durn it!

By the way, Crawford, Texas is the home of former President George W. Bush. Don't mention that to Cletus unless you have some time to spare, and no high regard for the retired President.

12

When Cletus and June left, it was just Barbara Jean and me standing there in front of her house. The sun was going down over the rolling hills, and you could hear cattle mooing. I think you call it mooing. Cows moo, so I assumed cattle mooed also. Sounds the same. It wasn't a question I'd bring up to Tommy the ranch hand, who would probably give me a blank stare, say nothing, and spit on the ground.

The air was still, and it was starting to cool down. Tommy, Alice, and Molly were back in the barn.

I was holding hands with my beautiful wife of about two hours, and she turned and smiled at me. Barb has one of the world's great smiles, and she's one desirable lady. Fellas, imagine the shapely beautiful blue-eyed blonde you dreamed of when you were a young lad. Barbara Jean looks like that. She wears old fashioned bright red lipstick that accentuates her pearly whites. Barb might be the best-looking woman in the United States wearing a real work-a-day cowboy hat. She's sexy just standing still and even better when she walks. Did I mention she's quite shapely?

Barb can put her thumb and forefinger in her mouth and whistle loud enough to get a horse's attention at 100 yards. I wish I could do that.

I'm okay looking. People don't turn away in revulsion when I walk past. Mid-forties, salt and pepper hair, lanky. My late mother said I was ruggedly handsome, but she tended to exaggerate. And after I became the black sheep of the family, she never had anything good to say about me.

On one level you could say I was happy and content. But on another level that $1.5 billion was gnawing at me. I wanted to get it back. Not so much the $1.5 billion, I wanted my own money back, the $50 million. And I hadn't told Barbara Jean about losing the money yet.

"Barb, we have to talk about money sometime soon," I said.

"You can never have enough." She smiled.

The day after we got married Barb took Tommy and Alice to the Feed Store. Barb has a Ford F-150 with a Crew Cab, which she alternates driving with her yellow standard shift Corvette roadster, and she drives any motor vehicle as though it was a horse she was riding in a barrel race at the rodeo. There's always a lot of gravel in her wake. Feed Store runs were made

13

in the truck, and took a while, for the store was the social and intellectual hub of Spicewood, where the local glitterati congregated, some in bib overalls.

I was sitting in my office just off the giant living room when I saw a dark blur going past the window. It was Enduro the stallion running free. The horse must have gotten out of his stall somehow.

This happens when you live on a ranch. Barb keeps a halter with a rope on it hanging in the coat closet just for this situation. A halter is the thing you put over a horse's head, it fits behind the ears and around the muzzle, and with a rope attached to it gives you leverage to lead the horse around. But first you have to catch the horse.

I was getting to the point where I felt comfortable around the horses. Enduro was the exception. Unlike all the other horses, I was afraid of him. Stallions can be aggressive and ornery. He had kicked me once, and bit me right in the stomach, which left a black and blue mark the size of a pizza. That made Barb laugh when I got undressed for bed.

But you couldn't just let a horse run around. Even though the property was fenced in, it was dangerous for a horse that is accustomed to being controlled to roam over hazardous terrain. So, I had to go out and catch Enduro and bring him back to his stall. I went to the refrigerator and grabbed some pieces of carrot, then took the halter and headed out the door.

I had seen other horses in this situation before. They enjoy their freedom and run around for sometimes an hour before they let you catch them. They are playful. The horses let you get close, then run away. Eventually they give in to wanting the carrot you have in your hand. I imagined having to walk all over this one hundred acre ranch before I would capture Enduro.

To my surprise, Enduro had stopped maybe 200 yards from the house, eating at the sagebrush. When he saw me and tried to run, it was evident he was stuck. There's an evil vine that grows in wild sage beds and it wraps around the horses' legs sometimes. Even the powerful stallion couldn't free himself, because the vines tighten like a bamboo finger trap if you pull away in a panic. As I got closer Enduro started whinnying and vainly trying to buck. I was experienced enough to not approach from the rear, in the kicking radius. When I walked

14

around to the front of the horse, I could see what was causing the panic. There was a big rattlesnake two feet in front of Enduro.

Enduro and I had this much in common; we're both terrified of snakes. My heartrate shot up to around 10,000, so much that I was dizzy. In the last year I'd been shot at and hit in the head twice in one day with a crowbar, entrapped in a 55-gallon drum, and this was worse. There wasn't time to go back in the house and get a gun. I picked up a good-sized rock. The snake seemed focused on the horse, so I smashed the rock as hard as I could on the rattler's head, and it worked! Killed the damn thing. To make sure I got another rock with a sharp edge and repeatedly slammed it down on the snake's body until I cut the rattler in half. That felt good. When I was sure the snake was dead, I stepped back and had to do some deep breathing until I calmed down.

Then I had to figure out how to pacify the horse and get it loose from the vine. His nostrils and eyes were huge, and his dark skin glistened with sweat. I decided to give Enduro a piece of carrot. This did the trick. It took me a few minutes to get the vines off his front left leg, then he stood quietly and let me slip the halter over his head. I fed him the other carrot pieces.

Only then did it occur to me that as I was gloveless and reaching through and pulling the vines, there might have been another rattlesnake or two under there. I looked at my hands. No fang marks. Not having a clue works out sometimes.

I was leading Enduro back to the barn when the truck drove in. Barbara Jean stopped and she, Tommy and Alice got out. The husband and wife ranch hands always reminded me of the couple in the painting *American Gothic*. Tommy wears glasses and is bald under his cowboy hat. All that was missing as they stood next to each other was a pitchfork for Tommy to hold.

I explained what had happened. Tommy wasn't in the position to give me any grief, or even to spit, because the barn was his responsibility, and it was probably due to his not properly latching Enduro's stall that the horse got out in the first place.

Tommy held out his hand as if to take the halter rope. "I'll put him back," he offered.

15

"Nah, that's okay, I'll do it," I said. Then I spit on the ground. I made up for inexperience by spitting real hard. I didn't want to drool one out of the side of my mouth. I'm not in Tommy's class as a spitter, but the message was delivered. It was about time I started marking my territory. I had to show Tommy and the other feed store types that I was only going to take so much of their passive aggressive condescending crap. Screw them. I had already lasted a lot longer on this ranch than Tommy would have lasted in my old job on the trading desk at the Big Investment Firm.

Enduro let me take him back to his stall, and was calm when I led him in, took off the halter, and bolted the stall door. I felt that we now understood each other better, that he and I were building a mutual respect.

Chapter Two

The next morning as I went to pet Enduro he tried to bite me. He didn't try all that hard, and I blocked him with my hand, so maybe we were making progress in becoming friends. But I had a bigger problem that hung over me. I had to wait all day to finally face Barbara Jean and explain the financial situation.

Barb and I had never gone over finances down to the level of who had what. She had a lot and she thought I had a lot. I figured that I would use the period of goodwill generated by saving Enduro from the rattlesnake to break the news to her about the $1.5 billion.

I had the knowledge advantage over Barb because I handled some of her money, but I never manage more than one third of the client's assets. I had a good idea how much Barbara Jean had. She didn't have a clue about my finances. She just thought I was a rich guy.

We sat at the kitchen table after our light supper. Barbara Jean ate a well-balanced diet, but small portions to keep her killer figure just right. She was a good influence on me.

"Barbara Jean, I have to tell you about the money situation," I said. "It's complicated."

"I've been waiting. I figured you'd tell me when you were ready. Let me tell you about me first. It's simpler, Barb said.

"Okay."

"Of course, you know the money you manage for me. Then I have a load of tax-free bonds with the other guy, and a third of the money in bank accounts and CDs, things like that. You told me to spread it around," she said.

I'm not a good listener. She went on for a while. I wasn't paying careful attention.

Barb said. "So, how much do you have?"

"Right now, a lot less than I had a month ago," I said. I needed to lay the foundation to support the construction of my complex tale. "Remember when I came out here when those people were going to kill you?"

"What kind of question is that? Of course, I remember," she said.

17

"Well, when you called, I had run the account up to $1.5 billion. I was about to sell, but I forgot to hit the enter key on the computer when I rushed out of the house to drive here," I said.

"How could you do that?" she asked.

"The next day when I woke up in the hospital, the $1.5 billion had turned into $1.50," I explained.

Barbara Jean laughed. "C'mon," she said.

"I'm not kidding. After transaction fees, I had to pay to get my account balance up to zero." I said.

"You're serious?" she asked.

"Yup."

"So, one day you were worth $1.5 billion and the next day your investments were worth nothing?"

"Yup."

When we sat down to have supper, I was sure that Barbara Jean loved me. It was very quiet now at the kitchen table. You could hear the hum of the air conditioning. I seemed to remember both of us recently taking vows that included 'for richer and for poorer', but in real life who says love isn't conditional?

"You're not telling me that you lost *my* money, are you?" she said.

"No, no I'd never do something like that with the money my clients trust me with. It was just *my* money," I explained.

"Was this part of that Bitcoin nonsense?" Barb finally asked.

"Yeah. I haven't explained what happened because I wasn't allowed by the government to tell you until we got married," I said.

Chapter Three
Moscow

Sierra Quinn couldn't believe this was happening.
She was about to enter the apartment of the President of Russia. He now preferred people to address him as "Lider," meaning "The Leader" in Russian. The person who had called her to arrange this meeting had given her instruction on how to act and gone over the pronunciation. "LED-yuh" was as close as an American could come to saying the title.

It wasn't the average dull life for the daughter of a beat cop from Queens. She had followed her father into the NYPD, became a detective and then been attracted by the dark side. Sierra Quinn became a murderer, someone who killed people for money while she was on the Police Force. She didn't have a regret, Quinn liked killing people, and the tax-free income appealed to her. She operated so far outside the norms of the system that she might never have been caught. Then she got involved with a couple of very lucrative killings paid for by a hedge fund manager who was running a Ponzi scheme.

The second of the well-paid killings was the shooting of movie star Lola Madison. Her boyfriend JR Johnson, along with Lola's bodyguard had killed the Ponzi scheme creep. The Wall Street crook had also run afoul of the Russians, who had been impressed with the way Quinn had handled herself. Oleg Turgenev, the head of the Russian criminal element in New York had helped Sierra flee the United States.

Robert Stanton Banks, the now deceased Ponzi scheme operator had been stealing money and used it to build a resort in Bali, Indonesia. Banks planned to leave the U.S. and settle under a new identity, having chosen that country because Indonesia had no extradition treaty with the United States.

After Banks died, the ownership of the resort was in limbo. Turgenev had gone to the bank in the Cayman Islands that had aided Banks in laundering money to pay for the resort and had convinced them to sell the property to him. His very effective method of persuasion was to threaten the bankers and their family members with gruesome death. Specifically, he threatened to put them while still alive, into 55-gallon drums, take them out to sea, and dump them overboard. Turgenev had

19

a well-earned reputation of carrying out such executions. Thus motivated, the Cayman Island bank sold the Indonesian property to Turgenev for $1.

Turgenev then installed Quinn as the president of the resort. She had no real duties, and Turgenev had just parked her in Bali, waiting to use her talents in murderous operations.

Turgenev and Quinn had most recently been involved in the Lider's failed plot to corner the Bitcoin market. But Quinn had nothing to do with the planning of that effort. She didn't understand Bitcoin, she just tortured and murdered people as ordered by Turgenev. All their efforts were in vain. When the Bitcoin episode came crashing down, she went back to Bali. Then a call came summoning her to Moscow.

Quinn had thought Turgenev would be calling her, but she hadn't heard from him. Instead, it was a new person, Colonel Nihisky, who instructed her to travel from Indonesia to Russia.

Quinn stood in front of the building in Moscow. She had no idea why she had been summoned, and had considered trying to flee, but knew that was impossible. There was no place on earth Quinn could hide from The Lider and his intelligence apparatus. It was better to come to Russia and face whatever consequences awaited her.

'Apartment' was far too humble a title for the big building. Maybe something was lost in translation. The edifice was an imposing two story ornate stone structure that looked like it was built in the 1800s, and if in New York could have passed for the home of, say, the late J.P. Morgan. The stone blocks were in layers, with indentations at the top of each layer, so it looked like any self-respecting rock climber could free hand from the street to the roof. There were Greek columns bordering the upper floor windows. Each window was topped by a stone carving centered with what looked like a coat of arms.

Two towering, uniformed guards stood flanking the front door. Quinn didn't know one Russian uniform from another, but these men were dressed in what might well be costumes of the toy soldiers in The Nutcracker Suite. They looked preposterous.

The guards gave what Quinn thought of as a rifle salute when she approached the doorway, stared straight ahead, and let her pass in the door. Inside was a man dressed in what looked like a Russian Army officer's uniform, the kind a high-ranking officer

20

would wear on a normal workday, but the crown of the hat was maybe twice as high as an American officer wore, it looked clownish. So far everything in Russia looked to Sierra like this; the uniforms, the signs, the cars were as though the country was trying to imitate the West but couldn't let go of their old heritage.

"Good evening Miss Quinn," the officer said. "I am Colonel Nihisky, aide to the Lider. Go right up the stairs, and see his secretary, The Lider is waiting for you in his office."

Quinn had been through stressful situations in her life that normal people would never experience, including shooting people who were trying to kill her. But she had never been as nervous as she was when the Lider's secretary opened the door to escort her into the office of The Russian President. Her contact and boss, Oleg Turgenev had told her that the Lider was a man who did not handle disappointment well. And the mission that Turgenev had sent her on was a spectacular failure that caused massive public humiliation, and huge financial losses to the Lider.

Sierra Quinn had heard stories of what the Lider had done to people who failed him. She half expected to be shot immediately when the doors to his office opened, but instead the Lider stood up and smiled at Sierra as his secretary closed the door behind her, leaving Quinn and the Lider alone in the room.

Quinn froze, but the Lider looked cordial and walked around his massive desk and gestured for Quinn to approach. When she got a reasonable distance from him, he stuck out his hand and they shook in a business-like manner. He gestured and spoke, "Please have a seat."

She sat in an ornate chair that looked like something that should be in a palace. It was uncomfortable. Maybe that was intentional. As Quinn surveyed the huge chamber, she realized that every item in the place looked like it belonged in a palace.

"This was the home of the last Czar's uncle, the Grand Duke of Moscovy. It has been repurposed for service in our Constitutional Democracy," The Lider gestured around the room.

Yeah, repurposed. What, did you get new drapes?

21

"I use this as my workspace. The office of the Russian President is in another building. I only use that for formal meetings. I hope that I speak English well enough that we can understand each other," he said

"Sir, you speak excellent English," Quinn answered.

"Thank you. I received many years of training as a youth. I like to think I speak English well. But sometimes I pretend that I cannot, when I'm in diplomatic situations, which I find to be a benefit. You understand?" the Lider asked.

"Yes sir."

"Turgenev told me you were an attractive woman, but he understated your beauty," the Lider said. "Please stand up."

She did.

"Turn around for me," The Lider said.

Quinn complied.

Where is this going? When Quinn was first on the NYPD, she complained to her Lieutenant that she was being sexually harassed by all the men she worked with. It was different times. The Lieutenant had told her that it didn't help that she was beautiful and built like "Blondie in the comic strips. Except you have dark hair."

You exude sexuality," The Lider said.

"Thank you," Quinn said. *Who was she going to complain to about The Lider sexually harassing her? And she did enjoy sex.*

"Have you seen Turgenev since your last mission?" he asked.

"No sir, I haven't seen him," she answered.

"As you know, I suffered a major public humiliation. I cannot have something like that happening again. Have you heard stories about executions, torture, beheadings happening to my underlings when they fail to carry out assignments?" he said.

Quinn didn't know how to answer.

"Those stories are true. I find that these… unfortunate…incentives help my surviving team members to focus." The Lider smiled and pointed his finger at her. "You were not to blame for the failure of the last mission. But Turgenev was too complacent. He was to blame. I *have* seen Turgenev."

The Lider stood up and raised his right hand to silence Quinn. He bent over, and from behind a curtain produced a huge glass jar which he placed on his desk with a thump. Inside the jar was

22

the unmistakable embalmed severed head of Oleg Turgenev. His mouth and eyes were opened in perpetual terror.

Chapter Four
Spicewood, TX

Finally, Barbara Jean spoke, "So you have no money?"
"Not exactly. But I lost all the money in my investment account, which was about $50 million, then I had temporary profits of over $1.4 billion, which added up to about a billion and a half when I ran out the door with the gun to save you," I said.

She folded her arms across her chest. "In the circle I run in, what you're describing is *no money*. All hat and no cattle." From the look on her face, I sensed that I wasn't going to get lucky that night. She stared at me.

"The circle you run in? You mean those intellectuals you hang out with at the feed store?" I asked.

"You lost all that money by forgetting to push a button?" she asked.

"Yeah. Remember I was going to save you...those people were going to kill—"

"You would have $1.5 billion if you had pushed the button?" she asked.

I nodded.

"How long would that have taken?" Barbara Jean asked.

"Two seconds," I answered.

"How long did it take you to make that money?" she asked.

"The new trading money? About four days," I said.

"You made over a billion in four days, then you didn't sell," Barb stated. It wasn't a question.

"Do remember that I saved your---"

She held her hand up. "So you married me for my money? Why didn't you tell me this before we got married?" Barbara Jean asked.

She wasn't listening. Barb was acting like I tricked her, so I could marry her for her money "Hey, let me tell you the whole story. What's the matter with you? Can I start at the beginning?"

She refolded her arms and glared at me.

24

Chapter Five
Fort Meade, MD
U.S. Cyber Command Headquarters

Toni Anne Laudano had a job that would never be done. She had an official title, but her real title was Smartest Person working for U.S. Cyber Command. Parade Magazine once did a story on the brightest people in the world and were going to include Toni Anne until Cyber Command got wind of the upcoming piece and insisted that she not be included for National Security reasons.

Toni Anne enjoyed being considered one of the smartest people on earth. She responded to the quashing of the magazine story by asking the head of Cyber Command, General Goldstein, "what, you don't think the fuckin' commies know about me?"

Because she was so important at her job, the General tolerated outburst like that from Toni Anne. He responded, "we don't want to rub their noses in it," and that was that.

Cyber Command's mission statement was to achieve and maintain Cyberspace Superiority. Toni Anne had just engineered her organization's biggest triumph, tricking Russia into using their most advanced cyber weapon in a futile attempt to corner the Bitcoin market, which brought about the collapse of that cryptocurrency and at the same time humiliated the Russian President. That had been a good day.

But in Cyber World there are many enemies of the United States. Russia, China, Iran, India, and Pakistan all have Cyber capabilities that mainly are aimed at subverting and stealing from the American government, corporations, and individuals. North Korea is aggressive, but a riddle, hard to pin down. The U. K. and Israel are allies of the United States with advanced Cyber capabilities, but the U.S. doesn't completely trust the U.K. or Israel; they have their own agendas which sometimes conflict with the United States. The U.K. and Israel don't completely trust the U.S. either, for the same equally valid reason.

It wasn't just nation-states that were in the game. There were increasingly capable private players. These were criminal organizations, many in developing countries, that were not

25

interested in political gains, they were solely focused on stealing money. The hackers ranged in size from single operators to large employers structured in bureaucratic hierarchies. Most of these organizations work with the full knowledge of the countries in which they resided. The corrupt governments just demand a percentage of their income, and either leave them alone, or in some cases provide protection for the crooks. All these organizations have one thing in common: they focus on the United States, for several reasons.

People in the U.S. are heavy users of the internet and buy a lot of products online, and Americans are gullible. It's in the American nature to trust people, that is not so in the rest of the world. The flimsiest scam, the "you won the contest, just give me your social security number so we can send you the prize," works remarkably well with Americans. Maybe it has to do with the optimism of the American people. But the biggest reason the scammers picked on the U.S.; it's just as bank robber Willie Sutton explained when asked why he robbed banks: That's where the money is.

Many hackers focused on individuals. This strategy makes the value of each transaction smaller, but law enforcement in the U.S. cannot possibly protect all these individuals, and many of the people who are scammed either never realize it, or never report the crime.

Some of the criminals went for the big score, cheating old people out of their homes or life savings, but others went for smaller but repeatable items. These hackers would put a small charge, say $6.99 on a victim's credit card that would occur every month, but go on forever. This is the kind of transaction that was seldom noticed and went unreported, and if caught, law enforcement could not pay attention to such trivial amounts. The key for these criminals was volume, to get large and growing numbers of victims, and thus have a repeatable source of cash flow. This level of activity operated way below the level of Cyber Warfare, the kind Cyber Command was tasked to stop.

Hacking is Cybercrime but Cyber Warfare is different even though the line between the two is starting to blur. Cyber Warfare was conducted only by the big boys, the nation-states. This is the most complex battlefield in world history by orders

26

of magnitude. To simplify, each country has two main branches of Cyber War:

1) Disinformation. This used to be called propaganda. All the countries involved spread small, medium and large lies using very sophisticated methods, increasingly using social media, in attempts to influence public opinion, and change the outcome of elections. The use of the Internet has made Disinformation much more powerful and effective than previous propaganda efforts.

2) Offensive hacking, subverting, and disrupting foreign computer networks, and creating defenses against those same things happening to their own countries. The major players each possess potent offensive capabilities that could cripple the information infrastructures of their enemies. But their enemies also have similar capabilities, so no country had ever launched a major offensive initiative because they feared the reprisals.

Toni Anne sat in the office of the leader of Cyber Command, four-star General A. B. Goldstein. The two geniuses had cooked up the recent plot to trick Russia into using their most potent Cyber weapon. The weapon had the opposite effect from Russian intentions, and The Lider's plan to corner the Bitcoin market had been a colossal and publicly humiliating failure. Because a cyber weapon, once used, is then dissected by all the other countries in the game, and therefore ineffective, the Russians had squandered years of development and now stood behind the pack in offensive capabilities.

Toni Anne stated the obvious, "The Lider is one pissed off Commie. We've taken away his major offensive threats for a while. He's got to be planning revenge, but we don't see any activity right now. What do you think General?"
Goldstein, the first officer in any branch of the service to be recruited directly out of college specifically to fight in the Cyber arena, thought for a minute. He was the tall, nervous type, who never put on weight, he had to be reminded when it was time to eat. Unlike the volatile, outspoken, and profane

Toni Anne, Goldstein was a man who could be quiet for minutes at a time while he formulated an answer.

"I've given that question a lot of thought. It's the one thing that keeps me up at night," he said.

Laudano laughed. Goldstein famously slept about two hours a night. "You mean you're down to sleeping one hour a night?"

The General ignored Toni Anne's comment. He was quiet again for a moment. "We have access to some HUMINT" he said, "the Russians may be going in a different direction."

HUMINT is spy jargon for Human Intelligence. In this context it meant the U.S. had a spy inside the Russian hierarchy. Although Toni Anne had the highest security clearance and the General's complete trust, some information was compartmentalized. "What direction is that?" Toni Anne asked.

"They may be farming out their hacking and ransomware operations to small time operators in their country and in the former Soviet Republics," the General said. "We know that the Russians have been hitting up those small time guys for a piece of the action, kind of a protection racket, but now they are actively supporting the independents. They are giving them more advanced technology."

"So instead of tracking one giant monster, we'll have to track thousands of baby monsters. Holy shit!" Toni Anne said.

"Yeah. Holy shit is right," said General Goldstein.

"You know what I don't get, General? Why do we just let these pukes steal from us? Why don't we do something about it?" Toni Anne asked.

"Well, we don't have any extradition treaties with the countries where the scumbags operate. What do you want us to do, go over and shoot them?" the General said.

"Good idea. I want to shoot them. Intellectual solutions are fine but seeing their buddies with their fuckin' brains laying on the floor is a more effective deterrent. We've got to get down to the level those scumbags understand," Toni Anne said.

"You're not alone. There are some other people in the Pentagon advising the President that we need to step up Kinetic retaliation," General Goldstein said.

"Kinetic. I hate those euphemisms. Why don't we just call it shit that blows up?" Toni Anne said.

28

"Okay. Some people over at the Pentagon want to at least threaten Russia that we're ready to use conventional weapons, or shit that blows up, if necessary," Goldstein said. 'We might be closer to that than you think."

Chapter Six
Spicewood, TX

Barbara Jean, you have to let me explain," I said.
She looked at me. It was not a friendly look. "Go ahead," she said.

"For one thing, when I proposed to you, I had all my money. I---"

"But you didn't have it when we got married. And you didn't tell me." Barb had me there.

"Let me tell you the story, starting from the beginning," I said.

"Alright," she said. When she wanted to use it Barbara Jean had a smile that could light up a room, but there was no sign of a smile now. Man, I'd never seen her like this. They say marriage changes things.

It took a long time to tell Barbara Jean the whole story. She listened for a while without interrupting.

I explained that the whole thing started when Movie Star Lola Madison was shot in New York. I had been dating Lola, until she started dating her bodyguard, Gabrielle McHugh. Lola was my client and was in the process of being swindled by Hedge Fund/Ponzi Scheme operator Robert Stanton Banks. Banks had ordered the killing of Lola in a futile attempt to keep his Ponzi scheme afloat. Gabrielle McHugh had been wounded during Lola's murder.

Gabrielle and I had ended up confronting Banks as he was just about to flee the U.S., and in a shoot-out in his lavish Wall Street offices, Gab and I each shot Banks, Gabrielle's shot being the fatal one.

After that I invited Gabrielle to recover from her wounds in my compound in Austin. Although Gabrielle was a lesbian, I had a crush on her and thought maybe I could convert her over to my side. Gab was a former Army Officer, a combat veteran Ranger who when recovered from her wounds decided to go back in the service, this time to serve in the intellectual world of Cyber Command. When she got back, she described me to Cyber Command's leadership as the Perfect Useful Idiot they could use in a complicated scheme against the Russians. It

30

turned out she had been setting me up the whole time she was in Austin.

I didn't mention the part about having a crush on Gabrielle to Barbara Jean, but I didn't have to. Being shallow, and a guy, during that same time period I was also in love with Barbara Jean Parker, which was convenient because she happened to be my first and current wife.

As I laid the groundwork for my saga, Barbara Jean looked at me in silence. "Where's the beef? When are you going to explain the important stuff; the money" she finally asked. There's something about a woman who owns 20 head of cattle, asking 'where's the beef?' that lends the phrase extra meaning.

"Cyber Command asked me to come up to Fort Meade, Maryland," I said. "They asked me to volunteer to set up a diversion, to divert the Russians, and the Lider."

"You volunteered?" Barb asked.

"They had me trapped. The Russians were already watching me because Cyber Command was talking to me. The carrot in the deal was that I could make maybe one, two billion dollars trading Bitcoin in a week," I explained. "They told me it probably wouldn't be dangerous."

"Probably not dangerous!" Barbara Jean said. "Then I end up getting punched out by a Russian hitman, and you end up with a fractured skull and broken ribs after almost getting killed. I wouldn't call that probably not dangerous."

"Yeah," I admitted.

"I'm beginning to think my father is right about political types. They used you, they got what they wanted, and what did you get? To lose your money?" Barbara Jean said.

This story wasn't coming out right in the telling. Which one of us didn't understand, Barbara Jean or me? Barb was throwing off a vibe as though I tricked her on purpose.

"Explain the money part to me," Barb said.

"When I agreed to cooperate, without explaining the whole plan to me, they told me to just go in and start buying Bitcoin in a big, aggressive way, to be the 'Big Swingin' Dick', so the Russians would notice what I was doing, and so they would think I knew something, maybe who was really behind Bitcoin all along."

"Yeah. So?" Barb asked.

31

"I really didn't know much, only that some operation Cyber Command was running would make Bitcoin go up," I said.

"You just jumped in?" Barb asked.

"I started buying. I had to use all my personal money to have enough to leverage up and get the huge Bitcoin position. The first few minutes I made $7 million, and then $100 million. The Russians weren't the only ones who noticed, and the whole world went crazy. The Russians were buying through intermediaries and crazy speculators everywhere just followed the trend. After four days I was up to $1.5 billion," I explained.

"Then what?" she asked.

"Then you called me when the two thugs were holding you captive. I had the 'Sell' all queued up. All I had to do was to hit 'send', but I rushed out to try to save you. I was under a lot of pressure." I said.

This generated a cold look from Barbara Jean. "Didn't Hemingway say: 'Courage is grace under pressure'?" she asked. Barb had been an English major at TCU. I might have considered that before I proposed.

"Yeah, Hemingway had so much grace under pressure that he shot himself," I said.

"Well, at least he was a crack shot. You'd probably miss," Barbara Jean said.

"You're giving me shooting lessons. I'll improve my aim," I said.

"Good!" Then Barb was quiet for a few seconds "So, you didn't have grace under pressure either. All you had to do was hit that one friggin' button!" she said.

"Are you calling me a coward?" I asked. "I was brave enough to come out and save you."

"Yeah, then *I* had to save *you*. I'm the one who eventually shot that Russian guy," she boasted. She sat up very straight and puffed out her chest. That was the one good part of this conversation. Barb has a great chest. "Have you contacted Cyber Command about your situation?"

"They contacted me. Toni Anne Laudano called me when I was still in the hospital," I said.

"*Toni Anne* who? Who is that?" she asked.

I instantly realized that I shouldn't have brought another woman's name into the discussion. Toni Anne the genius was

32

also a great looking woman who had come on to me when I was up at Cyber Command. *Was Barbara Jean using her superior womanly mental mind-reading wave rays to detect that I was attracted to Toni Anne? I started off this session to get myself out of deep water, now I was drowning.*

"Oh, she's this brainiac at Cyber Command. A real egghead type," I answered. I omitted the part of the description that Toni Anne was dark haired with blue eyes, looked and dressed like an innocent schoolgirl, but her high RPM engine was running just beneath the surface, and she openly talked about sex. She winked at me, which I found surprisingly attractive. Toni Anne also used profane language that made men in meetings with her uncomfortable, including General Goldstein. This behavior was tolerated only because Toni Anne was a rare genius, a true national resource, and dedicated to defeating our enemies, especially the Russians, who she always referred to as the "fuckin' commies."

"Sure," Barbara Jean said. She was staring straight through me.

We sat looking at each other for a minute. This conversation was at an impasse.

Barb said, "Then Bitcoin collapsed while we were trying not to get killed. What did ***Toni Anne*** say to you when she called?" *She could read my thoughts about Toni Anne. I better not play poker with Barb.*

"Toni Anne said she was sorry. Sorry that she hadn't hacked into my computer and sold before it was too late," I answered.

"She could have gotten you out at $1.5 billion, and she didn't!" Barb said.

"Well, she was busy with the Russians and $14 trillion at that point in time," I said.

"And you accepted this? You did their bidding for them, they got what they wanted, and you lost $1.5 billion, $50 million of it your own money? And you're just sitting there and taking it? You're planning on living off my money?" Barbara Jean asked.

I shrugged. I hadn't thought of the situation in those terms, but she did have a point.

"Well, what can I do?" I said.

"What can you do? Go up there to Fort Meade and meet with them. Tell them you want your money back!" Barb said.

33

"You want me to just call up a four-star general, General Goldstein and ask for my $50 million back?" I said.

"Why don't you call you girlfriend *Toni Anne*, and demand the meeting?" Barb said.

"I guess I can do that. I don't know what this will accomplish, though," I said.

"Well JR., here's the deal. I can't be married to a man that I don't respect. You didn't even tell me this before we got married! You need to grow some balls and go get your money!" Barbara Jean said. "My daddy may be a blowhard drunk, but you don't see him rolling over when he's in a negotiation about some oil leases on our land. He's tough, and I expect you to be tough."

I didn't care much for being unfavorably compared to Cletus Parker. *Tough negotiator my ass. At best he refuses to buy the Billy Bobs on the other side of the negotiation another drink until they make the offer they intended in the first place.*

I said, "I'm not sure they'll even see me. And I don't know about them giving me $50 million."

"Then let me give you a little extra incentive. You're not sleeping in the same bed with me, and by that, I mean not having sex with me, until you get that money. You can start sleeping in one of the other bedrooms. Or you can move back to your place in Austin for a while," Barbara Jean said. "And if you don't resolve the issue, we'll just annul the marriage."
I was only going to take so much. "Maybe we should just do that!" I snapped.

"Maybe we will! I could have married a hundred good looking men in Austin who want to live off my money. Get this thing done, or get out and stay out. You've heard about the InCels? Involuntary Celibate? That's you until you settle this." Barb said. "*Toni Anne*! Maybe she'll help you."

Since Barbara Jean was clearly reading my mind, I tried not to think of Toni Anne.

There's a theory that life is just a series of transactions. The transaction I just had with my wife of three days had not gone well. I had always heard from married men that the frequency of sex went down over time, but I didn't think that meant getting completely shut out after less than 72 hours. Barb went

34

out to the barn and had left me alone in the kitchen with my thoughts. *Her horse's ass daddy was a better negotiator than me!*

I weighed my alternatives. While my personal taxable investment account was gone, I still had some money in the bank, and my 401k was big enough to make most people happy, but you don't want to take money out of a 401k until you're at least 55 years old or you get crushed with tax penalties. I also still owned my swishy co-op on Fifth Avenue in New York City, and my compound in Austin, complete with house and casita. I might have to sell a few things, to get some liquidity to rebuild. It shouldn't be a big deal. A man of my great wisdom and sophisticated financial skills should be able to handle this with a minimum of struggle.

Barbara Jean was out in the barn with Alice. Molly the horse was off her feed and needed some attention. I walked out to the barn.

"Barbara Jean, something has come up. I've got to go to my house in Austin for a couple days," I announced to her, loud enough for Alice to hear even though she was a good distance away. I was putting on a bit of play acting to save face in front of Alice. For all I knew Barb had told Alice the whole story anyhow. They didn't have an employer/employee relationship, it was more like two best friends.

"There's some things I have to take care of to put the house on the market. So, I'm going now. I'll give you a call later." I didn't even sound convincing to myself. Though I'm an enthusiastic and persuasive liar, I'm a lousy actor. You'd think the two skills would be complementary.

"Okay," Barb said. She didn't bother looking up from cutting the string on a hay bale. I guess the Involuntary Celibate Protocol included not talking to me more than the bare minimum.

I went back to the house. When I had packed a few things and was ready to walk out the door, Alice surprised me by walking into the kitchen. She was fishing around in one of the drawers. "We're out of Bute in the barn. Molly's a little under the weather."

35

Bute is short for a longer word that I couldn't remember, a medicine they give horses. It's like horse aspirin, but you can't give it too often. Alice searched around and found the bottle.

Alice looked me square in the eyes. "JR, can I tell you something?"

"Sure Alice."

Alice gathered her thoughts. She wasn't a person to waste words. "JR, you must know how devoted I am to Barbara Jean."

"I think you're her real best friend in the world," I said.

She let that comment pass. It was quiet in the kitchen for a while.

"She needs you to assert yourself," Alice said.

"You mean I should go pick her up in my arms and throw her in our bed?" I asked.

"No," Alice said.

"What then?" I said.

"You need to go get your money back. You know Barb, beneath that tough exterior…" Alice said. "I'm not that good with words. She's real disappointed in you right now, she doesn't respect you."

"No Alice, you're good with words" I said.

"JR, excuse me for talking like this, but you need to grow up, to take things more serious," Alice said. "You need to be a man." Then she left to go back to the barn. After a minute I walked out to my truck to drive to Austin.

Chapter Seven
Austin, TX

I had been getting used to living on the open spaces on Barbara Jean's ranch, and now I was back in my urban abode, which consisted of a main house, swimming pool and a casita, a detached small house. It felt closed in. The next morning, I woke up in the quiet house.

One of the things you learn as a Wall Street trader is to never be afraid to call anybody, not that I had ever been a shy type anyhow. But I had to work up the nerve to call Tony Anne. I finally made myself commit and called her. The call went to her message recording, and I asked her to call me back.

Toni Anne surprised me by calling back in just a few minutes.

"Hey JR, how are you doing?" Tony Anne said.

"Not so great, Tony Anne. That's why I'm calling." I said

"What can I do for you?" she said.

"I want to set up a meeting with you and General Goldstein. I'm not happy about the way this issue was resolved. I got screwed." I said.

"What do you mean?" Tony Anne asked.

"You're the smartest person in the friggin' world and you don't know what I mean! I got hosed! You got what you wanted, and I lost my money. I did your bidding. You guys owe me." I said.

"What do you expect us to do?" Toni Anne asked.

"That's what I want to come and talk about," I said.

"Alright. We owe you that much. I'll talk to General Goldstein and call you back."

I thought that might be never and got down to the mundane task of managing my clients' money. The thought occurred to me that I could grow my business back to what it used to be, but my heart just wasn't in it. Over the years when I had gotten tired of taking guff from clients I didn't like I got rid of them, so now I was down to just clients that I did like. And I found when you approach clients or prospective clients and ask for their business, they smell desperation. It's like asking a woman out for a date when you haven't had one for months. The women want the men who are already dating other women, it

37

gives you a smell of approval and makes it safe that they're not dating some loser. Clients are the same. People are like dogs, they sniff each other, and if they sniffed me now, they'd get the odor of an Involuntary Celibate who needs money. It wasn't realistic to expect to grow my business back to the point where I'd be billing anywhere near what I'd need to get back up to $50 million in my account anyhow, so I had to figure out another way to get my money back.

The thought occurred to me that I could always tell Barbara Jean to go crap in her cowboy hat. That appealed to the immature jerk in my character. But the words of Alice stayed with me.

Yes, I had gotten Barbara Jean into that mess with the two thugs, but I put my life on the line getting her out of it, and all she was thinking about was the money, and that I wasn't as strong as that drunken fool Cletus Parker.

I looked at the markets and called a couple clients to do the standard schmoozing. You need to show them that you're paying attention. The market was choppy. One day it loved technology, the next day the crowd bought cyclical manufacturing stocks. My whole money management career I had bought aggressively when the market was low. Nothing was tempting me to buy.

My late mentor, the Legendary Texas broker Tom Good, had taught me that you wanted to buy from distressed Institutional Sellers who were panicking out of the market for some reason, and these reasons only came along every five or ten years. My client accounts all owned mostly Blue Chip stocks along with a scattering of technology and biotechs, just enough to keep them interested and have something to brag about to their clueless friends.

Tony Anne called me back about an hour later and surprised me by asking if I could be in Fort Meade tomorrow.

"I can be there," I said, "what time?'

"How about 9 a.m.?' Toni Anne said.

"You mean zero-nine hundred?" I asked.

Toni Anne laughed. "Gabrielle told me you can be a real jerk."

"I thought you knew that first-hand. You're speaking to Gabrielle? Do you still call her the Murder Bitch?" I asked.

38

"Sometimes. But I've got to tell you that I initially underestimated her. She's real smart---"

"As smart as you? I asked.

"There are only a few people in the world as smart as me, none of them in this building. That's just fact." Toni Anne said.

"So how about Gabrielle?" I asked.

"With her boss General Powers retired, Lt. Colonel Gabrielle McHugh is the second ranking officer to General Goldstein. She's going to make General as soon as it's not embarrassing."

"Embarrassing?"

"You can't promote somebody to be a General before they spent some time as a Lt. Colonel, then a full bird Colonel. It would get too many noses bent out of shape at the Pentagon. A lot of the old-timers are still pissed that General Goldstein made four stars so fast, and they'll never even get a second star." Toni Anne said.

"Is that something I should care about?" I asked.

Toni Anne paused, which was out of character for her; usually she had a rapid-fire answer to any question. "You need to learn to be a little subtle if you're going to get what you want out of this organization. If you just come in like a pissed off little spoiled rich kid like last time, you'll get your ass handed to you."

"You mean I didn't get my ass handed to me *last* time?" I asked.

"Last time *we* called *you* in, and you just walked into the trap like a sucker. This time you are calling us, and asking for the meeting," she said.

"So?"

"If you just come in and say, 'poor little me, I lost my money and you owe it to me', the General will throw you out on your ass. If you want something, you better have something to offer. This is the Big Leagues. We play with live ammo here. This isn't phony fuckin' Wall Street. There's no secret Slush Fund so we can just write you a check for $50 million. We've got to fight with Congress for every dollar." Toni Anne said. "Come up with something. Not what's in it for you. What's in it for the General?"

"Like what?" I asked.

"You've got between now and zero nine hundred tomorrow to come up with something. Just remember, I'm your friend. I

39

got you this meeting, and I'm the only one here that you can trust. I take care of my friends," Toni Anne said.

I stammered, "Yeah, you really took care of me last time. I bet your pile of money is still intact."

"Stop whining and come up with something that will get General Goldstein's attention. Think about: What's in it for him?" Toni Anne said.

"Alright, I'll come up with something,"

"Do better than *something*. Have a solid plan. Have bullet points. Remember that you're talking to a General. He likes to say; 'Prior Planning Prevents Piss Poor Performance,' Toni Anne said.

I didn't believe her about no secret Slush Fund. But I knew I wasn't going to get any of it. What kind of deal could I cook up?

It had been years since I had to make a *financial* proposal to anybody. I had made a *marriage* proposal to Barbara Jean, but I was confident that she was going to accept, so I didn't have to do a Power Point presentation, and since she was standing in front of me naked at that moment, brief and to the point was effective.

How do you make a proposal to a General? I thought once again about Tom Good. He would have told me that a General is just another person. Don't be fancy, don't use a lot of flowery language, just be convincing.

Once I got started talking to the General, I would be fine. But first I had to figure out what I had to offer and what I could reasonably ask for in return.

I opened Power Point on my computer. The white screen sat there staring me in the face. I not only had writer's block, I had life block. Where did I want this project and my life to head?

The program asked me if I wanted to use any Emojis in the presentation. I hate Emojis and didn't think Generals wanted Emojis. *That* would get me thrown out on my ass. This important decision made, I stared at the screen again for who knows how long. What did I want to ask for?

An opportunity. That's what I want to ask for, an opportunity to serve them again, with the chance of recovering my lost money. What were the specifics? I decided to put that ball in their court. I wouldn't walk in with a printed-up proposal. I'd

40

just tell them I wanted an opportunity and let them think up how it could be accomplished. They had to be working on one of their devious plots. I just wanted to help, and in return have a chance to get my money back.

Chapter Eight
Fort Meade, MD

I flew coach, not my usual first class, to Reagan National the night before my meeting at Fort Meade. I didn't like going coach, squeezed in the middle seat between two fat guys whose ectoplasm was oozing over the armrests and invading my personal safe space. But you must make little lifestyle adjustments after you've lost a billion dollars or so.

As is my habit I was a half hour early for my meeting at Cyber Command. As I sat in the lobby, I wondered who would come out to escort me to see the General.

Right at nine o'clock, zero nine hundred hours, it was Toni Anne Laudano. She looked as pretty as I remembered her. I had dated Lola, the Most Beautiful Woman in The World, but in real life Toni Anne was just as good looking and she had a real job. She smiled at me and shook my hand. She was attractive enough to make me consider my Involuntary Celibate status.

"I hear you just got married," Toni Anne said. "I don't screw around with married men."

So much for that plan.

"If it doesn't work out, we can talk," Toni Anne said.

I knew that once I was on the radar of Cyber Command, they had me under surveillance. I wondered if they knew about Barbara Jean's edict to me, but I decided that I was being too paranoid. But just then it did occur to me that for certain, they could hack into my computer any time they wanted to, so if I had done a Power Point presentation, they would have already seen it, and been prepared to shoot it down and do whatever they wanted to do in the first place.

"Did you do a Power Point, an outline of some kind? Where's your presentation for the General?" she asked.

"It's verbal," I said.

"It better be good," she said, "I warned you not to come in with some half-assed whiny bullshit."

"It's full-assed, and not whiny," I answered.

That drew a sideways look. "You didn't deny the 'bullshit' part," she said.

I shrugged.

42

I passed through the metal detector and an additional electronic wanding. Toni Anne and I started walking down the hall towards the General's conference room.

I looked at Toni Anne. In college I was forced to take some Liberal Arts courses to get my degree, so I took the easiest ones. I enjoyed Art History, the final exam consisted of being shown slides of famous paintings and required to name the artist. One of the paintings was "The Birth of Venus" by Botticelli. Venus is portrayed as a lovely, beautiful, idealized woman, with just the hint of an innocent smile. Today, Toni Anne reminded me of Venus in that painting. I was lost in thought for a moment.

"What are you grinning at?" Toni Anne asked.

I mumbled.

The Renaissance beauty turned to me, smiled and said, "Walk faster, we haven't got all fuckin' day,"

Chapter Nine
Moscow

If the Lider meant to intimidate Sierra Quinn by showing her the pickled head of Turgenev, it didn't work. Quinn loved gory, spattered blood and guts scenes, many of which she created. A lot of cops were like that. A lot of people were like that. Why did so many gawkers stop at an accident? At least Quinn admitted it to herself. She always knew her association with Turgenev would end with one of them dead and was relieved it wasn't her. Quinn had come to accept that the path she'd chosen would lead to an untimely and violent death. She hoped that the end would be sudden and not accompanied by hours of torture.

Quinn's goal was to kill a lot of people before that time came and see a lot of blood and guts spilled. She wasn't normal? So what? One of her wise guy detective partners in New York used to say: Normal is just the arithmetic average of all the abnormal people.

To prove to the Lider she wasn't timid Quinn got closer to the jar and bent down to stare at Turgenev. She blurted out, "He'll never be the head of a major corporation."

After a startled look, The Lider surprised Quinn by laughing, "I love American movies. Russian movies are so bleak. There's something about the American spirit. Russians could never make Austin Powers. A Russian comedy is ten minutes of a man stepping in an icy puddle, followed by an hour of talking."

Quinn considered that for a moment. "Sir, may I call you Lider?" she asked.

He smiled. "Yes. Your Russian accent is…. terrible."

Quinn smiled back. "I didn't have years of training in your language. Colonel Nihisky gave me a ten second course on the phone," she said.

"Fair enough," The Lider said.

"So, what's your favorite American movie?" she asked.

"That's easy," he said, "The greatest movie ever made, in any language. The Godfather! Would you like to stay here and watch it with me? I have a private theater."

"Why not?" she answered.

44

"A man in my position has had the…company…of many women. But I must admit, I've never had an American…. girlfriend." he said. "Is that the correct expression?"

"It depends on how long I stay afterwards," Quinn said.

Chapter Ten
Fort Meade, MD

Toni Anne and I walked into the General's conference room. It was big enough for a meeting of twenty people, but today it would be Toni Anne, General Goldstein, Gabrielle McHugh, and me. I shook hands with Goldstein and McHugh. The Cyber people all sat on one side of the table, behind them was the impressive seal of U.S. Cyber Command, I sat on the other side.

I looked at Gabrielle, Lt. Colonel McHugh. Within a period of less than a year I had seen her as Lola Madison's stone faced, ass kicking bodyguard who had shot and killed two men right in front of me within an hour, then a beautiful skimpily dressed woman sunning herself by my swimming pool and sitting on my lap in Austin, and now as a serious Army officer. I've met a lot of people in my travels, but none who could rival Gabrielle in her chameleon-like changes of persona. Would there be a next act, or was she residing in this character until she rose to General?

"Alright Johnson. I'm a busy man. What do you have in mind?" General Goldstein asked.

"General," I looked at Gabrielle. "Colonel. I'm not here to complain. I take responsibility for screwing up, if I had just remembered to hit a button, I'd have $1.5 billion. But you do have to admit those were extraordinary circumstances. What I'm here for today is to offer my services again. You must have other projects, and I offer something that nobody else has."

Gabrielle said, "What could that possibly be? You have no technical knowledge, no training in the field of intelligence---"

Goldstein held up his hand in the direction of Gabrielle to silence her. "Let him speak his piece," Goldstein said.

"The Lider really hates my ass. And so does Sierra Quinn," I explained. "C'mon. You guys are the masters of deviousness. You ought to be able work up some plan to take advantage of that. Use their emotions against them."

Gabrielle opened her mouth as if to say something, but she glanced at the General, who was stroking his chin. She said nothing.

46

"We hadn't been thinking along those lines," General Goldstein said. "If we come up with something I'll have Toni Anne call you. From the little I know about this Quinn character, it seems she's a sociopath, and I'm not sure the Lider is a man who would let his emotions get the better of himself."

Chapter Eleven
Moscow

Quinn was not completely naked. Pieces of her clothing dangled off her because the Russian President was not a man who waited to get what he wanted.

The Lider was on top of her. He still had his shirt and tie on, his pants were down around his knees. The Lider made a short proclamation in Russian, the same phrase, three times in a row. She didn't know the exact meaning of the words but got the message. He was done. She wasn't. He didn't care. He rolled off her and pulled his pants up.

"Why don't you get dressed?" the Lider said. He watched her.

She got dressed. The Lider didn't take his eyes off her.

This is creepy. Why am I not surprised?

They had been laying on a sofa in the back of the private screening room in the Lider's apartment. In front of them were maybe twenty oversized movie theater seats, upholstered in red velvet, separated by a central aisle. He gestured for them to sit in a couple seats on the aisle.

"You have a beautiful body, such beautiful breasts," he said.

"Thanks. I thought you might tear them off for a minute," Quinn said.

The Lider said. "I do get rough at times. You aroused me, satisfied me so much."

Quinn half smiled. *I wish I could say the same. I wonder if this sleaze bag recorded the whole thing with some hidden cameras. Probably.*

The Lider pressed a button on the arm of his seat, and a voice came back to him on a speaker. The President and the electronic voice had a short conversation, the only word of which Quinn understood was "vodka."

Quinn noticed the private theater had a peculiar smell. It took her a minute to place it. The smell was a disinfectant, like Lysol.

Wonder why they use the Lysol. It's to cloak some other smell. Maybe it's the smell of sex, maybe vomit, maybe the awful smell of death. Maybe all three.

48

In a minute a uniformed man wheeled a cart into the theater and next to the Lider. He set up an ice bucket which contained a bottle of vodka, and from out of a metal container produced two boxes of popcorn, one of which he handed to the Lider, who then passed one box along to Quinn. The Lider pantomimed placing the box of popcorn on a shelf on the back of the seats in front of them.

Vodka and popcorn. At least it's not caviar. I hate caviar.

The Lider was in a talkative mood. "We will watch *The Godfather* now. Instead of digital, I insist on the movies being projected on film, as they were originally intended to be."

He went on speaking, delivering a pretentious evaluation of *The Godfather*. The Lider pontificated on Michael Corleone's negative character arc, and how *The Godfather* is really an opera in spoken form. Any beret wearing NYU film major would have been proud to spout such bullshit. Quinn half listened.

The lights dimmed in the room. A curtain opened, exposing a movie screen. Before the movie started the Lider said, "When we are done with the popcorn, we will be served the finest Russian caviar."

On the screen, undertaker Amerigo Bonasera's face appeared. "I believe in America…" he started.

The same uniformed man wheeled out another cart and set up a small table which held a large container of caviar, some small pieces of bread, and a container of sour cream.

The Lider was the gracious host. "Please allow me to prepare your first one," he said. He took a piece of bread and spread a thin film of sour cream, then with a spoon dolloped on a portion of caviar. "There is no finer caviar anywhere in the world," he said as he handed the slice to Quinn.

Fish Eggs and 150 proof vodka. Don't they have pizza and beer in Russia? No M&Ms?

After having fixed a portion for Quinn, the Lider helped himself. Quinn nibbled at the caviar.

Ugh.

The Lider seemed to feel obligated only to fix the first serving for Quinn. "Please serve yourself," he said as he gestured to the table.

"It's so rich, along with the vodka," Quinn said.

49

And it sucks.

The Lider watched with a proprietary pride, as though he'd had something to do with making the movie, and when a favorite part was upcoming, he'd elbow Quinn, as if to say; 'watch this.' The wedding of Carlo and Connie was on the screen. Sonny's wife was using two hands, spread wider and wider apart to demonstrate his manhood to other women.

If I ever show other women The Lider's size, I won't need two hands. Just my thumb and forefinger.

The movie progressed to Sonny nailing the bridesmaid against the closet door. Although brief, it lasted longer than The Lider had on top of Quinn.

The Lider particularly liked the attempted assassination of The Don. He elbowed Quinn repeatedly during this scene.

During the talky parts of the movie the Lider seemed to lose a little interest. But when Michael Corleone was shooting Solozzo and Captain McCluskey, his elbow was working at maximum poking speed.

"I did that once," Quinn said, "I was inspired by the movie. Shot the guy right in the neck first, then in the forehead."

"Life imitates art, eh?" The Lider said.

When Sonny was ambushed and shot with about a hundred bullets at the tollbooth, the Lider clapped like a little boy who had just gotten what he wanted for his birthday. He threw up his hands and smiled at Quinn.

Is it possible that he's even more bloodthirsty than me?

As the movie continued, he consumed the caviar at a steady clip, and drank copious amounts of vodka. After several minutes the Lider was asleep, his chin against his chest. Quinn looked over at him. He was drooling.

The Godfather is a long movie. The Lider slept, snoring, until the car driven by Apolonia blew up, and he woke with a start.

"I must have nodded off," he said as he took a napkin and wiped his chin.

"Oh," Quinn said, 'this is such a great movie."

The movie progressed. Moe Green got shot in the eye.

"That's my favorite part!" the Lider said, laughing.

"Me too," Quinn admitted.

On the silver screen Carlo got garroted by Clemenza. "I like how he kicks out the windshield," the Lider said.

50

"Carlo got what he deserved," Quinn replied.

"Have you ever done something like that? Strangle someone with a wire?"

"I mostly just shoot people. Some I torture, but not with a wire, then shoot them," Quinn said.

"Efficient," The Lider said.

When the movie ended the lights in the room came back to normal. The Lider lightly held Quinn's arm, indicating that she should stay seated. The uniformed man came out and cleared away the debris from their decadent snack. Then the Lider rose to his feet, and held out his hand, gallantly assisting Quinn out of her seat.

What's next? Is he going to invite me to his bedroom where we engage in another three minute unsatisfactory rutting session, before he rolls over and snores all night?

"Please indulge me," the Lider said.

Oh No.

"I have a modest… umm. Collection," he said.

What was this going to be? A row of embalmed severed heads that he insists on showing me?

"I forgot to ask you before. Please remove your panties," he said.

"You…want me to remove my panties. Right here?" she asked.

"Yes," he said.

"Okay," Quinn said as she raised her skirt and dropped her panties.

"Please hand them to me," the Lider said.

She did so, and the Lider put them in his jacket pocket.

What a perv.

"It would not be appropriate for us to have a long-term relationship. I will have my car drop you back at your hotel. You will return tomorrow morning for a meeting. We will act professionally, as though there has been no interaction between us. Thank you for the lovely evening," the Lider said as he took her hand and kissed it.

A door opened and a man in uniform appeared. The Lider gave instructions to the man in Russian. "He will escort you to the car," the Lider said.

"Good night," the Lider said to Quinn.

51

"Good night," she replied.

Well, that was the shittiest date I've ever had. It's clear to me that he models his organization after the Mafia…. That sick bastard must have a panty collection of his conquests. And I've got to go to a meeting tomorrow with him and some other guys who are going to know. He's the kind of guy who brags…. I can't even shoot him…. Maybe the hotel will have room service still available when I get back so I might get some decent food.

"Oh, just a moment," the Lider said. He spoke to the uniformed man, who left the room.

"He'll wait for you in the hallway," the Lider said.

"Yes?" Quinn said.

"I don't use condoms, but I've had a vas… vas, how do you say it" he asked.

"A vasectomy?" Quinn suggested.

"Yes, that's it. So, you needn't worry about that aspect," the Lider said.

She wasn't going to get knocked up by the Lider. Great. Then again, that genetic combination might have produced some interesting offspring.

Chapter Twelve
Moscow

Sierra Quinn returned as instructed the next morning to the Lider's office. The first-floor security check-in was formal, and Colonel Nihisky greeted her as though the two of them had never met. The Lider went through the same farce when she was led into his office. This time there were others present. A woman was standing next to the Lider. The rest of the large group, maybe 50, were all men. Some looked western European, some Slavic, some with more Asian features.

This isn't a tryout for the Moscow Boys Choir. I've seen a lot of crooks, and these guys look like crooks.

"This is your interpreter," the Lider said to Quinn and gestured for the only other woman in the room to stand next to Sierra.

"I will speak to the men in Russian and allow time for the interpreter to translate," the Lider said.

"Miss Quinn, I will not introduce the other men in the room. You will be individually introduced to them only later if you have the need to know. I asked you here today to show these men my commitment to our next mission, and to put it bluntly, to let them know that they can go anywhere in the world, and if necessary, you will find them and shoot them," the Lider said. "We are not going to fail in this mission!"

"I am told Miss Quinn is an expert in the art of disguise," the Lider said to the men, "if she comes to shoot you, it is doubtful that you would recognize her."

Grim faced, Quinn nodded. *Oh great, he must be charming at a wedding! The Lider* is *a creative motivational speaker.*

Quinn smiled inwardly. At her fancy hotel's clothing shop, she had purchased and was now wearing over her regular underwear, a pair of ladies' underpants so oversized and old fashioned that they would be suitable bloomers for any 220-pound Russian peasant woman. She half hoped that after the meeting the Lider would somehow ask again for her panties but thought that was farfetched. Still, it amused her.

The Lider continued. "Miss Quinn, look at each man. I may be asking you to shoot one or more of them in the near future."

53

Quinn did as instructed. Most of the men made eye contact with her, but she gave them the 1,000-yard stare.

Now this was fun.

"As further motivation, I'd like to show you this," the Lider said. From behind the same curtain, he produced the embalmed head of Oleg Turgenev, and put it on his desk, just as he had done for Sierra last night. The Lider's joy in performing this demonstration was all over his face.

"Relax. If you perform your specific part of the mission, you won't be meeting Miss Quinn, or perhaps one of my other highly trained specialists. If you don't perform---Miss Quinn is a very good shot. And if I think you are disloyal to me in any way, 'marinovannaya svinaya golova'

The interpreter translated "marinovannaya svinaya golova means pickled pigs head," she whispered to Quinn.

Better than caviar.

The Lider stopped talking to let this point sink in, as he pointed to Turgenev's head. "Miss Quinn stay here. Alright, the rest of you are all dismissed. Go back to where you work and do your job," he said. "Don't let the door hit you in the ass."

That's how the captain of detectives used to end the meetings in his office back in Manhattan South. Some things transcend different cultures.

"Miss Quinn, you and I have a common enemy. JR Johnson. He ruined plans that each of us had during the Bitcoin fiasco. I now have plans for him. You may get to kill him, but not until I am done ruining his financial life, his reputation, his life in general. I caution you not to kill him until I specifically tell you to do so. I have no head of a woman in my jars yet. Do not disobey your orders unless you want to be the first," the Lider said.

Chapter Thirteen
Fort Meade, MD

General Goldstein stood up from the table. "There's no reason to continue this meeting. We'll get back to you if we have anything for you." He shook hands with me. Gabrielle stood and shook hands without any comment.

Toni Anne said "I might have something for you. Why don't you come back to my office." Both the General and Gabrielle looked at her. This comment had taken them by surprise. Goldstein shrugged, and Lt. Colonel McHugh was in no position to question anything Toni Anne did.

Toni Anne tilted her head at me. I understood. We were not to have any meaningful conversation in the hallway on the walk to her office.

"How's married life treating you?" she asked with a smile.

She knew. I wasn't being paranoid. They knew everything.

"Just fine," I answered. "I'm living out in Spicewood now."

She responded with a different smile and raised her eyebrows.

"Oh, all the time? You've completed your move out of the compound in Austin?" she asked.

Damn. "Well, I'm still tidying up a few loose ends," I said.

When we got to her office Toni Anne gestured for me to have a seat. It was not much of an office for a person of her power, but then again, she didn't have to impress anybody. A lot of her serious work was done in some secret room that most of the people in Cyber Command never got to see, she told me the last time I visited.

During our previous visit Toni Anne assured me that conversations in her office were not recorded. She gave me no such assurances this time.

"I just wanted to tell you that the General has a lot of things on his mind. I think he'll give your offer real consideration," she said.

This sounded like bullshit. And the genuine Toni Anne couldn't say two sentences without using language that would make a sailor blush. The last time I was in her office, after knowing me for five seconds, she told me I had my head up my

55

ass. "Okay, so what am I waiting for?" No response from Toni Anne. "Are you telling me that the General is preoccupied?" I asked.

"That's a good way of expressing it," she said.

"And how about the cold shoulder from Gabrielle?" I asked.

"Junior officers take their lead from their superiors. She isn't going to be your buddy in front of General Goldstein," Toni Anne said.

"Makes sense," I said. *But this whole conversation didn't make sense.*

"I don't want to waste any more of your time. But I'm trying to help you out. I'll talk to the General," she said. She stood and I followed her lead. As I walked to the door, she grabbed my arm and turned me around to face her.

"JR, I like you, and I appreciate what you have done for the country," she said. Toni Anne took my right hand in both her hands. She was so smooth that I didn't realize for a second that she had slipped a piece of paper in my hand. She winked at me. I liked it when she winked at me. It was reminiscent of the kind of gesture Lola would have done, and Lola had been a genius at manipulating people.

"JR, are you okay?" Toni Anne asked.

"I'm sorry, my mind was somewhere else…I was thinking…oh, not about *that,"* I said.

"Disappointing," Toni Anne said.

I slowly closed my hand and then put the paper in my right pocket.

"I've got to escort you out of the building," she said.

"No tour of the Control Room like last time?" I asked.

"Nah, we don't have to show you off to the mole. There's no mole now in the organization, that we know of," she said. "Or at least that *I* know of."

We walked without conversation to the main entrance. We shook hands again.

"We'll get back to you. And don't worry about the Involuntary Celibate thing. I'm going through that right now too," Toni Anne said.

56

Chapter Fourteen
Arlington, VA
Reagan National Airport

I was dying to know what was on that piece of paper. What was so secret that Toni Anne couldn't tell me? Was she afraid that they were bugging her office? After all she had done for the country?

Did you ever walk into a room and know everyone was watching you? That's what it feels like when you know you're under surveillance. I was so edgy that I didn't even touch the paper until I reached the airport lobby and went into a stall in the men's room. I took the piece of paper out of my pocket and unfolded it. The handwriting was tiny but neat.

It said: *I can't tell you what's going on. Trust nobody but me and John Wishbone Ives. I'll find ways of contacting you. You are being watched. I am being watched. It's appropriate to be paranoid. Get a burner phone, pay with cash, and call Wishbone.*

The phone number was listed.

It went on *DO NOT CALL HIM FROM YOUR IPHONE!!! Don't trust anybody else, even if they tell you that I sent them.*

There are rumors about changes in leadership at Cyber Command. You can trust General Goldstein, but if someone new comes in, do not trust them unless I tell you it's okay.

Oh. I have permission from one of the smartest people in the world, who's inside the government, that it is appropriate to be paranoid about the government watching my every move.

I knew a John 'Wishbone' Ives. It had to be the same guy. How many Wishbone Ives were there? But I hadn't seen him since we both worked together at the Big Investment Firm. He had been the only black person in the junk bond trading department. I christened him The Sole Soul Man, or just 'Sole.' John used to join my friend Elliott and I in the lunchroom once in a while. What we had in common is that we were all outsiders.

I left the New York operation to go to Austin, and John left the business a few months later when the junk bond market

57

blew up. We called each other a few times, but like a lot of relationships, it just petered out. I didn't know what he was up to. I guess I was going to catch up on all our lost time.

Chapter Fifteen
Austin, TX

For the flight home I modified my ticket in Washington from a direct flight to one with a stopover and change in planes in Oklahoma City. The ticket agent couldn't figure out why I wanted to do so, but I insisted on the new itinerary without any explanation.

I made that change so I could walk through the airport in OKC and buy a burner phone for cash at one of the kiosks. I figured that was good spy tradecraft, that it would be less likely that someone would be watching me in Oklahoma. My only training was watching movies and reading a few spy thrillers. I figured the authors of those books must do meticulous research, right? They don't just make things up, do they?

I considered calling Wishbone the evening I got home from D.C., but I drifted off to sleep. I slept well for someone who in recent months had been the would-be murder victim of a lawyer in New York, an hour later the Ponzi scheme operator tried to shoot me, then I was the target of Russian assassins, got conked in the head with a crowbar, and the frosting on the cake was to get bounced out of the nest by my wife of three days. And the smartest person in the world, who works for the government, told me to be paranoid about the government. Then there was the fact that I lost $1.5 billion. Well, you've got to let little problems like that roll off your back or you'll worry yourself to death.

I didn't even know in which time zone Wishbone was located, so I waited until 10 a.m. Central Time to call him.

He answered by repeating his phone number.

"Sole Man, is that you?" I asked.

"I was expecting you to call. We can't stay on the phone for more than 15 seconds at a time. Hang up and call me back," he said.

I called back. He gave me his address. It was in the East Village in New York City. "Be here tomorrow morning, by 9 a.m. if you can. Okay?" John said.

"Yeah," I said.

He hung up.

59

Chapter Sixteen
New York

I flew the overnight red eye to New York. Why is flying so tiring? It's not as though they've ever asked me to pilot the plane, but I always consider myself on alert, just in case. I have no qualifications as a pilot, but I'm a smart guy and think I'd look sharp in one of those uniforms. Flying coach takes even more out of you than first class. Now I had another incentive for getting my money back.

I was sure the surly male flight attendant didn't like me. I didn't like him either. Eventually we landed at LaGuardia Airport, which was designed for planes of the Wright Brothers and Lindbergh era. It seemed like modern jets had to do a Kamikaze-like steep dive to land there. Maybe the tall buildings of Manhattan, just across the East River, make the perspective look worse. I dragged my butt off the plane. As we shuffled down the aisle one six-inch step at a time, I felt like one of the steers being herded into a branding pen at Barbara Jean's ranch.

I took a cab to the East Village, its new, more gentrified name. It used to be called the Lower East Side, home of several neighborhoods, including the Bowery. As a youngster when I was even a bit disheveled, like having my shirt untucked, my mother used to say I looked like a Bowery Bum. But now even the Bowery has more upscale, artistic bums. Bum can't be an acceptable term. How about Alternatively Addressed Personnel? Maybe I'll send that in as a suggestion to the New York Times.

I had the taxi drop me off a couple blocks from the address that Wishbone had given me and walked. When I got to the address, I thought I must have made a mistake, because I was standing in front of an old funky looking movie theater.

I took out my burner phone and called Wishbone. I told him my predicament.

"You're in the right place. Just walk to the door and stand there." He hung up, the whole conversation in less than the stipulated fifteen seconds.

I waited a minute and the door opened. It was Wishbone. He looked great, almost the same as I had known him over ten

60

years ago, except that he used to have a shaved head and a goatee. Now he had short hair on top of his head and his face was clean shaven.

I wanted to start a conversation, but he put his finger up to his lips and gestured for me to follow him.

I followed as we walked past the concession counter and down a hallway past an office. Wishbone opened a door at the end of the hall.

When we got through the door and he had closed it, Wishbone turned to me and gave me a handshake with a slap on the shoulder.

"Hey JR, it's good to see you!" Wishbone said.

"Yeah, you too," I said. I looked around the dingy stairway.

"What kind of world have you and Toni Anne gotten me into?" I asked.

"Right now? It's a world of shit," he said with a smile.

I followed Wishbone up the stairs. After passing through another locked door at the top of the stairway we walked down a linoleum floored hallway that was clean, but dumpy. There was only one doorway. The door itself brought back memories, it was what I thought of as a 'New York apartment door', because it had about twelve locks. But none of them were locked, my host just turned the knob and pushed the door.

"Great security system," I said.

"I knew who was coming," Wishbone answered. "When I don't know who's coming, I'm a lot more careful." He pointed to a shotgun leaning against his worktable. There's something about seeing a gun in a room that sharpens your focus.

In contrast to the hallway, the apartment looked spectacular. It had modern furniture and an oriental rug. The large main room had a high ceiling and was a blend of industrial and high tech. A table held several large computer screens, and in front of the table was a kind of chair that I had only seen on tv commercials. It looked like it tilted seven different ways.

"That's a nice chair," I said. "What does something like that cost?"

"It depends," Wishbone said. "I, uh, get a lot of things at a discount."

I had to remember that I was in New York. Some of the products get discounted by falling off the back of a truck.

61

"What are you, the Phantom of the Opera? You live up above the theater? Do you swoop down and scare the patrons?" I asked.

"I own the theater. And you have to admit, my apartment is off the beaten path. I like privacy," Wishbone said.

"Alright. You mind catching me up? What are you doing? What do you have to do with Toni Anne?" I asked.

"Okay. For one thing it's safe to talk here. The walls are lead lined, and I have a real pro check for electronic surveillance. So we're clean. But as soon as we get on the phone, even burner phones, we're open to being listened to, by the NSA, the Russians, and lord knows who else. Uzbekistan hackers, the Israelis, North Koreans. A lot of people are interested in us," he said. "For your iPhone or anything with your phone number, just assume somebody, probably multiple entities, are listening to every conversation. When you use a burner phone, you don't know that they're listening, but they are always scanning, trying to listen. They all have sophisticated voice recognition systems, so if one of their computers locks on to us, they might well be listening. Its's a small probability, but it's not zero, and not worth taking the chance. They want to hear what we are doing, to give them an advantage, any advantage."

"An advantage in what?" I asked.

"An advantage in this crazy world of Cyber shit that you and I now live in," he said.

"I didn't ask to be in this world," I said.

"You weren't complaining when you were up one and a half billion," Wishbone said.

"True. I only want to be in the good part. The part where the bad guys try to kill me, I don't want to be involved in. Wait a minute, you know about all this stuff, all about me?" I asked.

"Yeah," he said. "I work for Toni Anne, for the government as a private contractor. I do some other things as well."

"Great. I hope you're doing better than I am financially. I'm doing so well that now I get to fly in coach," I said.

"Somewhere in the world, maybe in a leper colony in India, there's somebody who may have it tougher than you," Wishbone said.

62

Chapter Seventeen
New York City

Wishbone sat down in his high-tech chair and gestured to me to have a seat in an adjacent chair. "Take a load off. You look tired," he said.

"Your chair's a lot nicer than mine," I said.

"Tough," he said.

We laughed. "Look, I'm lost. Why am I here? What is your relationship to Toni Anne? What am I supposed to do?" I asked.

"Where do you want me to start?" Wishbone asked.

"Could you start at the beginning?" I asked.

"You mean the Celtics?" Wishbone said.

"I remember you played for the Celtics for a year before you came to the Big Investment Firm," I said. "As I recall you didn't do much."

"Hey, the coach hated me. Red Auerbach was the GM and drafted me even though the coach didn't want me," Wishbone said.

"You weren't what he was used to,"

"I went to Princeton. Majored in Math and played basketball. I was surprised when I got drafted in the second round by the Celtics. Didn't play much, tore up my knee, got cut after the first season and wound up on Wall Street, trading junk bonds," Wishbone said.

"Okay, it's coming back to me. You were the only junior trader in junk bonds who could do math. The rest of them not only didn't know anything; they didn't even suspect anything,"

"I got tired of being the fish out of water. I wasn't the standard model at Princeton. When I was with the Celtics I was the only Ivy League player in the NBA. Then I got to Wall Street and I was the only black guy in the junk bond department," John Wishbone Ives said. He wasn't one of those giants who you know on sight are basketball players. He was six-four, short for the NBA.

"Okay, I remember talking to you when the junk bond business blew up," I said.

63

"The junk bond business was there one month, and the next month every firm on Wall Street was laying off. Within a few months the few remaining junk traders just got folded into the rest of the fixed income desk," Wishbone said.

"So, you left the investment business then?"

"No. Management came to me and offered me another job at the Big Investment Firm, in Personnel. They wanted me to recruit minorities. Not because they really wanted to hire minorities, but they were getting a lot of political pressure," he said.

"So?"

"Hated it. I lasted a month. When I quit, I had saved enough money to go to graduate school and studied computer systems. Turned out I had a knack for it, so when I graduated Toni Anne recruited me to come and work for her company," he said.

"You mean her data encryption business?" I asked.

"Yeah. There were ten key employees besides her. We all got some stock. We worked crazy hours, but she worked the hardest, and she was by far the brightest. When she sold her business, I made a tidy sum of money, enough to retire on if I wanted to. I bought this theater and started my own data encryption consulting business in this very room," he explained.

"Why do you own a movie theater? You don't make any money on it, do you?"

"Nah. But this building is a good hideout, and I get to watch a lot of great old movies. We break even because I show the *Rocky Horror Picture Show* at midnight two Saturdays a month. The same stupid kids pay $20 and pack the place to watch the same stupid movie over and over. They buy a lot of popcorn and candy; we charge them 5 bucks for a Snickers. But they do get a safe place to smoke weed. We have to open all the fire doors on Sunday morning to air the place out. Some of the local gentry walk by on Sunday mornings just to breathe the second-hand smoke," he said.

"I never got the appeal of the *Rocky Horror Picture Show*," I said. "I'm more of a *Dr. Strangelove* guy."

"We've got a Stanley Kubrick film festival coming up. *Dr. Strangelove, 2001 a Space Odyssey, Paths of Glory—*"

64

I said, *"Paths of Glory*, that's a great one, underrated classic. How did Kirk Douglas not win the Oscar for that-"

Wishbone cut me off. "Then again, you might be too busy in upcoming days…. or dead."

"Dead? That again? I'm tired of that death stuff. Listen, if I'm dead, I'm not coming to the film festival." I said.

"Let me explain," Wishbone said.

Chapter Eighteen
Moscow

After the Lider's rousing motivational talk the room cleared out fast. Quinn stayed, as instructed.

"I want to tell you what I am up to," the Lider said. "As you know I suffered a humiliating defeat at the hands of the American Cyber Command. I have developed a new plan to get even. Better than even."

"I'm not sure I will understand all that Cyber Warfare stuff," Quinn said.

"You will understand this. The U.S. system is set up, like all the major cyber powers, to attack and defend against other large state actors---like two big armies in World War Two doing battle head on. You understand my point?" the Lider asked.

Quinn nodded.

"I am starting a guerilla war. Instead of our colossal government Cyber organization orchestrating attacks against the U.S., I am empowering the hundreds of, let's call them independent, hacking organizations in Russia and the former Soviet Republics to go after the U.S. Our centralized Cyber Force will monitor and provide technical support and protection to the guerilla forces. The forces will be able to steal vastly more money than before, and they must give our central government half of their earnings," the Lider explained.

'Why is that better?" Quinn asked.

"It is much harder to defend against multiple attackers, and they all have their own styles. So the attacks are less predictable. And, the Guerillas have the motivation of profit; a concept I have learned subsequent to my mastery of Marxism. And for the other side of motivation, that is why I called you in here today, and showed these men the head of Turgenev," the Lider said.

"What do I do now?" Quinn asked.

"You will have no activities within Russia. Go back to Bali. Colonel Nihisky will contact you when we need you. I anticipate that some of these people you saw today may not be up to their assigned tasks. They could possibly run, to America, and try to sell me out. Then I would need you to take care of them," the Lider said.

66

"Okay," Quinn said.

"There were men here today that I am certain will not be able to carry out their assigned tasks. I will liquidate them to provide motivation to the more talented survivors. Another one of them, while talented, has been making plans to move to America, but he overestimates the loyalty of his key lieutenant. The underling has been informing on him, selling him out to buy our favor. So, we know he wants to defect. And if he does..."

"That's where I come in?" Quinn asked.

The Lider nodded. "If you do kill him, we want it to be as public as possible, without you getting caught. We don't want something that can be covered up by the authorities in the United States. This traitor's bloody carcass needs to make the network news. I would like to see him impaled on one of the spikes of the crown of the Statue of Liberty."

"That would be cool. I might have to hire a helicopter for that one," Quinn said.

That's more like it. A chance to use my creative artistry.

Since they were alone in the Lider's office, a bold thought occurred to Quinn. She lifted her skirt and dropped her old-fashioned bloomers to the floor, then kicked them off. She reached down and put them on the Lider's desk without comment. He grimaced as though someone had put a dead rat on his desk. She smiled, turned, and left the office.

I guess I'm not going to be his girlfriend.

The next day Quinn was in Bali.

67

Chapter Nineteen
New York City

"If I do come to your film festival, I'm not paying five bucks for a Snickers," I said.

"Suit yourself. But no outside candy allowed. We're very strict about that," Wishbone said.

The power of suggestion. It must have been fifteen years since I had a Snickers, but now I wanted one. I wanted a Dr. Pepper, too.

"Alright, so why all the secrecy? What am I doing in the East Village, talking to a guy who owns a movie theater which is a front for his high tech who knows what?" I asked.

"Toni Anne is one of the best people in the world. A little different, but she's great. There's some political stuff going on in Cyber Command that not even Toni Anne knows about yet, and she needs me, and you, to help," Wishbone said.

"I'm listening. But I've got to understand what I'm getting into. Last time I got in half-assed, almost got killed, lost all my money. I've got to be convinced that I'm coming out of this whole, or I'm not doing it," I said.

"I can't give you any guarantees,"

"What can you give me?" I asked.

"A chance to get your money back,"

"What kind of chance? I've got a chance to get my money back at the racetrack," I said.

"A lot better chance than the racetrack," Wishbone said.

"So tell me what's going on. Everything. If I'm not convinced, I'm not getting in," I said.

"You might already be in, whether you like it or not, the Russians—"

I cut him off, "I'm not falling for that one again. 'The Russians are watching you, blah, blah, blah. Don't give me that bullshit. Just tell me what's going on, explain everything, and I'll decide what I'm going to do."

Wishbone grinned, "You're already getting smarter. You might make in in this world after all."

John Wishbone Ives spent the next fifteen minutes explaining the very complicated situation. I interrupted him a few times for

68

clarification, but he explained that he couldn't tell me everything. These people were devious beyond belief. I wondered if I was one of the parties getting tricked. Finally, he finished.

When he was done, I was quiet for a while. "Count me out. I need more assurances than that," I said.

"That's your decision?" he asked, "I can't believe it."

"Well believe it," I said.

We shook hands and he wordlessly escorted me to the door. He said, "just do one thing, keep the burner phone, okay?"

"Alright," I said.

Chapter Twenty
Austin, Texas

I had flown home in a bad mood. It wasn't like me to turn down an adventure, and I felt lousy about it. Still, I wasn't getting into something that I didn't understand. The only part I did understand was that the people who concocted the plot were masters at deviousness and could screw me anytime they felt like it.

But I did want to get my money back. I had concocted a plan where I'd show Barbara Jean my recovered money, and then we'd have it out over whether we'd get back together or go our separate ways. But right now, I had that one obstacle: I didn't have the money, and I didn't have an inkling of a plan about how I was going to get $50 million.

I got back to managing money for my clients. The market was medium/high, not a level where I'd do any serious buying. My clients got quarterly statements. They also could see their accounts online whenever they wanted, although most of them didn't look very often. That's why they had me for one leg of their at least three-legged stool. The other legs of their stool were managed by someone else, sometimes the client themselves, and I didn't pay any attention to assets that were not under my umbrella.

I told my clients that my ideal holding period for a stock was forever. I only sold if the company went sour for the long term. That's what people paid me for, to know whether a company was messed up temporarily or long term. I wasn't always right, but I'm better at judging stocks than most people.

Some of my clients asked me if I didn't buy or sell on a given day, what *did* I do? I answered that I'm like a duck, I look all calm and quiet on the surface, but beneath the water I'm always paddling, always thinking, reading. That was true until now. Now I was a dead duck, a decoy just floating around. My accounts were going up because the market was going up. If I couldn't get out of my funk and get motivated it was time to tell my clients that I was retiring.

My clients had no idea that I'd blown all my taxable investments on Bitcoin. I had taken a good-sized inheritance

70

that I received in my early twenties and turned it into $50 million, most of the gain coming from getting in the tech stocks in the 1990s and getting out. The selling was the hard part, because it threw off huge capital gains on which I had to pay Federal taxes. Being in Texas, there were no state taxes. But the taxes were still a huge bite and would have been a lot more painful if I had sold and then the tech boom continued after a rest. But it didn't continue, it was a Bubble, not a Forever Boom.

There aren't any Forever Booms. But it's tough to know when to get off the train. That's the hard part.

This funk lasted a few days. I called clients on the pretense that I wanted to discuss the Long-Term strategy for the accounts, but I called because I was bored and lonesome.

One client I didn't call was Barbara Jean. She could call me if she wanted to discuss her money, or anything else.

Two days later the computer flashed at me that I had an ACAT notice. I forget exactly what that stands for, but the T is for transfer. It means the client is taking their money away from me and transferring it to another broker or bank. The computerized notice just lists the account number, so I had to look up whose account it was: Barbara Jean Parker.

I'm a fiduciary. That means I have the legal and ethical responsibility of trust with my clients, I have to put their interests ahead of my own. When you get an ACAT regarding a client account you have the legal responsibility to do two things: 1) you must stop any trading in that account, and 2) you must call the client to verify in their voice that they intended to transfer. The second part has been instituted in the last ten years or so due to scams, where hackers faked a client's intentions and transferred the account to the Bank of Pluto or somewhere. Then the money would disappear from the banking system and never be seen again.

Most clients do you the courtesy of calling you before you get the computerized notice, so you don't have the embarrassment of making the phone call. One time a client fired me for being too conservative and called to tell me that I put the "douche" in fiduciary.

What could I do but laugh at that one? There's a tremendous temptation to get into a name calling match at that point, but it's

71

a bad idea. My mentor, Tom Good told me at that point to take the high ground and say, "Thank you for your business, and the best of luck to you. I'll take care of everything on my end. Have a good day." It's disarming, and sometimes the clients came back when a new investment guru didn't live up to the exaggerated promises that had been dangled before the client.

I had to call Barbara Jean. In the improbable circumstance that this was the work of hackers, if I okayed the transfer and the money was lost, I would be on the hook for it, the whole $15 million. And I was a little short of that kind of dough right now. I was tempted to just okay the transfer, but I sucked up my courage and called.

I got voicemail. "Barbara Jean. I just got notification that you are transferring your account. I need to speak to you, it's a legal requirement. The transfer cannot happen until you give me your verbal approval."

It was unlikely that I could force myself to go with the "Thank you for your business…" speech. It was more likely that I would ask Barbara Jean if her asshole father had some part in this decision.

Work was impossible. I just sat there. Maybe Barbara Jean wouldn't have the courage to call me. Then what would I do?

After a period of time, somewhere between 30 and 3,000 minutes, Barb called me back.

"JR, I got your message. It doesn't make any sense. What are you talking about?" she said.

"I got the notification on the computer that you are moving your account," I said.

"My account with you?" she asked.

"I just got the notification on my computer." I said.

"Well, there's some mistake or something. I hate to admit this, but when you told me that you just lost your own money and would never do that sort of thing with your clients' money that made me respect you more," she said, "besides, if I wanted to fire you, I'd do it in person."

I didn't know what to say. It was a good thing that I called her. Finally I said, "I've got to get to the bottom of this. I'll, uhh---"

"Call me back?" Barb asked.

72

"Yeah." From the tone of her voice, it seemed like the ice was melting a bit. "Barb, can I ask you a personal question?

"Go ahead," she said.

"Are you observing the Involuntary Celibate Protocol?" I asked.

"I can hold out a lot longer than you. Besides, some of the boys in bib overalls at the Feed Store are already sniffin' around. I'm pretty sure I could get lucky with one of the 300 pound guys. He's sweet on me. Goes by the name 'Homer,'" she said. "How's it going on getting the $50 million back?"

"I've got a solid plan," I lied.

"You didn't just make up this transferring the account thing just to have an excuse to call me, did you?" Barb asked.

"No…no, I'd never do something like that. This must be some glitch with the firm that holds all the assets. I've got to get to the bottom of this. It could have been a serious problem. It was just a coincidence that it happened to be your account," I said. I should have known then there are no coincidences.

"Okay then. I gotta go," she said.

"Bye,"

Chapter Twenty One
Bali, Indonesia

Sierra Quinn's phone rang, the special one that only got calls from Moscow.

Maybe it would be an assignment.

Quinn had been shooting target practice lately. She didn't need much practice because she usually was only a few feet from her victim. But it paid to train for contingencies.

It was Colonel Nihisky. "Miss Quinn?" he asked.

"Yes."

"Please hold for the Lider," Nihisky said.

"Okay."

"Miss Quinn?" the Lider said.

So now it was 'Miss Quinn, eh? He called me something else, in Russian, when he couldn't wait to get my clothes off. How do you say 'Slam, Bam, and Thank You Ma'am' in Russian?

"Yes, I'm here," Quinn said.

"We do not have a mission for you yet but should have one soon. Stay in practice. I did want to share with you the details of one of the initiatives we have implemented," the Lider said.

"Sounds interesting," Quinn said.

"Yes, I thought this would be of particular interest to you. One of our best hackers has already started ruining the financial life of one of your enemies, JR Johnson. The hacker has already started creating havoc with the money management business Johnson runs. This is just the first step, we have many more nightmares in store for Johnson," the Lider said. It will be more rewarding if we do it in pieces, rather than all at once. After all that, you, or someone else, can kill him."

"Sounds good," Quinn said, "I'd like to have that opportunity."

"You will if it fits into our operational plan. Does the name Toni Anne Laudano mean anything to you?" the Lider asked. "Did Turgenev mention it to you?"

"No," Quinn answered.

"That's not important. Laudano has the resources to protect Johnson, if she wishes to do so. We may take her out to prevent

74

her from meddling in the efforts of the hacker who is working on Johnson," the Lider said.

"Is that something I can do? I'd be glad to help." Quinn said. She was eager to get back in the game. She hadn't shot anybody in a while.

"No," the Lider said. "We have someone else in place. It's not time for you to go to the U.S. yet. But depending on how our plans play out, you may get the opportunity to put Johnson out of his misery."

"Great," Quinn said.

Chapter Twenty Two
Fort Meade, MD
Cyber Command Headquarters

Toni Anne had been summoned to the office of General Goldstein. He pointed and she sat down.

"Toni Anne, you must be aware of the scuttlebutt that's going around regarding changes," General Goldstein said.

"So, how bad is it?" Toni Anne asked.

"It's going to sound worse to you than—"

"Than what, General?"

"I'm getting lateralled over to the Pentagon to start up something called the Inter Agency Cyber Task Force," the General said.

"What's that? Am I staying here?" Toni Anne asked.

"You stay here. It's part of a bigger plan. That's all I can tell you now. Things are going to work out. In the meantime, Admiral Stockbridge is taking charge of Cyber Command," Goldstein said.

"That moron! I've been in meetings with him. He doesn't know his ass from a hole in the ground," Toni Anne said.

"He knows how to look like an Admiral. And he knows how to play the politicians," Goldstein said.

"That's all I need, a bunch of politicians running around here," Toni Anne said.

"You haven't heard the worst yet. Remember Congressman Safi?" the General asked.

"Let me see…Congressman Safi. White guy, asshole, wears a blue suit?" Toni Anne commented.

"Sometimes Toni Anne…. I'm going to miss you. Everybody who works for me at the Pentagon will just kiss my ass all the time," General Goldstein said. "Safi is politically very ambitious, and he's tight with Stockbridge. Rumor has it that Safi's going to run for President, and name Stockbridge as his running mate."

"And I have to report to Stockbridge?" Toni Anne said.

"Try not to get fired. Stockbridge is a real by the book guy, he won't put up with your insubordination," the General said. "Don't tell Stockbridge anything you wouldn't want

Congressman Safi to hear. Don't worry, Stockbridge is so dumb he won't even know what questions to ask."

"What the hell is going on?" Toni Anne asked.

"I can't explain it to you now," Goldstein said. "Trust me, everything will work out.

Chapter Twenty Three
Austin, TX

My burner phone rang, which hadn't happened since I'd been back from meeting Ives in New York. It had to be Toni Anne or Wishbone.

The voice at the other end said, "Hey." It was Wishbone.

"Yeah," I said.

"Toni Anne's been shot," he said. "Hang up and call me back."

"Toni Anne's been shot?" I asked.

"She's going to be okay," Wishbone said, "she's in the hospital. Toni Anne killed her assailant."

"Killed? How?" I asked.

"Hang up and call me back," he said.

I did so. Wishbone told me to meet him at 8 pm in the Cincinnati airport, Concourse B, at the McDonalds.

Chapter Twenty Four
Cincinnati Airport

The only way to fly to meet Wishbone was to buy a ticket to New York by way of Cincinnati and get off the plane at the intermediate stop. The flight attendant explained that this would invalidate my ticket to New York, and that my luggage was no longer the airline's responsibility.

"Fine, I understand," I said. "I don't have any luggage."

We covert types travel light.

The airport was almost deserted. It was easy to find my destination. The place looked like McDonalds on Concourse B at any airport in the United States, or the world. After Earth colonizes Mars, there will be a McDonalds on Concourse B, at Schwarzenegger Interplanetary Spaceport. From watching *The Martian,* we know they'll be able to grow potatoes in fertilized beds to make the fries.

I had to look around for Wishbone, who was sitting at a table as far away from the counter as he could get. After getting a McChicken and a coffee, my McDonalds standard, I went to sit with Ives.

"This is glamorous. Don't spies usually meet in St. Moritz, the Orient Express---"

Wishbone looked around and said, "Shut up. I think we're clean. We can talk."

"Why are we meeting here?" I asked.

"I like the wine list. Don't ask me too many questions. I just happened to be traveling."

"So what's going on with Toni Anne? She got shot?" I asked.

"In her apartment. She keeps a gun in her bedroom. A woman broke in, and they exchanged gunfire. Toni Anne got shot in the leg but managed to kill the intruder.
I just---"

"A woman? Do you know who it is? Is it Sierra Quinn?" I asked.

Wishbone didn't answer.

"Do you know who Sierra Quinn is?" I asked.

"I know who she is, but I haven't been able to talk to Toni Anne. I'm just a contractor. Cyber Command is on an

79

information lockdown, I can't get anything. Everybody's a suspect." Wishbone said.

"They don't suspect you, do they?" I asked.

"They're acting like it's a conspiracy. Everybody's a suspect. You, me, General Goldstein, everybody who's ever worked there," Wishbone shrugged. "You know there's a new boss at Cyber Command, an Admiral?"

"Admiral? What happened to General Goldstein?" I said.

"Goldstein got pushed aside, a so-called promotion to a phony job at the Pentagon. Admiral Stockbridge is the new head of Cyber Command. He's real tight with Congressman Safi," Wishbone said. "This guy Stockbridge is a pure bureaucrat, but he's a second-rate technical guy."

"You're losing me," I said.

"Stockbridge is coming in to play ball with Congress. Toni Anne calls him "Admiral Profile." To his face." Wishbone said. "There are some complicated reasons for him to be there. It changes plans that involve you. Stockbridge would never let you in the tent. He does look like an Admiral out of Central Casting though."

"You mean silver hair, tan, handsome in his Navy-Blue uniform?" I asked. "Spends his weekends playing golf with lobbyists, congressmen?"

"Exactly. In comparison, Goldstein doesn't know which end of a golf club to hold; works eighteen hour days, seven days a week. Toni Anne says the new guy leaves at five o'clock every day. He was only there a couple days before she got shot. Toni Anne briefed Stockbridge but doesn't think he understood what she was talking about," Wishbone said.

"So, what's on the agenda here?" I asked.

"Toni Anne and I cooked up Plan B before this happened. She'd never go to Stockbridge with this plan," he said. "It includes you getting your money back---"

"I'm in," I said.

"Not so fast. You have to know what you're getting into. By the way, Toni Anne seems to really like you… not that it's my business or anything, but I've got to know the dynamics of what I'm working with. Did you two ever---"

I cut him off, "Hey, I'm married, Toni Anne and I just have this---"

"Are you going to say "chemistry?" In New York when guys say that it means they're screwing outside the holy bonds of matrimony," Wishbone said. "I know one guy who's done so much experimental chemistry he should work for DuPont."

"Look Wishbone, let's put this to rest. Toni Anne and I have never done anything. If we're going to work together you should know that. Okay? Let's move on. What's Plan B?" I said.

"Toni Anne has cooked up a plan. There's a place in it for you…you can get your money back," Wishbone said. "But it might be superseded by another plan. No matter what, you've got to know something. And don't ask me how I know."

"I'm listening," I said.

"The Russians are coming with a big-time plan to screw us up with ransomware and hacking. Pulling out all the stops. They're going to use independent hackers from Russia and the former Soviet Republics. They're going to hit up American companies for major dollars and disrupt the financial system as a smokescreen. On top of that, they have special plans for one person in particular," Wishbone said.

'Who's that?" I asked.

"You. The Lider blames you for the Bitcoin thing," Wishbone said, "He's out to wreck you. There are a million dirty tricks they can pull on you. And they could kill you."

"Well, that's just great! I'm sure glad I helped out!" I said.

"People are trying to help you. First of all, before I give you all the details, I've got to be able to talk to Toni Anne in a secure location. Not her hospital room. She's in Walter Reed. I know some things she doesn't know," he said. "Then I can tell you more. Or maybe somebody else will end up explaining it to you."

"I'm completely lost. What am I supposed to do?" I said.

"I know it's confusing. I just can't tell you right now. Things need to get nailed down," Wishbone said.

"When can that happen?" I asked.

"Soon. Toni Anne needs to be brought up to speed. But I've got a very powerful friend who might help you," he said.

"I haven't got the foggiest idea what you're talking about," I said. "I feel like I'm watching a spy movie and went out to get popcorn, and missed the important part," I said.

81

Wishbone sat without talking. He rubbed his eyes and yawned. "You're right. Plans changed in the last few hours. But there's one thing we can accomplish tonight," he said.

"What?"

"Give me your phone," Wishbone said.

I handed it to him. He took off the back and fished an envelope out of his pocket. From the envelope he pulled out something that looked like a computer chip.

"What are you doing?" I asked.

"I'm installing a one-time use device on your phone. I can call you once. I emphasize once, without anyone else being able to listen in. No one will be able to triangulate on this call to be able to find your location. Once it's used, the device deprograms itself. It's a computer program that uses software to self-destruct without causing any harm to your phone," Wishbone explained.

"Why does it only work once?" I asked.

"Blunt reason?" he asked.

"We better be honest with each other," I said.

"If you take a call when you're in the hands of the bad guys, even if they torture you---"

"I can't make it work again," I interjected. "Reassuring."

"I'll save it until there's no other way out," Wishbone said.

"Cool," I said. "Where did you get this? Who—"

"This is not something you get at the Apple Store. Don't worry about where I got it. I have a special supplier," Wishbone said. "We have to give it two passwords. The thing is voice activated. I call you, then you say the first word, the screen flashes, and then you have seven seconds to say the second password. So what are two words that you'll remember, but wouldn't say together by mistake?"

I thought about that. What words would I remember, even after getting hit in the head with a crowbar, but that I wouldn't say together?

"The first word is something I wouldn't say in normal conversation?" I asked.

"Right. You wouldn't want to activate the countdown to the next password. If you do activate the first password, but don't shut off the phone within seven seconds, the function just cancels out. Nothing happens to your phone, but the special function will never work," he explained.

82

"Okay. First word: Albatross," I said.

"Why that? Wishbone asked.

"Albatross is three under par for one hole in golf. A hole in one on a par four, or a two on a par five," I said.

"Alright," he said. He tapped some letters and numbers on the screen of my phone. Wishbone held the bottom of the iPhone up to my face. "You have to say the passwords. It will recognize only your voice. You're sure you want that password?"

"Hey, an Albatross hardly ever happens, but I'll remember. And I'd never say the word in normal conversation," I said. "and I'm not going to say 'Hey, look at the albatross flying by the window.' I don't even know what a real albatross looks like."

'Didn't you ever read _Rime of the Ancient Mariner_?" Wishbone asked.

"Yeah, but it wasn't the illustrated edition. Hey, I went to Texas, it wasn't like Princeton. I hear you guys learned the classics from comic books with lots of pictures," I said.

"Stop being a shithead and pay attention." Ives said, "don't you take anything seriously? This—"

"Hey, don't give me _that crap_. My whole life has turned into a comic book. I lose over a billion dollars, Russians try to kill me, my wife throws me out, you give me this chip from Buck Rogers in the 23rd Century, and now I'm the Spy Who Came in From the Cold, or who's out in the cold, or---"

"Can't you shut up?" Wishbone said. We sat there looking each other in the eye for a good minute.

I was in a corner. If I walked away now, I'd have nothing. No plan, no wife, no money. "Alright, so I shut up," I said.

"JR, I know you have this independent streak. But if you want this operation to work, you have to do what I tell you. It's like the military, and I'm your commanding officer," Ives said.

"Why?" I asked.

Now it was Wishbone's turn to sit and think. "This is the last time I'm going to explain anything like this to you. Some information has to be compartmentalized, that's means—"

"It means if I don't know, I can't tell anybody, even if they're waterboarding me,"

83

"Right. But the villains here aren't the waterboarding type, it's too subtle. Waterboarding is popular because it doesn't leave any visible damage. Agencies that have government oversight like to waterboard people, so they have plausible deniability. These bad guys don't care what you look like when they're done with you," Wishbone explained.

"Remember, I'm the guy who got whacked in the head with a crowbar and stuffed into a 55-gallon drum and pushed into a lake," I said.

"That might end up seeming subtle compared to what these guys would do to you when they really want you to talk. Or they might just shoot you a few times," Wishbone said.

I decided not to make any more of the wisecracks that came to my mind. 'So, you're my commanding officer?' I asked.

"You have to do what I tell you. You can't ask questions. I'll explain things if I think you need to know," Wishbone said. "Can you handle that?"

"Alright," I said, 'what now?'

"Let's finish setting up your phone." He held the phone back up to me. "What's the second password?"

"Sierra," I said. "I won't forget that."

Wishbone gave me a grin. "Okay," he said.

"Hey, I just realized that you look different than when I knew you at the Big Investment Firm. You used to have a shaved head and a goatee," I said. "You looked sharp, distinctive. Now with short hair, clean shaven chin, you look---"

"—like I don't stand out in a crowd? I'm going for that look." Wishbone said. He pointed to a woman walking past the McDonalds. "Look at that woman. Don't look back over here. Describe what I'm wearing."

I couldn't.

"Okay you can look back now. That's the look I'm going for," Ives said.

I nodded. "Give me a hint. What's my mission?"

Wishbone stroked his chin. "Have you ever been to Korea?"

"North or South?" I smiled at my own witticism.

"North," Wishbone said.

Chapter Twenty Five
Bethesda, MD
Walter Reed Medical Center

Toni Anne Laudano was getting bored. She had been shot in the thigh and taken to Walter Reed, but since the bullet had missed any bone, it had not required surgery. It was her third day in the hospital.

She had VIP accommodations, but not the highest level, maybe something suitable for a colonel. The military was really into that stratification. A colonel would never get a room that was made for a general, even if the hospital was empty. Still, she had a good-sized private room. It told her where she stood in Stockbridge's order of battle. General Goldstein would have made sure she had the best accommodations, regardless of rank. A nurse hurried into her room.

"Admiral Stockbridge is on his way here. His aide called us so we could inform you," she said. The nurse was on edge. Someone with four stars on their epaulettes always got the medical staff nervous.

"Thanks," Toni Anne said. His aide called and spoke to the staff, who were told to inform their patient. General Goldstein would have just called Toni Anne himself, but this guy Stockbridge was all protocol and chain of command, he just didn't have the brain power to do the job.

Laudano's cellphone rang. Caller ID said: Gabrielle McHugh.

"Hi Gabrielle," Toni Anne said. She realized that was the first time she had used McHugh's first name. At the beginning of their working together, she had dubbed her "Murder Bitch", due to Gab's famous shooting of the lawyer, then an hour later the Hedge Fund manager in New York. Toni Anne had called her "Colonel McHugh" since her promotion. Lt. Colonels like being called "Colonel." It lumps them in with the full birds.

If Gabrielle noticed the informal name change, she didn't mention it. "Toni Anne, I'd like to come and visit you today," she said.

"Okay, but the Admiral is on his way here," Toni Anne said.

"I know. Can I come at lunch time, after the Admiral is gone?"

85

"Sure. Anything special on the agenda?" Toni Anne asked.

"Lunch," Gabrielle said.

They laughed. But Toni Anne knew that wasn't the real answer. Gabrielle didn't want to say anything on the phone. Toni Anne was sure that Admiral Stockbridge was spying on her, and now maybe Gabrielle McHugh realized that she too was under surveillance. The government doesn't need a court order to wiretap and otherwise spy on government employees. Wiretaps are only required to gather evidence that is admissible in a court of law. This situation would not result in a trial.

Chapter Twenty Six
Walter Reed Hospital

Admiral Stockbridge's aide had sent a nurse into Toni Anne's room to make sure she was "decent," as he put it, and when that was ascertained, the aide barged through the door, held it for the Admiral, and then the aide was dismissed and waited in the hallway.

"General Goldstein opens his own doors," Toni Anne said.

"I'm not General Goldstein," Stockbridge said.

"No shit,"

The Admiral was quiet for a good ten seconds. "I'm not accustomed to being addressed in that tone of voice," he said.

Toni Anne decided it was her turn to wait ten seconds to respond. "On top of all the usual problems Cyber Command has, now we have an unprecedented threat from literally hundreds of hackers and ransomware pirates in Russia and the former Soviet Republics, and you're worried about shiny shoes and saluting," she said.

"My technical people tell me that we should be able to handle the new threat with ease," the Admiral said.

"Your technical people? Since I'm not there everyone else is intimidated by you. They think you'll shoot the messenger if they tell you the truth, so they just tell you what you want to hear," Toni Anne said.

"I'm willing to put up with a certain level of insubordination from you. Everyone, including my predecessor, holds your intellect in such high esteem. But you've exceeded the level I'm willing to tolerate. You could be replaced. That's one of the items I'm here to discuss," the Admiral said.

"Oh, I wondered why you didn't bring flowers," Toni Anne said. "Cyber Command is too important for its' leader to be more concerned with military protocol than the truth. The very existence of our country is at stake. If you can't face that, maybe you should go back to inspecting battleships---"

"That's enough! I planned to be more diplomatic, but I'll just tell you straight out. You're being demoted. I'm bringing in a one star admiral to be second in command. You are to report to him. If you want to see me, you see him, and he'll arrange it if

87

he feels it's necessary. If you can't handle that, your resignation will be accepted. This isn't Goldstein's outfit anymore---"

"What a petty chickenshit you are! Who taught you your bedside manner? Newt Gingrich?" Toni Anne asked.

It was obvious that the Admiral didn't understand the Newt Gingrich reference.

But the Admiral did know how to act indignant. "I consider Newt Gingrich a friend," he said.

"I'm not surprised...Do you know the identity of the woman who shot me?

"Not yet," the Admiral said.

"That's not very impressive. What is it you're doing over there, polishing your belt buckles?"

"As I stated, I've had enough of you," the Admiral said.

Laudano went on, "So you want me to go through the Chain of Command? I don't like that. But I've earned a lot of points in the past couple years, so I get some special treatment."

Stockbridge said, "You're not going to get any special treatment from me."

"I'm friends with people a lot more important than you. You know whose private phone number I have?" Toni Anne asked.

"No, who's private phone number do you have?" the Admiral parroted.

"The President. And I have his permission to call him anytime 24/7 when I have a concern. Did you know that?" Toni Anne asked.

"No."

"General Goldstein knew. I guess the President hasn't gotten around to telling you yet. I've never called him. But that's about to change," Toni Anne said.

Admiral Stockbridge was quiet again. His face gave away nothing. He said. "Something else. I'm putting you on recuperative leave for 30 days. I've ordered the hospital to keep you for one more day. When you leave the hospital, you are to go home and stay there. You'll be guarded at your house. This isn't a work-from-home program. Your security clearances will be temporarily suspended. It's for your own good."

"I'm on house arrest!" Toni Anne said. "Your concern for my wellbeing is touching. What's with the security clearances? You don't trust me? Do you think---"

"We think your home may be monitored by foreign powers—"

Toni Anne erupted. "you mean you think I don't know the fuckin' commies are trying to monitor communications coming in and out of my house? What the---"

"Yes the Russians and others are monitoring your home. And I must advise you that we will be doing that as well," the Admiral said.

"You don't think I know that?" Toni Anne asked.

"I said you'd be discharged tomorrow. Do as I ordered, otherwise you'll be terminated from any association with the government," the Admiral said. "I had hoped this conversation would be on a more professional level."

"I'll express your disappointment when I talk to the President," Toni Anne said.

Chapter Twenty Seven
Admiral Stockbridge's Car
Capitol Beltway

The Admiral rated a limousine. He and his aide sat in the back.

"Give me the secure phone," Stockbridge said to the aide. The Admiral hit some buttons.

"Let me talk to Congressman Safi," he said when the phone was answered.

Safi came on the line. "Yes, Admiral. How did your meeting go with the foul-mouthed genius?" Safi asked.

"She didn't quit. I pushed her hard, I thought she might just tell me to shove it. But she did have a surprise for me." Stockbridge said.

"What was that?" Safi asked.

"Did you know that Toni Anne Laudano has the President's direct line, and permission to call him anytime 24/7 when she has a concern, without regard for the Chain of Command?" the Admiral asked.

"No, I didn't know that. How did that escape our research?" Safi paused. "Okay. Maybe we can use that to our advantage. I'll think about alternatives. I'll call you tomorrow," Safi said.

"Okay," Stockbridge said.

"And Admiral, when I'm President, that bitch won't have *my* phone number. If she's even alive." Then the congressman hung up.

In Washington power circles it was common practice for the more powerful of the two people on a phone call to hang up without saying goodbye. It established the hierarchy. Safi clearly thought he outranked Stockbridge, a four-star admiral.

Chapter Twenty Eight
Walter Reed Hospital

Gabrielle McHugh came into Toni Anne's hospital room just before noon. She did bring flowers, and a note was attached to the bouquet. It read:

I don't trust Admiral Stockbridge. Something is wrong. They are bringing in a one-star kiss ass admiral to be his second in command. Did you know about this?

Toni Anne read the note and nodded. "Thank you for the flowers and the nice card," she said. She tore the note into small pieces and threw the pieces into a plastic water glass on her bedside table. Then she poured water into the glass.

"Oh, look what I've done! Would you mind flushing the contents of the glass down the toilet? Toni Anne asked. Gabrielle did so.

"I'm going to call for the nurse so I can get a wheelchair to take you for a walk," Gab said.

"Good idea," Toni Anne said.

Gabrielle asked the duty nurse to step into the room. "I asked the Admiral for permission to bring Toni Anne for a walk," Gab told the nurse.

The nurse hesitated. "The admiral said it's okay, because Toni Anne is going home tomorrow," Gabrielle said. The nurse was nervous enough questioning Gabrielle but was not going to question an Admiral.

"Well, it's not in the doctor's orders, but if the admiral said it's okay… I'll get the wheelchair," the nurse said.

Toni Anne Laudano, in her hospital bathrobe, looked in the mirror. "Geez, do I look alright to be seen in public?" she asked.

"You always look good to me," Gabrielle McHugh said.

Toni Anne paused. "Forget I asked," she said.

Toni Anne was flagrantly heterosexual. Gabrielle was not, and had been the lover of Lola Madison, the now deceased movie star. Lola had been the sometimes girlfriend of JR Johnson. Toni Anne was interested in Johnson, but since he was married to Barbara Jean Parker, and Toni Anne had a strict no fooling around with married men policy, things were currently at a standstill.

91

Gabrielle and Toni Anne were quiet. It wasn't because they didn't know what to say, they were just afraid to say anything important, anything they didn't want the Admiral to know.

"Really, all kidding aside, you look fine. No problem. All the men will want to push your wheelchair," Gabrielle said.

"Push my wheelchair?" Toni Anne asked, "is that some kind of kinky euphemism… as in 'Hey baby, let me push your wheelchair?'"

They both laughed. "No, it just means they want to push your wheelchair," Gab said. "They might want to get kinky later."

"I'd like to have the stiches removed from my leg first," Toni Anne said.

As Gabrielle wheeled Toni Anne past the nursing station, the senior resident physician looked up. Gabrielle was wearing her uniform, and as a Lt. Colonel she outranked the doctor, so he said nothing.

After they had passed, the doctor called out to the duty nurse. "Who gave the patient permission to leave the room in the wheelchair?" he asked.

The nurse answered, "Sir, the Admiral who was just here said it was okay." The nurse didn't mention that she had heard that second hand, from Lt. Colonel McHugh.

The doctor muttered to the nurse, "Great, another Admiral thinks he's a doctor. Well, she is going home tomorrow. We've got bigger problems. It's okay."

Gabrielle and Toni Anne got in an elevator to go down. There were three doctors in the elevator, two male, one female. No one spoke. At the basement level, when the door opened the other passengers let Gabrielle push Toni Anne out before they exited.

"We're going to the cafeteria," Gab told Toni Anne.

As they progressed toward the cafeteria, Gabrielle said to Toni Anne, "The guys in the elevator were checking you out. I told you that you looked good."

"I might be an object of curiosity. Gunshot victims who shoot and kill their assailant get peoples' interest," Toni Anne said.

"Well, that's one thing we have in common," Gab said. "I'm the Murder Bitch, remember?"

This comment drew a quick glance from Toni Anne. "I didn't think of that…you shot the two guys in New York. We'll have to discuss that sometime…you know, when we can talk."

"Okay," Gab answered. "There's one more I want to shoot," Gab said.

"Just one?" Toni Anne asked.

Chapter Twenty Nine
Walter Reed Hospital
Café 8901

Gabrielle looked around. "This is nice compared to an Army cafeteria. And a fancy name, "Café 8901." Everybody is looking at us."

"You must be used to that," Toni Anne said. Gabrielle McHugh was a 6'3" beautiful woman, standing tall in her Army uniform.

"So, we continue to be objects of curiosity," Gabrielle said. "Let's hope the Admiral's *electronic* curiosity hasn't extended to Café 8901 yet."

Toni Anne held her hand over her mouth. "I'm sure it hasn't. Stockbridge is sneaky, but not creative. This was a good choice. His stooges haven't had the time to wire this place yet. We can talk here. Just in case, let's talk like this." She nodded her head to call attention to the way she held her hand.

They got food at the salad bar. Toni Anne carried their tray in her lap while Gab pushed the wheelchair, and they intentionally chose a table in the middle of the noisy room. Toni Anne was the only patient; all the other tables were occupied by what looked like medical types. When Toni Anne saw a doctor repeatedly peering over his shoulder in an attempt to eavesdrop, she said, "good afternoon doctor, can you hear us okay?" which was an effective deterrent.

"That doctor's not a spy, just a nosey pain in the ass," Toni Anne said to Gabrielle, loud enough for the offending doctor and his two luncheon companions to hear. They hurried to finish their lunches.

"Do you know that the Admiral hasn't sent anyone over here, a law enforcement type to interview me about the shooting?" Toni Anne said. "You'd think he'd at least pretend to be investigating."

"I hear they know. It was a Russian woman with loose connections to their embassy. It was the same woman who shot…your late husband," Gabrielle said.

"The woman who shot John Driscoll? That's interesting. When we know each other better, I'll tell you what it was like

94

to be married to a Russian mole. So, what do you want to tell me?" Toni Anne asked.

"The Admiral is up to no good. I don't know what it is," Gab said.

"The Admiral's an idiot, but a dangerous idiot. He is good looking though. If he was some homely guy, he'd be lucky to have made captain." Laudano said.

A Navy Captain was the equivalent to an Army colonel. "Are you implying I made Lt. Colonel so quickly just because of my good looks?" Gabrielle said.

"Stop fishing for compliments, it's unbecoming," Toni Anne said.

"I've already been read the Riot Act by Stockbridge. No more casual behavior, everything is by the hierarchical military book," Gab said. "And the new one star starts today. I met him once. He's got his lips locked to Stockbridge's ass. He doesn't seem like he knows anything about Cyber Warfare."

"If they get too rigid the best civilians at Cyber Command will quit. They could get jobs tomorrow in the private sector, paying three times as much. Only the mediocre will stay," Toni Anne said. There were more civilians than military among the highest intellectual levels of Cyber Command.

"I'm thinking about leaving," Gabrielle said.

"Don't do anything just yet okay?" Toni Anne said. "You might be more helpful on the inside."

"Stockbridge is going to know we were in the cafeteria so we could talk freely, outside of their snooping range. He'll confront me when I go back," Gabrielle said. "What should I tell him we talked about?"

Toni Anne laughed. "Tell him we talked about sex. A private matter, none of his business."

Chapter Thirty
Washington, DC
The Capitol

Congressman Safi was doing successive interviews on CNN, Fox, MSNBC and a couple other networks. This method was now preferred by politicians rather than a news conference because most viewers only watched one cable news channel, and this tactic made it seem like each channel was getting an exclusive. They all got the same message, with a little different spin, depending on whether Safi viewed the network as friendly or hostile to him.

"I am beginning a special sub-committee investigation into our lack of preparedness regarding cyber threats, with special focus on the recent hacking of our financial system that led to the entire banking structure being taken down for five unexplained minutes," Safi told each network.

In some manner each reporter asked the congressman if he thought the President might bear some responsibility for our cyber weakness.

"He is the Commander-in-Chief and let there be no misunderstanding; This is the equivalent of war," Safi answered. "We'll dig to get the truth and let the chips fall where they may. The American people *deserve* the truth."

Then each reporter asked some version of, "Congressman Safi, rumors have it that you are considering an announcement that you will be a candidate for President in the upcoming election. Any comment on that?"

"It's no secret that I have an exploratory committee looking into the feasibility of becoming a Presidential candidate. I have to tell you that I have not yet made a decision, but early response from around the country is very positive, very favorable." Safi said. "Patriotic Americans are very concerned about our lack of cyber awareness and are looking for someone who can lead us out of this area of vulnerability, as well as projecting strength in other important and presently overlooked areas."

When the last interview was over the bright lights in front of the congressman went dim. Technicians gathered up cables and wheeled lights back to their vans.

Congressman Safi's media consultant, John "Buddha" Alteiri stepped out of the shadows and the two of them began walking. "That was very good, but remember, we want to project a little more warmth along with the message of strength," the consultant said.

"Shut the fuck up," Safi said.

"That's the kind of warmth I'm referring to," Alteiri said.

Chapter Thirty One
The White House

The President was watching the television with Chan Wheeler, his Chief of Staff.

"Mr. President, it looks like this son of a bitch is just about to go public, saying that he wants your job," Wheeler said.

"Remember when Safi was over here for a meeting in the Oval Office once and made a comment on how the drapes looked a bit ragged?" the President asked.

"Yeah," Wheeler answered.

"Well, tell Safi not to call the decorator just yet," the President said.

Chapter Thirty Two
Washington, DC
Georgetown Neighborhood

Toni Anne Laudano was home. She had been released from Walter Reed National Military Medical Center that day and driven to her townhouse.

She was a recent widow. But she was not in mourning. Laudano had been married to John Driscoll, a man who she knew was a Russian mole who worked in U.S. Cyber Command. The American government had been pondering, with Toni Anne's full knowledge and consent, just how to eventually dispose of Toni Anne's husband when the Russians decided he was no longer useful to them and shot him in an alley near his Georgetown abode, thus eliminating that problem. There hadn't been a funeral.

Toni Anne Laudano had an immediate problem. She needed to talk with John Wishbone Ives. She was under intense monitoring from U.S. Cyber Command and probably other U.S. agencies like the NSA and from Russia and maybe some other governments as well. Any normal telephone conversation between them would be electronically overheard in real time by a handful of little spy weasels and replayed for their bosses multiple times.

But Toni Anne thought she might engineer a solution to the problem.

She had the President of the United States' personal phone number and his permission to call any time day or night. Very few people were in possession of this special number. Toni Anne's new boss, Admiral Stockbridge didn't have it. If Stockbridge had some urgent issue that he thought required the President's attention he had to call his boss, the Chairman of the Joint Chiefs of Staff and ask that the message be forwarded.

Toni Anne planned to ask the President in person for permission to use his private phone network so she couldn't be monitored in her conversation with Ives.

She phoned the President and thought she recognized the voice of the person who answered.

"Hello, this is Toni Anne Laudano. Who is this?" she said.

99

"This is Chan Wheeler."

"Chan, I need to speak to the President right now."

"Can this wait?" Wheeler asked.

"Chan, don't give me that Chief of Staff crap. The President told me I could call him anytime. Put him on."

In a moment the President came on, "Toni Anne. To what do I owe this pleasant surprise?"

"Mr. President, even though this conversation is secure, I need to speak to you in person. Tonight, if possible," she said.

"I wondered how long it would take you to call. I'll send a car for you. It will pick you up at 6 pm. Is that okay? The President asked. "Is that soon enough?"

"Yes sir."

"We'll have company," the President said.

Chapter Thirty Three
Washington, DC
The White House

Toni Anne's leg ached as she entered the White House through a side door that did not require her to climb stairs. She hated using the cane that had been supplied to her by the hospital, but it did make walking easier.

A civilian aide met Laudano at the door. He asked if she would like a ride in a wheelchair.

"Hell no! I'm not hurt that bad. I'll walk."

"As you wish, ma'am" the aide said. They rode without conversation up one floor, to the level of the Oval Office.

Toni Anne needed her cane but used it in a manner not proscribed by the physical therapist at the hospital. It seemed to Laudano that the recommended method had the cane on the wrong side, so she held it on the side of her bad leg. The therapist told her that would add to the strain on that leg, but he gave up when Toni Anne refused to follow his advice.

She was surprised that the hallway was empty except for two Marine guards, who stared straight ahead. Toni Anne was further surprised when the aide took her into the Oval Office, and it was unoccupied.

The President has a small conference room adjacent to the Oval Office. The door to the conference room is skillfully crafted into the wall of the office, is virtually invisible. and opened when the aide pushed it. Inside sat the President and General Goldstein.

The two men stood as Toni Anne entered the room. "You're using that cane incorrectly," the President said.

Toni Anne pursed her lips to avoid replying to the President's comment. General Goldstein laughed.

"Toni Anne! Are you too intimidated to reply to the President?" Goldstein asked.

"Yes, I am…a little intimidated."

The President smiled and gestured for them to sit down. "The Chief of Staff considered attending this meeting, but Chan decided against it when I asked him if he wouldn't be more comfortable being able to raise his right hand and swear that he

101

had no knowledge of what is about to be discussed in this room tonight, if it ever comes to that."

"Good decision," Goldstein said.

"Your timing in calling me was fortunate, Toni Anne. Otherwise, we would have had to make up some excuse to get you in here. I might have given you the Presidential Medal of Freedom. That would have been fun. I'd have loved to see Stockbridge's face if we announced that," the President said.

"Mr. President, I'm...uh...not understanding what's---"

The General interrupted Toni Anne. "There's no way you could have known what was going on. We've concocted a plan that even you would be proud of for its deviousness. The President will explain."

"I'm all ears, Mr. President," Toni Anne said.

"Congressman Safi wants this office. He's a dangerous asshole, we can't let that happen," the President said. "And his ambition has driven him into an alliance with very bad people."

"I'd love to hear you say that at a press conference," Toni Anne said.

The President laughed. "That would be great. But we have to be a bit more subtle."

The President and General Goldstein spent the next ten minutes outlining the plan to Toni Anne. They explained that Safi had promised Admiral Stockbridge the Vice Presidential slot on his ticket.

"You're giving Safi and Stockbridge enough rope to hang themselves." Toni Anne concluded. "But there's a lot of moving parts, a lot of things that can go wrong."

"That's why we need you," the President said. "We know that you have a scheme that's outside the government, that you plan to run in The Cold."

Toni Anne turned to look at General Goldstein. "How do you know that!" she said.

"Toni Anne, nobody doubts that you're the best technical genius in this game. But I'm a very good spy. In fact, I'm the best," the General said. "We're not going to need your plan, but we are going to need your help with our scheme."

"What do you mean---"

"Toni Anne, we need to bring you into the loop. I'll start by telling you this. Wishbone works for me," the President said.

"Huh?" Toni Anne said. "You *know* Wishbone?"

"I know him. He's CIA. Very deep cover," The President explained. "He reports directly to me."

Chapter Thirty Four
Austin Texas

To get home from Cincinnati after my meeting with Wishbone, I had to fly via Atlanta and Birmingham. I finally nodded off about two minutes before we landed in Austin.

I had to get in touch with the brokerage firm that cleared my trades and tell them not to transfer Barbara Jean Parker's account. I had to have Barbara Jean call them and tell them not to move the account, that she had never signed any instructions. Barb had to come up with verbal authorization passwords, like her horse's name, and her favorite teacher in elementary school, or something like that. This is far from an uncrackable code by sophisticated hackers, but it's something.

When Barbara Jean called me to tell me that the transfer was cancelled, I thanked her, then called the head of online security for the brokerage firm. He told me that the bank requesting the funds was a questionable entity in Cypress. I asked why that didn't show up as a red flag, something to be questioned before an account transfer was processed. He admitted the lack of verification was a shortcoming in their system, and that they were working on improving overall security.

"You better work on that harder," I said. "There's going to be a lot more shit headed your way. Sophisticated stuff."

"And you know that how?" He was getting snotty.

"Hey, what you just saw was the junior varsity," I said. "The big boys are coming."

"Sure," he said. "We get a hundred incidents like the one you just had every day."

"Hey listen, Skippy," I said. "You better start taking your job more seriously or get ready to get named in the class action lawsuits." Talking about lawsuits to someone at a financial institution is always a good way to get them to focus.

His tone changed. "There's no need for the personal insults. Of course, we take our jobs' seriously. There's nothing more important than protecting our clients' assets."

"That's funny, just a minute ago you sounded as though you thought acting like a cool guy was more important," I said.

104

No response.

"I'm serious. There's a whole new level of hacking shit about to come at you and every financial institution in the world. Don't ask me how I know. But if I were you, I'd get on the CEO's calendar today and tell him that your systems need to be ramped up pronto," I said.

"I'll give your comments every consideration," he said. That means *get lost*.

"If you screw up like this again, I'll pull my accounts," I said, even though I knew he couldn't care less. In fact, he'd be happy if I left, so he wouldn't have to talk to me again.

"Again, I'll take your comments—"

I hung up on him. That's a rude thing to do, but if I wasn't going to get his serious attention, I wanted the satisfaction of pissing him off. I thought of calling the CEO myself but decided not to waste my time. I couldn't tell the CEO what I knew, and pulling my accounts wouldn't do any good, because the Russians and their hackers from Everywhere-istan were coming for American companies and so many of them were complacent, and all but ignoring the risks.

And the Russians had already started with me.

Chapter Thirty Five
The White House

Toni Anne was stunned. She was used to running complex schemes designed to trick the world's most sophisticated Cyber Warriors and now what the President and General Goldstein were explaining to her made her feel like a rookie.

"I thought the CIA wasn't allowed to operate domestically," she said to the President.

The President and General Goldstein burst out laughing. "That's a good one, Toni Anne," the President said. "I'm not going to tell anybody. How about you, General?"

"Tell anybody about what? I don't know what you're talking about, sir," the General said.

"Keep practicing that line," the President said. "I've ordered coffee for everyone. He hit a buzzer on the table. "Bring the coffee in please."

A man dressed in the garb of a White House steward entered the room after knocking. He was pushing a cart, prepared to serve coffee to the three in the conference room. Tony Anne looked up at the man. It was Wishbone Ives.

How do you take your coffee, Ma'am?" Wishbone asked.

The President stood up. "Have a seat, Mr. Ives. I'll serve the coffee. Tony Anne, how would you like your coffee?"

The President was known on occasion to serve coffee to guests at the White House. He had done it for political adversaries of his, including Congressman Safi. The humble gesture disarmed people. When he was done, he sat back in his chair.

"Sir, you have established your common touch as the server, but I see you get to have the best chair," Toni Anne said.

"There are certain perks to the office," The President replied. "Why, would you like this seat? Are you thinking of running for President?"

Toni Anne said, "What, are you out of your fu---".

Admiral Goldstein said, "Toni Anne! You do realize who---"

The President held up his hand to interrupt the General. "I see you've gotten over being intimidated, Toni Anne. It's okay, General. I want us all to speak freely tonight. Toni Anne, to

106

answer your question, sometimes I do think I was out of my… friggin' mind to want this job, but now I'm in it, and I want to do the best that I can."

General Goldstein looked at Toni Anne and shook his head. She shrugged.

"Are you ready for the change in plans, Wishbone?" the President asked.

"Not yet. I had to talk to Toni Anne. JR Johnson is ready to play his role in this piece," Wishbone answered. "He doesn't know the details yet, though."

"Mr. President, this time Johnson should be given a realistic shot to recover his money," Toni Anne said. "It's not everybody who serves as a 'Useful Idiot' for the USA twice."

"No problem. He's all set, if he lives through it," the President said, "If he doesn't, he won't be needing the money."

Chapter Thirty Six
Minsk, Belarus

Sergey Kravanesko had a lucrative opportunity, and he intended it to be a success. If it was a failure, he was sure he'd be eliminated, killed in some gruesome manner. His employees would also be at risk. Every day he regretted having brought his son into the business, and now even more so. But Sergey had an exit plan.

Kravanesko had been at the meeting in Moscow with the Lider and the rest of the intelligent thugs who were tasked with the stepped-up hacking invasion of the United States, which had now only begun.

His Minsk, Belarus business office was in a building among the ugly Stalin Era blockish architecture that dominated the central city, built after clearing the rubble from the Nazi invasion of World War II. Kravanesko insisted that his employees be neatly dressed and that the offices be kept meticulously neat and organized. Many in his line of business were known for sloppy workplaces, and for employing slobs. Not for him. Disorganization led to misplaced work product and poor employee morale.

The offices were on the second floor of the five-story building, which was fine because the elevator worked about half the time, and never when you were in a hurry. The drab hallway had only one marked doorway, with a crisp white sign with blue letters that said in Cyrillic and English, Proectiridae Setey, Derzhatsya Podalsze. "Network Designs, Keep Out." The door was always locked, and the locals were sufficiently terrified by anything that hinted of authority to that they kept out when instructed by a sign to do so.

Sergey Kravanesko had excelled at math and physics as a boy and at university. After graduation, he took a job as an engineer with the local electric power utility. The utility was a boondoggle with three times as many employees as necessary, so he was assigned almost no real work and attended endless meetings organized by people told to look busy by their superiors. They had meetings to plan for future meetings.

When the world of computer hacking and ransomware became viable Kravanesko jumped at the chance. He quit the utility and once the online piracy business was up and running, he made over one hundred times his miserable salary at the power company. His family vacationed each summer in the South of France, not a local mosquito infested freezing lake on the outskirts of Minsk, where the workers he left behind in the bureaucracy spent their pathetic vacations.

With the rise of the internet so much potential money was there to be stolen that the Russian government from on high in Moscow decided to let independent operators run computer ransomware operations. Hackers in Russia and the former Soviet Republics were left free by their governments to steal as much as they could grab.

It wasn't as though running his hacking enterprise was without its difficulties. As an operator of one of the businesses, you had to follow strict guidelines. There were three major stipulations: One, no ransom target could be in Russia or any of the former Soviet Republics. Two, the independents were not allowed to meddle in anything political. That job was reserved for the Russian FSB, sort of a combination of the American CIA and FBI, which was tightly controlled by the Lider. Three, a 50% fee on all ransoms was payable each month for the protection provided by the government. The result was a Mafia. Kravanesko paid the local political boss, who in turn paid the brutal gangster with the laughable title of President of Belarus. The President then was responsible for sending a monthly payment directly to the Lider in Moscow. Belarus was nominally an independent republic, but in reality, a puppet state of Russia.

As in any complex and de-centralized enterprise, people got greedy and stupid. One operator in Minsk tried to shortchange his payment to the local boss. He was found wired to a tree with his hands chopped off, left to bleed to death.

Another five-person shop was guilty of the far more serious crime of hacking a Russian bank. All five were found in a barn, shot many more times than was necessary to kill them. Rather than just sweep the killings under the carpet, Minsk police officials investigated for one day, publicly concluded that the mass execution was an act of terrorists, and the case was closed as unsolved.

109

The local news media featured graphic pictures of the bullet ridden corpses. The leadership of this Mafia did not believe in subtle messages.

Kravanesko had recently seen the embalmed head of Oleg Turgenev in a jar on the Lider's desk in Moscow. Turgenev had been one of the Lider's favorite oligarchs. This was a business with serious consequences. Still, it was much better than dying of boredom and vodka as an automaton at the electric utility.

Being a part of this criminal organization had its advantages as well. When an unhinged employee of Kravanesko's wildly overestimated his own importance to the organization and threatened to go public with details of the true function of Network Designs unless his salary was doubled, Sergei mentioned this problem to the local political boss. The disgruntled employee disappeared that day from the face of the earth. The man became a non-person. Not one of Kravanesko's employees, nor the man's wife, ever asked about him, or even mentioned his name. Now, that was good for motivation and morale!

An unexpected bonus was that the non-person's wife became Kravanesko's second mistress. She was a bit skinny for Sergey's liking, but that offset the plumpness of his other mistress. The skinny one was now on Network Designs' payroll, at twice the salary of her permanently missing husband. She was listed as an outside consultant. Kravanesko mused that in a very broad definition that job description was accurate.

Chapter Thirty Seven
Washington, DC

Congressman Safi had an appointment in an unusual place for such a prominent politician. Safi was dressed in casual attire he never wore in public, for he sought to project the image of a soon-to-be President. But this night he wanted to go unnoticed. The Congressman left his brownstone in the housekeeper's car to a downtown D.C. parking lot at 10 p.m.

A tall black man was in the parking lot attendant's booth. He didn't look up from the television he was watching when Safi took his ticket, waited for the arm to raise, and drove in.

No one else was around that Safi could see. It was a parking lot full of cars with no people present. He drove the car up to the roof level as instructed.

As soon as Safi pulled away from the booth the attendant focused on the television which showed closed circuit footage of the roof level.

A woman waited for Safi. She was well dressed, thin, her dark hair almost covered by a silk scarf tied over her head. He got out of his car and walked over to her.

"Are you Patricia?" Safi asked.

She nodded.

"Why am I meeting with you? You're not my usual contact," Safi said.

"I'm your contact tonight," Patricia answered.

"You're certainly more attractive than my regular contact," Safi said.

This drew an icy stare from Patricia.

You have something to tell me?" Safi asked.

She spoke "Yes. I have a message from the Lider. We are about to commence the most intensive ransomware campaign in the history of the world. It is focused on the United States---"

"I already knew that. I'm very busy. What is so important that you make me leave my house in the middle of the night—"

Patricia drew a Glock 9mm with silencer from her jacket, pointed it at his heart, and in doing so froze the Congressman in mid-sentence. "Let's make this clear. We own you. When we tell you to come here and meet, you come here," she said. "The news I have for you is this: you will do everything we tell you,

111

without deviation. If you follow your orders, you will be the next President of the United States. If you displease the Lider, I have permission to kill you---"

"If he's trying to send some message of intimidation, I---"

"I am not a messenger. I'm an assassin. I've killed more important people than you. I enjoy my work," Patricia said. "Unless specifically forbidden, I shoot people. So, stand by for further instructions. And don't complain again. You could so easily be replaced."

Safi opened his mouth to speak, but no words came out.

"You know how easy it would be to shoot you right here?" Patricia laughed. She placed both hands on the Glock and aimed at Safi's forehead. "Did you know that there's no safety on a Glock? That's why I don't have my finger on the trigger. So, if you ever see me with my finger on the trigger, you don't have long to live." She put the gun back in her jacket, walked to her Mercedes, then turned back to face Safi. "You're lucky. Most people who've seen me point a gun at them had a life expectancy of about two seconds."

Safi said, "I don't scare that easily---"

"Then why are your hands shaking? Don't try to bluff me you little turd, I have a lot more experience at this sort of thing than you," Patricia said. "One other thing. If you do get to be President, don't think that means that you're safe. We can kill you under any circumstances."

Patricia got in the car and drove off.

Safi was grim faced as he got in his car. When he paid at the attendants' booth it took a long moment to get the tall man's attention.

The Congressman drove off. The tall man in the booth switched off the tv. "Thank you for speaking so clearly, Congressman," temporary parking lot attendant Wishbone Ives said.

112

Chapter Thirty Eight
Washington, DC

Patricia drove toward Reagan National Airport. Patricia Sizemore was the name on her passport because her real name, Sierra Quinn, was still on watchlists and could not be used.

Quinn was sexually aroused just by the thought of shooting the Congressman. She really needed a man, but Colonel Nihisky had warned her to not get involved with anyone while she was on this mission. Sierra had wanted to shoot the arrogant Congressman. It had been too long since she killed someone.

She turned in her Mercedes at the rental desk and took the shuttle for the terminal, to board a plane for Salt Lake City, her first stop on the long journey back to Bali. It had been a long way to travel just for this warning of the Congressman, but she followed her orders. The Lider had felt that it was necessary, and everyone followed the Lider's orders.

Chapter Thirty Nine
Austin, TX

I was home in Austin, trying to pay attention to my money management business. It was hard to focus, because anytime now I was expecting Wishbone to call me to arrange another clandestine meeting, this time to give me the specifics of whatever my role would be in the upcoming excitement.

My business number buzzed. My normal practice is to let the call go to voicemail, but out of boredom I picked up.

"JR Johnson," I said.

"What the hell is going on? You better have a good explanation, or my next call is to the SEC, or the New York Stock Exchange, or---"

"What? Patrick?" I asked.

"You bet your ass it's Patrick! What happened to my money?"

Patrick was a longtime client. He called when he was bored, or disappointed that he didn't own whatever stock was hot on CNBC that day. But his normal tone was whiny, not outraged like he was now.

"Patrick. What are you talking about?" I asked.

"I went to look at my account online. The account has a zero balance! I went to the transactions page and there was a message that the entire $6.8 million was transferred with my approval to your personal account! What the hell are you trying---"

"Hold on Patrick. There's some error---"

"You bet your ass there's some error. I never approved that! How could you do this to---"

"Calm down Patrick. I'm checking right now," I said. I tapped some keys to bring up Patrick's account on my computer. Zero Balance.

I looked at the transaction page. All of Patrick's stock positions had been transferred to my personal account.

"Patrick, there's something really wrong here---"

"Something wrong? I'm not going to let you steal from me. You'll go to jail, like Madoff! Or I might handle you like that Hedge Fund manager you shot in New York! What, did you learn from him, think you could pull off some stunt like this and

114

think I wouldn't notice until it was too late? You miserable mother---"

"Whoa, whoa, whoa Patrick! I'm as shocked by this as you are. I didn't do this. I'll get to the bottom of this and fix it---"

Patrick's outrage had kicked in and he wasn't about to listen. "My attorney always warned me that I trusted you too much! I talked to him before I called you. He said you have the legal right to move money around, and you probably did some sneaky move to take my money because you're in some kind of trouble. And now I'll have to sue you to get it back! I swear, if I don't get that money right back, you'll end up like that Hedge Fund guy that you shot!"

"Hey Patrick, that's enough shit from you! Your attorney couldn't find his ass with both hands. Now shut up!" This couldn't be happening, it felt wrong, like when Barbara Jean's account had been closed. "You asshole, you really think I'd steal your money?"

No answer.

"Huh Patrick, you really think I'd steal from one of my clients'?"

"Well…"

"Well, your ass! I'll get to the bottom of this and call you right back." I said, then I hung up.

I mused that the preceding conversation was not taken from the Suggested Sample Conversations Section of the Best Client Practices Handbook I had received my first day at the Big Investment Firm when I began training as a new hire on Wall Street. My mentor, Tom Good had always talked about the thin veneer of trust you had with clients. I thought I must have stripped off the veneer with Patrick. Or more accurately, the Russian hackers had stripped off the trust by manipulating the accounts.

Once again, I had to call the brokerage firm that handled the custody of my accounts. I called the operations department. After I dodged their automated account balance answering option, I managed to get a human, but not a smart human.

I gave my verbal password.

"I'm sorry Mr. Johnson, but that password is incorrect."

115

"How could that be incorrect? It's been my password for six years," I asked. "I'm looking at the account on my screen right---"

The account screen went blank.

"Mr. Johnson, your access to these accounts has been terminated," the not-so-smart human told me.

"What! I want to speak to your supervisor, right now," I said.

The next 45 minutes were spent talking to a rising hierarchy of progressively smarter people, but no one who seemed interested in helping me. They kept reminding me that the call was being recorded, then I was put on hold for various time periods to wait for the next person who wouldn't help me. The music on hold was awful, what I would call neo-classical-techno-crap.

Finally, the music stopped. Maybe the next person would help me! Then, a new recording came on: Due to extraordinary call volume, it would be necessary for me to leave a message, and someone would call me within one business day. Not that I was going to leave a message, but then the call was abruptly disconnected before I could hang up.

Modern technology has made many routine tasks super convenient when the technology works. When a system goes down the frustration is total, and a user feels helpless. Imagine what it feels like to be accused of stealing from a clients' account, then verifying that the clients' money has been transferred without your knowledge to your account. This client, egged on by his lawyer, has gone instantaneously from trusting you with his money to being ready to sue you and asking the authorities to take away your license. When you try to get to the bottom of the situation, you get an endless succession of bureaucratic bullshit, interspersed with music on hold, and finally a message informing you that no one else would be taking your call due to high call volume. So, try to wait until tomorrow, when someone else who won't help you might just be calling back.

My dilemma was not a return of a sweater to Lands' End. If all my clients' accounts had been hacked like this, the situation involved hundreds of millions of dollars, and I had no way to check. Come to think of it, Lands' End handled snafus like this much better.

Although the iPhone has many wonderful features, it doesn't afford the satisfaction of being able to slam it down like the old-fashioned phone I had on my desk when I worked on Wall Street. I couldn't slam it down! I did hit the red disconnect icon on the screen very decisively, but it was not satisfying.

So, I had a justifiably irate client, who thought I was stealing his money, and the money was housed in an account at a firm that no longer recognized my password. Most people would just have to live with the stress of this predicament.

Unlike most of the other clients of this brokerage firm, I did have the direct number of the CEO, and I called him. The CEO and I had worked together on the Equity Trading Desk at the Big Investment firm a million years ago. I got his administrative assistant, a man. I was informed that the CEO could not take my call.

"I don't think you understand. Unless he's currently having open heart surgery, he better pick up the fuckin' phone right now," I said.

"Sir, I don't---"

"Let me rephrase that," I said. "Even if he *is* having open heart surgery, he better pick up the fuckin' phone right now!"

My sense of urgency must have worked because the next voice I heard was the CEO.

"JR, we're having a major systems meltdown., it's a ransomware attack," the CEO said. "We can't get it under control. It's, it's---"

"I'm sorry for your problems, but I need you to do something for me," I said.

"What?" he asked.

"I need you to call one of my clients and tell him you're having systems problems, and that you promise it will all be squared away," I said.

Long pause.

"Are you serious?" he asked.

"Yeah, I'm fuckin' serious. Just make this one call and I'll leave you alone. It will just take a minute," I said. I thought he'd tell me to get lost.

"Alright. Give me his contact information. I'll do it right now," the CEO said. "I'm going on CNBC in a half an hour to

117

make a public announcement. I've got to go public with the ransomware situation. I'm not sure I get paid enough."

"You should have listened to your mother when she told you to become a Rock Star," I said.

Ten minutes later Patrick called me.

"Some guy called me, claiming to be the CEO of the brokerage firm. My lawyer said it could be some stooge you just put up to it, as part of your swindle---"

"Hey Patrick, fuck you! Turn on CNBC, you'll see the guy. And Patrick---"

"What," he said.

"When this all gets squared away, shove the money up your ass. Tell that mouth breathing so-called lawyer of yours to run the money---"

"He says he could do a better job than---"

"Shut up, you asshole," I said, then I forcefully touched the red disconnect icon on my iPhone. This time I got some satisfaction from the dynamic pressing action, but still not as much as if I had slammed down my old phone.

How to *Win Friends and Influence People*, in the age of the Internet.

This was spinning out of control. Could the Russians and their surrogates really get into any financial institution and just move the money around at will?

Chapter Forty
Minsk, Belarus

Sergey Kravanesko called Andrey Schmultz, his head programmer, and the real brains of the operation, into his office.

"Excellent job, Andrey. It looks like the Brokerage firm has just paid us the $2 million ransom. Make sure we return control of their systems to them as quickly as we promised," Kravanesko said.

"Yes sir. But—"

"What is it Andrey?" Kravanesko asked.

"We could have demanded a much bigger ransom. They would have paid," Andrey said.

"I agree, but we are just following orders from on high. It's part of a larger scheme. This is just the preliminary action. We'll be ratcheting up our demands. And Andrey?"

"Yes?"

"It is best that you forget this conversation," Kravanesko said.

"Yes sir," Andrey answered. But Andrey didn't forget any of his conversations with Kravanesko.

119

Chapter Forty One
Austin, Texas

I didn't sleep well the night before, worried about the status of my accounts with the brokerage firm. As usual, I started the day with the TV turned to CNBC.

My CEO buddy, head of the ransomware damaged brokerage firm was making a statement:

"After consulting with the best in-house and external experts in IT systems, our board decided it was in the best interest of our clients to pay the ransom demand. Per our agreement with the hackers, the amount paid is not public information. Our systems are up and running normally, with just a handful of accounts that have to be adjusted manually. I assure each and every client that no matter what it takes---"

I stopped listening. The phrase 'just a handful of accounts' is what got my attention. I just knew that included me, and it was like getting a dagger in the stomach.

It's normally an amusing situation seeing someone I know personally when they appear on CNBC. I realize the guy is just a guy, half the time they don't know what they're talking about, but the medium of television gives them such authority. I wasn't amused this time.

My phone rang. It was the head of operations at the brokerage firm.

"Mr. Johnson?"

"Yup."

"This is Rosemary Smith, Head of Operations---"

"Thank you for calling. What is the status of my client accounts?" I asked.

"For some unknown reason, when control of our systems was returned to us by the hackers, your clients' accounts were still frozen. All of your accounts had large suspicious transactions yesterday right before we were contacted by the hackers, most of your clients' assets were moved to your personal account," Rosemary told me.

The dagger in my stomach twisted.

"What are you doing to fix the problem?" I asked.

120

"Do you have printed copies of last months' statements for each client?" she asked.

"Of course," I replied.

"Can you please scan those and email them to us? We'll have to manually recreate them," Rosemary asked.

"I don't trust anything electronic right now," I said. "Where are you physically located?"

Although the brokerage firm headquarters was famously in Boston, their operations arm was in Albuquerque.

"I tell you what, Rosemary. I'm going to physically bring those statements to you, and we're going to go over every account to make sure that it is correct. I'll be there this afternoon," I said.

"Okay," she said. "I've been instructed by our CEO to personally manage this situation, so I'll be seeing you when you get here."

If you want to fly coach from Austin to Albuquerque this afternoon, it costs about $600. It's about 700 miles, as the crow flies, but you have to stop in Dallas and change planes. If you have a longer time to plan, you can fly 5,000 miles direct to Paris, France for less. Sometimes I think airfares are formulated by a team of chimps. I couldn't get to my destination until 6 pm, even at that exorbitant price. I called Rosemary and explained the situation.

"I have an idea. Let me call you back in a couple minutes," she said.

She was as good as her word. One of the company jets was flying from Boston to Albuquerque and would divert to Austin to pick me up. Could I be at the airport in an hour?

Yes, I could.

Rosemary gave me a warning. There was just one passenger on the plane. "He's a real jerk," she said, "and he's not happy about being re-routed and delayed."

"Do you outrank him?" I asked.

"Yes."

I went to the private aviation terminal at the Austin airport. You could get used to this kind of flying, since all you have to do is show up. There's no TSA screening, no line, no taking off your shoes and belt, no ticket required, no chance of you having to sit next to a smelly 300-pound guy sporting a doo rag and a

121

Hell's Angels leather vest. Maybe if I ever get the $1.5 billion back, I'll keep some for myself, enough to keep me on private jets for life!

I got on the corporate jet. There was a thin young man in a three-piece suit seated in the first row. His tie was snugged up so tight it looked like his head might pop.

"Howdy," I said. I thought he might like some real Texas atmosphere.

My charm didn't work. "I hope this diversion is important. It added an hour to my flight," he said.

"Who do you report to?" I asked.

He told me a woman's name.

"Who does she report to?"

He told me a man's name. Neither name was familiar. " Who does he report to?"

"He reports directly to the CEO. I'm sure—"

I held up my index finger to silence him, then got out my iPhone and scrolled a bit. When I got what I was looking for, I held up the phone so he could see it. "You mean him?" I asked.

"Uhh—"

"Do you want me to hit this button and call him, or would you rather just sit there nice and polite and just keep quiet on our little flight to Albuquerque?" I smiled. "What did you say your name was? Just in case, I want to get it right."

He said nothing.

I sat a couple rows back. The flight was routine and there was a car at the airport to pick us up. We'd get to ride together to the brokerage firm's huge operations facility. I didn't want to sit next to this overpaid nitwit and asked to sit in the front seat, but the driver insisted that we both sit in the back seat of the Lincoln.

We rode in silence. After about ten minutes, I asked, "do you remember the Hedge Fund manager who was running a Ponzi scheme, and got shot?"

"Of course. Robert Stanton Banks. Who doesn't remember that?"

"Well, I especially remember, because I'm the guy who shot him." I laughed.

Chapter Forty Two
Minsk, Belarus

Kravanseko called his son Boris into his office. The kid was dressed in a custom-made tight shiny silk suit, way over the top for the office of a ransomware piracy firm in Minsk. Boris was always the most expensively dressed employee of Network Designs, and the least productive. His young face wore the effects of his boozing and drug use. His eyes were permanently bloodshot and watery. He was pale even for Belarus.

"Boris, you look like shit. What were you doing last night? Kravensko asked.

Boris sat in one of the guest chairs, something no other employee would dare without being invited to do so. He half sat, half laid down, with one of his legs draped over the arm of the chair. He waved his right hand, as if to dismiss his father's question.

Kravanesko went on, "Never mind, I have something important for you."

"What," Boris asked, "I'm going to be busy tonight---"

"Yes, you're going to be busy. You're flying to Dallas, Texas, by way of France," Kravanesko said.

"I have big plans for tonight---"

"Boris, you're going to America permanently. I'm sure they have silly little whores and drug dealers there who can keep you busy. The entire family is moving to America after my current project is complete," Kravanesko explained.

"What am I supposed to do in America?" Boris asked.

"Be alive," Kravanesko answered.

123

Chapter Forty Three
Salt Lake City Airport

Sierra Quinn waited for her connection to LA, where she'd then get a flight to Tokyo on her way back to Bali. She enjoyed being an alluring, mildly dangerous looking woman, and liked watching men look at her. If they only knew! As the well-dressed men in the first class lounge checked her out. Quinn amused herself by classifying the gawkers as men she'd like to bed, or shoot, or both. Most men were classified in the "Shoot Only" category. It passed the time for her.

Her phone buzzed, notifying her of a text message. It read: Do not board the flight. Call Control.

Quinn wondered what time it was in Moscow but didn't much care. Not her problem. Colonel Nihisky answered when she called.

"Stay in place," Nihisky said. "We have a probable assignment for you. Accommodations have been made." Nihisky gave her the name of a Salt Lake City hotel. "You'll be contacted with further instructions when we have more information."

"Any idea of time frame?" Quinn asked.

"Soon," Nihisky said, then he terminated the call.

Chapter Forty Four
Brokerage Operations Center
Albuquerque, NM

Rosemary Smith met me at the door of the huge facility. The little dipshit who had accompanied me in the limo grunted and nodded at Rosemary and walked past. She barely acknowledged him.

When he was out of earshot she said, "He's here to show off for some of the people who report to him. It's a situation that could be handled on a conference call, but he likes to display his power by commandeering a corporate jet and coming out here. His subordinates hate him."

"There's a lot of that going around," I said, "That's why I work for myself."

"Screw him. Let's get down to work," I said.

As we walked to Rosemary's office, I commented, "Man, this place is huge."

"As I'm sure you've figured out, the company just keeps the presence in Boston to impress the big clients. This operations center would cost twice as much in Massachusetts. New Mexico has provided tax incentives for the company to grow our presence in the state. Massachusetts just keeps raising our taxes," Rosemary said.

"It used to be like that for the tech companies in Austin, but real estate prices have gone crazy in the last couple years," I said.

We got to her office and inside the comfortable space waited a man and a woman, Ted and Lisa, to help reconstruct the accounts.

After we sat at a small conference table and were introduced, I said, "I've got to be honest with you. I've decided to get out of the money management business. I'm being targeted by the hackers. They're real professional hackers, the best, and I'm very concerned that while it's me who is the target, my clients will suffer, so I'm calling all of them, explaining to them the situation, and helping them move to other money managers. This is in no way critical of your company." I didn't bother mentioning my conversation with their head of online security because it didn't matter.

Rosemary nodded. "I've spoken to our CEO about this. We think that's in everybody's best interest. If you didn't bring it up, we were going to... well, forcefully suggest it."

I was surprised at first by that statement, because firms want to retain clients. To make it clear, I was the client of the brokerage firm, and the people who trusted me to manage their money were *my clients*. The brokerage firm just held the assets. I was responsible for all the investment decisions, and I charged my clients a quarterly fee for the advice, which was automatically deducted from their accounts. The brokerage firm charged a miniscule separate fee to my clients for their services of holding the assets, sending out statements, maintaining online client access to their accounts, and tracking tax information.

Although I was not an employee of the brokerage firm; I was self-employed, the brokerage firm did audit my accounts each year and had a legal staff that assured that my transactions did not violate securities laws. The brokerage firm did hold and monitor all my many securities licenses and informed me periodically to fulfill continuing education requirement necessary to maintain some particular license.

Upon reflection I concluded; I was just a drop in the bucket to this giant financial firm, and since I was a target of the hackers, having my accounts would make them a target as well. When my clients all left me, and the firm that held the assets, the brokerage firm would lose all the liabilities that accompanied the accounts.

As soon as Ted and Lisa got down to the details of balancing the accounts, I found my mind wandering. I have a few good traits, but careful attention to detail is not among them. I'd have made the world's worst forensic accountant.

Ted and Lisa worked on correcting the accounts and passed on their completed work to Rosemary, who double checked each line item. She asked me if I'd like to check her work.

"No, what I really need to do is call all the clients, to tell them to transfer their accounts out of harm's way." I said. "Could I get an office so I can make all these calls with a bit of privacy?" I asked.

126

"Sure," Rosemary said, and she got up from the conference table and escorted me to an empty office.

Many of my Texas based clients had accounts at the Big Investment Firm's office in Austin, so my first call was to the branch manager of that office. I explained the situation to him.

He pretended to be sympathetic to my plight, but I knew he was happy that his office would be receiving hundreds of millions of new assets to manage. I told him I would be calling the clients and giving them instructions on who to call.

"Have you had any internet threats? Any security concerns?" I asked.

"No, no, we're fine. I was just on a conference call with the head of our Cyber Security team. Our firewall is very robust," he said.

I didn't tell him that might be coming to an end soon. I just needed to get my clients away from me, so they wouldn't be singled out for special treatment by the hackers.

When that call was concluded, my next call was to Barbara Jean.

When she answered I said, "Barb, you need to get a pencil and paper."

"Why?" she said.

I lost my patience. "Why do you think? Do you think I want to teach you how to draw over the phone?"

"You're as charming as ever," Barbara Jean said.

After Barbara Jean and I got over our impasse, I gave her the necessary instructions to move her account to The Big Investment Firm.

"I wish you'd make up your mind. Yesterday I had to make sure that my account stayed with you, now today the most important thing in the world is I have to move the money," she said.

"Things changed," I said.

"JR, it sounds like things are getting serious. Is there any risk of me losing my money?" she asked.

"Not as long as you keep it at the Big Investment Firm," I explained. 'It's insured. But the bad guys are coming after everybody's money."

"Okay," Barbara Jean answered. "Is all this folderol going to stop you from your plan to get your money back?"

127

"Let's just say I have a few balls in the air right now," I said.

"I hope you're successful. I have a special reward for you," she said.

"What?" I asked.

"How stupid *are* you?" Barb asked.

Chapter Forty Five
Albuquerque, NM

Oh. I wouldn't say stupid, I'd describe my condition as preoccupied.

It took hours to get in touch with all my clients and go through the complicated explanation of why to move their accounts. Some of them didn't want to do it, even after I explained the dangerous situation. I had to be forceful.

Only a few of them had seen the CEO on CNBC, saying that the firm had been the subject of ransomware, and that the accounts had been hacked. I had to explain the whole deal to each client, and it took a long time with some of them.

One of the clients told me that he had been on the verge of firing me anyhow. He wasn't happy with the fact that I hadn't participated in the Crypto and related Tech booms. I didn't bother reminding him that he only had a third of his money with me, and that my stated mission was to make conservative stock investments, and not to be speculative. Why waste my breath at this point?

That's the nature of the beast in the investment business. Some clients are always on the verge of firing you, usually because they're being promised unrealistic performance by some other money manager who's trying to steal the account. The ultimate example of touting unrealistic performance was Robert Stanton Banks, the dead Hedge Fund manager who had just created his performance numbers out of thin air. I got to shoot *him*. I'd like to shoot some of the other guys, but with Banks I had the excuse of self-defense, because he was trying to shoot me.

Now I had the odd experience of insisting that my clients fire me. All that work that I had done over the years to build up their assets and trust flew out the window in a matter of hours.

Rosemary Smith came into my temporary office. "JR, we need to have a word," she said.

"Okay," I said.

"We've balanced everything out. All the assets are back in the clients' accounts as they should be. Are all your accounts ready to transfer?" she asked.

"Yeah."

"The CEO has directed me to tell you...um...You understand it's not my decision to---"

"Just spit it out. What do you have to tell me?" I asked.

"Well. As I started to discuss before, when all the accounts are transferred out," she said, "we have to terminate our relationship with you---for legal liability reasons, you understand. So, you'll no longer have your securities licenses, unless you transfer your---"

"I'm not going to start over," I said. "In this environment? C'mon, be realistic, you're effectively putting me out of business."

It took a minute for that to sink in. I had a securities license continuously since I was hired by The Big Investment Firm all those years ago. I accumulated more licenses as I went along, like the license to manage money, and the license to act as a fiduciary. And now I didn't. I not only had no client assets under management, I had no clients, and no license to practice. It had been one thing when I had just been thinking of getting out of the investment management business. But that was my decision. Now they were telling me I had to go. That was different. I was just Joe Citizen.

"Jeez, this is like the scene in *Dirty Harry* where they make him turn in his badge and gun," I said.

"I suppose so," Rosemary said.

"I'm sorry you were the one who had to tell me. Your gutless CEO made you do it?" I asked.

"Well, he is very busy right now," Rosemary said.

"Excuse my language, but he's very busy being a pussy," I said.

Rather than being offended, Rosemary laughed. "He is kind of a pussy," she said. I liked Rosemary.

130

Chapter Forty Six
Minsk, Belarus

Kravanseko told his son, "Stand up and come over here,"
The kid complied, but stood with his hands in his
pockets, his shoulders drooped. He did his best to look bored.

"Look Boris, here's exactly what you're going to do. Don't
go home. Go straight to the airport. You're getting on an Air
France flight to Paris in two hours. You're booked to take a
flight from there to Nice, but you're going to change your
itinerary in Paris, and get on a flight to Dallas, Texas,"
Kravanesko said.

"Why all this?" Boris asked.

"Because we are at risk, and I'm getting you out first. When
my project is done the rest of the family, including me, will be
meeting you in Texas. We'll be setting up a cyber security
business in Austin, Texas," Kravanesko said.

"Why? ---"

"Krananesko interrupted, "Don't ask any questions. It's best
that you don't know any answers."

"What are you talking about? I don't want any part of this!"
Boris said.

Krananesko walked around his desk and grabbed Boris by the
lapels. "You don't have any options. You have to do this. If you
don't do exactly as I say, you will probably be dead in a day or
two."

That wasn't true, as far as Kravanesko knew, but it did get
Boris' attention. Kravanesko reached into his jacket pocket and
produced an item. "Here's your passport. There's a car waiting
for you in front of the building. It will take you to the airport."

Boris looked more attentive. "This is serious?"

"Yes," Kravanesko said. "You'll be met in the airport in Paris
by a man who will approach you and say, 'You're Boris? I'm
Boris too.' He'll hand you a paper with your new flight
information to Dallas. This man is your bodyguard. He will be
on the flight to Dallas, but not in first class with you. When you
get to Dallas, you are to follow this man's instructions.
Understand?"

"No," Boris said, "Our whole company is moving to
America?"

131

"Our family plus just one employee. Andrey will be moving along with us. We need his expertise, and he's the only one I trust. He knows what's going on, nobody else here knows anything," Kravanesko said. "Now go to the airport."

"Alright," Boris said.

"Good. Now just leave the office as though you're going to lunch. Try to act normal. There's a black car waiting to take you to the airport," Kravanesko said.

Chapter Forty Seven
Salt Lake City
Grand American Hotel

Sierra Quinn had gone as instructed to the Grand American Hotel. Her Russian handlers didn't spare any expense; this was the best hotel in Salt Lake City. She sat around for almost a day, watching television, and taking her meals from room service before her phone rang. It was Colonel Nihisky.

"A few moments after we hang up two hotel chamber maids will knock on your door. Their names are Debbie and Nancy. They work for us and will have instructions for your next assignment.... They have a special skillset. They are specialists in assisting people like you. I am terminating the call." He hung up.

I am terminating the call, Sierra said aloud and laughed. *Great personality, that Colonel Nihisky, a pleasure to deal with.*

Then again, he has a tough job. His immediate predecessor was decapitated, and that man's embalmed head now resides in a jar, which is displayed by the Lider when he sees fit. Maybe 'terminating' is a good phrase for him to use.

There was a knock on the door. Sierra looked out the peephole. It was two women dressed in the black and gray outfits of the chambermaids of the Great American Hotel. Quinn opened the door part way. "What are your names?" she asked.

"Debbie and Nancy," the first one said. Quinn let them in the room. The first one pushed a cart with cleaning supplies, standard issue chambermaid equipment.

The cart pusher said, "I am Debbie, this is Nancy," pointing to her partner. They were both 5' 6". They were intentionally plain in their chambermaids' outfits, but attractive.

"Are you twins?" Quinn asked.

"No, but we are sisters," Debbie answered. "We were sent here from Russia as teenagers. We live as Americans, but we work for...the Lider. You've heard of sleeper agents? Debbie and Nancy are not our real names, but it is best if you just know us by our American names."

"Fair enough," Quinn said. "You have instructions?"

133

"Yes, from Colonel Nihisky. You are to fly tonight to Dallas. A room is reserved for Patricia Sizemore at the Omni Hotel. You'll receive further instructions when you arrive. We will meet you there," Debbie said. She told Quinn her flight information.

"What is it that you do, that I can't do myself?" Quinn asked.

"We specialize in after action operations when someone like you has done their work," Debbie said.

"Okay," Quinn said.

Nancy stepped forward. "You have some time before your plane. We like to have sex with other women. Are you interested?" she said.

"I appreciate you getting right to the point, but no, I would like to have sex with a man," Quinn said.

"We have equipment that can replicate---"

"No thanks," Quinn said. "I thought I wasn't going to get to know your names."

"It isn't necessary to really know someone's name to enjoy having sex with them," Debbie said. "Because of our irregular lifestyle, we have not had what most people would consider normal sex lives. But we manage to enjoy ourselves."

"Forget it," Quinn said. "It's ok, but not for me."

"You're a very attractive woman," Nancy said.

"Thank you," Quinn said.

"If you ever reconsider…" Debbie said.

Chapter Forty Eight
Moscow
The President's Apartment

Colonel Nihisky approached the Lider's desk. "Debbie and Nancy contacted Quinn," he said.

"They invited her to have sex?" The Lider asked.

"Yes," Colonel Nihisky answered. "Quinn declined."

"Damn," the Lider said. "I would like to have that video in my collection!"

"Perhaps we'll get another chance," Colonel Nihisky said.

"Okay. For now, let's focus on the mission," The Lider said.

Chapter Forty Nine
Paris
Charles De Gaulle Airport

Boris Kravanesko was accustomed to flying to Paris. His family had changed planes often at CDG airport en route to their vacation home in Nice. He walked through the concourse still not believing that a man would approach him as his father had described. A huge man bumped into him.

Boris weighed maybe 150 pounds, and the burly man who bumped him must have weighed 300 pounds. They both backed off from the collision. The big man smiled.

"Boris! I am also Boris," he said.

"Alright," Boris said.

Still smiling, the big man said "Go to the Air France desk, right there. Take this paper and give it to the ticket agent. I'll see you when our flight gets to Dallas."

Chapter Fifty
Dallas
Omni Hotel

Quinn sat, bored in her deluxe room. She watched True Crime shows on cable. She was always astounded how amateurish the killers were.

This is what it was like being a professional assassin, a lot of boredom leading up to the action. But the action made everything worthwhile. And action was coming.

There was a knock at the door. Debbie and Nancy were waiting outside, dressed in the garb of the chambermaids for the Omni. Debbie pushed the cart into the room.

"We have verification from Moscow. A young man, Boris Kravanesko will be checking in, accompanied by a bodyguard. They're on the way from the airport. Kravanesko thinks he's a ladies' man. They'll certainly go to the bar," Debbie said.

"Tell me about the bodyguard," Quinn said.

"He's former military, but sloppy, poor attention to detail, he washed out of the Russian military, he has to take jobs in Belarus," Debbie said. "Kravanesko's father hired him. You shouldn't have any problem with the bodyguard."

"What about the father and the kid?" Quinn asked.

"Moscow said to tell you that you saw Kravanesko's father at the big meeting in the Lider's office. The father is planning to bring his entire family to the U.S. He sent Boris first to get him out of harm's way during the current crucial mission. The kid, he's a punk. Useless. He's accustomed to paying for sex. Likes drugs," Debbie answered. She produced a photograph. "This is him."

"So, I whack the bodyguard and the kid?" Quinn asked.

"Yes. You have to. We can't have the bodyguard running around." Debbie said.

'Okay. This should be fun." Quinn smiled.

137

Chapter Fifty One
Dallas
Bar, The Omni Hotel

Quinn had decided to dress ambiguously. She didn't want to look like a prostitute but wore a red dress just this side of slutty. Keep the kid off balance.

She saw Boris and the bodyguard standing at the bar. Quinn didn't want to waste time or have him get tied up with some other woman.

She walked up to Boris. "Hi, my name is Patricia. Would you like to come to my room and have a good time?"

Boris leered at her. "I usually like my women younger, but you'll do. Maybe I'll have a younger woman later. I can go through three or four women a night. Do you take American Express?"

"Yes," Quinn said.

The bodyguard whispered to Boris, who turned to Quinn. "My keeper here says I should take you to *my* room."

"That's ok. I'll do him too, but the price is double," Quinn said. "One at a time, you understand?"

The bodyguard shook his head at Boris. "No, he'll just be escorting us to the room," Boris said. "When he's sure everything is okay, he'll leave us alone. But I am very demanding. I'll pay you double!"

"Good," Quinn said. "One thing. The management of the hotel has cameras everywhere. Until we get in the room, we're just acting like three business people, okay?"

"Your country is so uptight. My country doesn't have these pretenses," Boris said.

"What country is that?" Quinn asked.

The bodyguard shook his head.

"I can't say. You'll just have to take a wild guess." Boris laughed.

The three of them got off at the Penthouse level. As they walked toward Boris' suite, Quinn saw Debbie and Nancy fussing in front of a supply closet.

Boris opened the door to his suite. It was showy, done up in Texas high roller style.

138

"Wherever you're from, you must do quite well," Quinn said.

"Yes. We do very well," Boris said. The bodyguard whispered to him.

"My keeper here wants to frisk you," Boris said.

"I have to use the powder room. She tossed her purse to the bodyguard. "Start with this. You'll definitely both want to frisk me when I come out."

The bodyguard went through the modest contents of the purse. "She has a device on her cellphone that lets her swipe in the information from a credit card. All the whores are using that now." He held up the phone with the square device attached. "Other than that, nothing interesting," he said.

Quinn emerged from the powder room, naked except for red bikini panties. She raised her hands and slowly shook her breasts.

"Who wants to frisk me first?" Quinn said.

"Are those real?" Boris said.

Quinn nodded.

"So, it is true what they say about American women," Boris said.

"You know who says I have a great body? The Lider!" Quinn said.

Boris looked puzzled. The bodyguard looked to a mirror on the side of the room and saw the bulge in the back of Quinn's panties. The bodyguard went for his gun, but he was clumsy, slow.

Quinn dropped to one knee and drew the Glock from her rear waistband. She held the gun in both hands as she shot the bodyguard in the forehead. His 300 pounds crashed backwards.

"A bulletproof vest doesn't do much good when you get shot in the head, does it Boris?" Quinn asked. "He's not going to help you now." Sierra was standing, pointing the weapon at the punk kid.

Boris stood with his mouth half open, turning his head from the dead bodyguard to the naked Quinn. He looked back and forth several times.

"Wait, how do you know my name?" Boris asked.

"You're as stupid as you look," Quinn said.

"I'll give you whatever you want," Boris said. "My family has great resources. I'll give you anything."

139

"You haven't got anything I want," Quinn said. She raised the gun and shot Boris in the chest. He went down. She closed in and shot him twice more in the head.

Quinn was excited. She could really use a man now to make the night complete. The killer went to the powder room and got dressed. Then she went to the door of the suite. Debbie and Nancy were waiting, equipped with the chambermaid's cart. They entered the room.

Nancy reached under the cart and produced a chambermaid's uniform and a gym bag, both of which she handed to Quinn. Sierra didn't bother going to another room, she changed clothes in front of the sisters, as they began their work.

Nancy said to Quinn, "You have a fantastic body. We also have great bodies. Perhaps when we're done with this mission—"

"Just get to work, okay?" Quinn said.

"We're leaving the bodyguard here," Debbie said. "The dead little shit we've got another plan for." She explained the plan to Quinn. "You leave now. Here's a key to the service elevator."

Quinn laughed. "That's a great plan. The Lider said he wanted to make a statement," she said, then dressed as a chambermaid and carrying her other clothes in the gym bag, left the suite.

Debbie and Nancy were busy stuffing Boris' body in the chambermaid's wagon, then covered the cart with a tablecloth, so the body was hidden.

Chapter Fifty Two
Dallas
The Omni Hotel

Quinn had slept soundly. She awoke thinking of the frightened look on Boris' face when he realized that he had run out of options and was about to die. Quinn smiled.

Sierra wondered what look she'd have on her own face when she realized it was her time to die. Quinn had concluded her death would not be from old age and hoped she would be defiant when the time came, not begging like that sniveling little creep last night.

She wondered if authorities would try to cover up Debbie and Nancy's handiwork. Quinn turned on the television and clicked to a local station.

A banner read; "BREAKING NEWS." That headline used to be reserved for important stories, but the message had lost its special meaning years ago. Now the newscasts proclaimed "BREAKING NEWS" when a cat was rescued from a tree.

But today the banner said: BREAKING NEWS-GRUESOME MURDER VICTIM FOUND AT SIX FLAGS AMUSEMENT PARK.

The morning anchor man was looking solemn. "The following story may be too disturbing for many viewers. We caution parents of young children to turn to another program." *That's a great way to stop people from changing the channel.*

A female reporter with a couple pounds of hairspray was speaking. "Authorities are disclosing details of a bizarre apparent murder. Here's Tarrant County Sheriff Bill Ed Taylor moments ago."

The picture cut to an impromptu news conference. A heavyset, crew cut Sheriff with three stars on each side of his collar of his uniformed shirt wiped sweat from his brow with a handkerchief as he spoke to over a dozen microphones.

"Sheriff's deputies received an anonymous call regarding an...incident at Six Flags Amusement Park in Arlington at 3:10 this morning. The Park is normally closed for the night, but when they reached the scene, they found the Batman Roller coaster lit up and operating, carrying a single passenger. The off switch was disabled on the coaster, and the deputies could not

141

stop the ride for several minutes. Park management had been called and arrived on the scene in approximately ten minutes. When the ride was stopped and the car carrying the single passenger was, um…also stopped … at the beginning of the ride, it was determined that the passenger was dead. He had been shot three times, once in the body and twice in the head. The deceased was carrying a passport from Bela…Bela…"

"Belarus?" asked one of the reporters.

"Yeah, there," Sheriff Bill Ed said. "His identity is being withheld pending notification of next of kin."

"Who is notifying the next of kin?" a question came from the press.

"I don't know, the Bela-Roosians. I guess," the Sheriff said. "The FBI told us they'd handle that part, you know, talking to the foreign government."

"Aren't there security guards at the park?" a reporter interrupted.

"Yes. There were two security guards. They were found bound and gagged near the entrance to the Batman roller coaster. They were taken to the hospital and examined but were released. We are questioning them now," the Sheriff said.

"Any other details?" a woman reporter asked.

"Well, uh, I guess it's going to get out, so…the victim, uh, his male, uh organ…um…*his penis*, had been cut off and upon investigation was found in his mouth," Sheriff Bill Ed Taylor said.

As hard as he tried not to, Sheriff Bill Ed couldn't stifle a quick laugh.

Within minutes this clip was being shown on every cable tv news station in the country, which Quinn watched as she went from station to station.

That was a clever touch. Debbie and Nancy are good at their work.

Now that the national media had the story, they seemed to be competing for who could use the largest typeface for: BREAKING NEWS. Once the letters took up the entire screen, one station put them in italics.

When the story had reached the frenzy stage, Debbie and Nancy unleashed the final touch. They sent grainy cellphone video of Boris' corpse riding the Batman Roller Coaster to

142

every media outlet in the U.S. The ten second clip showed the coaster slowly cresting the highest point of the ride, then plunging down the steep descent. Boris' head flopped around like a rag doll.

Every station advised viewers about the graphic nature of the video, then showed Boris' ride up to thirty times in a row. Many stations showed it in slow motion, but with Boris' head masked with an electronic blob. The clip went viral on the internet. There was no electronic blob used on the World Wide Web. YouTube froze for several minutes due to excess demand.

Chapter Fifty Three

It was evening in Belarus. The staff at Network Designs were still at their desks. Runi, a young but promising hacker approached Andrey Schmoltz's desk.

"Have you seen the video on YouTube?" Runi asked.

"What are you doing wasting time on YouTube?" Andrey demanded, "you're supposed to be working."

"I'm sorry, but the chatter is all over the Net. It's not something I normally do,' Runi explained. "May I show you?"

Andrey nodded. Runi typed and moused and produced the video of Boris on the Batman Roller Coaster on Andrey's computer. Although the Tarrant County Sheriff's department had not released the identity of the rider, this was not a convention shared by the ethics of the internet. The title below the video said: Boris Kravanesko's Final Ride.

Andrey knocked on Kravanesko's open door, waiting for permission to enter. Sergei looked up and waved him in.

"Sir, I have very bad news for you," Andrey said.

Kravanesko looked puzzled. "What is it? Some technical thing?" he asked.

Andrey closed the door. "It's about Boris. May I show you on your computer?"

When Kravanesko had watched the video several times he rolled his chair back from his desk and reclined, looking at the ceiling. "I never should have gotten Boris involved with the business," he said.

Andrey said nothing.

It was quiet in the office as Kravanesko sat with his chin in his hand. Finally, he said, "I have to go tell his mother. Would you take me home?"

"Of course," Andrey said.

Andrey opened the office door. The workers had all seen the video and pretended to be busy, looking solely at their computer screens as Kravanesko and Andrey walked through the open plan cubicle area. The workers knew they were being recorded by multiple video cameras, so there was no celebration, or even acknowledgement that the universally despised Boris had met such a justified fate.

Andrey drove his car, a used Volvo. It was not in the class of Kravanesko's huge new Audi, but the Volvo displayed some prosperity to the population of Minsk. Andrey thought that soon he'd be driving whatever car he desired.

There was no talk in the car as Andrey drove Kravanesko on the ten-minute trip to his home. Andrey stopped the car. Kravanesko opened his door, and said, "It is important to continue operations as planned. I would appreciate it if you would return to the office and make sure our overnight staff carry out their assignments."

"Yes sir. I will stay all night and make certain that all operations are continued without interruption. I do have to make a brief stop before returning to the office," Andrey said.

Kravanesko nodded. He assumed that Andrey meant he had to stop at home to talk to his wife, but that assumption was incorrect.

Andrey parked the Volvo on a side street in central Minsk and walked into a noisy bar. Sitting in a booth in the very back of the establishment was the local Party Boss.

The Boss gestured for Andrey to have a seat. "Thank you for the excellent information, Andrey," the boss said.

"I was surprised that the kid was eliminated so fast," Andrey said.

"It was determined that the message must be sent immediately to Kravanesko," the Boss said. "I will be meeting with him and reinforcing the message."

"What now? When will Kravanesko be eliminated?" Andrey asked.

"When he is no longer useful," the Boss said. "I am waiting for input from Moscow."

"Will the senior Kravanesko also get a roller coaster ride? We do have an excellent amusement park here in Minsk," Andrey said.

The boss snorted. "Moscow may have other plans. Will you stay for a drink?"

"No thank you. I should get back to the office so as not to arouse any suspicions," Andrey said.

145

"Alright. I'm sure they're all shitting their pants now. That's what we wanted," the Boss said. "Not only here, but every hacker working for the Lider anywhere will get the message."

Andrey arose from the booth and started walking toward the front of the bar.

"Andrey, come back here for a moment." the Party Boss said.

Andrey did as instructed but remained standing.

"You will be the owner of Network Designs after Kravanesko is eliminated, as we've discussed all along. You will be rewarded for your loyalty. It is important for you to be patient a bit longer. Don't do anything to tip off Kravanesko," The Boss said. Andrey nodded and left the bar.

Chapter Fifty Four
Austin

I was back home from Albuquerque. The phone rang.
I don't pick up when the caller is not identified, but this caller
ID said: Austin Longhorn Moving and Storage.

"JR Johnson," I said.

"Mr. Johnson, we've been waiting for you to call," a
woman's voice said.

"Why? What are you talking about?" I asked.

"We've got to arrange moving you out of the house. Don't
you remember?" she asked.

"Huh?" I said.

"Mr. Johnson, I know this is awkward. We must move you
out of the house today. The new owner has been very patient.
The Bank called us yesterday when the foreclosure was final---
"

"What Bank? How could I have a foreclosure? I don't even
have a mortgage," I said.

"Sir, this is embarrassing," the woman said.

"What bank are you talking about?" I asked. The phone
started to cut off. I could only hear every other syllable, then the
phone went dead.

I looked up the list of recent calls on my phone. There was no
record of Austin Longhorn Moving and Storage. I googled
Austin Longhorn Moving and Storage. There were companies
with similar names, but not that exact name.

It dawned on me that this was just another part of the hacking
attack. Even though I knew I had no mortgage, it shook me up
when this very convincing woman had told me that my house
had been the subject of a foreclosure. What were these people
capable of doing? I had to call Wishbone.

I used the burner phone to call Wishbone. He answered right
away.

"I'm not ready for you yet," he said.

"But I've got something---"

"Remember the fifteen second rule," Wishbone said. Then he
hung up.

147

A minute later the burner rang. "You got a problem?" Wishbone asked.

"Yeah," I said.

"Okay, I'll get back to you today," Wishbone said.

I had no clients to worry about anymore. But that meant that I had no income from the money management business. I had my own bills to worry about, and I had no substantial liquid assets. Weeks ago, I had lost all the money in my very substantial taxable investment account in a few minutes when the cryptocurrency market had imploded. That meant I would have to dip into my checking account to pay the bills, and that amount was pitiful in comparison to what I spent on a monthly basis. I decided that I needed to sell whatever I could to raise some substantial cash. I could sell my compound in Austin, sell my co-op in New York, maybe even sell my 401k and pay the tax penalties. I needed cash to get me through this indefinite period.

I almost never used the co-op on Fifth Avenue across from Central Park, so I decided to start with that. But exclusive co-ops in New York have different rules. You don't just call ReMax and list the place for sale. It was necessary to go through the co-op board, and I had to call the President of the Board, a guy with three last names. I had never paid any attention to the byzantine set of rules the co-op board had established when founded back in the Grover Cleveland administration, but I knew they were onerous.

I could never get this guy's name straight. It was something like Warner Winthrop Hamilton. Maybe it was Winthrop Hamilton Warner. I wrote down the six possible permutations on an index card. Eastern elite types don't have to worry about keeping these things straight, because they are all given an alias shortly after birth. "Biff" is too cliché, but it's a name like "Blake" or "Topper." Don't ask me where these names come from; my stick-up-the-ass old money family followed this practice with my three siblings, all of whom were older than me. For example, my sister's given name was Margaret Pennington Johnson, but my mother decided her AKA would be "Bitsy." My parents must have run out of ambition by the time their fourth child came along, because I was just my initials, "JR." I always assumed there must be some top-secret book available only to the elite, like *Acceptable Alternate*

148

Precious Names for Your New Heir or Heiress, but my parents never bothered with it in my case.

My sister is a big-time doctor now, married to another doctor. She goes by Dr. Bitsy Johnson-Dickerson. Yeah really. When you call her at work, a receptionist answers, "the office of Dr. Bitsy Johnson-Dickerson." I know, it's enough to make you spit up your breakfast. In the very few interactions we've had in recent years, I called her "Margaret", which irritates her, my goal accomplished.

I forgot the co-op President's preppie nickname, and he would never have spoken to me if I had been audacious enough to address him that way. That name could only be used by peers.

After all, I had gone to the University of Texas. I'd have to do some digging before I called him.

I made some calls. The co-op President's last name was Hamilton. After several false starts I managed to locate him. Mr. Hamilton was an Emeritus partner at one of the big white shoe law firms. Emeritus partner means he's retired, but still keeps an office at the firm; it gets him out of the house and away from his wife. After all, it would be fatal for his liver if he spent all his time at the Harvard Club of New York.

I called the law firm and got Hamilton's secretary. It seems Mr. Hamilton was quite busy; she'd have to take a message and maybe he'd be able to get back to me. The New York Times crossword puzzle must have been a tough one that morning. I stressed that this was regarding the co-op.

Three hours later Hamilton's secretary called me back. "Please hold for Mr. Hamilton," she said.

"Okay," I said.

"Mr. Johnson, you called me?" Hamilton asked.

"Yes Mr. Hamilton, I called regarding the co-op," I said.

"Yes?"

"Mr. Hamilton, I am interested in selling my apartment," I said.

Long pause. "Hmm," Hamilton said. I waited. I could hear him taking a deep breath.

"As I'm sure you're aware Mr. Johnson, you do not actually own your apartment. You own the right to a perpetual lease, subject to the terms and conditions…"

149

This went on for several minutes. Hamilton was a law school graduate, but his undergrad major must have been in Pontification. He and his predecessors on the co-op board had enjoyed showing off that they took Contract Law at Harvard and Yale and had cooked up such a convoluted quasi-ownership scheme for the entire co-op that made it very difficult to sell your piece of the pie, the only avenue was to potential buyers who were pre-approved by the co-op board, which met only the second Tuesday of every second month. Not only could you not have a mortgage on your apartment, but you could also not use your ownership as collateral to borrow. To do so voided any ownership interest, and this clause was stringently enforced. There was a waiting list of approved buyers, but because of the pre-approval, approval, and post approval periods one could not expect a liquidity event within a one-year period.

A 'liquidity event' meant getting paid by the buyer of my co-op apartment. This was indirect. The buyer paid the co-op board for the privilege of owning the right to the perpetual lease, then the co-op board would pay me, after taking a two percent fee. Lawyers like built in fees.

I could only ask the co-op board to put things in motion by sending a notarized letter to the board. The English language translation of the whole thing was: The Board had no intention of being The Money Store for some pissant who needed three or four million in a hurry. I was screwed.

"Alright. To whom do I send the letter?" I asked. Because I live in Texas, I don't get the opportunity to say 'whom' much.

"I'll have my administrative assistant pick up to give you that information. Goodbye," Hamilton said.

I took down the information from the assistant and intended to send the letter someday. But since it was going to take me at least a year to get any money out of selling the co-op, this wasn't going to do me any good. In that time I'd either have settled my problem or be dead.

The whole experience gave me another incentive. I wanted to outlive Mr. Whatever-His-Name-Is Hamilton. As I thought about him, his preppie nickname popped into my head. It was "Henley." A photo of him and his dried-up prune of a wife had appeared on the Society page of the New York Times when I lived in the building while I worked on Wall Street. Mr. and

150

Mrs. Warner Winthrop Hamilton had attended some charity fund raiser. The caption mentioned he was known as "Henley" to his friends.

Why hadn't I thought of the easy way to get money? Every month I got a letter from my bank saying that based on my home equity on my Austin property I was preapproved for a credit line of up to $2 million. I'd just call the bank and draw down a small part of the credit line. That would keep me comfortable while I resolved all the other issues.

Meanwhile my conversation with Wishbone kept coming back to me. He had to be kidding about me having to go to North Korea, right? I'd give him a call.

Chapter Fifty Five
Austin, TX

Alright, so I couldn't get any money out of the co-op in New York. I had a pathetic checking account balance at Oilmen and Ranchers National Bank of Texas, but they're the ones who kept sending me the letter offering me the big line of credit.

Just as I prepared to call the bank my burner phone rang.

"What do you want?" I said.

"A little grumpy today? Come to New York tomorrow 1 pm EST, my place," Wishbone said, then he hung up.

That's the nice thing about the communications protocol that Wishbone and I had. No small talk. He didn't have to ask me how Bitsy was doing before getting down to business.

The Oilmen and Ranchers National Bank of Texas is a fancy name for a little bank, but it's where I kept my checking account. I never had much of a balance, I just moved money over from my investment account to pay monthly bills, and I wanted a local bank for my ATM card.

I found the last letter regarding the line of credit the bank had sent me and called the name of the person who signed it, Vice President Cliff Auburn. I got right through to him and explained my situation.

"I'd like to take down a small amount from the line of credit you've extended to me," I said, "maybe $50,000 to start."

There was a long silence. Finally, Cliff Auburn said, "Mr. Johnson, I'm going to have our President, Mr. Murphy, pick up."

"Okay," I said. I knew the bank president Paul Murphy a little. We had played golf a couple times. He always hit the ball too far right off the first tee. Maybe the president had to approve the initial transaction in a line of credit account.

"Hi JR. Cliff tells me you want to draw down some more from your line of credit?" Murphy said.

"What do you mean? This is the initial transaction," I said.

"JR, have you been drinking or something?" Murphy asked.

"What are you talking about?" I said.

152

"JR, two days ago, with all the proper paperwork and e-signatures, you maxed out you line of credit. We wired the $2 million to the Bank of Malta for your purchase of the property there," Murphy said.

"What! I never did anything like that!" I said.

"JR, you called me from Malta. We told you we were recording the call, and you gave permission. We processed the transaction, and the money has been wired. You owe us $2 million. You don't remember this?" Murphy said. "Would you like to hear a replay of the call?"

"You bet your ass I would," I said.

"Ok, hold on a moment," Murphy said. The recording came on. It was my voice, and I was asking for a $2 million line of credit to buy a mansion in Malta. The call went on for five minutes.

"I know that sounds like my voice, but that's not me," I said. "I've never been to Malta. I couldn't find it on a map!"

"JR, we've got your e-signatures. They match up perfectly with your signature. All the documentation is proper and legal. Are you sure you're alright?" Murphy said.

"I'm alright! But I deny ever doing that!" I said.

"JR, you owe us $2 million. It's a 25-month loan, no payment the first month, then the monthly payments are $81,666.68. Maybe you need to see a doctor or something," Murphy said.

"I completely deny any involvement with this," I said.

"JR, let's not have to get the lawyers involved. We do have a lien on your property in Austin," Murphy said.

I hung up.

153

Chapter Fifty Six
New York

Punctual as always, I walked up to the front of Wishbone's theater and called him on the burner phone. He came down and let me in and we silently went to his apartment.

"Hey Wishbone, before we talk about your issues, I've got to tell you what happened yesterday," I said.

"What?" Wishbone asked.

"I found out I took a $2 million line of credit on my house in Austin and spent it all on a mansion in Malta a few days ago," I said, "except I've never been to Malta and didn't borrow the money. The bank even has me on a recorded line. It's sounds just like me asking for the loan. They've got my e-signature on all the documents."

"That's a big mortgage for an unemployed guy," Wishbone said.

"I don't think that's funny," I said.

"The Russians are messing with you. They're really good at that sort of thing," Wishbone said.

"So, what are we going to do about it?" I said.

"Toni Anne can probably fix that eventually'" Wishbone said. "We have to do the mission first. We can't help you now, the Russians would find out, so you've got to just roll with the punches."

"I've got to let the Russians just take all my money?" I said. "I'm beyond broke. Now I owe $2 million."

"I had the opportunity to meet with Toni Anne and we tightened up the details to our little caper. We're not quite ready to brief you yet." Wishbone explained.

"I am going to get a chance to get my money back?" I asked.

"Yup. I've got a promise on that," he said. "There's a slight chance you might have to do something in New York. Just in case, I've got something for you."

"What is it?" I asked.

He reached into a drawer in his table/desk. "Here, you might need this," he said, handing me a Glock. He also handed me what I thought was a silencer.

"Is this a 9mm?" I asked him. "And this thing is a silencer?"

154

"You know about these things? Can you hit the broad side of a barn?" he asked.

"I've had some training," I said. I didn't tell him that my training was from my now estranged wife, Barbara Jean. Her blowhard father liked to brag that she could shoot the balls off a male mosquito at 100 yards. "When I started, I couldn't hit the broad side of a barn."

"And now?" Wishbone asked.

"Now I can hit the *narrow* side of a barn," I said.

"Reassuring," he said.

"Hey, I shot Robert Stanton Banks in the neck," I reminded him of when I had shot the Hedge Fund manager.

"From four feet away, and it was a lucky shot, and Gabrielle had to finish him off, because he was about to kill you," Wishbone said.

"You ever shoot anybody?" I asked.

I had asked that question to be a ball buster, I was sure the answer was "no." But Wishbone didn't answer, he gave me a hard look. It made me think that the answer was "yes."

"At the end of this little adventure there are some things I have to tell you... if we're both alive," Wishbone said.

"There you are with that death stuff again," I said. "I want the outline of the plan... the version where I end up alive and with the money at the end," I said.

Wishbone looked at me.

"Well, I meant to also say that you end up alive, too, you know, as a secondary objective," I said.

He tried not to, but Wishbone smiled. "You really can be a jerk. Strangely enough, that might keep you alive," he said.

"Okay, Wishbone, tell me the plan," I said.

"I'm not authorized to tell you yet. It is probably going to be simple; you'll just deliver a message," Wishbone said.

"That's all? What are you not telling me?" I asked.

"Hey, have you ever been tortured?" Wishbone asked.

"I had this girlfriend when I worked on Wall Street. You must remember Gretchen Barnes. You both worked on the junk bond desk," I said.

"I remember her," Wishbone said.

"She dragged me out to a weekend in the Hamptons with a bunch of junk bond traders. Is physical torture worse than that?" I asked.

I explained how I had explored the sale of my New York co-op, and how that was a dead-end.

"You had this conversation with the head of the co-op board on your regular iPhone?" Wishbone asked.

"How else was I going to have the conversation?" I said.

"That's good. The Russians heard that conversation, they heard your conversation with the bank in Texas, they know you're getting desperate," he said. "They'll get complacent when they know their measures against you are working," he said. "And they think we don't care about helping you."

"But having no money sucks," I said.

"That's the way things have to be," Wishbone said. "If you end up going to North Korea your trip will be free. All expenses paid."

"What do you mean? You guys can supply me with money," I said.

Wishbone shook his head. "I told you. We can't help you. If we do, the Russians will be able to tell where the money is coming from, and they might figure out the whole thing. You've got to find some way to get your own money. It will look more credible if you struggle."

"So how do you expect me to get money?" I said.

"Oh, I forgot," Wishbone said as he handed me a briefcase. It was very heavy. "There are two hundred rounds in there, preloaded in clips. You just need to eject a clip and slap in a new one if you ever get in a---"

"Hey, I saw *John Wick*. You expect me to be *John Wick*? That was just a movie, you know," I said.

Wishbone shrugged. "You wanted in the plan. You want a way to get your money back," he said.

"So how do I get any money in the meanwhile?" I asked.

"You've got a gun. That helps persuade people," Wishbone said. "If you don't learn how to improvise, you're not going to make it through this deal."

We established that I was to leave the Glock and the ammo in a pay locker at the airport. I was to get another weapon and ammo when I got to Texas. This was my New York gun.

156

As I left Wishbone's place, I thought of one other source of funding.

Chapter Fifty Seven
New York

I had a couple hours before I had to get to the airport for my flight back to Austin, so with my gun tucked into my jacket and my 200 rounds of ammo in the briefcase I took a taxi to midtown with a plan to see Kevin Dowd.

Kevin is the lawyer I used in New York for a lot of my client related activities, and he had been dragged into the situation with Lola and the hedge fund manager. He was a corporate guy, not a criminal lawyer but had referred me to one when I needed that sort of representation. Then the lawyer he recommended tried to kill Gabrielle and me and was shot dead by Gab. An hour later Gab and I shot and killed Robert Stanton Banks. It had been an exciting evening. Dowd was astounded by what had happened, and his life had been at risk as part of the complicated situation.

Wishbone had cautioned me not to try to enter an office building armed as I was, because the buildings all had metal detectors and security guards these days. I went to an upscale bar, The Squire, near Dowd's office and called him.

He picked up. "Hey Kevin, it's JR," I said.

"JR, it's good to hear from you. How are things in Austin these days?" Dowd said.

"Complicated," I said. "I'm here in New York today. How about coming to The Squire for a few minutes? I have a very profitable business transaction to propose to you," I said.

"You're serious?" Dowd asked.

I said, "It will be worth your while."

"Okay, I'll be there in ten minutes," he said.

I used the time to organize my sales pitch. As in all effective sales presentations, it's important to stress what's in it for the other guy.

Dowd walked in the bar. I waved to him, and he came over and sat at the table. A waiter appeared. Dowd ordered a scotch.

"Are you picking up the tab?" he asked.

"No," I said.

He looked unhappy at that comment. "You have a proposal for me, and you can't even buy me a drink?"

158

"Wait til you hear what I have to say," I said.

He folded his arms. "Alright, go ahead," he said.

When the government is forced to release a secret document, but doesn't want anybody to know the details, they do something that is called "redacting" the document It looks like somebody crossed out all the good details with a black magic marker.

I gave Kevin Dowd the redacted version of the story. I couldn't tell him about Wishbone, and Toni Anne, and I certainly couldn't tell him about some nebulous plan for me to visit North Korea. The conclusion of the pitch was that I needed short term money, and there was a way for him to profit from this situation that would be mutually beneficial.

"So," Dowd arched an eyebrow and tilted his head, "what exactly is your proposal?"

"I'll set the wheels in motion to sell my rights to the co-op---"

He interrupted me. "You don't actually own the rights to the co-op, but rather---"

"Shut up," I said. "I've heard enough of that lawyer shit to last me a lifetime. You know what I mean; I'll sell the friggin' co-op, okay?"

"Yeah," he said.

"Since I won't get the money for a year, you're going to loan me $100,000 at one-hundred percent interest, the principal and interest payable when I get the payment from the co-op board," I explained.

"You can't encumber the co-op in any way!" Dowd said. "That would threaten any claim you have on the rights of ownership! Didn't Hamilton explain that---"

"Holy shit!" I said, "are all you guys the same? This would be strictly off the books, just between you and me. And it would have to be all cash, of course."

"Absolutely not," Dowd said. "I can't begin to tell you all the reasons why I can't do that. It's unethical, it's illegal, it's immoral---"

"But you're a lawyer. None of those reasons apply," I said.

He pursed his lips. "Okay, how about this one? If you get killed, I end up holding the bag. There's no way for me to get paid back. And it sounds like you're in dangerous territory."

159

I held up my hand and he stopped talking. "I am in danger. How about this?" I opened my jacket enough that he could see the Glock, then I closed the jacket. No one else in the bar seemed to notice.

"Is that a weapon?" Dowd asked.

"It's a Glock 9mm. With a silencer attached." I picked up the briefcase, put it on the table and opened the case. "See this? It's 200 extra rounds, already in clips. Of course, the weapon is loaded, these rounds are just extras."

"Are you threatening me?" Dowd asked.

"Why else would I show you the gun?" I said, then closed the briefcase. "I'm a desperate man."

"I can't believe you would shoot me," he said.

"Let's look at this as a risk/reward situation. I could shoot you right here and nobody would even hear it," I said. "I could escape during the confusion. I've been trained. Why take a chance?"

I was lying. Of course, I hadn't been trained. And I was lying about no one hearing the Glock being fired. Even with a silencer the Glock made a very loud thump, something Barbara Jean had demonstrated to me during a shooting lesson behind her barn. But I thought Dowd wouldn't know that because people see a silencer in the movies and it's unrealistically quiet.

"You're going to shoot me unless I give you $100,000 in cash?" Dowd asked.

"No. We're going to visit your ATM," I said. I was improvising as Wishbone had told me I would have to do. "Drink up, we're leaving."

Dowd tossed down the rest of the scotch in his glass.

"Now get up and don't do anything stupid," I said, as I put my hand inside my jacket. "Don't worry, this is only going to cost you two grand."

"What do you mean?" he asked.

"You're going to withdraw your daily maximum and give it to me," I said.

"My daily maximum is only one thousand," he said.

"Remember what I said about not doing anything stupid?" I asked. "Lying like that to me is real stupid. I know what kind of account you have. Where's the closest ATM?"

160

He pointed to the right, and we left the bar and headed right. It was less than a block, and no one was using the machine when we got there.

I stopped 20 feet before the machine and stood close to the building, hoping to be out of sight of the camera on the ATM.

"Go up and withdraw the money. Nice and easy, nothing to it," I said.

Dowd approached the machine and inserted his card. He appeared to be entering his PIN. "There's something wrong! It won't take my code. Maybe I'm screwing up because I'm nervous." He entered the PIN several times, the machine beeped, and a glass slid down in front of the screen.

"There, I shut it down. What are you going to do now, shoot me?" he said.

I was furious, and took out the gun and shot the security camera above the ATM. "You're lucky I haven't shot you yet," I said to Dowd. He was standing with his hands up, his back against the ATM. "Get out of the way," I said.

In a rage I emptied the clip into the ATM, aiming at random. I'm not sure what I was trying to accomplish, but the façade of the machine fell away, exposing the innards. There was a metal box. I assumed it must be where the cash was stored. I tried to yank it free, but it didn't move.

I looked around, afraid that people would be watching. But this was New York, people were walking away with their heads down. They were smart enough to know that it didn't matter that the JP Morgan ATM got ripped off. That was no big deal to them, as long as they didn't get shot, or asked later by the police to be witnesses.

Dowd was still standing there with his hands up. "Put your hands down you doofus, or I *will* shoot you," I said.

I was calm as I ejected the spent ammo clip, put it in my jacket pocket, and opened the briefcase to get another clip. I loaded and shot at the metal box. Why not, it worked before.

The metal box came free. I looked in and saw cash stacked in 20s, 50s and 100s. I started grabbing the money and stuffing it into my jacket pockets, then loaded as much as I could in the briefcase. I didn't figure I had time to get all the money out of the box. I stood back.

161

I addressed Dowd. Time to keep improvising, "Ok pal, here's the deal. I'm not supposed to tell you this, but I'm working undercover for the CIA. When the cops come, you say that I was just some random guy, and you tried to foil my attempt by intentionally putting in the wrong PIN. That will check out. Just stick with that story, don't be a candy ass. You'll look like a hero. Do I have to tell you that the CIA can be very vindictive? They still kill people, you know?"

I started to walk to the curb, then turned to face Dowd. "I'll explain the whole thing to you when it's over. If I'm alive…Hey, you should have gone for the first offer. Remember what I said about sticking with that story. If you're a standup guy, the CIA will protect you. If not…"

"You've become a psychotic," Dowd said.

"And don't send me a bill for your time, either" I said.

Who says you can't get a taxi in NYC? I stuck my hand up, a taxi pulled over and I got in. I changed cabs three times in Manhattan before I finally took a cab and told him to use the Tri-Borough Bridge to get to LaGuardia Airport. I paid all the taxi drivers cash and I was a generous, but not outlandish tipper. It's fun having pockets full of cash, it gives the feeling of real money, not just some dots on a computer screen.

While crossing the East River on the bridge I happened to catch my reflection in the glass that separated the passengers from the driver of the cab. I looked at myself. The son of an elite family, from a long line of distinguished doctors, the valedictorian of a top prep school, and the solid number six golfer on the University of Texas golf team. I was the former boyfriend of the world's most beautiful movie star, a respected money manager. Now I was married, at least for the time being to a Texas oil heiress. And, as of today, I was guilty of several serious Federal Crimes, including I figured, kidnapping, armed robbery or something akin to it, and grand larceny.

You could say I was committed to carrying out the plan. I didn't know exactly what the plan was, but I was going to get my money back.

Chapter Fifty Eight
Moscow
The Lider's Office

The functionaries who met with the Lider that morning must have noticed that he wasn't paying full attention to them. He seemed to be fascinated with something on his computer screen.

As the visitors who stood in front of his desk gave their reports, the Lider was watching the YouTube video of Boris Kravanesko's roller coaster ride, over and over. He watched it more than one hundred times. When one bureaucrat finished talking and was dismissed, The Russian President asked his secretary to summon Colonel Nihisky.

Nihisky marched into the Lider's office and clicked his heels. The Lider asked, "Have you seen this video?"

"Yes sir," the colonel answered. The Lider must have known that.

"Let's watch it again!" The Lider gestured for Nihisky to come around the desk and stand next to his chair, then he started the video again.

"Isn't that great?" The Lider asked.

"Yes sir," Nihisky answered. No other answer was acceptable.

"This is the most fun I've had in a long time. Quinn and the sisters, Debbie and Nancy seem to work well together," the Lider said.

"They are all good at their jobs---"

"*That's* a video I want. The sisters having sex with Sierra Quinn," the Lider said.

"Sir, I'm not sure, umm, we---"

"Never mind for now. I've got to maintain my focus. What's next for the senior Kravanesko?" the Lider asked.

Nihisky answered, "The local party boss is meeting with him today. I have given the Boss discretion regarding when Kravanesko will be eliminated."

"Good. I can use another specimen for another glass jar," the Lider said. "People are already forgetting Turgenev. It's a pity, but I've found that terror is the best motivator. I'm sure all the ransomware pirates have seen the video and have gotten the

163

message," the Lider said. "The glass jars are very expensive, you know. They are made out a specialized glass imported from Sweden. But they're worth the price."

Chapter Fifty Nine
Minsk, Belarus

The Party Boss phoned Sergei Kravanesko. He asked him to meet at the same bar in which he had met Andrey. That bar served as the Boss' unofficial office.

Kravanesko arrived at the Uzhin Vie Klube, which translated into "Supper Club" a local joke, because the Club was just a seedy bar that served greasy snacks. Nevertheless, the place usually did a bustling noontime business because it served cheap booze. It was deserted except for the Boss sitting in his usual booth, farthest from the door, and a single bartender who just nodded to Sergei. Since the Boss owned the place, the emptiness sent a silent message to Kravanesko.

The Party Boss gestured for Kravanesko to sit opposite from him.

"It's a pity what happened," the Boss said.

"Thank you for your condolences," Kravanesko said without enthusiasm.

"I wasn't offering condolences," the Boss said. "What happened to your son was inevitable when you made the mistake of thinking you could send him to America without consequences during this most important operation. This is currently the Lider's most critical program, and you think you have the wherewithal to sneak away without being detected? The pity is that you think you can escape without completing the job the Lider assigned to you."

Kravanesko was stunned, not by the message, but by the bluntness by which is was delivered. He said nothing.

"What do you have to say for yourself?" the Boss demanded.

Kravanesko blurted, "Why did you bother with my son! He was inconsequential! He---"

"He's inconsequential now," the Boss said. "You saw the pickled head of Oleg Turgenev on the Lider's desk. You must know there are more pickled heads. Can you imagine the process that results in the head being put into the jar?"

When it was clear that the Boss would wait until there was a response, Kravanesko finally said, "Yes."

165

"If you want to live until tomorrow, continue to do the specific job you have been assigned. I suggest you begin each day with this thought," the Boss said.

Kravanesko nodded.

"You can go now," the Boss said.

Kravanesko knew he would die a gruesome death soon.

When Kravanesko was gone from the bar the Boss picked up his phone. "Andrey?"

"Yes sir," Andrey answered.

"Be ready. Kravanesko's time is up. I can see in his eyes that he'll be useless in the operation. I've decided to move up the timetable. We're going with the loud option," the Boss said.

Chapter Sixty
Minsk, Belarus
Offices of Network Designs

Kravanesko knew it must be Andrey who had betrayed him. No one else knew his plans. There were no other suspects.

When Kravanesko returned from the Boss' bar, although he felt like every employee was staring at him, he tried to act normal as he invited Andrey to step into his office. Andrey complied.

Sergei Kravanesko had reached the decision that since his life was as good as over, he would first take Andrey's life. Kravanesko imagined he would be hideously tortured before being murdered but would have the satisfaction of killing the treacherous rat who had set up his son.

Andrey looked calm as he closed the door behind him after he entered Kravanesko's office. For the first time during his employment, Andrey sat in a guest chair without having been invited by Kravanesko.

Kravanesko sneered at Andrey. "To think I trusted you!"

Andrey smiled and shrugged.

"Let's see how complacent you are now," Kravanesko said, as he pulled a Marakov pistol out of his desk drawer. The Marakov is a Russian knock-off of the German designed semi-automatic Walther PP. "You know that I'm an expert shot?"

"Yes, but I'm not worried," Andrey said.

"Why, do you think I won't shoot you?" Kravanesko asked.

"All the ammunition has been removed from the gun," Andrey said.

Kravanesko aimed the Marakov at Andrey and pulled the trigger. The gun clicked. Andrey smiled.

Andrey got a remote-control device out of his pocket. He pressed the single button on the remote.

"What are you doing?" Kravanesko asked.

"I have just buzzed three gentlemen through the outer door to the offices. They'll be coming in here in a moment," Andrey said.

167

The door burst open. In came three enormous men in black ski masks. One of them was carrying a chainsaw.

A novice must put a chainsaw on the ground and place one foot on the saw to steady it as he pulls the cord to start the engine. An expert can hold the chainsaw in one hand at waist level and pull the cord with the other hand. The man in Kravanesko's office was an expert.

The employees of Network Designs heard the chainsaw and the screaming. It was brief, but the memory would stay with each of them.

Then the three enormous men left Kravanesko's office, one carrying a black body bag over his shoulder, another carrying a bloody chainsaw. The third was carrying a black plastic bag by the attached cord. It swung beneath his hand and contained Kravanesko's head.

None of the employees made eye contact with the killers. Then Andrey came out of Kravanesko's office. He addressed the staff.

"I am now the CEO of Network Designs. You should take this experience as a learning opportunity. I should not have to remind you that it is in your best interest to forget what you have seen here today, and not to discuss the inner workings of Network Designs with anyone. As long as you follow those rules, you can continue your excellent opportunity to make a great deal of money. Keep working."

Chapter Sixty One
Moscow
The Lider's Office

Colonel Nihisky met with the Lider.
"Sir, I have a report on the Minsk situation," the colonel said.

The Lider nodded, meaning to go ahead.

"The Party Boss met with Kravanesko. He did not offer any sympathy, but rather blatantly threatened Kravanesko. He mentioned Kravanesko's head might soon be sitting in a jar on your desk," Nihisky said.

"That's a good idea," the Lider said as he smiled. "Kravanesko's head in a jar on my desk for the next meeting of the ransomware scum! I won't have to say much to get the point across."

"The deed has been accomplished. Kravanesko's head should be here, in the jar, tomorrow," Colonel Nihisky said.

"Good. I need a new centerpiece," The Lider said.

Chapter Sixty Two
LaGuardia Airport

When I got out of the cab at LaGuardia, I was expecting to be confronted by a heavily armed police SWAT team, but no such thing happened. Things were normal. I entered the terminal and bought a magazine just so I'd get a plastic bag. Then I went to the men's room and went into a stall and transferred my Glock and some of the cash into the bag. I found the section of the airport that housed the pay lockers and put the bag and the briefcase into a locker, just like I'd seen Jason Bourne do. Nobody looked twice at me, and I boarded the plane and got into my, ugh, coach seat without incident.

Until the plane took off, I was nervous that the FBI or some sort of law enforcement would storm in and arrest me, and I was relieved when we flew off, away from the scene of the crime. I was, so far, a successful ATM robber. This was the happiest I had ever been in a coach seat on an airplane. I began to read the magazine that I had purchased: *Guns and Ammo*. Time to familiarize myself with my new field as much as possible. *Guns and Ammo* is a lot like *Golf Digest*; just cross out "New Titanium Drivers Review" in the headline of the article and replace with "9mm Striker Driven Pistols Review," and they're pretty much the same.

All plane flights should be like the trip from NYC to Baltimore. You go up, fly for a bit, and land. I had to change planes and took the opportunity to call Wishbone. In an extended series of 15 second phone calls, I explained the current situation and asked him to make a threatening phone call to Kevin Dowd. "Make sure he doesn't rat me out," I said.

"Hey, you're learning," Wishbone said, "I'll take care of it, with pleasure."

Chapter Sixty Three
New York City

Wishbone used a clean burner phone to call Kevin Dowd.

"Hello," Dowd said.

"Kevin, this is a friend of yours calling," Wishbone said.

"What do you mean, a friend?" Dowd asked.

"A friend is someone who wants to make sure you're safe," Wishbone answered.

"So how are you going to make sure I'm safe?" Dowd asked.

"As long as you stay with the story JR told you to stay with, you're safe," Wishbone said.

"And if not?" Dowd asked.

"I'll make sure you're not safe," Wishbone said, then hung up.

Chapter Sixty Four
Austin

The Desperado, me, was back in his hideaway. I had a little over $4,200 in cash, and a couple thousand back in the locker in New York. A week ago that wasn't much, but now it seemed like a lot. Perspectives change.

When we had gotten engaged, Barbara Jean had given me a Sig Sauer pistol, a high-end handgun. I learned how to use it, but it was stolen by Sierra Quinn during the unpleasantness when Quinn and her accomplice had knocked me out and stuffed me in the 55-gallon drum. Barbara Jean had ended up shooting and killing the goon, but Quinn sped away from the scene with the Sig in her vehicle.

After I began living with Barbara, we didn't think about replacing the Sig Sauer, because I now resided at her ranch, which I referred to as the Texas Firearms Repository and could get a gun any time I wanted.

But now that I was back living in Austin, I needed my own gun. A Texas gun, since my New York gun was in the airport storage locker. I would only use it in New York, or somewhere that I could go from the City without taking a plane.

Barbara Jean had an arsenal at her house, and given my finances, a free gun was my first choice. I called my wife. She answered.

"You got your money back yet?" she said as a greeting.

"Not yet, but I want to come by the ranch," I said.

"What for?" she said.

"I'll tell you when I get there," I said.

There was a pause. She didn't say anything. "What's the matter, you got a gentleman caller?" I asked.

"Yeah, I'm entertaining the Dallas Cowboys defensive line right now, but I can tell them they have to leave," Barbara Jean said.

I'm sure she was kidding.

"Just the starters, or the backups too?" I asked.

After Barb didn't answer I said, "I'll be right out."

"Get your pants on fellas," I heard Barbara Jean call out, then she disconnected.

172

Chapter Sixty Five
Spicewood, TX

I stopped my pickup at a post 20 feet from the front gate of Barb's ranch. Barb had a remote control to open the gate, but people who had the code for the keypad had to get out of their vehicles and tap in the code. Not many people had the code, as far as I knew, just Barb's parents and me. Others had to hit a button that engaged an intercom and wait to be buzzed in. I entered the code, and the electric gate began to open. It stayed open long enough to allow getting back in your vehicle and to safely drive through the gate, which was especially important for her fat ass father Cletus.

I was reassured that the gate opened at all. At least Barbara Jean hadn't changed the passcode, so maybe she did see our situation as temporary. I drove in, the gate closed behind me and I went down the long gravel driveway to the main house.

Barbara Jean was waiting out front. She looked great, even for her. Barb smiled at me. When my movie star girlfriend Lola was alive, I used to say she could just smile her way into the vault at Fort Knox. Barbara Jean was in that category.

"You look above average today," I said, "it makes me wish I had the $50 million back."

"But you don't, so don't even think about it," Barbara Jean said.

"My thoughts are my own. But seeing you stand there creates additional incentive," I said.

She clasped her hands above her head and shook her body. I think you could call it shimmied. Barbara Jean looked like a cowgirl belly dancer. Are women born knowing how to do that? Either way, I liked it.

"So, what's so urgent? And why couldn't you talk about it on the phone?" Barbara Jean asked.

I was prepared. I took an index card and a pen out of my shirt pocket. I wrote: We can't talk about this. I'm being listened to. I'll write out what I need.

"C'mon! Really?" Barb said.

I nodded. I wrote: I need a gun, a Glock 9mm if you can spare it. And as much ammo as you can give me.

173

She smiled. "Part of the plan, or are you just crazy?"

"A bit of both," I said.

I needed money, too. I just knew she must have a coffee can or two, of hundred-dollar bills hidden somewhere. I wanted to ask her for as much cash as she could give, but my pride just wouldn't let me. I'd just get the gun from Barbara Jean and think of some other way to get money.

This is Texas. It's easy to buy a gun, but Barbara Jean didn't bring that up in conversation. Barb took me to her walk-in gun safe, which was more like an Armory. She was proud and happy to give me the Glock and a couple hundred rounds of ammo in a grocery bag.

Inside the safe I thought it was okay to talk.

"Barb, I've got a solid plan, and some people helping me get the money back," I told her.

"Oh, is your friend **Toni Anne** helping you?" Barbara Jean asked.

"She just got shot," I said.

"Is she---"

"No, she's not dead, she'll recover. But this is getting serious," I said.

It was hard to tell how she viewed the news of Toni Anne being alive. "Is some Russian hitman going to punch me out, try to kill me? Like last time?" Barbara Jean asked.

I was quiet for a good minute. That wasn't something about which I had given any thought.

"Well?" Barb asked.

"The action should take place a long way from here," I said.

"Like where?" Barbara Jean asked.

"Probably Washington, North Korea. Maybe New York City," I said.

"Sure. You're so full of it!" Barbara Jean said.

"I'm not sure where. There's no reason anything should happen around here," I said

"I'm not sure I should be giving a gun to a man telling Fairy Tales," Barbara Jean said.

Chapter Sixty Six
New York City

Wishbone had known of JR's actions with Kevin Dowd and the ATM even before JR called him. Now that Toni Anne knew he was CIA they could have more candid conversations during their nightly call, which was routed through the White House and was scrambled. Although the call was protected by the White House's technology, Cyber Command, and thus Admiral Stockbridge would know from their surveillance of Toni Anne that she was on a scrambled line and could not monitor the conversation.

"Your man JR Johnson looks like he might have the makings of a field agent," Wishbone told Toni Anne.

"What do you mean?" Toni Anne asked.

Wishbone explained what had happened with JR and Kevin Dowd, and how JR had shot up the ATM and extracted the cash.

"How are you keeping track of him?" she asked.

"We're the CIA," Wishbone said.

"So, answer my question," Toni Anne said.

"You mean even before he called me up and told me? We are tracking JR's whereabouts by monitoring his phone location. And I have connections in NYPD. We routinely turn off the cop's surveillance cameras in areas of the City where we have something going that we don't want them to know about. NYPD can't, or doesn't want to, figure out what's going on with their camera network," Wishbone said. "They don't mind being a bit ignorant as long as the Federal dollars keep pouring in."

"And?" Toni Anne said.

"And, we had video of JR Johnson walking up to the ATM with his lawyer Kevin Dowd as a hostage and shooting up the freakin' machine. He got a lot of cash out of it, then hightailed in a cab. He changed cabs a bunch of times before going to the airport," Wishbone explained.

"I wish we could help him out more," Toni Anne said.

"But we can't. You know that," Wishbone said, "we don't want to blow the cover on the whole operation."

175

Chapter Sixty Seven
Spicewood, TX

In an attempt to get some sympathy from Barbara Jean I said, "If I get killed, I don't want a funeral."

"I had a little taste of what the people you are up against are like," she said, "if you get killed, don't worry about a funeral, because we'll never find the body." She laughed. I like a gal with a lively sense of humor.

I opened the passenger side door of my pickup and put the paper bag full of ammo on the floor. "What should I do with the gun?" I asked Barbara Jean.

"Don't try to hide it. Just put it in plain sight, right on the passenger seat," she said, "this is Texas, you could get away with having a 50-caliber machine gun on the seat as long as you weren't trying to conceal it. If you do get stopped, the cops will probably suggest that you get a bigger gun."

"Okay," I said, but I was still nervous. I got into the truck, started it up, and opened the window so Barb could talk to me.

"JR, what's going on? You don't expect me to believe some story about North Korea, do you? What are you trying to do?" Barbara Jean asked.

"I'm getting my money and my wife back," I said.

"Really?" she said.

"Brace yourself," I said. "I shall return." Then I floored the truck, skidding on the gravel of Barb's driveway, and I was off to Austin.

"Brace yourself," was something I said to Barbara Jean when I wanted to have sex. I told her it was the equivalent of foreplay.

Chapter Sixty Eight
Austin

I missed Barbara Jean. I tried to convince myself that it wasn't just for the sex, it was for the companionship, the conversation, the cuddling, how great she smelled when we spooned in bed, her smile, the food preparation. But right at this moment, it was mostly for the sex.

I pushed that thought aside. It must be great being a mastermind spy, like Toni Anne, cooking up all these plots. But I was no mastermind, I was just a drone who was going to carry out the plot, and I waited for my assignment.

How was I going to get more money? I could burn through this much cash in a hurry. I had no idea how long it would be until I got my money back. Screw it, I thought, I'd cash in my 401k. I could worry about the tax penalties later, maybe while I was in the federal penitentiary.

A different investment firm held my 401k assets. I had bought distressed blue-chip stocks in 2009, during the Great Recession, and held on to them. I didn't pay much attention to this portfolio; I had just sold the few stocks that hadn't worked out over the years and held on to the winners. Since then, the market had quadrupled, and I had done a little better than that. The quickest way to get money out of the 401k was to borrow it. If you pay it back within 60 days, there are no tax penalties.

I went on the website for my 401k. My password didn't work. I called the company. "Your call is very important," a recorded voice told me, I should hold for the next available operator.

While I was holding for the next available operator, I had a very bad feeling.

Why hadn't I thought of this? I should have taken the money out when all of this nonsense had started.

At least the music on hold was tolerable, it was plain classical. I was on hold for so long that my mind wandered. It reminded me of my childhood. My mother allowed solely classical music on our family stereo in the parlor. The only rebellious thing I could ever remember my sister doing was playing a Beatles record on the hallowed stereo, an act seen as so hideous it was reported to my brain surgeon father when he

177

got home to preside over dinner than evening, and dad had seized on the opportunity to deliver a lecture on the insidious effect of rock and roll, he had even read a scholarly journal article which had quoted a study that prolonged exposure to such music decreased IQs among the study group.

Upon enhanced interrogation, my sister, dear old Bitsy, had confessed that she had borrowed the record from a friend. That was a major relief to my parents. At least no assets from the family trust had been squandered, and it was agreed that the offensive recording would be returned, and the matter was settled. The other girl's parents could worry about that girl turning *her* mind to mush while depleting that family's trust assets, one $2.99 album at a time.

My mother was one of those out-of-touch old money nincompoops who lectured her children on always counting our change and keeping a careful inventory of postage stamps. "That's how you protect your wealth," she'd say. She skipped over the part where her parents left her millions back in the 1960s, along with Manhattan real estate. I'm convinced she thought people without money were the ones who squandered postage stamps and didn't count their change. Didn't everybody inherit?

My mind was wandering again. Time to focus. After several complete symphonies, an operator picked up. I identified myself. "Please hold," she said.

Chapter Sixty Nine
Moscow
The Lider's Office

There's a theory that language shapes one's thought, that is, people who speak different languages see the world differently. Scholarly studies had been written for the U.S. State Department; some think the theory is nonsense, it's a matter of heated debate.

Many Russian technical terms are not direct translations from English. For example: the western astronomical term, "Black Hole" is expressed in Russian as "Dark Star," or "Temnaya Zvezda," the two terms implying different concepts.

The Lider had a meeting that received his complete undivided attention. Kuznetzov, The Commanding General of the FSB brought in his subordinate, Hemo, the Director of the Glubokaya Poddelka Program. It was one of the few terms that the Russians translated directly from English and meant: Deep Fake.

Deep Fake technology produced believable audio and video that was totally false, purely the creation of its' makers. For example: a Deep Fake video could show Tom Cruise, Marilyn Monroe, and John Glenn at a news conference supposedly recorded yesterday announcing that newly disclosed research indicated that the Moon Landings never happened but had been filmed in an abandoned warehouse in Tucson. This wasn't some spliced together quasi-realistic Hollywood creation, it was digitally created and when done well was impossible to tell from the real thing without detailed analysis by experts.

Until this time the U.S. and China were acknowledged to be the leaders in Deep Fake technology. North Korea was known to be lagging, but working hard to catch up, and Russian efforts were thought to be weak.

But Russia had been playing possum and had intentionally leaked amateurish examples of Deep Fake output. Just a small group within the FSB knew of their real capabilities, which were the best in the world. The Lider had realized the potential of Deep Fake technology and had spent a sizeable percentage of the national defense budget on it for years.

179

Hemo brought a sampling of four videos of foreign leaders. The first video showed U.S. President Gerald Ford. His physical appearance was as he looked in 1975. Ford was addressing an American Legion Convention. His voice and gestures were perfect, even the occasional vocal flubs and physical awkwardness. The text of his speech praised the inspirational leadership of Russia's current President, and he concluded that the United States would be far better off abandoning its' military capabilities, completely disarming, surrendering its' national sovereignty to Russia and putting its fate into the benevolent hands of the Lider. His final line: "The Lider can do a far better job governing Cleveland, the Great State of Ohio, and the United States of America than the Congress, the Supreme Court and your current humble President." The audience wildly approves and gives him a standing ovation as thousands of red, white, and blue balloons are released from the ceiling of the convention hall.

Videos two and three were similar, except the speakers were Israeli leader Benjamin Netanyahu and German Chancellor Angela Merkel speaking to groups in their respective nations.

In the fourth British PM Boris Johnson was dressed in a pink leotard and a tutu and tapped danced while he sang "On the Good Ship Lollipop."

Upon the Lider's invitation the General and Hemo flanked the Russian President as he watched the video on his computer. Following his lead, the subordinates were grim during the initial three videos and laughed when the Lider laughed at the prancing Boris Johnson.

"This is so good that I think if Boris Johnson saw it, he might think that we drugged him and filmed him in the tutu!" the Lider said.

The General blurted, "Sir, we intended no frivolity, we just included the last one to show how far we can take the technology---"

"---I know you take this very seriously General. I am very impressed with your work. No apologies are necessary." The Lider paused and clasped his hands.

"Thank you, sir."

"Impressed does not begin to describe how I feel about your work. If we use this correctly, we can control the world. This

180

technology is more powerful than nuclear weapons," the Lider said. "We must be first to use it, before adequate defense measures can be created to counteract it, and before it becomes so commonplace that people will be more wary."

The General said, "Sir, the technology is ready. To make specific videos we do need time. The videos cannot be ---"

"I understand, General. I want to be ready for its maximum use in the next American Presidential election. But first, let's test the waters in a smaller manner," the Lider said.

The Lider explained the Deep Fake video he wanted produced.

Chapter Seventy
Austin

When I was in college, I thought that the ultimate feeling of dread was watching when my opponent in an intercollegiate golf match lined up a one-foot putt on the last hole that would beat me. Life experience has since taught me that there were other events with more serious and dreadful consequences. I was to learn more in this area.

In two separate incidents in New York, Sierra Quinn had shot and killed Lola, and my friend Elliott. Later that week I had two men point guns at me with deadly intent. Weeks ago, a Russian goon, at the instructions of Quinn, had knocked me out with a crowbar and entrapped me in a 55-gallon drum with the intention of drowning me in a pond. I woke up and when I realized that I was in the oil drum; now that was a feeling of dread.

But as I waited on hold to discuss my 401k, I experienced a new form of dread. *The How Could I Be So Stupid?* form.

I had hesitated to withdraw from my 401k because it set off tax problems. But if the account had been hacked there would be no, tax problems, because there would be no money.

I just knew that due to my inattention the 401k had been liquidated or moved or borrowed against and I would have lost all the money. *How could I be so stupid?*

When a voice came on the phone it took a few seconds to realize this was in fact a live person. It's not always easy to tell in these circumstances.

I went through the verbal dance of identifying myself, including reciting the middle name of my first dog, or something like that. When the voice was satisfied that it was me, I asked about my account balance.

"As of yesterday's close, the balance was $57.57," the voice informed me. That was several million less than it had been in the previous month.

"Can you please refresh my memory. How did that happen?" I asked.

"Sir, two weeks ago you liquidated all your stock positions and put the proceeds into Vladcoin. You must remember, we made you sign a form that acknowledged that you were

182

executing this trade on an unsolicited basis, not as a result of any recommendation of our firm. I can send you a copy of the document that you electronically signed," the voice went on.

I remembered Vladcoin. It was a startup cryptocurrency that had been exposed as a fraud and lost nearly all its value in the last couple weeks. But I had not directed any transfer of funds in my 401k in months. I never signed anything. The bad guys were getting good at ruining my life.

I didn't know what to say. Eventually I said, "Thank you, I'll get back to you," then I hung up.

I should have listened to my mother. If I'd only saved, say, 20 million postage stamps over the years, I'd be even. Sounds like a big number, but I calculated that over 20 years it's only 2,739 stamps a day, at current prices.

Chapter Seventy One
Austin

Barbara Jean called me, a first since I had been placed on the Involuntary Celibate Protocol.

"JR, I'd been thinking," she said.

"Oh, anything good?"

"I think you need some more shooting lessons. It's not a good idea to have you walking around with that Glock without knowing how to handle it," Barb said. "So, I think you should come out to the ranch for some more instruction."

"Well, I'm very busy, but I think I can work you into my schedule, how about if I come out now?"

"Alright, bring the Glock, but don't bother bringing any of the ammo. I got a new shipment delivered."

"You get ammo delivered?" I asked. I was always learning something new about Barbara Jean.

"I'm a good customer," Barbara Jean said.

"I'll be right out," I said.

Chapter Seventy Two
Spicewood, TX

I felt odd, embarrassed to be entering Barbara Jean's ranch. I didn't want to encounter Alice and especially didn't want to see Tommy. They weren't around when I drove up to Barb's house.

I knocked on the door of what had been my home a few days before. Barbara Jean answered. She was all business.

"When I learned to be a Gun Instructor, they taught us that we have a responsibility to the pupils and to society, to not let someone go off thinking that they know how to shoot safely when they are not fully trained."

"You took formal lessons to be a Gun Instructor?" I asked. "Didn't you know enough already?"

"I wanted to be officially certified. I taught my class how to shoot, back when I was a Sunday school teacher. There's a lot you don't know about me."

"Learnin' them youngsters to shoot for The Lord, huh?" I asked. "Sunday school in Texas sounds like a lot more fun than where I grew up in Maryland."

"Everything is better in Texas," Barbara Jean said as she suggestively shook her shoulders.

Right then I wished I had that $50 million in my pocket.

I wondered what Barbara Jean would think if she knew that I had shot up an ATM in New York City. That couldn't be part of the standard Sunday school firearms training package.

Barbara Jean said, "I am all set up for training out behind the barn," then gestured for me to exit through the front door. I wondered what the message she was giving me by not walking me through the house and out the back door; that's the easiest and most natural way to get behind the barn, but I wasn't going to worry about subliminal messages at this point. Learning how to shoot better might just help me get my money back, and even save my life.

As we walked toward the barn, I checked out Barb. She was wearing a shirt that made her look flat chested. I knew this was definitely not the case. I wondered how women manage to alter their appearances like that, flat chested women sometimes look voluptuous, and shapely women like Barbara Jean can wear

185

tops that make them look mannish. I had seen thousands of combinations and permutations of this phenomenon. I concluded that this was a mystery that I would never solve, it was merely a further example that women were mentally far superior to easily manipulated men but resolved to diligently continue my studies in this area as long as I was alive.

The shooting lesson focused on aiming. It was important to leave both eyes open but concentrate on using your dominate eye. We experimented for a couple minutes before determining that I was right eye dominant. After maybe 20 minutes of serious practice, I was much improved in hitting my intended targets, not that I was anywhere near Barbara Jean's proficiency.

"If it ever comes time for you to shoot anybody, you want to accomplish two things. You want to kill your intended target, and you do not want to harm any innocent bystanders," Barbara Jean said. "That's enough for today."

We wordlessly policed the area, picking up spent cartridges. I had fired more rounds than I realized during the lesson.

"Can I come here same time next Tuesday?" I asked

. "We'll arrange something, but not next Tuesday," Barbara Jean said.

"How's that?" I asked, realizing that it was none of my business.

"My father comes all the way down from Crawford for his monthly poker game at the Grange Hall near the Feed Store. He drops off Momma June, then drives to town. He wins a lot because he's the only one who doesn't drink during the game. He told me he plays cautiously until the other guys get drunk, then he cleans up. You'd think they'd catch on, but it's been going on for years," Barbara Jean said.

"They play for big stakes?" I asked.

"Big money. You know these oil men. Half of them drive around in old beat-up pickup trucks. You'd never know they have ten, twenty thousand in cash tucked into their cowboy boots for the poker game," Barb said.

"Almost doesn't sound fair," I said.

"Some months he lets them win, say four or five thousand. Then the next month he gets them for big money," Barbara Jean said.

186

"He's trickier than he looks," I said.

"Hey, as my father says, 'they don't have to drink', why not take advantage of them?" Anyhow, when the game is over the old man drives out here and gets drunk and passes out on the couch. Then he and my mom drive back to Crawford the next day."

I chose to say nothing.

"It's funny, sometimes the old man has so much cash stuffed in his boots that it's hard for him to take them off. Thousands of dollars, sometimes a hundred thousand. He always leaves me a couple thousand on the coffee table, like he's leaving a tip for the chamber maid." Barb said.

"Next Tuesday, huh?" I asked.

Barb nodded.

"Sounds like fun." I said.

"They happen to be coming up today. Telling me about the Will, the Trust. Their lawyer made some changes. They should be here soon. You'd best be leaving," Barbara Jean said. "It will avoid any awkward explanations.

As I drove toward the gate, I saw Cletus Parker's big Escalade parked outside the property. He had opened the door of the vehicle and stepped down, then walked to the keypad to gain entry.

Cletus reentered his Caddy and drove through the open gate, and I took advantage of the opening to drive through on the way out. It was plenty wide enough for two vehicles to pass side by side. I didn't want to talk to Cletus, and I could see that June was in the passenger seat. I gave them a big smile and wave and kept going. Not knowing whether she had told her parents the current state of her marriage, I'd let Barbara Jean make up some story to explain my behavior.

I was getting antsy to have some action, any action that would get me closer to my goals and had begun to carry two phones with me all the time: my iPhone and the burner. I didn't want to miss a call from Wishbone.

Halfway back to Austin the burner phone rang.

"Hello Wishbone," I answered.

"It's Toni Anne," the voice said.

187

I worried that something, like violent death, had happened to Wishbone. "Is everything all right?" I asked.

"No, but it's not any more fucked up than usual," Toni Anne said. "Hang up and call me back."

We went through the dance of the fifteen second phone calls. We established that she was calling me on this number because she needed to arrange a meeting with herself, Wishbone, and me. It was going to be in Washington, D.C.

"Let me give you the address," Toni Anne said.

'Let me guess. 1600 Pennsylvania Avenue," I said.

"That's happens to be our eventual destination, you little shithead," Toni Anne said, then she gave me the address where I should wait to be picked up. "How do you like them apples?"

Chapter Seventy Three
Washington, DC
The Congressional Office Building

Admiral Stockbridge visited several Congressmen that morning. It was traditional for military brass to call on politicians because the military depended on the Congress for funding and going hat in hand to the Representatives reinforced that Stockbridge was beholden to them. Stockbridge merely went through the motions with his first three meetings. Each Congressman arranged to be photographed with the Admiral, so the Representatives could send the image back to their constituents and prove that they were close to the heartbeat of the Intelligence Establishment. The Admiral hated having to kiss the asses of all the self-important politicians, but he was a master of the art and only half listened to these idiots. Stockbridge kept his focus on the main goal.

After the next election Stockbridge was confident he'd be Vice President. And who knows what could happen then? Safi was getting on in years. Every morning when Stockbridge got dressed, he imagined himself as President. He wondered if he could wear the Admiral's uniform as Chief Executive, at least on some occasions; after all the President was the Commander-In-Chief.

For any chance of that scenario happening, Stockbridge knew he must carry out his assignment at Cyber Command with the utmost care.

The real purpose of Admiral Stockbridge's trip to Capitol Hill was his fourth meeting that morning. He called on Congressman Safi.

Safi had called Stockbridge and in a terse exchange ordered Stockbridge to arrange the meaningless visitations with the other Congressional flunkies. The two of them could then talk in Safi's office, the one place he was sure was secure, and their meeting would not draw undue attention from the White House. He had a private security firm sweep his personal office and was confident that no one could listen in to any conversation.

189

When the two of them were alone and the door was closed, Stockbridge said, "So, Congressman, why this meeting? Or should I say Mr. President?"

"Let's not get carried away, Admiral. We have a lot of work to do before I'm... before *we,* are President and Vice President," Safi said.

Chapter Seventy Four
New York City
East Village

Wishbone was wearing expensive headphones. To an observer it would seem like he was listening to music on a high-tech sound system. But he was having much more fun than that since he was listening live to the conversation between Congressman Safi and Admiral Stockbridge. Most of the time the conversations in Safi's office were recorded for future review, but Wishbone wanted to hear this one as is happened.

It turned out that the private security firm with the impeccable reputation that had electronically swept Safi's office was in reality a company that Wishbone controlled. This conversation was so important that Wishbone would report what was said directly to the President that night.

Chapter Seventy Five
Dallas

Sierra Quinn had used the Express checkout option of the
Dallas Omni Hotel the morning that Boris Kravanesko's
rollercoaster ride had been broadcast, so she didn't *have* to stop
in the lobby. She did stop. Sierra wanted to see the Dallas cops
coming and going.

Just like everywhere on earth the police were great at
responding to a crime long after it happened, and any potential
suspects had left the vicinity. The place was crowded with
forensic types and detectives trying to look busy and important.
The local detectives tried to blend in, but their clothes made
them stand out. It reminded her of her days on the job in New
York. Whenever the homicide detectives were in one of the
upscale hotels in their cheap suits they might as well have had
neon signs on them flashing "Cop," Some of the detectives
bought suits that were twice as expensive as their co-workers,
but it didn't help; it looked like they were cops wearing higher
priced cheap suits. It was the same in Dallas, the same
everywhere she guessed.

Quinn wondered what they would make of finding the dead
Russian bodyguard in what had been Boris Kravanesko's suite.
It didn't take a very good detective to conclude the stiff hadn't
been an effective guard.

TV crews were kept outside the building. Reporters with
microphones in hand were talking to cameras and lights. *What
could they be reporting? Nothing new*, Quinn surmised.

One of the detectives did check her out, but not as a suspect.
She, in her expensive clothes, gave him a cold look, and he
abruptly turned away. Her appearance was very different than
the cops would find on the security footage from last night of
the two men and one woman leaving the bar and going to
Boris' room. The bell captain helped Quinn get a taxi for the
airport.

As she was getting in the cab a plain sedan pulled up and
parked in a restricted area. The two men who got out of the car
wore sunglasses and suits, ties, and white shirts that might have
been purchased directly from the J. Edgar Hoover Well Dressed
FBI Agent Catalogue. They never looked at Quinn. Later that

192

day when the FBI agents looked over the list of hotel guests the name Patricia Sizemore didn't raise any interest.

Quinn instructed the taxi to take her to DFW airport and went to the Delta first class lounge. She didn't have a destination, or any new orders from Colonel Nihisky. It seemed like a good idea to get away from the hotel, and she'd wait in the airport for a couple hours to see if Nihisky would call or text her. If not, she'd fly to Salt Lake City, one step closer to Bali, and wait there for a few hours. Her standing orders were to return to Bali if she hadn't received instructions directing her otherwise.

When police and FBI looked at the surveillance video, they noticed that two chambermaids had entered Kravanesko's suite, but three chambermaids had left. The cops also noticed that the chambermaids wore caps that obscured their faces.

But later that day when Wishbone watched the same video, he had advanced technology that let him use artificial intelligence to construct faces for the chamber maids. Two of them were unknown, but Wishbone identified the maid who left by herself.

Chapter Seventy Six
Washington, DC

Why was I here in DC to meet with Toni Anne and Wishbone? After all, Wishbone was the guy who made me meet him in the Cincinnati airport for anonymity's sake, and now we were rendezvousing at what was probably the world's most famous address. I was such a novice in this world, an easily distracted checker player among the chess masters.

My instructions were to stand at the corner of Jefferson Drive and 14th Street near the Smithsonian, at 7pm, and I got there five minutes early. Try doing that sometime, standing at a street corner in an unfamiliar city, and attempting to look inconspicuous, back from the street far enough not to be in the way of pedestrians, but close enough to be seen by whoever was picking me up in a car.

I assumed I was being picked up by a car, that it wasn't a drive by shooting. If they wanted to kill me, they could find easier and more efficient ways. Why would anybody in this country besides my sister want to kill me? I told you I was in over my head.

There weren't many pedestrians around here at this hour. Most of them looked like tourists who were lost, and one of them asked me for directions to the Lincoln Memorial. I told him to go to Grant's Tomb and turn left. I pointed. He and the missus nodded as if they understood and kept walking.

Grant's Tomb is inconveniently located at 122nd Street and Riverside Drive, in Manhattan. It's a dump and doesn't get many visitors. Why was I so mean to these tourists? I think it was because I was nervous, but I felt bad about it. At least the questioner seemed to be an American, so I wasn't being a dick to foreigners.

At the appointed hour a limo with dark windows pulled up. The rear right-side window lowered. Toni Anne said, "Looking for a good time?"

"Yeah, I am looking for a good time. But I don't suppose I'm going to have one."

Toni Anne laughed, and the door opened. "Get in."

194

The limo had a glass that separated the driver from the passengers. There was one other passenger who sat beside Toni Anne. It was Gabrielle McHugh, the Warrior Princess and past object of my unrequited affection. The very same Gab who was such a pain in the ass when I visited Cyber Command.

"If you have any champagne in here, we could tell the driver to take a detour for a couple hours and have a little private party," I suggested.

"We mustn't keep the President waiting," Toni Anne said.

"We're going to see the President?" I asked.

"Why do you think we're going to the fuckin' White House?" Toni Anne asked.

I shrugged.

"Besides, I thought you were more of a Pearl Beer man," Gab said.

"I'm flexible, hey, you're talking to me now?" I asked Gabrielle.

"My role is evolving," Gab said.

"You're going back to shooting people?" I asked Gabrielle.

"We'll see," she said.

"That's something we all have in common. We've all shot somebody," Toni Anne said.

"See, if we had champagne, we could make a toast," I said.

It was a short but complex route to the White House. The street grid of Washington, DC was supposedly laid out by an architect. If so, it must have been an architect who hated people and wanted them to get lost. It was a good thing I wasn't driving.

The limo had to stop at the security gate in the entrance to the White House. The guard asked only to see credentials of the driver and waved us through.

"We must be on some kind of special list, huh?" I said, "they didn't even check our IDs."

"When you're coming here to be executed, they're lax on security," Toni Anne said.

"Ha-ha," I said. I was nervous and wanted to ask a million questions, but Toni Anne and Gabrielle looked so calm. I didn't want to seem any more out of my element.

Ho-hum, just another undercover nighttime trip to the White House.

195

The limo didn't drive to the grand front entrance that you see on tv but pulled around to the back. Without ceremony or escort, we got out and walked in, entering the building through a very ordinary looking glass and metal door. Toni Anne limped and used her cane but walked first. When I hesitated, Gabrielle shoved me ahead of herself, none too gently.

"What, are you afraid I'm going to run away?" I asked Gab.

"If you did, the snipers on the roof would pick you off. I'm just protecting you," she said as she pointed to the door. "Go in." Gabrielle trailed me.

"Thanks. You haven't always done a great job of protecting me," I said.

"Shut up," Gab said.

Snipers?

I was surprised that there was no Marine guard, no security, not even a rent-a-cop. Wishbone stood in the hallway, nodded to us, and said, "follow me."

We did so. The part of the building we were in was utilitarian. Wishbone opened an unmarked door. Inside was a plain sheet rock painted off white room with a linoleum floor and a small cheap conference table surrounded by six olive drab folding chairs. There was a flat panel display on the wall, but nothing else that distinguished the room.

"Why are we here?" I said, "this room is just---"

The door opened. The President of the United States walked in.

Everyone else stood, so I stood. The stupid thought of whistling a few bars of 'Hail to The Chief" went through my mind, but I didn't whistle.

"Good evening," the President said. "Would you excuse us for a minute. I'd like to talk to Mr. Johnson alone."

Good thing I hadn't whistled.

Toni Anne winked at me as she, Gabrielle, and Wishbone exited the room. What was it about the winking that I found so attractive?

The President shook hands with me and asked, "Can I call you JR?"

"Sure," I said.

He sat and gestured for me to do so. "You can call me Mr. President," he said.

196

"I was planning on that," I said. "Sir."

"Sir is ok too," the President said. "Now that we have established that, I have something to tell you---just you. Understand?"

"Umm. Could you make it clearer, sir?"

"You're not to tell anyone else this information. Except for the Beloved Chairman when you're interrogated in North Korea," the President said.

I laughed. "Why didn't you just say that?"

The President didn't smile. "I can see why you get along with Toni Anne," he said. "The same wise guy approach to authority. Be careful. Toni Anne is one of the smartest people in the world. We need *her*. You, on the other hand...I've seen your grades, your file."

"Wow. You mean the teachers were right when they said items on my permanent record would come back to haunt me later in life?" When I get nervous, I run off at the mouth. "I guess when you're President you can see anything you want to see, any personal information on anybody---"

He interrupted, "now that you've brought that up." The President reached for a remote-control device in the middle of the table and pointed it at the screen. On came surveillance footage of me shooting up the ATM and stuffing my pockets with money in New York. It was odd, almost clinical watching with no sound. "Only the CIA has this footage, not the NYPD or FBI. We routinely blackout other agencies surveillance cameras in areas of the major metropolitan areas when we have something of a national security interest going on that we don't want everybody else to see. The CIA gets priority. Since 9/11 everybody understands that. Even the FBI doesn't complain. Sometimes it helps not to know things when you testify under oath to Congress"

It's a different experience sitting with the President of the United States watching a video of you committing an armed Federal Crime.

"Why are we watching this, sir?" I asked.

"Oh. Let me reassure you. You're not going to be prosecuted or anything. I'm just showing you this to demonstrate that although you have no formal training, we are enthusiastic that you have natural ability to improvise. You may remember I used to be the Director of the CIA."

197

"This is a motivational speech?" I said. "Maybe when this mission is over, I can apply for a high-ranking job at the CIA."

"That's enough bullshit from you," the President said. "Your academic credentials qualify you for maybe sub-assistant to the Secretary of Agriculture."

"Could I apply for that slot?" I asked. "I think that would be a lot less dangerous than what you people have in mind for me."

"Sure. But that job wouldn't give you the chance to get your $50 million back," the President said. "Tax free."

The President showed me the message I would carry to the Beloved Chairman.

"Memorize this. Exactly. Every word," he said.

This day had become a bit out of the ordinary for me, doing covert work, talking to the President of the United States at the White House, getting a message to deliver to a homicidal communist world leader. "The North Koreans might rough you up a bit. They claim it's part of their way of establishing your bona fides. I think they just enjoy it. You look like you're in good shape. You can take it."

"Might rough me up a bit? Does that mean they're going to kick the shit out of me?" I asked.

"Probably," the President said. "They're professionals. They know how to inflict pain without causing any permanent damage."

Oh. He was a politician, used to giving people the rosy side of the scenario. He meant the North Koreans definitely were going to kick the shit out of me.

"It's vital that you deliver this message *exactly* as written," the President said. "I'm trusting you to take this piece of paper with you. Read it to yourself hundreds of times during the next 24 hours, then destroy it. Burn it. To make it easier to memorize it has been written in the form of a rhyme, so it's like learning a song."

I read the message. It began: A sheep in sheep's clothing…

"I wish you complete success in your mission. I want you to get the money. Of course, you won't get it unless the mission is successful," he said.

"Mr. President, can I ask you one question?" I said.

"Go ahead."

"Is it true that the Beloved Chairman had his own uncle executed in a crowded stadium, by a firing squad using 50-caliber machine guns?" I asked.

"I hear he was a bad uncle," the President said. "Listen Johnson. I want to tell you personally that we will honor our part of the bargain regarding the money. But if you fail, or get in trouble, we never heard of you. Understand?"

"I'm not even getting a souvenir pen?" I said

"No." The President laughed. "Good luck Johnson." He left the room. Toni Anne, Gab, and Wishbone reentered a couple minutes later.

After they filed in and sat at the conference table. Toni Anne asked me, "Did you enjoy meeting the President?"

"He swore at me," I said.

"Well, you aren't here to get an Eagle Scout badge," Toni Anne said.

"I didn't get a souvenir pen either," I said.

'What a dork you are," Gabrielle said. Toni Anne and Wishbone nodded, making it a unanimous opinion.

"Well, I'm the dork taking all the risks. You other candy asses are just sitting around," I said.

"That might change," Toni Anne said. "And by the way, I'm the one who got shot lately."

I thought that Toni Anne would run the session, but it was Wishbone who handled the briefing. "There are a few things I've got to explain to you," he started.

A few?

"First of all, I'm CIA," Wishbone started.

"I thought you were an independent contractor working for Toni Anne," I said.

"I didn't know he was CIA until a few days ago," Toni Anne said. There was a silence in the room as Toni Anne and Wishbone looked at each other.

"That explains the source of the gadget on my phone," I said to Wishbone.

"Let's focus on the mission going forward," Wishbone said. "We've got the Russians focusing an unprecedented attack of ransomware and hacking on the U.S. JR, you know that firsthand. The Russians have political allies right here in Washington."

199

"There are people in our government helping the Russians?" I asked.

"Yeah," Wishbone said. "You don't need to know about that, your job doesn't have anything to do with that side of things. I only tell you that because this mission is out in the cold. It's not official CIA or Cyber Command or Pentagon. There are only a few people who know, and we have to keep it like that. JR., I hate to put it this way, but you can't talk about this to anybody. If you start shooting off your mouth, you'll be silenced."

"I'll be killed by the U.S. Government?" I asked.

"Just keep your mouth shut, and you'll be fine," Wishbone said. "From our point of view. Also, the Russians may want to kill you, and not everybody we've sent to North Korea, well, not everybody sent there has been accounted for."

That got my full attention. *So, it wasn't just my sister who might want to shoot me.*

"I like to be accounted for, preferably while breathing," I said. Then out of my mouth I heard my voice saying, "Hey, I'm in this to get my money back. I won't say anything, I'll just do my job," but in my mind I thought, *they're going to kill me? Would Gabrielle shoot me?*

"You need to know about North Korea," Wishbone said.

"Ok," I said.

"We have been using the government of North Korea for years to be a buffer against China," Wishbone said. "All that stuff with the missile tests and belligerence is a show. But make no mistake, they're real communists, and they're crazy, but both governments use each other. For example, Cyber Command just stood idly by when the North Koreans hacked Sony Pictures in Hollywood. Remember when they were pissed off about the movie Sony made about the Beloved Chairman?"

"I tried to watch that movie. It sucked. Sony deserved to be hacked," I said. "Can't Hollywood make a good comedy anymore? It's just---"

"We'll talk movies when you come to my theater for the film festival. Let's focus. The U.S. and North Korea are not friends…but we share a common enemy. Those nuclear missiles could be targeted at China, you know. The North Koreans are afraid that China will invade them," Wishbone said.

200

"What does North Korea want?" I asked.

"The Beloved Chairman and the small leading faction in North Korea have great lives, and he loves having absolute power. They want to preserve the status quo. They use us to help them do that, and we use them to limit Chinese expansionism," Wishbone said.

"Is that working? It seems like the Chinese are getting really aggressive," I said.

Toni Anne, Gab and Wishbone all exchanged glances. Wishbone smiled, then said, "You have no idea how right you are. We're working on that. First, we've got to get this job done. Focus on this, you're going to get your money by pulling off this stunt against the Russians. The U.S. government has other people to scheme global strategies."

"I have the feeling I'm in the room with some of them," I said.

"Forget it. Try to do your job and be alive, okay?" Wishbone said.

Wishbone talked for another five minutes. I felt like a naïve little kid. "Who knows this? Does Congress know?" I asked.

"Almost nobody knows," Wishbone said. "It used to be that certain long serving members of Congress could be trusted with intelligence. Now, none of them can be trusted, so we just feed them with info that the foreign governments already know."

Gabrielle hadn't said a word since Wishbone started his briefing. She sat with her hands folded on the table, with a hard look on her face, like the look she used to get when she was Lola's bodyguard. That was a thousand years ago, it seemed.

Wishbone had stopped speaking. The room was silent. I could hear myself breathe, and my heart was racing. Finally, I said, "Why is Gabrielle here?

"I'm tired of sitting in Cyber Command, polishing a chair with my ass," Gabrielle said.

That statement made my mind wander a bit. I'm really a literal-minded adolescent. I thought of Gab's ass polishing a chair. It was a pleasant thought. I remembered when she sat on my lap by the pool in Austin wearing a bikini.

"JR, pay attention," Gab said.

"I, uhh, it's just that---"

201

"I talked to Toni Anne, told her that I was ready to move out of Cyber Command, back to the Kinetic side of things," Gabrielle said.

"Kinetic?" I asked.

"Shit that blows up," Toni Anne explained.

"Oh, you mean shooting people and stuff like that?" I asked Gabrielle.

"Yeah," Gabrielle said.

"It's nice to do what you're good at," I said.

"I'm good at everything," Gab said.

"I bet," I said. Toni Anne laughed.

"Let's get back on track," Wishbone said. "A lot of things have to happen just right before any potential trip to North Korea. We have to bait the trap just right."

"What is the Kinetic part?" I asked.

"If things go as planned, we may go over and shoot some of the ransomware pirates," Gab said. "This couldn't be an official U.S. government action, so I'm out in the cold too."

"How are you going to do that?" I asked.

"Did you ever hear of a stealth helicopter?" Gabrielle asked.

"No," I said. "We have stealth helicopters?"

"Yes, and the Russians also have stealth helicopters. I might just have to "borrow" one," Gab said. She made air quotes.

"Cool," I said.

Wishbone explained for another few minutes. For now, my assignment was to go back to Texas and wait for an unspecified time. Toni Anne, Gab, and I exited the White House through the same door we had entered. The limo was waiting.

After 47 right turns the limo dropped me off at the same corner where they had picked me up. Toni Anne opened the door and I got out.

"See you honey," Toni Anne said.

"Yeah," I said.

"See you---*honey*," Gabrielle said. The door closed and the limo drove off.

I felt that Gab saying "honey" was perhaps insincere. Still, I like being called "honey" by a woman, even a fat old waitress in a diner. *Especially* by a fat old waitress in a diner. There were no tourists around to ask me directions to the Lincoln

202

Memorial or Grant's Tomb, so I flagged down a taxi and made for the airport.

Chapter Seventy Seven
Fort Meade, MD
Cyber Command

Admiral Stockbridge sat alone in his office. He had already received his morning briefing, which consisted of his second in command, the one-star admiral, escorting one or two of Cyber Command's smart people into Stockbridge's office, then the two admirals sitting mostly silent while the designated briefers talked about what had gone on in the world of Cyber Warfare in the last 24 hours.

Stockbridge believed in the saying that it's better to be quiet and let people think you're a fool than to open your mouth and confirm their suspicions. He nodded a lot, and the one-star nodded along with him. The senior staff at Cyber Command referred to them as "the bobble head dolls."

The two admirals at Cyber Command weren't the only authority figures in Washington who didn't understand much of the information in the briefings they received. Stockbridge looked the part of the competent 21st Century Techno-Warrior and believed that was more than half the battle. It had gotten him this far, and the Vice Presidency or better, was just over the horizon.

Still, Stockbridge slipped up occasionally and asked a colossally stupid question that caught the briefers off guard. They'd have to backtrack and dumb down the briefing. Stockbridge could sense their contempt but ignored it.

This morning the Admiral hadn't paid much attention to the briefers. He was preoccupied with yesterday's meeting with Congressman Safi. Stockbridge mused that although the two of them were soon to be running mates, they still addressed each other as "Congressman" and "Admiral." That was okay with Stockbridge, he was career military, and many superior officers never referred to their subordinates by their first names, only by their rank or last name. A junior officer would never refer to a superior officer by his first name in public, and rarely even in private, unless the two of them were friends, and the junior was invited to do so. Maybe Safi was establishing the protocol that would be used when he was in the White House.

204

Safi had told him of his meeting with "Patricia" the messenger the Russians had sent to threaten him in the parking garage. "I've given that much thought, and have concluded that the Russians are bluffing, that they are operating from weakness," Safi had said. "If they wanted to kill me, that woman could have shot me right there. I bet she's not even a killer, probably doesn't know how to fire a gun, she's just somebody they use as an agent. The threat wasn't even that convincing."

"What's your point, Congressman?" the Admiral had said.

"I---we, have to send a message to the Russians that we are not all that intimidated. A public message," Safi said.

"Are we in the position to do that?" Stockbridge asked. "The Russians could go public and expose our relationship with them. We'd be ruined! Or sent to prison!"

"Calm down, that would never happen," Safi said. "Sometimes you military men make me laugh. You're not experienced enough in the byzantine realities of politics."

"Meaning what?" Stockbridge said. The abruptness of the question was intentional.

Safi paused for a long second, then smiled. "Don't be offended Admiral. Relax. I am formulating exactly what and how the message will be delivered. You'll learn the subtleties of politics by working with me."

"Alright," Stockbridge said. "What kind of message were you thinking about delivering, Congressman?"

"I haven't decided, but it won't be subtle. The action may be announced by Cyber Command, may be announced by me. I'm considering exactly what to say and how to say it. The Russians will understand," Safi said.

"Sir, at Cyber Command we need White House approval to make any major announcement---"

Safi interrupted, "---relax Admiral, leave it to me. I know how to play this game."

Chapter Seventy Eight
Delta First Class Lounge
Dallas-DFW Airport

Quinn's iPhone indicated she had just received a text. It was from Colonel Nihisky, and read: Status? Reply via text message.

Quinn typed: At DFW, awaiting instructions.

Nihisky's reply: Fly to SLC, check in same hotel. Await further instructions.

Quinn: Okay.

Quinn used her Patricia Sizemore credentials and credit card. The credit card bills went to a bank in the Cayman Islands and were ultimately paid by the Nitup Resort in Bali. Patricia Sizemore had an unlimited credit line. She could get used to this international business executive lifestyle, as long as she could still shoot people, and it would be nice to get laid occasionally, by someone other than the Lider. It would be good to find a man who would at least pretend he was interested in satisfying her.

There had been a man like that back in Bali, a guest at her resort. But she'd had to shoot him before their relationship could be consummated. Bad luck for him. That man had been buried at sea, if that's what you could call being sealed in a 55-gallon drum and dumped off a boat into the ocean in the dark of night.

Maybe she'd get the chance to kill that idiot Congressman. Things change.

206

Chapter Seventy Nine
Austin, TX

I decided that I better workout on a more regular basis. It's good to be in shape as you prepare to get the shit kicked out of you by the North Koreans. Try having that hanging over your head. I considered learning some martial arts skills, maybe watching some YouTube videos, but then I concluded that the Glock would be my personal defense strategy, and that any hand-to-hand action with a professional would be a pathetic losing effort. I'd just shoot him or her before they could put their hands in front of them, crouch down, and shout "karate!" or whatever people do in real life.

My workout was scheduled for the first thing in the morning, then I ate breakfast. I had the rest of the day to do nothing.

Out of force of habit I watched CNBC every morning to see what was going on in the financial markets. But I had no client's money to manage, and no money of my own to invest.

It's easy to become complacent when you're a rich guy, I'd gotten used to being able to buy anything I wanted within reason. Now, my cash reserve was dwindling, and I wondered how I was going to buy gas for my truck, food for my table, and pay my cable bill. How would I pay for an airline ticket if I was summoned back to DC? I came up with an idea.

Improvise, both Wishbone and the President of the United States had told me. I improvised.

The first part of my plan was to print instructions on the computer printer. I figure that was much better than writing with Magic Marker in my own hand, because if the instructions were recovered somehow the handwriting couldn't be traced back to me. I have bad, but distinctive handwriting. Each instruction was printed on an 8x11 sheet of paper with the letters in 48-point print, so even an old guy could read it without glasses.

The first printed page read: SHUT UP AND LAY ON THE GROUND.

When my printing was done, I set out to buy a ski mask. This might be an easy thing to do in Burlington, VT, but not so easy

207

in Austin, TX. A hunting store would probably have those masks, but I didn't want to buy from a store with surveillance cameras, so I decided to try the Goodwill outlet.

I spent a long time rooting around the disorganized Goodwill, during which I declined getting help from staffers who asked, "May I help you, sir." I didn't want any of them remembering a handsome man who was looking to purchase a ski mask. I had almost given up and was considering making a mask out of a pillowcase, then I did find one ski mask.

It looked like a girl's size and was pink with a snowflake motif. I hid my disappointment, it was not the sort of kick-ass commando look I was going for, but it would do the job. An unexpected bonus was that the items in the store didn't have any barcodes or other kind of identification that would be scanned at checkout. The disinterested cashier rang up my $3.50 item and handed me a receipt that had the amount, but no description.

When I got home, I tried on the mask. It was tight and hot, and I had a tough time lining up the eyes. The mouth opening didn't come close to my actual mouth, but that was okay, because I wasn't going to do any talking. That's why I printed the instructions.

Chapter Eighty
Spicewood, TX

It was Tuesday, getting toward sundown. I sat in a beat-up old farm pickup truck I had stolen from a field. Stealing it was no big deal, people leave the keys in trucks like these. Country folks trust each other. They weren't expecting a big-time international operative like me in their midst.

I had my pink ski mask and my printed instructions in my jacket. The Glock was next to me on the seat. I drove to the parking lot near the feed store.

Cletus Parker left the Grange Hall. He tried not to smile as he got in his Escalade. I guessed that he must have won a bundle in this month's poker game.

The Escalade moved out of the parking lot and turned for Barbara Jean's ranch. I followed in the farm truck, hoping Cletus wouldn't drive too fast. This farm truck seemed like its top end was maybe 50 mph.

I needn't have worried. Unlike his daughter, Cletus was a slow driver. Maybe he was just old. I kept my distance, and no other traffic was around. It was a few minutes to Barbara Jean's.

A ditch ran along the right side of the road, the ranch was on the left side of the road, and Cletus put on his turn signal.

How thoughtful.

By the time I pulled up behind him Cletus had gotten out of his Caddy to enter the code into the keypad. I intentionally came up too fast and had to stomp on the brakes. The brakes weren't good, and I skidded gently into the back of the Escalade.

"What the hell are you doin'?" Cletus said. "Is that Bobby Miller's truck?"

Cletus couldn't tell if I was Bobby Miller because I was wearing the ski mask. And I was pointing the Glock at him from four feet away.

209

Cletus fished around under his jacket and shocked me by pulling out a Colt .45 revolver. He aimed it at me.

I lurched forward and swiped my right hand across my body, hitting his right wrist just as he pulled the trigger. Man. That thing was loud. I was sure the bullet passed just by my ear, and by the sound of it, the round hit Bobby Miller's truck.

Before the clumsy Cletus could fire again, I put my right foot behind his left foot and shoved him to the ground, then stomped on his right wrist. He dropped the Colt, and I kicked it ten feet away. I was glad I had decided to wear work boots, more stomping power.

This was not going the way I had planned. I didn't want to have to hurt him, but now this fat turd had taken a shot at me. The wrist stomp had probably done some damage, and his head hit the ground hard. I was learning. In tactical situations, you've got to have a plan, but be flexible when the plan goes out the window. My plan had lasted maybe five seconds, now I was improvising. It's hard to stay calm after someone has taken a shot at you, and my impulse was just to shoot Cletus and take his money. Bad idea.

The shot had been so loud that my ears were ringing, and I couldn't hear what Cletus was saying as he laid face up on the dirt, but you didn't have to be a lip-reader to know that he was cussing me out and threatening me. I did pick up a "Goldang it!"

It was tough to suppress the urge to cuss him back. This was an easy guy to insult, and I was furious. But I couldn't let him hear me. Not that the big mouth know-it-all had ever listened to me, or even shut up while I was talking, but even Cletus would probably be able to identify me by my distinctive voice.

Instead, I reached inside my jacket for the printed instructions. I held up the first one: SHUT UP AND LAY ON THE GROUND

"I am layin' on the ground, you moron," Cletus said.

I used my Glock to point at the two words: SHUT UP.

I shuffled the papers. The next instruction said: GIVE ME YOUR MONEY.

Cletus fished in his shirt pocket and pulled out some bills, maybe a total of $80.

210

I took the wad of cash and threw it in his face. The bills blew away in the light wind. I shuffled the papers again and produced the following: THE PEOPLE YOU PLAY WITH ARE TIRED OF YOU CHEATING.

This had the desired effect. It outraged Cletus. "Cheating my ass! It's not my fault the other dadgum guys…" He petered out, like he was having a hard time talking. Cletus must have hit his head on the ground harder than I thought. It would be too bad if he died. Wouldn't it be a shame? Really.

Barbara Jean did love the fat bastard, and if he died it would cause unwanted complications.

The ski mask was hot, and that combined with my physical exertion and excitement made sweat run down my forehead and into my eyes. I tried to blink it away, but it was hard to see.

I silenced Cletus by bending close enough to him to have the Glock maybe two feet from his face. The next paper read: I'M TAKING OFF YOUR BOOTS.

Then I shuffled through the papers again and produced the desired message: DON'T MOVE OR I'LL EMPTY THE CLIP IN YOUR FACE.

Cletus laid there like a beached whale. Now I was having fun. I yanked off his cowboy boots. Only the left boot had money in it. The cash wasn't under Cletus' foot, as I had imagined, but stuffed around the ankle section. There were fifties and hundreds, a good amount, but hard to tell how much. I stuffed the money in my jacket pockets. I'd count it later.

I tossed the expensive boots on to the gravely ground past his vehicle. This really pissed off Cletus. Stealing his money was one thing but messing with his custom-made boots took the hostility to a whole new level.

"You suck-egg weasel!" he said. That was his ultimate insult.

I stuck the Glock in his face, and he shut up. I got the next paper instruction: GET IN THE TRUCK.

I gestured with the gun for Cletus to get in the passenger side of the farm truck. He was dizzy from hitting his head when he fell and hobbled barefoot over to the truck.

The ski mask was hot and itchy. I got in the driver's seat of the truck, which had an old-fashioned bench seat. I pointed the Glock at Cletus and gestured for him to sit as far from me as possible.

211

I adjusted the uncomfortable mask, then Cletus shocked me. He lunged across the seat and grabbed the bottom of the mask, trying to pull it off!

"Let's see who you are under there, you yellow-belly!" he shouted.

If he saw me, I'd have to kill him. Instinct kicked in. I smashed him in the face with the butt end of the Glock. His head snapped back, his nose bloody, and he released his grip on the mask. I pressed the gun right up to Cletus' forehead and pushed. He sat back.

I turned the ignition key. Nothing. The engine didn't turn over, the starter didn't even click. Dead. I must have damaged the old heap when I bumped into Cletus' Escalade.

Time to improvise.

I considered getting the two of us into Cletus' vehicle but rejected that plan. The Caddy probably had all kinds of GPS or OnStar locational electronics, maybe even a panic button that Cletus could hit.

My original plan had been to drive the two of us about a quarter mile down the road and make Cletus get out. I figured that would give me plenty of time to drive a half mile further to my truck, which was parked behind a clump of trees on the other side of a ditch and make my getaway. Cletus would take forever to waddle the quarter mile barefoot. Now what?

I decided to take Cletus across the road and make him lie down in the ditch. It would take him a while to crawl out and get across to the gate of Barbara Jean's ranch. Hell, it took a couple of minutes for this fat bastard to just sit up from a reclining position.

I pointed the gun at Cletus, motioning for him to get out. "Who put you up to this?" he said. That was good, I had planted the seed that it was one or more of the poker players, so they would be the suspects. After all, who else would know that he kept the money in his boot, and that he would be at Barbara Jean's ranch at this time?

I didn't wait for Cletus to waddle out, opened my door, got out, and walked around the back of the truck, to go to the passenger side and, if necessary to yank Cletus out. He shocked me again by scooting across the bench seat and sitting behind the steering wheel. He slammed the dashboard hard with the

212

heel of his hand, then foolishly, I thought, turned the ignition key.

The engine cranked right over and started!

Cletus rammed the truck into reverse and tried to run me over. He stomped so hard on the gas pedal that the truck spun its wheels before lurching at me. I wasn't even behind the truck, more off to the side, so I stepped out of the way, no big deal.

I had to hand it to Cletus. He had more fire in his belly than I thought. And it's a big belly. But an idiot with fire in his belly is still an idiot. I'm sure that Cletus is one of those guys who think John Wayne movies were real, and he was John Wayne.

The truck was out of control as it went past me, across the road, and into the ditch. Cletus had attempted to straighten the wheel, but only made it so the truck was diagonally situated as it hit the ditch. The truck flipped over, the rear wheels still spinning. The horn blared continuously.

Oh shit! I had planned this thing so Cletus wouldn't get hurt. Now what? Was he dead?

The truck horn stopped. I froze. I decided to go over and check him out. Cletus was laying on the ceiling of the flipped truck. He seemed unconscious, but he was moaning. I opened the driver side door.

I put my hands under his arm pits and started dragging him. His limp body made it like pulling a huge bag of cement. He moaned a few times.

Good, now let's hear you squeal like a pig, I wanted to say.

The moan meant he was alive. and with great difficulty I dragged his fat ass maybe 30 feet away from the truck, but still in the ditch. I figured that was far away enough in the unlikely event that the truck exploded. I went back and switched off the ignition on the truck, reasoning that would cut down on the odds of a fire.

Improvising time again. Cletus would probably live, but I couldn't stay here.

There was no other option than to take the Escalade. I had no idea how long it would be until the county sheriff came, or another vehicle would come down the road. It was too far to run, maybe three quarters of a mile to my truck, and even the Billy Bob County sheriff would find it suspicious if he saw me running down the road.

213

Cletus had left his engine running with the door open. I got into the Caddy and headed for my truck. Part way there I got the idea to abandon the Escalade maybe 200 yards short of the thicket of trees where my F-150 was parked. I got out of the Escalade, turned the wheel toward the ditch on the right, then I realized that I had to get back in to step on the brake pedal while I put it in Drive. I jumped out and Cletus' vehicle gently headed into the ditch. I was disappointed when it appeared that no damage was done to the Escalade.

I had abandoned Cletus' vehicle because I didn't want the cops to find it where I had parked my truck. Not knowing anything about forensics, I didn't know if some kind of evidence leading to me would be left behind by the F-150, but why take the chance?

It was dark now. I ran the couple hundred yards to my truck, tucked away behind the only trees around. Just as I reached it, another truck came by, headed in the direction of Barbara Jean's ranch, but they couldn't see me parked behind the clump of trees. I waited for a minute to start my F-150, then slowly started driving in the other direction, with my lights off at first. I was careful not to hit the brake pedal, thus lighting up the back. In my rearview mirror I could just make out the other truck stopping at the ditch where Cletus' Escalade was crashed. When I thought it was safe, I turned the headlights on and got up to speed and headed for Austin.

Chapter Eighty One
Washington, DC
The Congressional Office Building

There weren't many people who knew about Congressman Safi's deal with the Russians. Even most of his inner circle was clueless, but John Alteiri, the media consultant was in the know.

Just as Safi had promised the Vice Presidency to Admiral Stockbridge, Alteiri had been promised the job of White House Press Secretary in the Safi administration. At that time, Safi had decided it was worth the risk of bringing Alteiri into the scheme.

John picked up the nickname "Buddha" in college when he gave into his early male pattern baldness and shaved his head. That along with his pot belly made the nickname fit, even his wife called him Buddha.

Alteiri was tired of his career, being media strategist to egomaniacal politicians, and figured that after serving as Press Secretary for one term while Safi was President he could write the best seller that every media person in Washington aspired to write and spend the rest of his life as a talking head on cable tv.

Alteiri despised every politician, male or female, he had ever worked for, and after a few cocktails with his trusted journalist buddies always postulated his equal rights theory of politics; that is, with hard work and perseverance a woman in politics could be just as egotistical, vicious, and backstabbing as any man.

As his skills increased Alteiri worked for ever more important politicians, for ever more increasing salaries. His clients had one thing in common: when Alteiri was their media consultant, they won. Politicians would pay any amount to win, especially since it was not their own money, but contributions largely from major individual donors and lobbyist groups. Alteiri just had the knack, a natural sense of how to handle the media as that world morphed from traditional newspapers and television and more into the digital realm.

Before being hired by Safi, Alteiri had been warned by a few journalist buddies about the Congressman's abrasive personality. John Alteiri thought he had seen it all and could

215

handle any politician, but after accepting the job Altieri became convinced that Safi was the worst human being he had ever met. Narcissistic, vain, friendless, shallow, extremely over-confident, and demeaning of his subordinates were just some of Safi's characteristics. He never admitted he was wrong, he cheated at golf the one time Alteiri had played with him and was supposedly banging a few of his female staff members. Safi was wildly ambitious. A perfect recipe for a successful politician.

The first political function that Alteiri had attended with Safi was when the Congressman received the Catholic Layman of the Year Award in his home district in California. Safi's wife had stayed in Washington, but a female staffer accompanied them. The last Alteiri had seen that night of the Layman of the Year was Safi and the staffer entering the Congressman's hotel room. Safi had noticed Alteiri watching and glanced back with a look of triumphant privilege.

It was over a year later now and the Congressman was about to announce his candidacy for President. Safi and Alteiri met in the Congressman's private office. "I've decided to give Stockbridge the mushroom treatment on this situation... You know, keep him in the dark and covered with shit?" Safi said as though that was an original witticism.

For Alteiri that passed as a joke from Safi. He had heard the mushroom treatment thing a thousand times and forced himself to smile. It was going to be tough to accompany Safi through the Presidential campaign and a four-year term in the White House, but he focused on the big payday and lifestyle improvement he'd have after writing the best seller.

Still, the deal Safi had made with the Russians worried Alteiri so much he had a hard time sleeping. But now that he was in, Alteiri reasoned, the only way out was to see it through.

The Congressman had called Alteiri in a couple weeks after the media consultant had started working in his office and told him the outline of the scheme. The Russians had contacted Safi with an offer that he had accepted.

The offer: The Russians would launch an unprecedented level of ransomware attacks against U.S. companies, from Russia, and from countries of the former Soviet bloc, countries they could control. After netting huge sums of money in ransoms, the Russians would let U.S. Cyber Command, as championed

216

by Safi, shut down the attacks. Safi's Intelligence Committee would then expose the current President for his unpreparedness in Cyber Warfare, and Safi would take the new Cyber commander, Admiral Stockbridge as his running mate. The Russians promised a Disinformation campaign in the Presidential election using an undisclosed new weapon that would assure Safi a victory.

That was all fine with Safi, but he decided to show the Russians he was their equal. He made contact with them and demanded another meeting with Patricia at the same parking garage in Washington.

He decided that he would tell Patricia he wasn't afraid of her, or of the Russians, and they must operate as equals. Otherwise, he'd unleash an unspecified threat. He was bluffing, he had no specific threat. They wouldn't know that, and if necessary, he could come up with something. After all he had Stockbridge in Cyber Command, they could cook up some threat.

Chapter Eighty Two
Washington, DC

Quinn traveled as Patricia Sizemore from Salt Lake City to Washington for the sole purpose of meeting Safi.

The two met under the same circumstances as the prior meeting. She even rented the same model Mercedes. She and Safi approached each other on the top floor of the parking garage.

"I'm Patricia, remember?" Quinn asked.

"Yeah," Safi said.

"What is it you want?" Quinn asked.

"First, I want to say that I'm not intimidated by you," Safi said.

"Another man told me that once. It was the last thing he ever said," Quinn mentioned.

"Hmm. I don't believe you," Safi said. "Tell the Lider that I'm not doing anything different, for now."

"You arranged this meeting to tell me that?" Quinn asked.

"As the Lider knows, I virtually control Cyber Command now," Safi said. "As long as the Lider treats me as an equal, nothing will happen. But if I have to send a message, it will come through Cyber Command."

"That's it?" Quinn asked.

"Yes," Safi said.

Quinn wordlessly got in the Mercedes and drove to the airport. She she had recorded the audio of the meeting and forwarded it to Nihisky.

Chapter Eighty Three
Austin

It was the morning after my big heist. I hadn't slept all that well, not out of worry of being caught, out of disappointment.

When I had arrived home, I counted the money that was in Cletus' boot: $14,650. I had taken all that risk for a fourteen-thousand-dollar payout, not the hundred grand that I had hoped for when I made the plan. In the investment world there's something called the risk/reward ratio, and if I applied that concept to my robbery, it was a failure.

At least I could afford to restock my refrigerator with Pearl Beer. I drank all the seven beers in the fridge last night in an effort to calm down and go to sleep. It was like drinking water, my nervous system was so wired up. Maybe if I had gone to Med School like my father had wanted me to, I'd understand better.

I had slept what seemed like five minutes at a time, and dreamed of shooting Cletus, or Cletus shooting me, of Barbara Jean shooting me, During the dreams, whenever a shot went off, I woke with a start. If that was what sleep was going to be like going forward, I'd rather just stay awake.

Just when everything seemed like it couldn't get much worse, the phone rang. It was Barbara Jean.

"Hello," I said.

There was no response for a few seconds. Then Barbara Jean said, "JR how could you?"

Oh shit!

I had gone this far, I had to tough it out.

"What are you talking about?" I asked.

"This is the most terrible day of my life," Barbara Jean said.

"What do you mean?" I asked.

"How could you not tell me about this?" Barbara Jean asked.

"Look Barbara Jean, we're not getting anywhere. What are you talking about?" I said.

"Come out to the ranch. We need to confront this now," Barb said.

"Ok, I'll be right out," I said, and hung up.

219

Chapter Eighty Four
On the road to Spicewood

I can't remember a time in my life when I didn't want to get somewhere as much as I did not want to get to Barbara Jean's ranch. It would have been okay with me if the world collided with an asteroid. I drove slow, especially by Texas standards, other vehicles zoomed by me, and their drivers turned to give me dirty looks or the finger. I ignored them, except for a woman that I flashed the "Hook-em Horns" hand signal, which caused her to give me the finger with even more vigor. In normal circumstances I would have laughed, but nothing was going to make me laugh now.

I know a guy who went to West Point. He told me that when you're a freshman, or plebe, the upperclassmen tell you that you are lower than whale shit. That's what I was. Lower than whale shit, the lowest thing on earth.

For I was going to Barbara Jean's house, and she was going to confront me. Somehow, they knew it was me who had robbed Cletus. Beyond that I didn't know what to expect. Would the police be there? Was I going to jail? Worse of all was I going to be dressed down by that puffed-up idiot Cletus? If I went to jail, I wouldn't be able to go through with the plan that the President had for me, wouldn't be able to get my money back.

I got to the ranch, did the keypad, and drove down the long path to the house. I expected bad, but I didn't know how bad. As a I drove a county sheriff's car came heading away from the house. His lights and siren were not on, and he passed me without a look. I was confused. Maybe he was going to block the entrance in case I changed my mind and did a U-turn in an attempt to escape.

I got to the house. There were no other cars, and I took a deep breath, walked to the massive double door, and knocked. Maybe this was an ambush.

"Why in tarnation are you knocking at the door? Come in," I heard Cletus say. I went in.

Cletus was sitting on a couch with an ice bag on his forehead, but looked good under the circumstances, and June was sitting next to him, doing the wifely pat on the hand thing. Both of

220

them looked at me. I couldn't read their expressions; I'd call it neutral.

Barbara Jean was not neutral. She'd been crying, not what I expected.

I decided to play dumb, and if confronted to deny robbing Cletus, all the way to the electric chair if it came to that. "What's going on?" I asked Barbara Jean.

"We'll talk to my parents in a few minutes. Come with me," she said.

I followed her into the small room that I used as my office. Barbara Jean kept her laptop in there. It was on, and I saw YouTube at the top of the screen.

The playback had been paused at what looked like the very beginning of the video. I could see a grainy still of me with two other people, and below the video read: Jeffrey Epstein, Ghislaine Maxwell, and JR Johnson. Below that I could see that the video was posted less than an hour ago and already had 456,000 views.

"Explain this," Barbara Jean said, then she hit enter.

The video started. Panic went through my mind, my body. Had I ever met Jeffrey Epstein and that woman? I scanned my memory. Had we met sometime in New York?

No, I had never met Jeffrey Epstein and Ghislaine Maxwell. I'd been drunk in New York, but never that drunk so I wouldn't remember something like this. I was sure of it. Then the audio started.

I started speaking. It was my image, my voice, my gestures. The video looked to be surveillance recorded in a noisy hotel bar. Parts of the discussion were unclear, but the video included subtitles. Random people walked between the camera and the subjects once in a while.

"I can hook you up with a virtually unlimited supply of 14- and 15-year-old girls," I said. "I have them on an isolated ranch in Texas. I keep them as sex slaves."

"When can I have delivery?" Epstein asked.

"Tomorrow," I said. "You and your friends can be having sex with these girls tomorrow night."

"Great," Ghislaine Maxwell said.

221

The video went on for 2:46. The three of us discussed financial arrangements. I concluded by shaking hands with both of them and saying, "I guarantee you won't be disappointed. These girls are the best you've ever had."

The video concluded, then began to play again from the beginning. Barbara Jean hit the hold button.

Even though I knew this had never happened, it sure looked and sounded like me. Panic ran through my mind, could I have done this? Of course not. But how was this possible? The video had more than a half million views, the total was going up like a pinball machine. At least some, probably the vast majority of viewers would believe this video to be true.

"Well?" Barbara Jean said.

I felt sick to my stomach. "Barb, that's not me. It some kind of elaborate fake," I said.

"Let's say for a second that I believe you. What kind of enemy could you have made that could do that? Who *would* do that? What have you gotten yourself into?" Barbara Jean said.

I tried to gather my thoughts, but my mind was bouncing from one subject to another. "Do your parents know about this?" I asked.

"No, but they're going to know. It's on the Internet! Everybody in the world is going to see this!" Barbara Jean said.

"Well, what's going on with your parents then?" It looked like I had a Get Out of Jail Free Card. This wasn't about Cletus getting robbed! At least I had that. But this was worse. I began hoping again that earth would collide with an asteroid.

'We'll talk about my parents in a minute. We have to get to the bottom of this first," Barbara Jean said.

"How am I going to get to the bottom of this? I have no idea!" I said.

"JR, if this is true, you realize that we can't be married," Barb said.

"Of course. But it's not true," I said.

"But if it's *not* true, what kind of trouble are you in?" Barbara Jean asked.

"I don't know." I shrugged.

"Does this have something to do with those people in the government that you're involved with?" Barbara Jean said. "I can't be married to you; I can't be around you if this is the kind

222

of life you're in for. Remember that I almost got killed because of the stupid horseshit Bitcoin thing where you ended up losing all your money."

My mind was settling down. I had to think this through, time to put one foot in front of the other.

"The people I'm involved with would never do this to me, but they can figure out who did fake the video." I was bluffing a bit here, I really didn't know if Wishbone and Toni Anne could figure it out, but I thought they could. "I have to make some phone calls."

"Well, get on the phone and call!" Barb said.

"I can't call from here," I said. "I can't explain. I'll call when I get home."

At that point our conversation hit an impasse. We stood and looked at each other for what seemed like a long time. What else would go wrong?

"We've got to talk to my parents. Let me explain a complication," Barb said.

She explained that her father had been robbed coming home from the poker game. He had a few bumps and bruises, but the doctor had checked him out and he'd be okay. The county sheriff had questioned him and just left. That had been the police car that I passed in the driveway.

"Who do you think robbed your father?" I asked.

"He's really disappointed. He thinks it was a professional criminal hired by one or more of the guys he plays poker with." Barbara Jean said.

"Really?" I said. Barbara Jean looked like she was buying my performance. Maybe I was a better natural actor than I thought.

"C'mon, let's go out and talk to them," Barb said.

We went out into the living room. "Daddy, why don't you explain to JR what happened," Barbara Jean said.

"Well, goldang it, you just ain't gonna believe it!" Cletus started. "This big guy, maybe six foot six, 250 pounds held me up…"

Cletus was right. I didn't believe it. His version of the events was so far from the truth that the county sheriff would never even suspect what really happened. Cletus was the hero of the tale.

"But don't you think that I didn't get a couple of hard punches in!" Cletus said. "That no good weasel is home with a ribeye steak on his face, trying to get rid of the bruises, I'd guess. But it's probably some professional criminal they brought in just for the job, not from around here. He was wearing one of those commando masks, but I ripped it clean off him, got a good look at his face. Not somebody I recognized."

"The police are sending out one of those sketch artists," June said.

"Oh," I said. I reckoned that the pink ski mask would not be mentioned.

"How much money do you think he took?" Barbara Jean asked.

"I won big, but you never count your money at the table. It was probably around one hundred grand, consarn it" Cletus said.

I wished at least that part of Cletus' tall tale was accurate.

"That guy had some kind of big weapon that I had never seen before, and I seen a lot of weapons. I think it was a machine pistol of some kind, a military grade weapon," Cletus said.

I had a feeling that this legend was going to grow over time and repeated telling by Cletus.

I was careful not to ask any questions. I was afraid I might slip up and ask something that hadn't been discussed by Cletus. It was better to be quiet, and Cletus wasn't a person who had trouble shooting off his mouth

It took a while for Cletus to run out of lies. He contradicted himself a few times, but nobody called him on it. June and Barbara Jean were used to this sort of thing. Finally, he stopped talking.

"A truck was passing the other way, and the man stopped and helped Cletus get out of the ditch," June explained.

"Ahh, I was preparing myself to get out of the ditch anyhow," Cletus said. "But it was neighborly of him to stop."

"That's...some...story," I said.

"I'm real disappointed. You never know what some people are willing to do to get your money," Cletus said.

"True," I said.

Barbara Jean said, "JR, why don't I walk you out to your truck?"

"Ok," I said.

When we got outside, she said, "I know. He's lying…more like exaggerating. That's just him. But somebody did rob him and hit him in the face."

"You don't think he might have staged the whole thing, do you?" I said. I thought mentioning that might take her off my tracks entirely.

Barbara Jean paused. "I hadn't thought of that. I don't know." She was quiet for a minute. "My poor mother. And now I've got to tell her about the video. I've got to *show* both of them the video. I'd rather tell them than to have them hear about it from somebody else."

The time spent listening to Cletus and coming to realize that I wouldn't be caught for the robbery had given me a false sense of a reprieve. That was over now. The video of me selling teen age sex slaves to Jeffery Epstein was still out there, and who knew how many people had watched it by now?

"JR, you swear to me that's not you in the video?" Barbara Jean asked.

"Of course," I said.

"Say the words," Barbara Jean said.

"I swear that's not me. That never happened." I said. "But I've got to get this cleared up. Even if I do, some people are always going to think it's true. What a nightmare. I've got to call my contacts."

"Alright. I'll handle telling my parents. Take care of yourself, JR. And I don't want this to end up with a Russian hitman pointing a gun at me like last time," Barbara Jean said.

"I assure you, that's not going to happen," I said.

Barbara Jean was maybe eight feet away from me. She gave me a cold look. No hug. We were a long way from being reconciled.

225

Chapter Eighty Five
Austin

I drove back to my compound in Austin. The driver of every vehicle that passed stared at me. They all knew it was me in the video with Jeffery Epstein.

I knew that wasn't so. But it seemed like it was true. It's easy to be paranoid when a scandalous video featuring yourself is on YouTube.

I called Wishbone. "No fifteen second bullshit! We're having a regular conversation until we resolve this thing," I said.

"Okay, we'll take our chances. Just get a different burner phone after---"

I interrupted, "Enough of that shit! What the fuck are you people letting happen to me? You're dangling me out there—"

"JR, we didn't know the Russians were this good at Deep Fake---"

"What?" I said.

Wishbone explained, "That video was made with something called Deep Fake technology. We and the Chinese are the best at it, we didn't think the Russians could produce anything that good."

"Great! That's just fuckin' great! What are you going to do about it?" I asked.

"I don't blame you for being apeshit," Wishbone said. "Calm down, get a new burner, then call me tomorrow. We have to go back to the fifteen second protocol, or I can't talk to you, understand?"

"Yeah," I said, then disconnected.

Chapter Eighty Six
Austin

I was just beginning to calm down when my iPhone rang. It was Warner Winthrop Hamilton, the co-op President.

"Mr. Johnson?" he asked. Those were his words, but what he meant was 'hey scumbag!' In a patrician manner.

"Yes," I said.

"There's a morals clause in your lease. We, the board have decided to activate the clause until such time as your current situation has been adjudicated," Hamilton said.

"Oh, you guys have been surfing the web?" I asked.

"I beg your pardon?" Hamilton asked. He knew what I meant. They had seen the Epstein video.

"What do you mean adjudicated? I'm not charged with anything," I said.

"Nevertheless," Hamilton said. "Your request to sell your leasing rights has been frozen. Pending the outcome of...certain issues."

"I haven't even sent in a request yet," I said.

"Nevertheless," Hamilton said.

"You already said that," I pointed out.

"We are tabling the situation without prejudice, Mr. Johnson. We believe in your Constitutional rights," Hamilton said.

"I thought some of the co-op board members *wrote* the Constitution," I said. They were pretty old, and they had the same last names as some of the framers of the Constitution.

"Good day, Mr. Johnson," Hamilton said. He disconnected.

Prick. I really had wanted to tell him to shove it, but something told me not to do so. Maybe it was that I knew there were three or four million dollars of my money sitting illiquid in my co-op apartment and the Board could keep me tied up in court forever if they felt like it. That's one thing lawyers are good at: delaying.

I had bigger problems.

Then I had a pleasant thought. Bitsy would see the video. My two doctor brothers would see the video. It would ruin their days, maybe weeks, or months to come. They'd be so ashamed. Their colleagues would be whispering behind their backs.

227

"If only he'd gone to Medical School," Bitsy would say to my brothers.

Chapter Eighty Seven

Wishbone and Toni Anne decided to meet at the White House. Toni Anne invited Gabrielle to join them.

"What is she doing here?" Wishbone asked, pointing to Gabrielle.

"I want her here," Toni Anne said.

"Let's talk about what we are going to do about the commies releasing this video," Toni Anne asked. "This video of JR Johnson and Epstein and Maxwell is devastating."

"What is it you want to do?" Wishbone asked.

"Counter-measures, and I've cooked up some great ones" Toni Anne said. "That moron Stockbridge won't even understand what's happening, or do anything, but I'm still on recuperative leave. I've got Deep Fake stuff on a server that General Goldstein funded under a dummy appropriation but nobody else knows about. I've saved them in case there was a situation like this. Why should I even talk to Stockbridge? Wait until you see these! And I have the President's permission to release them."

"Like what?" Wishbone asked.

"Some real deviant stuff, starring the Lider," Toni Anne said.

"Good quality?" Wishbone asked.

"No grainy video. This is Hollywood quality. Let's take a look," Toni Anne said.

Tony Anne picked up the remote control on the table and played the videos in succession "Let's start off by releasing the pissing video. It makes a point without being too graphic. We'll keep the one of the Lider giving oral sex to the stallion as the ace up our sleeve."

"Yeah, we don't want to offend the Animal Rights people," Gabrielle said.

"I don't know, I think it shows genuine affection for the horse," Toni Anne said. "Maybe we could include the caption: No fuckin' animals were harmed during the filming."

Wishbone and Gabrielle laughed. "Toni Anne, you have such a way with words," Wishbone said.

"It's a gift," Toni Anne said.

229

Chapter Eighty Eight
Moscow
Office of the Lider

Colonel Nihisky entered the office. The Lider looked pleased. Nihisky said, "Sir, I have bad news for you."

The Lider folded his hands on his desk. "What would that be?" he asked.

The colonel searched for words. "Sir, I mean… you have to watch something."

"What?" the Lider asked.

"May I use your keyboard, Sir?"

"Go ahead," the Lider said.

Nihisky walked around to the Lider's side of the massive desk, tapped some keys and cursored to the video. The title of the video was: The Lider at Play.

The video started innocently enough. The Lider was in a hotel room and took off his shirt.

"I am proud of my physique!" the real Lider said to Nihisky. The colonel nodded. The two of them continued to watch the video.

The man took off his pants and was completely naked. His penis was maybe one inch long.

"That's outrageous! I'd have to use a pair of tweezers to take a leak!" the Lider said to Nihisky." What kind of virility does this show the world?"

The Lider laid on the floor, and three extremely fat old naked women came on camera and began urinating on him. The women were drinking vodka straight from bottles. The Lider had an ecstatic look on his face as he smeared the urine all over himself, moaned with pleasure, and groveled at the feet of the women. He licked urine off the rug. The women pissed huge streams onto the Lider's head.

"That's not realistic! Women can't piss like that. They look like cows pissing on a flat rock," the Lider said.

Nihisky said nothing.

The video stopped with a freeze frame. One of the women had just vomited on the Lider's face, which pleased him. A caption appeared, in Russian and English: To Be Continued…

"Where did this originate?" the Lider asked.

230

"Sir our experts have determined that this came from the U.S., from Cyber Command, and although they could have obscured its origins completely, they left tell-tale signs that they sent it," Nihisky said. "They want us to know they posted it."

"This is the message that idiot Safi told Quinn he would be sending! He had his stooge at Cyber Command do this. We must retaliate immediately. We have to show that we own him," the Lider said.

"You don't think this is retaliation for the video we released with JR Johnson?" Nihisky asked.

"No, Safi and Stockbridge don't care about him. I've got other plans for Johnson," the Lider said.

"Will we be sending another Deep Fake video?" Nihisky asked.

"Think bigger. It's time to kill somebody. I've always found that to be an attention getter," the Lider said.

Chapter Eighty Nine
Salt Lake City

Sierra Quinn thought she'd be bored, sitting around for days with no new mission. She was wrong.

Soon after she got to her hotel room, Colonel Nihisky texted her. The sisters, Debbie and Nancy would be visiting her within the hour with the parameters for her new mission.

"Room service," Debbie said as she knocked on the door. Quinn let them in, Nancy pushing a service cart.

"You don't have any food in that cart do you?" Quinn asked. "I'm hungry."

"No, sorry," Nancy answered. "But we do have the instructions for an interesting mission."

"You'll get to use your skills," Debbie said. "Congressman Safi is going to Denver to address a National Chamber of Commerce session. The Lider wants to send a message. We'll help you."

Debbie and Nancy went over the details with Quinn. When they were finished outlining the mission, Debbie asked, "Any interest in having sex with us?"

"No thank you," Quinn said.

"It never hurts to ask. You're such an attractive woman," Nancy said. What she didn't say was that Colonel Nihisky had offered them a bonus of up to $500,000 if they could get a video of them getting extremely intimate with Quinn, depending on how pleased the Lider was with the performances. It wouldn't be the first video of this sort Debbie and Nancy had supplied for the Lider.

The three would meet in Denver the next day.

Later that night Debbie and Nancy privately discussed telling Quinn about the sex video incentive and offering to split the bonus with her.

"Let's finish the next mission first," Debbie suggested. Nancy agreed.

"It's just sex." Debbie said, "for $250,000 she could pretend she was enjoying it." They laughed.

"I've pretended for less than that!" Nancy said.

232

Chapter Ninety
Denver

Congressman Safi was in town for what he called a "Hit and Run." He'd give his standard bullshit speech to the Chamber of Commerce National Convention, during which he said the word "freedom" seventeen times, sleep overnight and fly back to Washington in the morning. The Congressman couldn't get paid directly for the speech, but the Chamber could make a big contribution toward the Political Action Committee that would be formed when Safi announced his candidacy for President. To Safi that arrangement was better than getting personally compensated because the PAC would get the money tax free and spend it on his Presidential campaign. He'd get the big six and seven figure fees for making speeches after he left the White House.

The only staffer to accompany Safi was Media Consultant Buddha Alteiri. He'd have plenty to do, schmoozing with the local and national media at the event.

The Chamber of Commerce provided the best suite in the hotel for Safi, and a more modest room for Alteiri. Safi decided the two of them would have a light dinner in Safi's suite before the speech. Due to the two-hour time difference between Washington and Denver, room service was asked to deliver at 4 pm. The congressman was obsessed with brushing and flossing his teeth prior to a public appearance and blocked out time for that purpose after a meal. People might not remember what he said in the speech, but they'd remember his near-neon white teeth.

At exactly 4 pm Debbie and Nancy knocked on the door to Safi's suite. The Congressman, seated on a couch, gestured for Alteiri to open the door. He did so.

As Safi and Alteiri approached the dining table in the suite, Debbie slipped a strong nylon bungee cord over Safi's head and pulled it to chest level. There was a metal clasp in the back. Debbie tightened the cord and locked the clasp.
Simultaneously, Nancy did the same thing to Alteiri.

"What is the meaning of this?" Safi said, as he struggled to breathe. The tight cord cut into his arms.

233

Debbie said nothing as Nancy walked to the door and opened it. In walked Sierra Quinn. She was wearing a tasteful expensive red dress, with just a discrete bit of cleavage, her hair and makeup in the glammed-up mode. She looked like a trophy wife of one of the bigwigs attending the convention. Her hands were behind her. Quinn pulled her Glock from behind her back.

The two men froze as Quinn approached. Quinn confronted Safi. She held the silenced Glock to Safi's forehead.

"The Lider doesn't think you're taking him seriously enough," Quinn said to Safi. "You might notice that my finger is not on the trigger. Yet."

"What do you want?" Safi managed to croak.

"The Lider wants you to realize your position in this relationship. You are the servant, the Lider is the master," Quinn said. She laughed.

Quinn walked over to Alteiri. "You are John Alteiri?" she asked.

"Yes," he said.

"Good, I hate…well…*dislike*, killing the wrong guy," Quinn said as she shot Alteiri in the forehead. He crashed backward on to the dining table, knocking over a chair and breaking some plates and glasses.

Quinn walked back to Safi. "My finger is on the trigger now," she said as she held the gun to Safi's forehead. She pulled the trigger.

Safi gasped. The gun clicked. Quinn laughed.

"Gee, I must have counted wrong. I thought there were two bullets in the clip," Quinn said.

Safi's knees buckled, and he fell to the floor.

"Here's the deal," Quinn said. "Don't release any more videos."

"I don't know what you are talking about," Safi said.

Quinn gestured to Nancy who removed a loaded clip from a shelf on the cart and handed it to the assassin. Quinn ejected the clip in the gun and rammed home the new clip. She pulled back the action, chambering a round, ready for firing. "Don't make me put my finger back on the trigger," Quinn said. "Just listen."

"Alright," Safi said.

"The surveillance cameras have been temporarily disabled for this floor. Here's your story: Two guys, you think Caucasian, came here to rob you, and Alteiri decided to be a hero, so he got shot. If you don't stick with that story, you'll be as dead as he is in a couple days. I told you we could get to you. Just do what you are told to do from now on." Quinn said. "Don't initiate anything in the Lider's direction. Understand?"

"Yes," Safi said.

"So, as they say in show business, don't call us, we'll call you," Quinn said.

Safi said nothing.

"Ok, take their watches, wallets and cash," Quinn said to Debbie and Nancy. Then Quinn said to Safi, "This has to look like a robbery. It's okay to be vague with the details. You're in shock. The assailants were average height and build, dark hair. They wore stockings over their faces."

When Debbie and Nancy were done taking the valuables from Safi and the dead Alteiri, Quinn said to Safi, "I really don't like you, but I follow orders. Don't give the Lider a reason to order me to shoot you, because if he does, I'll do whatever it takes to kill you."

Quinn walked toward the door. She stopped and turned. "The Lider wants you alive, but I want you dead. He can change his mind depending on the situation. Catch you later," she said to Safi, then she left.

Moments later Debbie and Nancy wheeled the service cart to the door and left Safi bungeed and lying on the floor.

Chapter Ninety One
Austin, TX

I had bought a new burner phone from a street vendor in downtown Austin after being instructed to do so by Wishbone. I forced myself to go through my morning workout. I figured it was important to maintain discipline.

My breakfast consisted of a hardboiled egg, half a grapefruit, and a couple pieces of toast. I was halfway through eating it when I couldn't wait any longer and phoned Wishbone.

"JR. I was just going to call you," Wishbone said.

"That sounds like something some of my ex-girlfriends used to say," I said. "How were you going to call me when you don't have my new phone number?"

"Alright, just listen. Google "The Lider at Play," and watch the video, then call me back," Wishbone said.

I watched the video. Who knew being pissed on could be so rewarding? Even to a man with a one-inch dick? I called Wishbone. We went through the 15 second thing.

"What's next?" I said to Wishbone. Do you think the Russians will retaliate by releasing another video of me?"

"Probably not. They didn't think the U.S. was going to use Deep Fake, but they must know we have a lot worse stuff in the vault," Wishbone said.

"What do you think they're going to do?" I asked.

"Our best guess is they're going to go full bore with the ransomware attacks," Wishbone said.

236

Chapter Ninety Two
Moscow

The Lider had convened a meeting with the heads of the security services. The mood was grim. The Lider was unpredictable in normal circumstances, who knew what he'd be like after the pissing video was released.

"Relax. No one is coming in this meeting with a chainsaw. At least not today. I want to get everyone on the same page," the Lider said.

No one relaxed.

"Can this pissing video be taken down, restricted somehow?" the Lider asked.

No one wanted to answer. The Lider pointed to Hemo, the head of the Deep Fake project. "Well?" he asked.

"Lider, one of the attractive characteristics of Deep Fake technology, from an offensive standpoint, is that once a video is released, it is impossible to eradicate from the web. We can try to get the genie back in the bottle, but the practical answer is "No." Hemo said.

The Lider was known to have ordered the deaths of the entire list of attendees at a meeting a few years ago. The topic of that meeting was a botched intelligence operation. The victims weren't shot as they sat there, but six high ranking bureaucrats had met with tragic accidents over a two-week period. The men in the room were all too well aware of this event. In fact, most of them were in their current positions because their immediate superiors had been liquidated by the Lider after attending that meeting.

"I thought you told me that the Americans would not use Deep Fake technology," the Lider asked Kusnetsov, the GRU General.

Kusetsov swallowed. "Sir, our best estimates were that the Americans viewed Deep Fake like they view Germ Warfare; they have it, we know they have it, and the threat of it is enough to be a deterrent."

The Lider expressed no emotion as he sat. No one in the room dared speak.

237

"Was the release of the pissing video an overt action, approved by the American President?" The Lider asked.

No one volunteered to answer, so The Lider asked, "Kusnetsov, what is your opinion on this issue?"

"Sir, we do not think the release of the...offensive...video was authorized by the White House. It was released from servers controlled by Cyber Command," Kuznetsov said. "And Cyber Command left enough digital breadcrumbs...clues, to make sure we know they are the ones responsible.

"And?" the Lider asked.

"Sir do you want me to disclose sensitive information to the entire group?" General Kuznetsov asked.
"Go ahead," the Lider said.

"The new commander at Cyber Command, Admiral Stockbridge, is under the control of Congressman Safi. Safi wants to be President, and he..."

"Go ahead, General. Everyone here has to know, so we can formulate a coherent strategy," the Lider said.

"Very well. As some in this room know, we have approached Congressman Safi and offered him significant help, including a major Disinformation campaign, to get him elected President. He, in turn has agreed to be compliant to us in important areas. Safi has promised Admiral Stockbridge the Vice Presidency on his ticket, Kuznetsov said.

"And so?" the Lider asked.

The General continued, "Congressman Safi has recently come to think of himself as our equal partner, instead of our puppet---"

"Exactly! Safi, through his minion, Admiral Stockbridge, must have ordered the release of the pissing video! Without the approval or knowledge of the White House," the Lider said.

The Lider paused to let the information sink in, for the benefit of people who were just hearing it for the first time.

"Safi must have thought releasing the video would make us back off. However, we have escalated our response," the Lider said.

No one wanted to ask the obvious question: What was the escalation?

"Hours ago, three of our unconventional operatives held Congressman Safi and his Media Advisor captive in their

238

Denver, Colorado hotel suite. Both men were bound, and the Media Advisor was assassinated not five feet from Safi. The congressman was told he was our servant and not to ever think about disobeying our orders again. Safi was also instructed to say the whole incident was a robbery gone wrong. You'll be seeing news stories about the heroic congressman surviving the brazen robbery," the Lider said.

The men attending the meeting nodded in approval.

"We don't think there will be any further video releases from Safi. Meanwhile I am calling in the ransomware pirates for a meeting. It's time to ramp up their operations to full speed," the Lider said.

Chapter Ninety Three
The White House

The President decided it was time for another late-night meeting with General Goldstein, Wishbone and Toni Anne.

They met again in the room off the Oval Office. "Wishbone, get us up to speed," the President said.

"Safi is sticking with his bullshit story that the incident in the hotel room was a robbery," Wishbone started, "A contact of mine says the Denver Police are skeptical, but publicly are going with the story at face value."

"The police have to do that. What else are they going to do? Accuse Safi?" the President said.

"I ran into Buddha Alteiri a few times, on a professional level. It's too bad," General Goldstein said.

"Alteiri knew about the deal Safi had made. He shouldn't have gone to work for that asshole," Toni Anne said.

"Toni Anne, that's pretty cold," General Goldstein said.

Toni Anne shrugged. "I think we all agree the Russians shot the wrong guy."

"Not for *their* purposes," Wishbone said. "There's more. Toni Anne, the President has approved me reading you in on the following intel: We have a mole in the Kremlin."

"No shit?" Toni Anne Laudano said.

"Yes, and it's a good one," the President said.

"And listen to this. I just got this from our mole before our meeting: The Lider has no idea it was Toni Anne who released the Pissing Video. He thinks it was Stockbridge, at the direction of Safi. That's why the Russians shot John Alteiri. It was a message to Safi," Wishbone said.

"That's incredible!" the President said.

"I'd like time to think through all the permutations," General Goldstein said, "but at first blush, it seems like we have Safi by the balls!"

"Yeah, and now it's time to squeeze 'em!" Toni Anne said. She grimaced and clenched her fist.

"Looks like you have experience in that area, Toni Anne," the President said.

240

"Thanks, Mr. President," Toni Anne said, "I'm gifted in many areas, not just computer science and math."

"Alright, that's an unexpected gift on one front," the President said. "Let's focus on what else we have to do."

"The Russians are going to go full bore with the ransomware attacks," Wishbone said.

"We're going to have to let lots of American companies pay a pile of ransom," General Goldstein said.

"Well. As we know, about half of that money will be redirected to Political Action Committees to support my re-election," the President said. "And, of course, that is in the self-interest of the red-blooded American ransomware victims, even though they don't realize it. The North Koreans will get their cut."

"Don't forget the payment to JR Johnson," Toni Anne said.

"That's a big payment for the job he is doing," General Goldstein said.

"It's okay. A totally untraceable payment to him. It will make him whole for playing the stooge in the Bitcoin situation," the President said. "And he'll only get it if he's alive. I did give him my word."

"Sir, you didn't give him your word that he'd be alive," Wishbone said.

The President shrugged. "This isn't a risk-free business."

Chapter Ninety Four
Moscow
The Lider's Office

A meeting of the ransomware pirates had been convened on one day's notice. Still, when the Lider requested your presence in Moscow, you had no choice but to comply whatever the hardship. Some of the attendees had to travel great distances, for the former Soviet Union is a big country.

The attendees stood in front of the Lider's desk. There were no chairs provided for them to sit. He walked into the room.

"I have found that short meetings are the most effective. This will be brief. Everyone is here from the previous meeting," the Lider said. "Kravanesko will be here in a moment."

The door opened and Colonel Nihisky pushed a cart into the room. It was covered with a velvet cloth. The Lider walked to the side of his desk and with a flourish like a magician, removed the cloth.

"Voila! Here's Kravensko," the Lider said, his voice rising.

On top of the cart was a large glass jar. Inside the jar was the embalmed head of Boris Kravanesko. His face displayed the now familiar look of permanent terror.

"Kravanesko was foolish enough to betray me. Look at his face!"

The Lider's tone turned philosophical. "It must be hard to look brave while you're having your head removed with a chainsaw. He sent his son to America as sort of an advanced scout. You've seen the roller coaster video?"

When there was no response, the Lider raised his voice. "Surely you've seen some interesting videos recently. You've seen the roller coaster video?"

Every head nodded, and all murmured to the affirmative.

The Lider spoke softly. "It is time to unleash the full force of your ransomware attacks. Every technical assistance is available from our intelligence service, merely for the asking. All you need to do is your jobs, and you will be wealthy men. Understand?"

Every head nodded.

"I should not have to tell you that I expect your complete loyalty. Use your imaginations. Imagine a future in which you

242

have been loyal...Now imagine a future in which you have been *disloyal*. We have an unlimited supply of these large jars," the Lider said.

After what seemed like an interminable interval the Lider asked, "Any questions?" The room was silent.

"Very well, this concludes the meeting. Get out," the Lider said.

The room emptied quickly, leaving the Lider and Colonel Nihisky alone.

"They left as if somebody farted," the Lider said, then he laughed.

"Yes sir," Nihisky said. "That was an excellent meeting sir."

"Yes, it was, wasn't it," the Lider said. "Now call in some fat old women. I feel like being pissed on."

Nihisky froze.

"Just a joke, Colonel," the Lider said.

Chapter Ninety Five
The White House

Chan Wheeler personally phoned Admiral Stockbridge's number. The Admiral's assistant answered.

"This is the President's Chief of Staff, please get Admiral Stockbridge on the line, immediately," Wheeler said.

Wheeler waited three minutes before Stockbridge came on the line.

"Good morning," Stockbridge said.

"Do you not understand what immediately means?" Wheeler asked.

Stockbridge mumbled.

"Admiral, enough of your meanly mouthed bullshit! The President wants to see you right now, immediately. That means get in your car and get your ass up to the White House. Now. Understand?" Wheeler said.

"Alright," Stockbridge said.

"Immediately," Wheeler said, "Just you, do not bring an aide, understand?"

"Yes," Stockbridge said.

"Alright," Wheeler said, then he hung up.

Wheeler walked into the Oval Office. "We should have some fun with Stockbridge when he gets here, Mr. President."

"I bet he's on the phone with Safi right now," The President said. Both men laughed.

244

Chapter Ninety Six
Washington, DC
The Beltway

In the backseat of his limo, Admiral Stockbridge was on the phone to Congressman Safi.

"Congressman Safi, I've been called on the carpet by the White House," Stockbridge said.

"Regarding what?" Safi asked.

"I don't know, but I got a call from Wheeler. He was very rude, confrontational. He told me to drop everything and get to the White House," the Admiral said. "What should I say?"

"Stonewall them," Safi said.

"Stonewall them about what?" Stockbridge asked.

"See, it shouldn't be too difficult," Safi said, then he hung up.

Chapter Ninety Seven
The Oval Office

The President sat at his desk; hands folded. He hadn't spoken to or greeted Admiral Stockbridge. The only other person attending the meeting was Chan Wheeler. The Admiral sat in a chair in front of the President, Wheeler stood to the President's right, facing Stockbridge.

"Just what the fuck do you think you're doing, Stockbridge?" Wheeler asked.

"I came here as ordered," Stockbridge said.

"C'mon Admiral, you can't be as stupid as people say. You know that's not what I'm talking about. I'll ask again." This time Wheeler shouted. "Just what the fuck do you think you are doing?"

The Admiral sat silently.

"Okay, play dumb," Wheeler said. "You're a natural at it. Let's review the current situation."

Wheeler had a remote-control device in his hand. He hit a button, a panel on the wall slid open, exposing a flat display. The Chief of Staff hit another button. The video of the Lider being pissed on played. No one spoke.

"Why did you order Cyber Command to release this video?" Wheeler demanded.

"What?" the Admiral asked. It was quiet in the Oval Office. No one spoke for a good minute.

Finally, the President spoke. "You're trying my patience, Admiral."

"Sir, I don't know what you are referring---"

"Shut up Stockbridge! Even a moron like you can't get away with playing that dumb," Chan Wheeler said. "We'll go along with you for a minute."

Stockbridge looked confused.

"Look Stockbridge, everybody knows that a server at Cyber Command released this Deep Fake video. All our intelligence services, the Russians. We all know that you ordered the release of this because you were told to do so by your pal, Congressman Safi," Wheeler said.

246

Stockbridge sweated, tugged at his collar. He looked confused.

The President spoke. "I am responsible for the foreign policy of the United States. Not you, not Safi."

"Yes sir," Stockbridge said.

"Yes sir! That's what you have to say for yourself! You fuckin' moron," Wheeler said. "If this was Russia, you'd be down in the sub-basement getting shot right now."

Addressing the President, Stockbridge said, "Sir, I don't---"

"Shut up," Wheeler said. "The President put you in your job to pay off some political favors. You're on very thin ice. The only reason the President doesn't fire you today is that it would look embarrassing for him to admit that he put such a disloyal fuck-up in a position of responsibility."

Wheeler paused to let his comment hang. "You might want to relay this conversation to Safi. Now get the fuck out of here before we have you thrown down a flight of stairs and tell people it was a tragic accident."

Admiral Stockbridge left without a word.

When Stockbridge was safely out of earshot the two men in the Oval Office laughed.

"Stockbridge doesn't have a clue what just happened," Chan Wheeler said.

"Who says you can't have fun in this office?" the President said.

Chapter Ninety Eight
Fort Meade, MD
Cyber Command

Admiral Stockbridge was quiet on his 45 minute ride back to Cyber Command. He did not want to call Safi until he had some idea of what was happening.

As soon as he got into his office, Stockbridge called in his second in command. The one-star admiral reported.

"Have you seen the pissing video of the Lider, Admiral?" Stockbridge asked.

"Sir, with respect, I think everyone in the world has seen the video," the one-star answered.

"I hadn't seen it until I went to the White House. I'm confused. The President and his Chief of Staff, that evil bastard Wheeler, are convinced that we at Cyber Command released it."

"Oh!" the one-star said.

"Is there any possibility that we released the video?" Stockbridge asked.

"I don't know sir," the one-star said. "I don't know the procedure for releasing something like that, or if we even do things---"

"Well, don't you think you ought to find out!" Stockbridge snapped. "Alright, convene an emergency meeting of the department heads. Let's get to the bottom of this."

"Do you think it could be that bitch Toni Anne Laudano who's behind this?" the one-star asked.

"No. She doesn't have access to any of our servers. She's been completely cut off. I have assurances on that," Stockbridge said.

Chapter Ninety Nine
Fort Meade, MD
Cyber Command

The one-star admiral had called Gabrielle McHugh for a meeting.

"Colonel McHugh, I've got to be brief. There's an emergency meeting that I've got to organize. But meanwhile, I have to tell you that you've received new orders, transferring you to the Pentagon. You're to report tomorrow, to something called the Inter Agency Cyber Task Force. Is this a surprise to you?'

"Yes sir," Gab said. She had to hide her sexuality all her life so she was far more practiced in lying than the average person. Convincing this empty suit admiral was no challenge.

"Well, as I said, I'm quite busy with something. Apparently, this Inter Agency thing reports to General Goldstein. I never heard of it," the admiral said.

"Sir, if it's alright, I'll clean out my office and leave now," Gabrielle said.

"Yes, it's alright. Good luck to you," the admiral said. He handed Gabrielle the orders, a pile of bureaucratic stuff.

"Thank you, sir," Gab said. The nitwit one-star hadn't even asked her any hard questions. If she wasn't in the building Admiral Stockbridge wouldn't think of asking her anything, either.

249

Chapter One Hundred
Fort Meade, MD
Cyber Command

The one-star walked into Admiral Stockbridge's office.
"Sir, the department heads are assembled in the conference room. Before we go in, I should tell you one thing," the one-star said.

"What?" Stockbridge said.

"Toni Anne Laudano was seen in the Pentagon today, walking into General Goldstein's office," the one-star said.

"Good. Maybe Goldstein will hire her. It would get her out of our hair, no more of her disruptions. She could go work on the backwaters with Goldstein," Stockbridge said.

"That's what I think too, Sir," the one-star said.

Chapter One Hundred One
Fort Mead, MD

Six department heads were scattered around the 20-seat table in the Main Conference Room. Admiral Stockbridge walked in, trailed by the one-star.

"Good morning. You've all seen the video? The one with the Lider, being…urinated on?" Stockbridge asked.

"Yes sir," the six said simultaneously.

"Is there any chance that this video originated in Cyber Command?" Stockbridge asked.

"Sir, what do you mean by originated?" Colonel Nick Civitello, the department head of North American Networks asked.

Stockbridge raised his voice a bit. He was angry, but he was cautious that foolish questions could reveal how far he was in over his head.

"Colonel Civitello, I mean: did Cyber Command produce, somehow film or create this video?" Stockbridge asked.

"Sir, something like that, Deep Fake technology, is not in our mission statement. Certainly nothing like that is in our budget," Civitello said. The other department heads nodded. All of them had risen through the bureaucracy knowing how not to lie while at the same time not disclosing the truth.

"Could that video have been stored on our servers, and sent out to…the world, by Cyber Command?" Stockbridge asked.

Sheldon, the head of Hardware Technology answered. "Sir, we completely sweep all of our storage every five minutes, 24 hours a day, 365 days a year. We have nothing like that." Sheldon was Toni Anne's closest confidant. He spoke the Zeroes and Ones language of the machines as well as any human on earth. He operated on such a higher plane than Stockbridge that he in particular could mislead the Admiral while technically telling the truth.

"So, you're all telling me that Cyber Command did not produce that Deep Fake video, and it was not released on Cyber Command servers?" Stockbridge asked.

No one answered.

"Civitello, answer the question," Stockbridge said.

251

"Not to the best of our knowledge, sir," Colonel Civitello said.

"What does that mean, "not to the best of our knowledge?" Does that mean NO?" Stockbridge demanded.

"Sir, it means that as far as anyone in this room knows, the answer is no," Civitello said.

"Alright. Is it possible that Toni Anne Laudano somehow hacked our system and released the video through Cyber Command?" Stockbridge said.

"Sir, on your orders, Toni Anne was completely shut out of our system," Sheldon said. That was another technically correct statement.

"That's what I thought," Stockbridge said. "Frankly, I think Laudano's reputation is overrated."

None of the attendees commented.

"That's all. You're dismissed." Stockbridge left the room, his second in command trailing.

None of the other attendees made any comment. They knew they were being monitored. After the Admirals were safely out of the room they left to return to their departments.

Chapter One Hundred Two
The White House

General Goldstein was in for another late-night meeting with the President. This time Chan Wheeler was in attendance.

"Chan, I'm surprised you're here," General Goldstein said. "I thought you wanted to have plausible deniability if it ever came to testifying under oath."

"I'm in too deep," Wheeler said. "But I'm getting old. I may have a hard time remembering things. I've been practicing saying: I do not recall, Senator."

"Okay General, it's time to organize the Kinetic Response Team. That's the order I'm giving you. Who are you thinking of to head up the team?" the President said.

"Gabrielle McHugh. I trust her completely, and if things go south, she'll never lead anybody back to me, or to the White House. She has a lot of tough guy friends from her time in the Rangers, including just the man to borrow a Russian stealth helicopter. And the team has a new name: Inter Agency Cyber Task Force"

"Good. Get to it. Be ready to go in a week. You won't hear from me unless I give you the order to go," the President said.

The General went on, "other than Gabrielle, we're not using any active-duty personnel. It will just be contractors that she hires. That way---"

"General, I don't want to hear the details. I trust you, go do it. Now get out of here. I've had Chan spending the day to see if it's constitutional for me to pardon myself if this thing blows up in our faces," the President said. Goldstein left.

The President and Wheeler sat facing each other. "Cheer up Mr. President, this is going to be great. Think positive."

253

Chapter One Hundred Three
The White House

Chief of Staff Chan Wheeler had his secretary call Congressman Safi's secretary. After a delay long enough to establish what an important person he was, Safi came on the line.

"Yes?" Safi said.

"Congressman, this is Chan Wheeler. The President thought it was best for me to call you, due to the back-channel nature of some of this discussion, instead of calling you himself."

"Alright," Safi said, "what is it?"

"First the President and I extend our condolences for what happened to John Alteiri," Wheeler said. "The President will call Alteiri's widow personally."

"What else?" Safi asked.

"While what you do politically is none of the President's business, he feels that if you are considering running for this office that you formally announce your candidacy. That way you'll get Secret Service protection, and something like that tragedy in Denver would never happen again," Wheeler said.

"Tell the President that I'm touched about his concern," Safi said.

"Goodbye," Wheeler said, and he hung up before Safi could comment.

Wheeler then walked from his office to the Oval Office. He and the President were alone.

"Mr. President, I talked to Safi," Wheeler said.

"And?" the President asked.

"And what do you expect? He was a complete asshole, sounded like he could care less about you calling Alteiri's widow. He'll probably spend the next three days parsing out every word of the conversation," Wheeler said.

"Good," the President said.

254

Chapter One Hundred Four
Austin, TX

I sat alone, an Involuntary Celibate who had just finished his morning workout. They say many people workout with no real purpose in mind, but I had a specific goal: to survive having the shit kicked out of me by the North Koreans. Not being a martial arts expert, I didn't know what particular exercises were best to toughen up your nose to avoid having it broken.

Wishbone had told me that assuming I get back from North Korea, and having successfully completed my mission, I might expect the Russians to want to kill me. It might sound strange, but I was more worried about the certainty of getting beaten up by the North Koreans, than getting killed by the Russians. Both were bad, but the beating was more tangible.

I had a bank account with no money in it, credit cards that were cancelled, an investment account with a negative balance, and a 401k with a balance of $57.57. My assets in my New York co-op were frozen, and someone who had stolen my identity had taken a home equity line of credit of $2,000,000 on my Austin home compound. I did have some cash, most of which I had stolen at gunpoint from my father-in-law. I paid my bills by going to a bank and purchasing money orders, so I could put gas in the truck, pay my cable bill, and eat.

The other day my property tax bill came in the mail. People think taxes are low in Texas, but not so property taxes. The bill every six months was over $20,000. It would be a while before I paid the property taxes and I consoled myself that if I got killed, I'd never have to pay that bill. It's important to keep things in perspective.

You can only be so broke. Beyond flat broke. That's where I was. Overall, this is not the Financial Plan that Suze Orman recommends on her televised programs. I'm sure that Suze has not factored in having pissed off the President of Russia so much that he has directed the power of his entire government to ruin you financially. That didn't seem like a fair fight.

I made a mental note. If in the near future the Russians were shooting me, my last words should be: at least I don't have to pay the property taxes. I figured those last words wouldn't be on par with Julius Caesar or Nathan Hale, but should put me in the top one percent, so I had that going for me.

I did have something else going for me that the average totally broke guy doesn't have. If I played my part in the upcoming scheme, and the cyber warfare arms of the United States and North Korea did their thing, I'd get at least $50 million. It wasn't a sure thing, though. I'd been screwed big time by the U.S. government before. Remember they stood idly by as I got screwed out of $1.5 billion?

I was on standby, waiting for Wishbone to call me and tell me to go somewhere to some airport for the first leg of my all expenses paid junket to Pyongyang, which I hear is lovely this time of year. Unless you're going there to get the shit kicked out of you.

Has anyone else in the history of the friggin' world ever been in this situation?

After wallowing in my self pity for too long, I reverted back to old habits and turned on CNBC. There was: BREAKING NEWS.

Big deal. When was there not Breaking News?

This time it was significant. An unprecedented volume of ransomware attacks had hit U.S. companies within the last 24 hours. Prior targets like hospitals and municipalities had been spared so far, but for-profit companies, across the spectrum had been hit hard. Airlines, pipelines, banks, insurance companies, auto manufacturers, software giants, chip makers. It seemed that the ransomware pirates were going after only selected names in each industry, and they were demanding much larger ransoms than previous levels.

The White House had yet to comment. Congressman Safi, the Chairman of the House Intelligence Committee was scheduled to make a public announcement at 10 a.m.

Wishbone had told me this whole scenario would be coming. It would set everything else in motion.

Chapter One Hundred Five
The White House
The Oval Office

Chan Wheeler was alone with the President. "I hear Safi finally got someone to replace John Alteiri as his Media Advisor. He had to pay up, double Alteiri's salary," he said. "Combat pay."

The President said nothing and nodded.

"He sees this situation as his big opening. He'll rip into us and announce his candidacy for President at the same time," Wheeler said.

The President grinned. "What a tool! He's falling right into our trap."

"But he does have nice teeth," Wheeler said.

Chapter One Hundred Six
Washington, DC

Congressman Safi stood in front of the bright lights at the press conference.

He started, "Good morning. The current national crisis forces me to make two announcements this morning:

"First: The cause of the current ransomware crisis can be laid right at the feet of the White House, and specifically the current President. I am today calling for an immediate emergency hearing of the House Intelligence Committee. The companies being threatened, and the American People, deserve to know what factors caused this very serious breakdown in our National Security preparedness. It is my opinion that the current Commander of Cyber Command, Admiral Stockbridge was left holding the bag by his disorganized and unprepared predecessor, General Goldstein. Admiral Stockbridge, who has only been on the job for a short time, has the wherewithal we need to get out of this crisis, and I believe we will prevail. We will be calling witnesses to explore this theory, including General Goldstein. Our nation must find out what happened, and ensure it never happens again."

"Second: I had planned to make this next announcement in a ballroom full of supporters and balloons, but the seriousness of the current situation compels me to say this now: I am announcing my candidacy for the office of the President of the United States. I assure the American people that the fact that I am running for President in no way will stop me or cause me to not be objective in presiding over the upcoming hearings."

"That's all. I've got to get to work. Thank you for your time."

As Safi turned away, a reporter shouted a rehearsed question. It had been planted with that reporter by the new media advisor.

"Congressman? Are you going to subpoena the President to testify to your committee?" the reporter asked.

Safi stopped walking. "We will leave no stone unturned," he said. Then he continued walking out of the room, ignoring the cacophony of other shouted questions.

258

Chapter One Hundred Seven
The White House

The President watched Safi's news conference with Wheeler.
"Even that imbecile knows the President can only be
subpoenaed in a criminal case." Wheeler said.

"I think we'll have the last laugh," the President said.

The President and Wheeler went over the details of the
interview the President was scheduled to have that afternoon.
The White House rotated individual interviews with the major
networks, and it would be the good fortune of today's
correspondent to be able to break a major story.

Chapter One Hundred Eight
The White House

All the lights and sound equipment were in place in the Roosevelt Room. The woman news correspondent sat in a chair facing the President. The interview would be taped, so any flubs could be edited out. Every President got this treatment from the networks; it was part of the deal the news organizations made to get the interviews.

It's difficult being either party in this interview format, but the knowledge that it's not live makes it a bit easier. The President hated wearing makeup, but with the bright lights and the advent of high definition tv, he knew he'd look like a zombie without at least some powder on his face. Between every few questions the interview would pause, and the makeup artists would wipe sweat off the participant's faces and apply a bit more powder.

What looks so casual and almost cozy to the viewers is taped in a room with multiple hot lights hanging from stands, cables running every which way on the floor, and crowded with people, some television technicians, two makeup artists. Members of the White House staff are there to worry about every word and camera angle.

There were three cameras, one taking a wider shot of both of them, and two dedicated cameras filming each of their upper bodies. It was the job of the tv director to ultimately edit which camera's shot would be shown during each part of the conversation. A skilled director makes all this look easy, something the viewer never even thinks about.

The correspondent held a yellow notepad on her lap, but the President had no notes, no teleprompter in this format. He and Wheeler, along with two staffers had rehearsed the answers to questions that would likely be asked by the correspondent.

If the President was not prepared for, or didn't like a certain question, he was skilled at changing the subject in midstream, answering the question he felt like answering. The job of the correspondent was to keep the President on track without being rude or too confrontational. The public expected the correspondent to be deferential to the President, due to his office, not so much the man. About 20 percent of the American

260

public always told pollsters that they "disliked/hated" every President, and that number didn't waiver despite who held the office, but still a vast majority of the public expected the news media to be polite to any Chief Executive.

By convention the interviewer always referred to the subject as Mr. President, while the President always called the interviewer by their first name. This protocol was used even when the President privately despised and/or distrusted the interviewer, which was often the case. The interview began.

"Mr. President, I had a list of questions prepared, but in light of today's revelations of the ransomware attacks, and Congressman Safi's comments this morning, I'd think we should start with that topic. What can you tell the American people in response to the current crisis?"

"Well Anne, thank you for asking me that," the President began. "You're right, people need to know what's going on. You'll recall there was a major uptick in ransomware attacks several months ago, for example the attack on Baylor University. After that, U.S. Cyber Command, as directed by General Goldstein, sent a letter to the CEO of every major company in our nation outlining steps to protect against the kind of attack that is currently happening."

The President held up a copy of the letter. "The CEO of your organization received this letter. Were you aware of that, Anne?"

"No sir," Anne said.

"I wouldn't expect that you would know, you have other things to do, but the important thing is that these instructions were sent." The President said.

"What has been the response to the letter? Was it effective?" Anne asked.

"That's a very perceptive question. Companies received not just the letter, but instructions on how to contact our government cyber experts and get the knowledge to set up very effective firewalls against just the kinds of attacks that are hitting right now," the President said. "The companies that didn't comply were contacted a second time."

"If so, why are companies having so many problems---"

The President interrupted, "That's another great question. The answer, to the best of our preliminary assessment: most

261

companies followed our advice and guidance. Some companies, for reasons known only to them, chose not to follow the advice, and they seem to be the ones who are currently at the mercy of the ransomware pirates."

"Couldn't you mandate that companies upgrade their cyber defenses?" Anne asked.

"Not under existing laws. When this situation is resolved, we hope to work with Congress to pass stricter legislation in this area, especially with any company that does business with the government. It's a delicate area because nobody wants the government to have excessive power. But for now, we'll have to say: you can lead a horse to water, but you can't make him drink," the President said.

"Congressman Safi says that the situation is your fault, and that Cyber Command, under its new leadership is capable of counteracting the current cyber threats," Anne said.

"Is that a question?" the President said.

"Mr. President, do you have any comment of Congressman Safi's statements?" Anne asked.

"My only comment is, Cyber Command is a major component in our multi-faceted defense against cyber threats. I am expecting Admiral Stockbridge's assessment and recommendations, hopefully any moment now…. with that in mind, and in light of current events Anne, I've got to pull up short on our promised interview time. But let's look at this as just the first part of an interview. So, when this situation is resolved, you get to finish the interview. Is that okay? The President said.

"Of course, Mr. President. Any idea of when that might be?" Anne asked.

"As soon as possible," the President said.

"Cut," the director said, and the lights dimmed. One of the makeup artists handed the President a white towel which he dabbed against his face. When he finished and glanced at the towel is was stained with orange powder.

Speaking to no one in particular the President said, "At least they don't make me wear a red rubber ball on my nose."

"Not yet," Wheeler said from behind one of the cameras.

Anne laughed. "Thank you, Mr. President," she said.

The director was not as polite. "Damn it Chan, why didn't you tell us about this?" he asked.

262

"We have this little job of running the country, I was busy," Wheeler said. "You got a good story, and you'll get to finish in another interview. Stop your whining."

The President was already gone from the Roosevelt Room. Wheeler left.

Chapter One Hundred Nine
Fort Meade, MD
Cyber Command

Admiral Stockbridge sat in his office, accompanied only by his one-star second in command.

"I just received a call from the Chairman of the Joints Chiefs. He's looking for our response to the current situation so he can inform the White House," Stockbridge said.

"What's our response going to be sir?" the one-star asked.

"I don't know," Stockbridge said. "We need to convene another meeting of the department heads to get some ideas. In a hurry. Let's have the meeting right here in my office. Maybe a less formal setting will encourage open ideas. Take care of that, will you?"

"Yes sir," the one-star said.

Chapter One Hundred Ten
Fort Meade, MD
Cyber Command

The six department heads sat in Stockbridge's office. Stockbridge was behind his desk, the one-star was in a chair to his left, facing the six experts. There was no idle banter.

"Let's get right down to it. The Chairman of the Joint Chiefs is looking for an update from me. What are we going to do to fix this situation?" Stockbridge asked the group.

No one spoke. Stockbridge asked, "Colonel Civitello, what is your assessment?"

"Sir, as you know the mission of my group is to monitor the networks in North America---"

Stockbridge interrupted, "So Colonel, you're monitoring. What is your assessment of the situation of the companies currently being held up for ransom?"

Civitello said, "Sir, uhh, I uhh—"

Sheldon said, "I can answer that question Admiral. Colonel Civitello is not in a position to see if he can fix this, it's just not his job. It is my job, and my answer is: we can't help the companies that are currently under attack. Pardon my language, but those companies are fucked, they have to pay the ransom."

"That's what you expect me to tell the Chairman of the Joints Chiefs of Staff? "They're fucked, they have to pay the ransom?" You really don't have a better answer?" Stockbridge said.

"Sir, I'm sure the Chairman wants to know the truth. Sugar coating an answer right now isn't going to do anybody any good," Sheldon said.

"How about if I fire you right now and call in your immediate subordinate? Maybe we'll get a different answer," Stockbridge said.

"Go right ahead Admiral. You better fire everybody in the department, one after another. By the time you get down to the custodial staff, maybe they'll tell you that the situation can be fixed," Sheldon said.

Even though Cyber Command was a mixed military and civilian outfit this level of insubordination was not acceptable.

265

Stockbridge and Sheldon stared at each other, the rest of the people in the room looked down at the floor. Finally, Colonel Civitello spoke.

"Sir, I know the tensions are running high right now. But with Toni Anne not here, Sheldon is the smartest person in the building. May I suggest that we continue the discussion?"

Stockbridge waited five seconds. "Alright. Sheldon, explain to me the reason for your answer."

"Admiral. The level of sophistication which has been used by the ransomware pirates is way beyond even the best private hackers that we have seen. These attacks are clearly coming from Russia and the former republics. We are 100 percent confident that the hackers are receiving support from Russian military intelligence," Sheldon said.

"And we're not better than the Russians?" Stockbridge asked.

"Sir, we are better, but only a bit better. It's vastly easier to protect against a ransomware hack than it is to get rid of it after it has already infected the computer. It doesn't help to think we're the only smart people in the world," Sheldon said.

"So why can't we fix the computers that have been hacked?" Stockbridge asked.

"Sir, to oversimplify, software runs on five levels. Most ransomware attacks are on outermost, the fifth, or maybe the fourth level. We can fix those. But these new attacks have penetrated to the first, or the core fundamental level. If you gave one computer with this level of virus to our best people, they might be able to crack the fix in a month, but not for certain even then. There are literally trillions of possible permutations of the viruses. Since there are thousands of effected machines, and a limited time frame, it is not feasible to fix them," Sheldon said.

"Impossible?" Stockbridge asked.

"Yeah, let's be honest. Impossible," Sheldon said.

"Why didn't the effected companies comply?" Stockbridge asked.

"Who knows? Lazy, dumb, arrogant, too cheap. Maybe a combination of those reasons," Sheldon said.

"So, we tell the companies to pay?" Stockbridge asked.

"Yes, but that's when we face the biggest risk," Sheldon said.

"What's that?" Stockbridge said.

266

"Most times the ransomware pirates take the money and release control back to the victims. But not always. Sometimes they change the rules, for example, make demands for double the ransom. That's happened," Sheldon said.

"What can we do to prevent that?" Stockbridge asked.

Sheldon looked at the other department heads. No one wanted to answer, so Sheldon said, "Nothing."

Chapter One Hundred Eleven
Austin, TX

It was around 9 a.m. My phone rang. It was Wishbone calling.
"Hey Wishbone," I said.
"Ready for a trip?" he asked.
"Yup."
"Be at the Austin airport, private aviation terminal, 8 a.m. tomorrow," he said.
"Okay. Should I bring anything besides my toothbrush?" I asked.
"You might not need the toothbrush so much," Wishbone said.
"Oh. Quick trip?"
"I meant you might have less teeth to brush as a result of the trip," he said. "I was just trying to be funny." He disconnected.

I decided to call Barbara Jean, but I didn't plan what to say.
"Hello, JR," she said.
"Barbara Jean, I have to go on a trip. Let's call it a business trip,"
"Where are you going?" she asked.
"I can't say, but it's a major part of the plan,"
"You and your tall tales. I never know whether to believe you," Barbara Jean said.
"You're a good judge of character," I said.
"I hope you're successful. I don't want the embarrassment of having two ex-husbands,"
"Your level of concern is touching," I said.
"Really JR, I want you to succeed. I want you back. But I drew the line in the sand, and that line stays there,"
"I know. Wish me good luck," I said.
"Good luck, sweetie," Barbara Jean said.

Chapter One Hundred Twelve
Austin Airport
Private Aviation Terminal

I had a debate with myself last night. Should I bring my passport? Since I was going to a foreign country, I decided to bring it.

I took an Uber to the airport and walked in the private aviation terminal around 7:45. There were counters for private air services, but I wasn't going on any of those. I looked around. There were a few Asian people, but nobody with a military style hat with a red star pinned on the front. I figured my contact would find me. If they couldn't that would be okay too, I'd just go home and tell Wishbone I had done my best.

A well-dressed tall white guy with a tan and slicked backed hair came up to me with a big smile on his face. "JR, is that you? You old dog!" He shook hands with me and slapped me on the back.

"Do I know you?" I asked.

He kept up the handshake and pulled me closer to him with his other hand on my back. In a threatening voice, he said, "I'm Alan MacKenzie. I'll be escorting you on the first part of your trip. Follow me."

As we walked out of the building toward a sleek jet, painted brilliant white with no markings except for numbers on the tail, MacKenzie said to me, "No luggage?"

"No, just my passport," I said. "And phone."

"You won't be needing those."

"Where are we flying to?" I asked.

"You know," MacKenzie said.

"I mean, are we flying straight there?" I asked.

"No. This plane doesn't have that kind of range."

"So where are we stopping?" I asked.

"It doesn't matter. You're not flying the plane. Just sit in your seat and shut up," MacKenzie said.

"Oh. Fly the Friendly Skies, huh? Is MacKenzie your real name?" He sounded like he might be Canadian.

269

"You can start the shutting up part right now," he said. I decided he must be American. Canadians are generally nicer.

We walked out of the terminal across the tarmac and got on the 12-seat jet. It was the luxury model. Big wide leather seats and a personal video screen for each. MacKenzie motioned for me to sit in the front row, so I did. He sat toward the back. I could hear muffled voices of pilots talking pilot talk, presumably to the tower, but their door was closed so I never saw them. I buckled up. With no fanfare or announcement, the plane took off.

The flight was smooth. Man, I could get used to this. There were headphones in a plastic bag in a pouch of my seat. I took them out of the bag and plugged in. This activated the screen, which displayed letters in English and some other languages. It read: Video Entertainment System.

The easy-to-use touch screen device displayed my choices: Movies, Sports, News. There were also selections for Google and YouTube. For laughs I chose News, thinking it would be a choice between a May Day Parade complete with nuclear capable missiles, and a three-hour speech by the Beloved Chairman, but instead it had, Fox News, BBC America, and CNBC. That was too standard, so I searched the movie section.

Wow, I liked this airline. Who picked out the movies? There were hundreds of classic films, and I selected *Dr. Strangelove.* You know, Slim Pickens riding the atomic bomb down to start the Doomsday machine, the annihilation of the human race? What could be more appropriate for what might prove to be the final movie I ever saw?

I looked out the window once in a while to try to see what route we were flying, but I've never been very good at that. The terrain was the dry American west. Maybe the plane was heading north.

I've seen *Dr. Strangelove* a dozen times, but I'm the sort who can watch the same movie again and again. It was still fun. MacKenzie startled me when he appeared at my elbow. He gestured for me to lower my tray. After I did so he left for a minute, returning with a package of three Oreo cookies and a container of milk.

"What, no Animal Crackers?" I said.

"Just eat the cookies."

270

More out of boredom than hunger I ate the Oreos and washed them down with the milk. I like milk to be very cold, and this was too warm. It tasted funny. I got sleepy. Very sleepy.

Chapter One Hundred Thirteen
Somewhere in the air

I woke up and my mouth was dry. The sky was dark. I looked around, but didn't see anybody, so I took off my seatbelt and stood up.

A man emerged from the galley at the back of the plane. I had a hard time focusing. He was Asian, medium height and trim, dressed in a crisp military uniform. He walked toward me.

"Alan?" I said, "you've changed."

"Shut up," the man said, "and sit down in your seat."

"Well, you have the same dynamic personality," I said, as I sat down.

The man approached. "I am Colonel Li. I will be accompanying you on your final leg of the trip to Pyongyang."

Colonel Li was a handsome man with sharp features. He looked like he wouldn't have a hard time ordering an execution or carrying out an execution himself.

I was groggy. "Hey, those must have been some Oreos," I said. "How long was I asleep?"

"You slept for about nine hours. The milk was laced with a sedative. You didn't miss anything."

"I missed the end of the movie."

"You can watch it again," Colonel Li said, then he moved to the rear of the plane and sat.

I wasn't in the mood to watch *Dr. Strangelove* again, so I watched *Day of the Jackal*. I had forgotten the scene toward the beginning of the film where the French security service tortures the suspected terrorist, and before he can spill the beans has a heart attack and croaks. I hoped this was not an omen.

I didn't know when the flight was going to end. Part of me wanted the flight to end soon, just like you feel on any long flight. There's got to be some part of the normal human brain that craves being released from a speeding aluminum tube. But another part of me wanted the flight to go on forever, because I had some sense of what was waiting for me in North Korea. Should I ask for more milk and cookies?

The Day of the Jackal was two and a half hours long. I don't want to spoil it, but DeGaulle lives in the end. The movie concluded and the plane seemed to be steady, with no

272

movements or sounds that indicated slowing down or preparing for landing. I figured that not telling me how much longer the flight would take was part of the drill, a ploy to make me anxious. So, I decided not to be anxious, and queued up another classic: *Blazing Saddles.* I could identify with my favorite character in the movie, the Waco Kid, having recently been to that fine city. But *this* Waco Kid was on a flight to Pyongyang. To have the shit kicked out of him and ultimately meet with the Beloved Chairman. Nothing to be anxious about. Maybe I'd get lucky, and the plane would crash.

Chapter One Hundred Fourteen
Fort Meade, MD
Cyber Command

Admiral Stockbridge's secretary buzzed him on the intercom. "Sir, the Chairman of the Joint Chiefs is on the line."

"Stockbridge, sir," the Admiral said.

"Stockbridge, what the hell are you doing? You were supposed to give me a Situation Report ten minutes ago! The President's waiting. I have to call you?" The Chairman said.

"Sir, we are efforting to---"

"Don't give me that horseshit! What's the situation?" the Chairman said.

"General, we are of the opinion that the companies facing the ransomware shutdowns have no choice but to pay the ransoms. The companies that have implemented enhanced security procedures are not threatened, in our opinion," Stockbridge said.

"You expect me to tell the President that the U.S. intelligence community can do nothing? That we should recommend the companies currently shutdown due to ransomware to just pay the ransoms?" the Chief asked.

"Yes sir," Stockbridge said.

"Stockbridge, it has come to my attention that Cyber Command had a program of reaching out to companies that had not yet complied with Cyber Command's security upgrade instructions, and that you curtailed that program as soon as you took over. Is that true?" The Chief asked.

"Sir, I wouldn't say curtailed. When I came in, I suspended all non-vital programs pending review---"

"---And this was one of the programs you suspended? Notifying companies of how to protect themselves from ransomware?" the Chief asked. "How is that non-vital?"

Stockbridge replied, "Sir, I know that looks bad now, but—"

"---Stockbridge, don't waste your breath. You do realize that I can fire you, that the Secretary of Defense can fire you, that the President can order me to fire you, that the President can directly fire you himself? You're safe for now because I'm sure there will be no personnel changes during this crisis. But

274

afterwards, your seat is going to be very hot. Do you understand me?" the Chief asked.

"Yes sir, "Stockbridge said.

"And never make me wait for a call from you again!" the Chief said. "Or I won't wait for the President to tell me to fire you."

Chapter One Hundred Fifteen
The Pentagon

The Chairman put the phone down. A man who had been listening on another line put his phone down.

"Well, Goldstein, how did I do?" The Chairman asked.

"Great sir," General Goldstein answered.

"That idiot Stockbridge never asked me how I knew that Cyber Command had discontinued the program regarding contacting the companies on procedures to upgrade their anti-ransomware systems," the Chief said.

"Stockbridge is in so far over his head that he doesn't even know what questions to ask,' General Goldstein said.

"I don't want to know any more about what's going on?" the Chairman said.

"That's right, sir," Goldstein said.

Chapter One Hundred Sixteen
Somewhere in the air

Now the plane made the unmistakable sounds of preparing to land, and my ears were popping from changes in pressure. I always hold my nose and blow out at this point. The Video Entertainment System shut off *Blazing Saddles* just as Lili von Shtupp was doing her big musical number. The screen displayed: Fasten Seatbelts.

The landing was smooth, and the video displayed the same lame stuff as a commercial flight: keep your seatbelt fastened until we come to a complete stop. Colonel Li ignored this, he walked up the aisle and stood next to me while the plane was taxiing. He looked at me but said nothing.

"Are you checking to see if my seatbelt is still fastened?" I asked.

"Shut up," he said.

I decided to shut up.

The plane taxied for a few minutes, then stopped. Colonel Li hit a switch near the door which was in front of me on the left side of the plane. The hatch opened and a set of stairs automatically slid out from under the door. Two soldiers came up the stairs and entered. They were carrying rifles, which was awkward in the limited space.

I don't understand one word of Korean and don't know what the insignia on a North Korean soldier's uniform mean, but even I could tell that these were two enlisted men, and that they were terrified of Colonel Li. He barked some orders at them. They stiffened and said the equivalent of "Yes sir!" Some things don't require translation.

"Go with these men," Colonel Li said to me.

"But I haven't finished the movie."

"Disco Duck," Colonel Li said to the soldiers. That may not be exactly correct, but it sounded like that.

"Disco Duck" apparently meant for one of the soldiers to hit me in the ribs with the butt of his rifle. It knocked the wind out of me, and I got into the aisle. One soldier led the way, the other walked behind me, poking me with the muzzle of the rifle.

277

"I hope you have the safety on," I said to the soldier who was poking me, "that's how accidents happen."

Colonel Li barked another order. The soldiers stopped. Colonel Li walked up to me. "I advise you to shut up."

"You've mentioned that," I said.

Chapter One Hundred Seventeen
Pyongyang Airport

We had walked down the steps and were standing on the tarmac, maybe 100 yards from the closest part of the terminal. Colonel Li gave another order.

"My job is done; I am handing you over to our Internal Security Division. Goodbye, Mr. Johnson," Colonel Li said.

"That sounds so final. Let's go with: Until we meet again."

"Ha!" Colonel Li said. He walked toward the terminal.

I looked around, trying to get my bearings. The place looked like any airline terminal in the world, except it couldn't be New York, because in New York there would be papers blowing around. Pyongyang airport was perfectly clean. Littering laws must be strictly enforced in North Korea. The soldiers stood ramrod straight and quiet. I just stood.

In a moment a white Mercedes limousine pulled up to us. One of the soldiers opened the rear driver's side door and motioned for me to get in. I did so. The soldier closed the door. The two enlisted men stood at attention on the tarmac as the car sped off.

I thought that it had been unnecessary to have a couple of armed soldiers escort me to the car. Colonel Li wore a sidearm, he could have shot me if I misbehaved. I concluded that the whole thing was an attempt to intimidate me. The funny thing is: it was working.

In addition to the driver there was a man in the front seat. He wore what I thought of as a Chairman Mao outfit, a khaki suit with rounded stand-up collar and no insignia. He showed no emotion. I amused myself by giving him the private nickname "Chuckles."

"Just sit there and do not try anything stupid," he said.

"What do you expect me to do? Jump out and try to swim to Hawaii?"

Chuckles snorted.

"By the way, where did you learn to speak English? Did you go to school in Australia?"

"Do not feel as though it is necessary to talk," he said.

279

"Ever?" I asked.

No comment from Chuckles. The driver could have been a robot.

I analyzed Chuckles' statement. Although it was more polite than telling me to shut up, somehow it was much more ominous.

The car went fast. There was almost no traffic on a limited access highway toward what I assumed was the city of Pyongyang. As we approached the city, whatever traffic there was got out of our way.

Pyongyang must be a model city, all of North Korea couldn't look like this. It was beyond clean, I would say sterile, and there were almost no pedestrians. There were definitely no 14-year-old boys riding skateboards down metal handrails. In the center of the city the buildings were modern, stark. As individual buildings they were okay, but taken in total, well, I'm no architectural critic, but I would call the effect of the whole picture: Totalitarian Brutalism.

The car exited the limited access highway and headed down a wide boulevard. In a few minutes we stopped in front of a tall building. It had a façade of black stone, maybe marble, with black glass windows.

A couple of armed soldiers came up to the car. One opened the front door for Chuckles, the other opened the door for me.

"We are going in the building," he said.

"Is this like the Hotel California? You can check out anytime you like, but you can never leave?" I asked.

Chapter One Hundred Eighteen
Pyongyang, North Korea

The lobby of the building was plain but clean. There was no receptionist's desk, no directory, no sign with changeable plastic letters saying: Welcome JR Johnson. The floor was black and polished. At the far end of the room was a double door of black glass, and above the doors was an impressive sign, gold Korean characters carved into the black marble. A guard stood on either side of the doors. The guards were tall, perfectly dressed, motionless, and looked like they might be models for a propaganda poster of the Ideal Communist Man.

"What does the sign say?" I asked.

"Jinri Sayeok," Chuckles answered.

"My Korean is a little rusty," I said.

"Ministry of Truth," Chuckles translated.

I laughed. "You're kidding, right?"

Chuckles halted in his tracks, so I stopped too. He looked at me.

"This is not a place we come to tell jokes, Mr. Johnson, Only the truth is spoken in this building. And we will make certain that you tell the truth, as well."

Chuckles opened the right door and held it open for me. The polished marble décor extended into this section. There was a bank of elevators on the right. He hit a button, the elevator dinged, just like everywhere else in the world, and we got in. He hit a button for a floor. The door closed and the elevator gave the unmistakable sinking sensation of going down.

Chapter One Hundred Nineteen
Pyongyang, North Korea
The Ministry of Truth

W e're not going to the penthouse?" I said.
"What?" Chuckles asked.

"We're going to the basement. Is that to make it more convenient? The same floor as the morgue?" I said.

"There is no morgue in this building, Mr. Johnson. In the rare event of a mortality, it is not necessary to do a postmortem. We would know the cause of death," Chuckles said.

"Cuts down on the paperwork, eh?" I said.

No comment from Chuckles. The elevator came to a clunking stop. The door opened and we got out. The basement hallway was dingy, lit only by bare bulbs spaced far apart. The floor was bare concrete and sticky. In contrast to the main floor, the décor here was what I would classify as Early Dungeon.

"I see your interior decorator hasn't made it down to this floor," I said.

Chuckles said nothing.

There was a welcoming committee of three waiting for us. An officer dressed in the same uniform as Colonel Li and two goons. The officer was short, bald, and had a pockmarked face. The goons looked like goons. I thought that goons of any race, creed, or color all looked the same. Maybe there was an organization: *International Brotherhood of Goons*. They could have conventions in Las Vegas. I imagined the big electronic display: *Welcome International Goons! Free Buffet!*

My reverie was interrupted when the colonel gestured with his head, and we started walking down the corridor. One of the goons pushed me. He was a strong pusher and shoved so hard that I almost fell on my face before recovering my balance.

"Watch your step, Mr. Johnson," Chuckles said.

We came to an unmarked door. One of the goons opened it, and the other goon shoved me in.

The room was lit by a single bare bulb and had concrete walls. It smelled like shit, piss, puke, blood, and fear.

282

"You guys should really do something about the ventilation system. OSHA would never approve of you having to work in an environment like this," I said.

The goons tore my shirt off.

"Hey, I just got that from Brooks Brothers," I said.

It was a light blue long-sleeved button-down shirt. The goons couldn't get the shirt over my hands, the cuffs were buttoned. They tugged harder but couldn't get the shirt completely off.

"Please allow me," I said. Chuckles said something to them in Korean. They let go of me and I unbuttoned the cuffs and took the shirt off. I tossed it to one of the goons. He threw it on the floor.

Take that, you imperialist shirt!

There was a table in the room with chains, leather straps, other paraphernalia. One of the walls had two metal rings hung at about the eight-foot level. A goon shoved me against that wall. I stood still.

A goon held each arm in turn while the other snapped a leather cuff on my wrists. Then they attached a chain to each cuff and threaded the chains through corresponding rings on the wall. The goons pulled tight enough that I had to get on my tiptoes. They pulled more, so my feet were just off the floor. Then the goons secured the chains on hooks.

"I saw a room like this in a movie I ran across on cable," I said. "Except there was this blonde in chains with a tight leather outfit and a whip. Not that I usually watch that sort of thing, I just stumbled across the movie channel surfing---"

My witty repartee was interrupted by Goon Number One punching me in the gut. My stomach spasmed, I puked up my undigested Oreos, and he didn't get out of the way fast enough, so the puke got all over his shirt.

"What is this, your first day on the job?" I asked. Some of the puke slid down my chin.

One of the biggest problems with being tortured is you don't know when it's going to be over. Another problem is you don't know if they're going to kill you, either on purpose, or unintentionally. A third factor is: they keep asking you the same stupid questions, over and over.

Then there's the getting hit part. That's not fun either. When they hit me in the face, I assumed they could have punched

283

harder, but shots in the ribs and stomach seemed full force. Just to mix things up and keep me mentally off balance there was the occasional kick in the balls. North Koreans, with their training in the martial arts, are very strong kickers.

One unanticipated bad part: when it seemed like I was losing consciousness they'd throw a bucket of freezing water on me. At first it was refreshing, but after several dousings it made me cold, and I started to shiver. I was shivering so violently that I was shaking the chains and causing the metal rings that held the chains to clang against the cold concrete wall.

All in all, I was not enjoying my trip to Pyongyang so far. The single thing that kept me going: Wishbone, Toni Anne, and the President knew this would happen, and they sent me anyhow. If I got through all this and didn't get my money, I resolved that I would kill them. All of them. I did my best to focus on this thought.

It was tough to tell if Chuckles outranked the officer. Only the officer gave orders to the goons. Chuckles and the officer alternated asking questions, but there was no rhythm to the process. Sometimes they'd ask rapid fire questions, sometimes a single question, other times nothing. The goons did not speak or express any emotion.

The most frequent question: Mr. Johnson, Are you going to tell the truth to the Beloved Chairman?

Being tortured makes it hard to keep track of time. After some period, the officer gave an order to the goons, and all four North Koreans left the room and shut the door. They were gone for what seemed like a long time. I knew this was calculated to increase the terror factor but focused on how I would get my revenge if necessary. My rational mind knew they would be back, but there was an ever-increasing kernel of fear that they would just leave me there until I starved or bled to death.

Chapter One Hundred Twenty
The White House

A CEO of one of the big banks had called the White House, demanding to speak to the President. Chan Wheeler and the President were alone in the Oval Office.

An aide came in and explained who was on the line.

"Thank you, we'll take it from here," the President said. The aide knew that meant he was dismissed.

"You take care of this moron," the President said to Wheeler.

"This is Chan Wheeler," he said as he picked up the phone.

"I demand to speak to the President," the CEO said.

"Noted. You can speak to me," Wheeler said.

"I said I want to speak to the President," the CEO said.

"That's not going to happen. You can either speak to me, or speak to no one," Wheeler said.

"Well, what is this horseshit about us having to pay the ransom? With all the taxes we pay---"

"Excuse me, but wasn't your company contacted twice by Cyber Command regarding how to upgrade your firewall?" Wheeler asked.

"Yes, but—"

"But what? You chose to ignore the warnings?" Wheeler asked.

"We were studying the implementation," the CEO said.

"The government is not going to be your fairy godmother this time and bail you out," Wheeler said. "You're screwed. Even the best people can't fix this problem. Pay up."

"That's outrageous! I'll go public with this conversation," the CEO said.

"Go ahead. We'll make sure that the public knows that you were given more than adequate time to make the changes, but chose not to, unlike all your major competitors. You'll have lots of time to work on your golf game soon…which I hear is shitty, by the way," Wheeler said.

"Up yours, Wheeler," the CEO said.

"I'll give the President your regards," Wheeler said, then he hung up.

285

Before they could discuss the phone call, the President's special phone rang. Wheeler looked at the caller ID. "You're very popular, Mr. President, it's Toni Anne Laudano,"

"I'll take that one," the President said.

Toni Anne told the President that she needed to have an urgent meeting. The President explained that he and Wheeler could be there. He'd have to check with General Goldstein, but Wishbone was in New York.

"That's ok. Wishbone doesn't need to be there. You can tell him later. It's up to you," Toni Anne said.

"Toni Anne, *everything* is up to me," the President said. "This isn't something you can tell me on this secure line?"

"I'd feel much more comfortable discussing this in person, Mr. President. You'll understand when I get there," Toni Anne said.

The President, Wheeler, and General Goldstein were waiting in the room off the Oval Office when Toni Anne was escorted in.

The President smiled. "So, Tony Anne what's so secret and important that you had to tell us in person?"

"It's the money," Toni Anne said, "it's way too much."

Chapter One Hundred Twenty One
Pyongyang, North Korea
Basement of the Ministry of Truth

I had lost track. How many rounds of beatings had I been through? Between rounds my four commie friends left the room, only to return to more beatings accompanied by the same questions. There was no more temptation to make any wisecracks. I would have confessed to anything to get out of that room, but they weren't asking me to confess.

Any pretense to being a tough guy was long gone. The worst pain did not emanate from the places on my body that had been hit, the worst part was the constant pain in my shoulders, as a result of being hung from chains for hours. There were times when I screamed from the pain.

Did you ever hear yourself scream? It's doesn't seem real, but the pain makes it so.

It was beyond anything I had ever experienced, or even imagined. People say you can get used to anything, that it's mind over matter. There are people who say that torture doesn't work. Those things are not true, the people who say them have not been hung from chains in the Ministry of Truth, wondering if this will go on until they're dead.

During the current round of beatings only Chuckles spoke, and he asked the same question, over and over: Are you going to tell the truth to the Beloved Chairman?

"Yes," I mumbled.

"I can't hear you, Mr. Johnson," Chuckles said.

"YES," I yelled as loud as I could muster. It wasn't that loud.

Chuckles said, "Very well." He nodded to the colonel, who gave an order to the two goons.

Each one went to a chain on the wall and undid it, so my feet hit the floor. I couldn't lower my arms normally but could get my hands down to about level with my shoulders. The pain was less acute. The goons undid the chains.

Was I done? Were they going to let me go?

Then one goon grabbed me from the back and lowered me to the floor, face up. I was a couple feet from the wall. He leaned over and loosened the cuffs on my wrists. The sensation was overwhelming, I didn't realize how much my wrists had hurt.

287

Goon One tossed the cuffs to Goon Two, who was standing by my feet. Goon Two put the cuffs on my ankles and attached the chains. Goon One shoved me, sliding me feet first on the slimy floor over to the concrete wall, and each one hauled away. When this was accomplished, I was once again suspended, this time upside down. The blood rushed to my head. I passed out.

Chapter One Hundred Twenty Two
The White House

You can never have too much money, Toni Anne," Wheeler said, "what do you mean?"

"Remember when we calculated that the sum of the ransoms would be about $50 billion? When the North Koreans got their 50%, and after JR Johnson got his bonus, there would be about $25 billion to divert to the phony PACs that would contribute to your campaign?" Toni Anne asked.

"Sure," the President said. "Even $25 billion is too high. There are do-gooder journalists out there looking for dark money. We might have a hard time hiding that much dough. Don't forget we're going to get some legitimate contributions from real PACs and loyal citizens who want to buy some influence. So, what's the problem?"

"Remember Sheldon, my temporary replacement at Cyber Command?" Toni Anne asked.

"Yup," the President said.

"He's found a low-tech method for staying in communications with me. It involves trash cans. I won't bore you with the details."

"And?" the President said.

"He's been keeping track of the ransom demands, and how much the companies are going to pay. The commies are getting very greedy this time," Toni Anne said.

"How much"" the President asked.

"Around three hundred and thirty billion dollars. Some in Crypto, some in U.S. dollars," Toni Anne said.

The President whistled. "How are we going to hide that much money?"

"Isn't that a good problem to have?" Wheeler asked.

The room was quiet for a couple minutes while the attendees considered the situation. Finally General Goldstein spoke.

"As a refresher, remember that the North Koreans get their hands, electronically, on the money. Then they give us our half. There's no way we can screw them out of their half," Goldstein said.

289

"That's ok, they'll be happy. And we know they'll give us our share, we have too many secrets we could divulge hanging over them," the President said. "But how are we going to hide our money? We can't spend $165 billion on my re-election campaign. And I'm not directing funds to any congressional campaigns. They could never keep their mouths shut."

Wheeler got out his cellphone and used the calculator function. "I don't know, that much money for your campaign might be great. We could directly bribe every voter, give each one 2,000 bucks!" Wheeler said.

"Ha!" the President said, "that might be a little obvious, Chan."

"So how much do you want to go to the PACs, Mr. President?" Toni Anne said.

"Not more than $15 billion. Any more than that and we risk getting caught. As it is, we're pushing the envelope," the President said.

"I have an idea, Mr. President," Toni Anne said.

Chapter One Hundred Twenty Three
Pyongyang, North Korea
Ministry of Truth

When you're hanging upside down after being beaten in the face and the blood rushes to your head, the specific areas that have been hit throb. So many areas had been hit that my whole face, and most of my head throbbed. Each pulse of my heart sent regular increases of pain. It felt like my head might explode.

I came to this realization slowly as I became conscious. I had been doused with another bucket of freezing water. After a moment I jolted, having inhaled the ammonia capsule being held just about in my nostrils by one of the goons. The jolting made me hit the back of my head on the concrete, which served to heighten my consciousness. It's difficult to get a perspective on things when your hanging upside down.

I was so miserable and hopeless that if they shot me, I wouldn't have minded. Even upside down and delirious I could tell it was the same four commie buddies in the room. The two goons were standing by me at the wall, and Chuckles and the unnamed colonel were by the doorway speaking to each other in soft voices.

The colonel gave an order to the goons. They left the room and returned with two plain metal chairs, which they arranged in the middle of the room, facing each other.

The colonel gave another order, and the goons released the chains and lowered me to the floor. I wasn't about to hope for anything.

As I laid on my back on the cold slimy floor, I spoke to Chuckles, but my voice was weak. "What are you going to do now? Strap up one ankle and one wrist and hang me sideways?"

"That's an interesting suggestion. We can go on for much longer. It sounds like you've given up hope, Mr. Johnson. Is that so?" Chuckles asked.

"Yeah, I guess," I mumbled.

"That's good," Chuckles said.

Chuckles nodded to the colonel who said something to the goons. The goons took the cuffs off my ankles.

291

Chuckles said, "Mr. Johnson, you can get up and sit in this chair." He pointed to one of the metal chairs.

Easier said than done. I couldn't get up, didn't have the energy or balance. It felt good to lay on the cold, slimy, filthy floor.

The colonel spoke to the goons again. They picked me up and placed me on the chair.

It was touching how gentle the goons were. Especially in comparison to kicking me in the balls a thousand times when I was defenseless, hanging against the wall.

I couldn't sit up straight. The room was spinning, so I put my head between my legs.

"Take a few moments to compose yourself," Chuckles said.

I was still shivering, half naked, and I could feel blood running down my face. Still, I felt pretty good. It was a lot better than being chained upside down against a concrete wall.

The old Henny Youngman joke came to me: How's your wife? Compared to what?

Chuckles had gone out of the room and returned with something in his hand. It was a can of Coca Cola. "Here, Mr. Johnson, drink some of this, you'll feel better."

He handed me the can, but I didn't have the strength to open the top. Chuckles opened it for me. I took a sip. When I put the can to my lips, I could feel how swollen they were.

Just one sip was a magic energy boost. "This is great, but you don't have any Dr. Pepper?" I mumbled.

"I'm afraid all we have is Coca Cola, Mr. Johnson." It was a new voice, coming from the doorway.

I looked over. It was The Beloved Chairman. His hair was perfect, considering his hairstyle choice. He wore the same Mao style suit as Chuckles, but it was perfectly tailored and the cloth was very fine, maybe silk.

"That's a very nice suit," I said.

"Thank you," the Beloved Chairman said. He walked into the room and sat in the other metal chair facing me.

The colonel said something to the goons, who hurried out of the room with their heads bowed, careful not to make eye contact with the Beloved Chairman.

I took another sip of the Coke. I wondered if it had poison or some drug in it. Then I thought: *if you can't trust the Coca Cola Company, who can you trust?*

"You probably are wondering why we put you through this ordeal," the Beloved Chairman said.

"Yes," I said.

The Beloved Chairman said something to Chuckles. Both Chuckles and the Colonel left the room. They closed the door, almost, leaving it just a crack open. It was just me and the Beloved Chairman, about to have a friendly chat.

"They are standing right outside the door, afraid that you might try to assassinate me. You're not going to assassinate me, are you Mr. Johnson?" he asked me.

"No," I said. "I don't have the strength to assassinate this soda can right now," I said.

"Good. I feel safe," he said. "Now let me explain the situation to you."

Chapter One Hundred Twenty Four
Pyongyang, North Korea
Basement of the Ministry of Truth

One moment I had been laying on the cold concrete floor, having resigned myself to being beaten to death in a dark hopeless place. Wishbone had told me that some of the people sent to North Korea were never accounted for, and I thought I would be one of them. Barbara Jean would never know what happened to me. Maybe my mutilated body parts would be fed to the dogs of the Beloved Chairman.

I was in pain, but the terror was over, at least for now. I resolved to do anything that would prevent the torture from starting again.

*That **was** worse than a rainy weekend in the Hamptons trapped indoors with a houseful of junk bond traders. Not that I want to do that again, either.*

Now I was sitting in a chair, drinking a Coca Cola, face-to-face with this Communist. Despite his bizarre hair styling he seemed rational, smart, someone used to handling people. It reminded me of my experience meeting my very own President.

"Do you have any dogs?" I asked.

"Yes, I do," the Beloved Chairman said. "I am particularly fond of German Shepherds. Why do you ask?"

"Idle curiosity," I said.

"Let's get the important part over," he said. "Tell me the message from your President." He got out a small notebook and a pen.

"A sheep in sheep's clothing…" I started. The rest of it went on like that. The whole message wasn't that long, and the sing song rhyming structure made it easy to remember. It seemed like nonsense, except the Beloved Chairman wrote down every word.

"Are you sure that these are the exact words? You've been through a lot in the last day," he said.

"Yes, I memorized it," I said. "I would have told you without the torture. Was that necessary?"

"I promised you an explanation. Our two governments have a working understanding. I wanted to make sure that you gave me the exact message." he said.

294

That didn't make sense to me. I thought back to my meeting with the President when he explained that the North Koreans just seem to enjoy torturing people. This was above my head. Maybe this whole thing is some game the two countries play.

"I insist that these sorts of messages are delivered in person, not electronically. No one can digitally intercept a spoken message delivered in the basement of the Ministry of Truth," he said. "Makes sense?"

"Yes." *If you're batshit crazy.*

Did your President explain the meaning of this message?" he asked.

"No."

"This message is a code. It gives us the exact routing information for a large sum of money that is going to be paid in ransom by U.S. companies to the ransomware pirates, who are controlled by the Russian government. At the right moment, we will intercept it. Steal it. Then we keep half the money and send the other half to your government. Well, not exactly to your government, to phony entities that get routed as your President directs. What happens to that money is none of our business," he said.

At least that part made sense to me. I nodded.

"What happens to the money *we* get is none of *your* business," the Beloved Chairman said.

I shrugged, which caused an electric pain to shoot through my shoulders. It made me hold back on any witticisms I had in mind. I wasn't going to say anything that would make me get chained up to that wall again.

"To make sure that the code you gave me is valid, we will be keeping you here until we have the money. It should be soon, certainly within 24 hours," he said.

I panicked. The Beloved Chairman read the look of terror.

He smiled. "Oh, Mr. Johnson, I don't mean here in the Ministry of Truth. You will be taken to a private hotel. Very nice, unlimited room service, courtesy of the Democratic People's Republic of Korea."

"I was that obvious?" I said.

"You've been through a lot, Mr. Johnson. But…" He let the sentence hang.

295

"But what?" I asked.

"If you lied to me, you will be brought back here, to the Ministry of Truth. It's a very unpleasant way to go. With that in mind, are you certain there isn't anything else you'd like to tell me? Perhaps you misspoke about one of the codes?" he said.

Holy shit! What if I forgot something, or said something wrong? What if the President intentionally set me up, by telling me the wrong codes to trick the North Koreans?

"Sir, to the best of my knowledge I have told you verbatim what I was instructed to tell you," I said.

"I like you, Mr. Johnson. Each letter of the words you gave me is translated into binary code, ones and zeroes. Do you understand binary?"

"I knew it for the test in college. Got a B plus," I said.

"This better be an *A plus* effort, Mr. Johnson. The letter 'A' is 1 in binary. 'J' is 1010, it goes on from there up to 110010 for the letter 'Z'. So even this short message you gave me generates a long string of zeroes and ones. I hope the codes work. Just so you know, there is no margin of error," he said.

"Meaning?" I asked.

"Meaning, if for any reason the codes don't work, if they are one digit off, you will be brought back here and tortured to death. No excuses accepted." He smiled. "I am confident everything will work out."

"Me too," I lied.

"A word of advice. Try not to be too shocked when you look at your face in the mirror. Our experience shows that your appearance should return to near normal in a few months," he said.

"Oh," I said. I hadn't thought about that. The Ministry of Truth wasn't big on mirrors.

A few months! On the other hand, I might not be alive in a few hours. Dogmeat for the German Shepherds.

"The hotel has worldwide satellite television. Do you like to watch basketball?" the Beloved Chairman asked. "Are you a fan of Dennis Rodman?"

"Sure," I said.

Yeah, among washed up basketball players with purple hair and nipple rings, Dennis Rodman's my favorite.

"My uncle and I love to watch American basketball. The best players in the world," he said.

296

"Don't you have more than one uncle?" I asked.
The Beloved Chairman smiled "Not anymore."

Chapter One Hundred Twenty Five
The White House

The Morning Briefing was just breaking up. Many earnest people who had gotten up at 4 a.m. to practice just what they would say had briefed the President on the current state of the world, including the ransomware situation. The President listened. He knew some things they didn't know, that most of them would never know.

The Secretary of Defense spoke. "Mr. President, may I make a comment?"

"Sure."

"Sir, it's remarkable how calm you are in this moment of crisis. It reminds me of a quote by Kipling---"

The President interrupted---Mr. Secretary, in the interest of time, could we hold off on the Kipling quote? You can save it. How about for my eulogy?"

Everyone laughed, except the Defense Secretary, who forced a smile. It was evident the meeting was over, people filed out of the Oval Office.

"Chan, stay here a minute, will you?" the President said.

When it was just the two of them, Chan said, "That little ass kisser really wants to still be Secretary of Defense during your second term, doesn't he?"

"It would help if he knew an F-22 from an F-35," the President said.

The two stood there in silence for a minute. Chan and the President were friends of over 40 years. They had been roommates at Stanford freshman year, and Wheeler had fixed his friend up with a date when he couldn't get one for some fraternity function. Still, as soon as he was elected, Chan had called him only 'Mr. President.' The President had never once suggested that Wheeler call him by his first name, even in private.

The President asked, "Have you given any thought to Toni Anne's proposal regarding what to do with all that extra money?"

"Have you considered that we both open offshore accounts and deposit the money there?" Chan said.

298

"I have. You know why we can't do that?" the President said.

"Why? We wouldn't get caught," Wheeler said.

"You know who would catch us? The North Koreans! We can't have that hanging over our heads. Can you imagine the leverage the Beloved Chairman would use on us if he knew we personally stole the money?" the President said.

"It might be hard to explain, say $75 billion dollars in each of our offshore accounts to the American people," Wheeler said.

The President said, "Chan, don't assume that we'd split the money evenly."

"It was hypothetical," Wheeler said.

"Besides we each have enough money, and after I leave the White House, I'll get paid seven figures per speech, and you can get a job pimping for Goldman Sachs for ten million a year. We'll be okay. Maybe I'll even co-write a book with James Patterson," the President said.

"Don't write the book, that's a worse crime than stealing the $75 billion," Wheeler said.

They laughed. "No, I think we should go along with Toni Anne's idea, fund her proposed project. The North Koreans will love that, and we'll be doing something great for the country…without all that pesky congressional oversight," the President said.

"Still, $75 billion in an offshore account has a nice ring to it," Wheeler said.

Chapter One Hundred Twenty Six
The Pentagon

General Goldstein met in his office with Gabrielle.
"Do you like being back in the operational side, Gabrielle?" Goldstein asked.

"Yes sir, it's where I belong." Lt. Colonel Gabrielle McHugh said. "I'm leaving for Poland as soon as we're done here."

"You have your plan all set?" the General asked.

"We have as few moving parts as necessary. I'm going in, but the other three guys going with me are private contractors. They don't have to know all the reasons I'm there. These guys are all ex-Asymetric Warfare Group," McHugh said, "they know not to ask too many questions."

Goldstein said, "Asymetric, we're they here?...refresh my memory---"

"Sir, the Asymetric Warfare Group was a very baddass elite force, headquartered out of Fort Meade. It got disbanded four years ago. These three guys thought the Army was going soft, so they quit to become private contractors. They're not people who would function well in normal life, but---"

"But all our warriors can't be Sheldon, sitting behind a computer terminal," Goldstein said.

"Yeah, you can't program people to death. The unfortunate reality of the world is, as Toni Anne says, you have to blow peoples fuckin' brains out once in a while," Gabrielle said.

"Toni Anne. She should write a self-help book." Goldstein said.

They laughed. "It would be a best seller," Gab said.

"Can I ask you a serious question, Colonel?" Goldstein said.
"Sure,"

"Does the morality of this sort of thing bother you?" he asked.

"No," Gabrielle said.

"That's your entire answer?" Goldstein asked.

"Should I have said: No, *sir*?"

"Well alright. On another subject, can this guy you picked really steal and fly the new Russian Stealth helicopter?" Goldstein asked.

300

"Can he do it? He's a native Russian born speaker. An expert pilot. He can't wait!" Gabrielle answered.

"Okay. Say, what weapon have you decided on?" Goldstein asked.

"There are several good choices, but I went with the HK 416," Gab answered.

"Why that one," Goldstein asked.

"Two reasons: it's manufactured in Germany, so it gives us at least a horseshit alibi, like 'who us?' A lot of countries use this weapon, it could have been the Czechs, the Georgians, the South Koreans, the Dutch…even the Russians have been known to use it. Everybody will know we did it, but---"

"What's the second reason?" Goldstein said.

"Sentimental reasons. It's the gun we used to kill Osama Bin Laden," Gab said.

Chapter One Hundred Twenty Seven
Fort Meade, MD
Cyber Command

Admiral Stockbridge had convened a meeting of three. He met with his one-star second in command and Sheldon. The one-star was useless, it was Sheldon's information that he wanted.

"Sheldon, what is going to happen now?" Stockbridge asked.

"The companies are going to pay. All the big ones, anyhow. A couple of the smaller guys are holding out, but they're just being stubborn, they'll end up paying," Sheldon said. "They have no realistic alternative."

"When is this going to happen?" Stockbridge said.

"Today. The deadline is 6 p.m. Eastern Time," Sheldon said.

"Do we have any way of tracking the payments?" Stockbridge asked.

"Sir, these are thousands of transactions, demanded by dozens, or hundreds of ransomware pirates," Sheldon answered.

"We're not going to track the money?" Stockbridge asked.

"We are going to track whether the victim companies have their computer systems released by the pirates," Sheldon said.

"And if not?" Stockbridge asked.

Sheldon shrugged. "What we have prepared the victim companies to do is immediately after their systems are released by the pirates to put up the new firewalls against the hackers. Immediately, like in a few seconds," Sheldon explained.

"The systems can be fixed in a few seconds?" Stockbridge asked.

"No sir, it's a three-step process. The first step takes their whole network offline, so nothing can get in, but the system doesn't work, either. Step two: in a few minutes, depending on the system, the firewall upgrades are installed. The final step puts the system back with normal function and opens up their network," Sheldon said. "The whole deal takes five, six minutes."

"Sounds simple," Admiral Stockbridge said.

"Conceptually it's simple, sir. The technology isn't simple, it was developed by some of the smartest people in the world. But it is simple to implement. If the victim companies had just

302

implemented this upgrade they would have collectively saved billions of dollars," Sheldon said.

"Do we have any idea how much money it is in total?" Stockbridge asked.

"I don't have that number, sir," Sheldon replied.

"Alright, keep me informed. Give me an hourly update, and if necessary, interrupt at any time with crucial information. That's all." Stockbridge said.

Sheldon left the Admiral's office. Once again, he had not lied, but he hadn't told all he knew, either. Stockbridge just didn't know what questions to ask.

Chapter One Hundred Twenty Eight
Bialystok, Poland
Near the Belarus border

NATO was about to hold a regularly scheduled exercise which included Polish, Dutch and American forces. The General in charge of the joint exercise force was an American.

Gabrielle had flown from Washington, DC to London, then from London direct to Bialystok on a C-17 Globemaster. The massive jet transport plane carried two Abrams M1 Tanks, and Lt. Colonel Gabrielle McHugh, in the cargo bay. The pilot of the Globemaster was told that he and none of the crew were to talk to their passenger.

When the plane landed Gabrielle McHugh reported to the American General in command. The General's Command post was set up in a group of tents well away from the city of Bialystok.

"Lt. Colonel McHugh reporting sir," Gabrielle said to the General after being escorted to his office. She saluted. Gab was wearing the standard Army Combat uniform, camouflage on a green background, with any insignia patches in black.

"Buck Goldstein is a friend of mine. He told me not to ask you any questions," the General said.

"Yes sir. I will be observing in an unconventional manner. I will not be reporting on anything to do with your command," Gabrielle said. "I am self-contained, I won't be needing any resources from you sir. I am reporting to you as a courtesy."

"General Goldstein said that I was to extend you help if you asked for it, during your...unconventional observing. I hope you won't be needing it. Good luck with...whatever it is you are doing," the General said.

"Thank you, sir," Gabrielle said. "I would like a ride into Bialystok if that's not too much of an inconvenience, sir."

"We have a truck going that way," the General said. "The sergeant out there will hook you up."

"That would be fine, thank you, sir" Gab said, and left to find the sergeant.

304

Chapter One Hundred Twenty Nine
Bialystok, Poland

Gabrielle sat in the passenger seat of a five-ton truck. The driver was a nervous private who stared straight ahead and didn't say a word during the 20-minute drive, which served Gabrielle just fine. When they reached the city center, Gab said, "drop me off right here, Private.'

"But ma'am we're just a couple klicks from---"

"Right here Private," Gab said.

"Yes, ma'am," he said.

Gab grabbed her bag, got out and stood still until the private drove off. Then she walked to the local bus station, went in the ladies' room and changed into a black sweatsuit. She produced a real German passport at the ticket counter and speaking German, bought a ticket for Minsk, Belarus.

A plausible cover story had been worked up for Gabrielle. She was traveling as a German volleyball referee, going to Minsk for an international tournament. Having gone to school for several years while her father a U.S. Army colonel was stationed in Germany, her German was excellent, certainly good enough for answering questions from a border control agent in Belarus.

The bus was dirty, the driver had food stains running down his once white shirt, and there were only a few passengers as they pulled out ten minutes late of the Bialystok bus terminal. They would drive across the Belarus frontier and stop in the first town, Grodno, where they might be questioned by border control. Then Gab would switch for the bus to Minsk. Once in Belarus she would be asked to show her passport only if she was checking into a hotel. She would not be checking into a hotel.

Chapter One Hundred Thirty
Pyongyang, North Korea

After the Beloved Chairman left my torture chamber Chuckles and the colonel reentered. Chuckles tossed me a black hoodie with a Chicago Bulls logo on the front.

"Put this on, Mr. Johnson," Chuckles said. "Put the hood up. We wouldn't want people to see your face and get the wrong impression."

The miraculous effect of drinking the Coca Cola enabled me to stand up and put on the hoodie. I was led out of the building and back into the white Mercedes limo.

These people really know how to treat a torture victim.

It was the same set up as before. Chuckles and the driver in the front seat, me in the back. The boulevards are wide in Pyongyang. But there's almost no traffic. Maybe the wide roads are for the parades when they drive the rocket launcher trucks and tanks.

I wasn't about to ask.

We drove for maybe five minutes to a modern three-story building and went down to a below ground parking lot. Chuckles got out of the limo and escorted me to an elevator. We didn't see another person as we went to the third floor, walked down a hallway, and Chuckles handed me a key.

"This is your room," he said.

My hand was shaking. I couldn't get the key in the door. Chuckles intervened and opened it, then allowed me to enter first.

It was a modern room with a king-sized bed. The décor was light wood, hardwood floors with oriental rugs. There were no mirrors.

Chuckles pointed to a door. "That's the bathroom. There's a very nice shower, and bathrobes." He pointed to a phone. "Just pick up the phone. 24-hour room service. They have Advil. I suggest you order some."

I looked around. The TV was huge. The thought occurred to me that as I would soon be watching TV, they would be watching me.

306

"I will leave you alone now," Chuckles said. "If all goes as planned, you will receive new clothing for your flight back to the United States. If not, you will be taken back to the Ministry of Truth."

"That's a big bet on a coin toss," I said.

Chuckles shrugged, turned, and left the room.

After Chuckles left, I walked into the bathroom. It had a wall of mirrors. At first, I avoided looking at myself, but then I decided to get it over. I glanced at my face.

It was bad. But it wasn't a monster looking back at me. My lips were cracked in three places, and my eyes were swollen almost completely shut. I looked like Rocky after the first fight with Apollo Creed.

"Adrienne! Adrienne!" I said in my best Rocky voice, for my own amusement, and I figured it would confuse the North Koreans who I was sure were watching and listening to me.

Maybe they would think I lost my mind, and they would take pity on me. Unlikely, I decided.

I turned on the shower and went back in the bedroom to take my clothes off. Putting the hoodie over my head aggravated the shoulder pain. I wondered how many Advil you can take. Then I took off my pants and underwear.

The goons had succeeded; they did kick the shit out of me. I also pissed my pants. There had been no bathroom breaks during the hours of torture at the Ministry of Truth, that's why the room smelled the way it did. If I was going back to the Ministry of Truth maybe they'd let me wear the bathrobe I found near the shower. It was really nice.

Advice for any potential travelers to the Ministry of Truth: Try to remember to piss before they hang you upside down.

I walked back into the bathroom and after emptying the pants pockets of my passport and phone, I deposited the pants and underwear in a wastebasket. When I looked in the mirror at my body, I was shocked. In front, from my thighs up, almost my entire body was black and blue, including my swollen genitals. Even my pecker was bruised and discolored. It looked like an eggplant. Well, not the size; the color.

The shower was not the pleasant experience I had been expecting. The water stung my face and caused my body to hurt more. I stood under the stream of water as long as I could

307

tolerate it, maybe a couple minutes, in an attempt to rinse off the layers of filth and got out.

I hadn't noticed the towels before, but they were top notch, even better than the towels at Barbara Jean's house, and she ordered hers monogrammed from Niemann Marcus. If I ran into the Beloved Chairman again maybe I could ask him where he got the towels so I could get some as a present for my wife. That was contingent on whether I was alive, got the $50 million, and still had a wife.

I'm not much of a bathrobe guy, but this one was luxurious, thick, oversized. I'd have to get one when I was a 50 millionaire again. I was thinking positive.

Lounging on the bed, I noticed a menu on the nightstand. It was in many languages. There were some Korean dishes I recognized, like kimchee, but there was also Western food, including a cheeseburger and French fries. I picked up the phone, and a voice said, "Yes, Mr. Johnson, how may I help you"

"Is this room service?"

"Yes sir."

"Could I please have a cheeseburger medium, with French fries. And a Coke. Could I also have a bottle of Advil?" I asked.

"Yes sir. It will be there as soon as possible." The voice said.

I could then tell I was in a totalitarian dictatorship because: The food arrived in five minutes, it was exactly what I ordered, it was hot, and there was a plastic squeeze bottle of Heinz ketchup on the tray. Also included was a large bottle of Advil. The waiter who delivered the food was quick, efficient, and did not shake me down for a tip. These are not things you see in Western democracies.

I took four Advil and washed them down with the Coca Cola. Eating was more of a challenge. My initial bite into the cheeseburger caused shooting pain in my jaw, so I was reduced to cutting minuscule pieces of food with a knife, so small I didn't have to chew. At that moment I realized I did have all my teeth, doing a quick inventory with my tongue to confirm.

After eating a bit, I sat back on the bed, planning to watch a basketball game, any basketball game, for I assumed the Beloved Chairman would find out what I had watched, and I wasn't going to do anything that would make him put me back in that cellar in chains at the Ministry of Truth.

I loved Big Brother! I loved Dennis Rodman! Don't chain me back to the wall!

I did have a problem. The remote control had three different power buttons, one button each for Cable, TV, and Satellite TV, lots of arrows and different channel controls. I couldn't turn it on!

So, I gave up and tried to eat some more. The door burst open. It was the Beloved Chairman, flanked by two officers. The officers had their sidearms drawn and aimed at me.

I blurted out, "I was trying to watch a basketball game!"

"What?" the Beloved Chairman said.

"Oh," I said. I calmed down a bit. Even in North Korea they probably wouldn't execute you for not watching Dennis Rodman.

"Mr. Johnson, a few minutes ago, we entered the information you gave us in the coded message from your President!" he said.

"And?" I asked.

"It worked perfectly. We have stolen the money and forwarded half of it as directed by the Americans." The Beloved Chairman said.

"So, why the drawn weapons?"

"We like to keep people off balance," he said.

"It works." My pounding heart exaggerated the pain, especially in my face.

The Beloved Chairman said something to the officers. They holstered their guns.

"A word of explanation. The Russians were distrustful of their own ransomware pirates. All the money was sent to one bank account in Cypress. We were able to steal in in a second, in a single transaction," he said.

"I don't understand," I said.

"The Russians wanted to get the money in one chunk, then dole it out individually to the pirates. If the pirates had each received money from the victims in different accounts, it would have been exponentially more difficult to steal it in the few seconds it was available. The Russians didn't trust the pirates to pay them."

"I understand," I lied. I didn't care. Maybe I could get Toni Anne to explain it all to me when this thing was done.

"You're free to go. Some new clothing will be brought up immediately, then you will be flown back. Keep the hoodie. Dennis Rodman brought over 100 of them as a gift to me on his last visit." He turned and left the room, followed by the two officers.

The same room service waiter knocked on the door minutes later and brought new clothes for me, in the correct sizes, including an identical blue button-down shirt from Brooks Brothers. What a country!

Chapter One Hundred Thirty One
Minsk, Belarus

The railway station is adjacent to the bus terminal in Minsk. No one had asked Gabrielle for her passport in Grodno when she changed busses. The Belarusian bus had been spotlessly clean and sleek. The driver was neatly dressed, and when the half full bus from Grodno pulled up at the Minsk terminal Gab was able to exit the area without incident.

She was dressed in a loose-fitting black sweatsuit and wore a black knit hat, that would later convert to a ski mask. The train station was located in the same ugly Stalinist block as the office building home of Network Designs. Gab was just four hours early.

The code names of her three contractors were Manny, Moe, and Jack. She was to meet Manny at the bus station at 11:30.

As Gabrielle surveyed the downtown, she was struck was the odd juxtapositioning of very modern glass and metal office buildings adjacent to, and sometimes mixed right in with, the hideous post-World War II Stalinist architecture. Minsk was participating in the worldwide technology boom; it was just that some of the participation involved stealing money using the internet.

Meanwhile she walked about a mile to the Chizhouka Arena, site of the ongoing volleyball tournament, found the coffee shop and sat in the most obscure area she could find. An abandoned Russian language newspaper was on her table. She picked it up and went through it, but her Russian was mediocre, and she couldn't get much out of the articles. No one paid any attention to her. Gabrielle mused that this is what it was like being on an operation: hours of boredom punctuated by moments of violence.

A tired looking old cleaning lady with a broom told Gabrielle something in Russian. Gabrielle thought she meant it was closing time. That was fine, it was just before 11 pm, and she walked back to the station.

Manny was there sitting on a bench. He nodded at Gabrielle and walked out the main door. Gabrielle followed five minutes later.

311

The plan was to enter the office building via the loading dock which was in an alley not visible from the street. She'd meet Manny and Moe who were waiting for her. They'd give her a weapon. The three of them then had to wait until 1:50 am local time. Gabrielle would proceed to the main entrance facing the street and be the lookout. Manny and Moe would go up and shoot all the employees of Network Designs. The President of the United States had decided it was time to go kinetic with software pirates. They had to learn that they were not safe just because they operated in a country with no extradition treaty with the U.S. There wouldn't be any prisoners or survivors.

Chapter One Hundred Thirty Two
Minsk, Belarus

Gabrielle McHugh walked in the alley up to the loading
dock. Manny was looking for her and opened the door
when she approached. He closed the door as quietly as he could
when they were both inside.

Moe was waiting, sitting on a counter. "Colonel," he said.

"Moe," Gabrielle said. Now addressing both men, she said,
"okay, we've got to cool our heels for two and a half hours.
This place looks alright, yes?"

"Yeah, I checked it out. Nobody is in the building except at
Network Designs. Not even a night watchman," Moe said.
"This loading dock area is a good place to wait. There's even a
head over there." He pointed to a door. "Don't flush, though."

"Hey Moe, this isn't my first op," Gabrielle said.

"Sorry, Colonel," Moe said.

"You miss the Army, Moe?" Gabrielle said.

"Not since they turned into the Special Pussy Forces...oops,
sorry ma'am, no offense," Moe said.

"None taken," Gabrielle said. "This is going to be one fucked
up deal unless our helicopter gets here to fly us out. What's the
status on that?"

"Jack is the perfect guy for this mission. He has the big balls
and the flying skills to pull it off. Speaks perfect Russian. As
planned, we got real credentials from Russian High Command
for Jack. That's a lot easier now than it used to be, we just
bribed the right Russian," Manny said.

"Do we know the Russian helicopter is there?" Gab asked.

"Yup, the new Kamov KA-53S, the best stealth helicopter in
the world," Manny said, "invisible to radar, no infrared
signature."

The first stealth helicopter designed by Russia was an attack
model, the KA-52. It had room for only the two pilots. The
newer Kamov KA-53S was designed to carry commando units
with light weapons on quick undetected strikes into enemy
territory.

"What's his plan?" Gabrielle asked.

"The Russian pilots will be asleep. He's going to barge in the
Belarusian ops area with his High Command creds and demand

313

a snap inspection of the chopper, then insist on sitting in the pilot seat to make sure it's fueled up. Then he's just gonna take off!"

"Sounds good," Gabrielle said.

"Yeah, at 1:45 they'll probably be asleep in the Ops area. They won't know what hit 'em," Moe said.

It got quiet in the loading dock for about an hour before the scheduled time for the mission. Manny and Moe were preparing themselves for what they were about to do. At 1:45 Gabrielle said, "let's go."

They three of them walked out of the loading dock into the main hallway. Gabrielle went straight to the main street side door, Manny and Moe up the stairs.

Gabrielle stood inside the front door. A local policeman was unlocking the door! Gabrielle stood to the side; the policeman couldn't see her. He walked in.

Gabrielle pointed he HK 416 at the cop. "Hands up," she said in English, then instantly regretted her choice of language.

"I just bathroom. I need bathroom. That's all," he said, as he put his hands up.

She noticed he had a pistol on his belt. "Put your hands behind your back," she said. As she tried to put his hands in zip ties he went for his pistol with his right hand. Gabrielle smacked him in the head with the butt of her HK 416, and he went down. He seemed conscious so she pressed the muzzle of the assault rifle to the back of his head.

"You idiot! Don't make me kill you!" Gab smacked him again with the butt of her weapon, this time knocking him out.

Gab removed the cop's pistol from his belt and kicked it down the hallway, then put the restraints on the cop's hands. Then she duct taped his mouth.

314

Chapter One Hundred Thirty Three
Minsk, Belarus
Offices of Network Designs

Andrey came out of his office, his face showing nothing. All seven hacker programmers stood. "C'mon boss, don't keep us in suspense. What's up?" Runi said.

"All the victims paid up! I've released their systems back to them. We're waiting for…you know… to pay us our share. It should just be a moment," Andrey said.

"Give us the money…give us the money," the hackers started to chant. Andrey began leading them with his hands like an orchestra conductor.

The group was so caught up in their impromptu cheering that they did not notice the door opening.

Manny and Moe shouldered their weapons and began firing in the auto mode. The outside windows shook from the deafening sound. An HK 416 fires at a rate of over 800 rounds per minute, so their 30 round ammo clips were out in a matter of a few seconds. The two mercenaries ejected their clips and reloaded.

Seven bodies lay on the floor. The room was now quiet except for the soft moaning of Runi. Moe advanced on the bodies. He put his weapon on semi-automatic and shot Runi in the head, then pulled the trigger six more times to apply the coup de grace to the others. When the reverberation stopped the room was noiseless.

Manny and Moe were dressed entirely in black, including the ski masks which exposed only their eyes. Moe gestured to Manny to hit the light switch. When the lights were off the two put on infrared goggles. The purpose of the goggles was to be able to spot the infrared signature of the body of a person who was hiding.

Manny and Moe spotted no stray bodies, but when they looked at the carpeting, they saw traces of liquid. It had to be warm to show up on the goggles, so it was probably blood, along the carpeting leading to another office. Moe indicated that he would lead.

Moe kicked the door open. In the dark, he could make out the infrared signature of the torso of a man leaning on a huge desk.

315

Andrey Schmoltz was wounded. He had kept Sergey Kranvanesko's Marakov pistol. It was now loaded. Andrey hit a switch, which lighted up the room.

Moe was wearing his infrared goggles and the room light was so bright that he was momentarily blinded. He whipped off the goggles, but in that moment, Andrey had begun to fire the Marakov pistol. Andrey was not trained in shooting but got off three wild shots.

Two shots missed, but one hit Moe in the left eye, and Moe fell back, dead.

Manny took off his goggles when he saw the room light go on and entered the room and sprayed Andrey with multiple shots. A coup de grace was not necessary, there was gray matter laying on the floor next to the Belarusian's dead body.

Moe was dead, there was no question; the back of his head was blown away. Manny knew what he had to do. When that was done, he ran down the stairs to the first floor.

Chapter One Hundred Thirty Four
Minsk, Belarus

Gabrielle was standing near the door, looking out. The policeman was still unmoving. Gabrielle had dragged him 20 feet into the building.

Gabrielle turned and saw Manny. "Where's Moe?"

"Didn't make it. Dead," Manny said.

"You cleaned up the situation?" Gabrielle asked.

"Yeah. The targets are all confirmed dead. And I set the whole fuckin' floor on fire. We should be getting out of here," Manny said. "What's with this guy?" He pointed to the cop. "Is he dead?"

"No, a local cop. He was looking for a place to take a piss," Gabrielle said.

"You should have killed him." Manny said. "I should have known. We shouldn't have brought a pussy on an op. We don't want witnesses!"

"I'm making the decisions here," Gabrielle said. She had been through the macho stuff with the guys, ever since her first day at West Point. She'd talk to Manny later about this.

There were sirens outside, close.

"Let's get over to the park now. If we wait till the chopper gets here, we may have to shoot our way out. You go first," Gabrielle ordered.

Holding his HK 416 under his arm, Manny walked out of the building, followed by Gabrielle. No one else was on the scene. A second-floor window exploded, and fire shot out. The sirens got closer.

Victory Square Park is across the street from the office building. The two black clad operatives ran to the border of the park. No helicopter was there.

"Alright, so what happened up there?" Gabrielle said.

"The targets were all together. We thought we got them all, but one crawled away, into a smaller room. Even though he was wounded, he managed to get a gun out of a desk and shot Moe." Manny said. Then I killed him."

"Him? You mean the target?" Gab asked.

"Yeah, the target. Moe was dead, half his head was gone." Manny said.

317

"So you started the fire?" Gabrielle asked. She pointed at the building.

"Yeah," Manny said.

"It's some fire," Gab said. "It will be a great distraction. All we need now is for the helicopter to get here."

"I took one of the incendiary grenades from Moe's pack, put it in his mouth and pulled the five second timer," Manny said. "Wanted to burn his body beyond recognition and destroy his teeth. Then I took his other incendiary and my two and set them off near the seven targets in the main room. I took Moe's weapon, then got out of there." Manny handed Moe's HK 416 to Gabrielle.

None of the contractors carried any identification with them on this sort of op. Manny had wanted to destroy Moe's teeth so there would be no chance of identification through dental records.

Two fire trucks had arrived at the building. More crashing sounds came from pieces of the glass façade hitting the sidewalk, and the trucks were noisy diesels. There was so much of a racket that when the helicopter landed in the middle of the park Gab hardly heard it.

She shoved Manny, who was looking at the fire. "Let's go," she said.

They sprinted to the chopper. The cargo door was open, and Jack was back in the pilot's seat, as planned. Gab slid the door shut. The interior of the helicopter was very quiet, unlike any other chopper that Gab had experienced.

Jack looked over his shoulder. "Where's Moe?"

Gab said, "Didn't make it. Take off."

The Kamov KA-53S, the world's best stealth helicopter, lifted off from Victory Square, Minsk. It was so quiet compared to the pandemonium coming from the burning building that not one fireman looked up.

Chapter One Hundred Thirty Five
West of Minsk, Belarus
Altitude 3,000 feet

Gab leaned forward to talk to Jack. "Moe got killed. One of the targets got off a few shots before Manny took him out," she said.

Jack was quiet for a minute. "That's why we get paid so much," he said. "We started the fire?"

"Yeah," Gab said. "Did you have any trouble stealing the helicopter?"

"No. It was simpler than planned. I scared the shit out of the sentry at the gatehouse when I flashed my Russian High Command creds. Told him this was a surprise inspection, and that if he so much as picked up his telephone I'd find out and shoot him. The two guys in the control room were asleep. I just walked out on the tarmac and stole the chopper," Jack said. "I was a real prick to the sentry, just like the Russian officers are. They're even bigger pricks than American officers."

"Oh?" Gab said.

"Oh, sorry ma'am," Jack said.

"That's alright, now I've been called a pussy and a prick on the same night by you guys," Gab said, "are you ok flying this thing?"

"Yeah, look at this. Separate switches for radar deflection and infrared heat suppression. They can look, but nobody can track us. And this thing is fast. In about forty minutes we'll be landing over the border in Poland," Jack said.

"I bet the Russian are looking. They're probably lining up people and shooting them at the airbase right now," Gab said. "It's bad to lose a stealth helicopter."

319

Chapter One Hundred Thirty Six
Moscow
Office of the Lider

The Lider waited in his office. Only Colonel Nihisky accompanied him.

His personal phone rang, the call he had been anticipating from General Kuznetsov. The Lider picked up, "Yes Kusnetzov?"

"Sir, I have…news on the money transfer," Kusnetzov said.

"What is it?" the Lider said.

"Sir, the money is…gone" Kusnetzov said.

"Gone? What do you mean gone? We don't have it?" the Lider said.

"No sir," Kusnetzov said.

"What happened?" the Lider demanded.

"Sir, the funds were all transferred---"

"Kusnetzov, come over to my office immediately. Alone. Be prepared to explain the situation to me." the Lider said.

The Lider turned to Colonel Nihisky. "Colonel, go get your sidearm. You may have to execute Kusnetzov. It's a shame…it makes such a mess. I'll have to replace the carpet."

Nihisky rose to leave the office.

"And Nihisky. Do not conceal the weapon. Wear it on your belt so Kusnetzov can see it," the Lider said. "Before you go, do you have Sierra Quinn's number on your phone?"

"Yes sir."

"Give me your phone, I want to speak to her directly," the Lider said.

Chapter One Hundred Thirty Seven
Moscow
The Lider's Office

The Lider called Quinn's number.
"Yes," she answered.
"Do you recognize my voice?" the Lider said.
"Yes sir," Quinn said.
"It may be time for you to kill this person," the Lider said.
"This is a contingency plan." He gave a specific order.
"Good, I've been waiting for this," Quinn said. She'd be
headed for Spicewood, Texas again.

Chapter One Hundred Thirty Eight
Moscow
The Lider's Office

Colonel Nihisky reentered the Lider's office, his sidearm holstered on his belt.

"I was unable to reach Quinn. I had a hunch about her and the sisters. It's not important. We can try her tomorrow. Let's concentrate on important matters." The Lider tossed the phone to Nihisky. The colonel didn't have to know everything. The Lider had reached his office by knowing when to compartmentalize information.

Moments later General Kusnetzov walked into the office. He stood at attention and clicked his heals, "I'm here as you ordered, sir."

"Kusnetzov, you are sweating profusely. Is it that hot out tonight in Moscow? Or are you nervous about what you have to tell me?" the Lider asked.

Kusnetzov remained standing. He said nothing.

"At least sit down," the Lider said. "Tell me what happened."

General Kusnetzov dabbed his brow with his handkerchief. "Sir, the funds were routed and rerouted over hundreds of thousands of nodes around the world. That is standard procedure in a ransomware situation, making the transactions untraceable. All the funds arrived at the bank in Cypress, and when confirmed, the ransomware victim's computers were freed, also standard procedure. This took a matter of two minutes. Then as scheduled, the bank attempted to transfer the money to our account. The money was gone, vanished."

"Get it back!" the Lider said.

It was quiet in the office. The Lider glared at Kusnetzov, who stared back.

"I take it by your silence that you can't get the money back," the Lider said. "Explain better. What happened? Who took it?"

"For a brief period, less than a minute, the money was held by the bank itself. It has to be somewhere, electronically speaking. Someone knew it was coming, because there was a worm there, waiting for the money. It was transferred out, to a thousand locations, and subsequently to thousands of other locations," Kusnetzov said.

322

"A worm?" the Lider said.

"An embedded code, hidden below the surface. Very clever, and the work of the highest-level cyber warfare," Kusnetzov said.

"An inside job? The bank itself stole from us? Interrogate the people at the bank," the Lider said.

"That is already being done. Very vigorous interrogation has yielded nothing, our man in Cypress thinks the bankers are telling the truth. The Cypriots don't know what happened," Kuznetzov said.

"Who then? Who has the money? Was it the U.S.?" the Lider asked.

"It doesn't have the signature of the U.S. Not the kind of technique they have been known to use. And---"

"And what?" the Lider said.

"The thieves had to know that the money was coming to that specific account. How would the U.S. know that?" Kusnetzov asked.

An aide knocked on the door, then entered, walked over to Colonel Nihisky and whispered something to him. Nihihski said, "Excuse me sir, I will be right back." Nihisky followed the aid out of the Lider's office.

General Kusnetzov blurted, "Sir---"

"Hold off General," the Lider said. "Let's wait to see what Nihisky has to tell us."

During the silence in the Lider's office General Kuznetzov wiped his brow with his handkerchief.

The Lider sat at his desk and repeatedly tugged at his right ear lobe. Nihisky reentered the office and stood in front of the Lider's desk.

"Sir. General. Our new prototype stealth helicopter, the Kamov KA-53S, has been stolen. It was last seen at the military airport in Minsk," Colonel Nihisky said.

"What was it doing in Belarus?" the Lider asked.

"It was there to observe a NATO wargame exercise," Nihisky answered.

"Lider, if I may?" General Kusnetzov said.

"Go ahead, General," the Lider said.

"One of our theories regarding the theft of the ransom money. It could be that one of the ransomware pirates, our own people,

323

stole the money. We do have one of the most advanced operations in Minsk. Network Designs. You must remember---"

"You think I don't remember Network Designs? That was Kravanesko's operation," The Lider said. "His head is in that jar, remember?" The Lider pointed with his left thumb in the direction of the jar.

"Maybe the ransomware pirates used the stealth helicopter to make their escape, after stealing all the money," General Kusnetzov said.

"There is something else going on with Network Designs. Their office is on fire. Crews cannot get close; the fire is too intense. It appears to have been set by some incendiary devices." Nihisky said.

"That cannot be coincidental," the Lider said.

"Witnesses say there were gunshots heard before the fire started," Nihisky said.

Chapter One Hundred Thirty Nine
Somewhere in the air over the Pacific

No cookies and milk on this flight. The same white Mercedes had taken me to the airport, this time unescorted by Chuckles, just the robo-driver and me. The same private jet took me from Pyongyang. The very same Colonel Li accompanied me on the jet.

When I entered the plane Colonel Li said, "I see you've enjoyed our hospitality."

"I'm hoping to come back soon," I said.

I had taken the bottle of Advil with me from the hotel and popped three more after the plane took off, swallowing them without the aid of water. I wasn't going to eat or drink anything on this flight if I could avoid it.

Exhaustion hit me and I dropped off to dreamless sleep. It is tough work being suspended by chains for hours on end.

A thump startled me awake, then I realized it was just the lowering of the landing gear. I looked out the window, but it was dark. Nothing I could see gave me a clue to our location, it was just some airport.

When the plane came to a stop Colonel Li walked up to me from the back of the plane. "I will be leaving." The plane stopped, Colonel Li opened the door and left.

In a few minutes I could hear the sounds of the plane being refueled.

My old buddy Alan MacKenzie entered the plane. No big smile this time. "I'll be escorting you on the rest of the flight," he said. MacKenzie opened the door to the cockpit, spoke to the pilots, then came back to me.

"It will take some time to refuel. I've got to go make some arrangements inside the terminal. I'll be back before we take off," he said.

"Swell," I said.

MacKenzie left. My iPhone buzzed.

This phone works out here, wherever we are? After all I've been through? I was glad I had let the salesman talk me into buying the protective case and screen protector.

You never know when you're going to be tortured by the North Koreans, although that's not mentioned in the sales brochure

325

After I answered the voice on the other end said, "JR, remember how we can use this phone for one encrypted call?" It was Wishbone.

"Yeah," I said.

"Do you remember your passwords?" he asked.

My brains had been scrambled a bit in the last day or so. Still, I remembered after some thought.

"It's time to speak them now," Wishbone said. When I didn't answer, he said, 'say the passwords to your phone!"

"Oh. Albatross," I said. The phone displayed a countdown clock. "Sierra," I said. The phone displayed: Encripted.

"Listen. We're monitoring the flight plan of the plane you are on. They've just told the tower they're going to change destinations." Wishbone said.

"Where are we going to be headed?" I asked.

"China," Wishbone said. "Beijing."

Chapter One Hundred Forty
Some airport

What?" I said.
"Where's MacKenzie," Wishbone said.
"He went into the terminal. Where am I anyhow?" I asked Wishbone.
"Guam. Listen. MacKenzie must have sold you out," Wishbone said.
"What does that mean?"
"The Chinese must be paying him a huge sum to deliver you to China. The pilots must be in on it, too," Wishbone said.
"How do the Chinese know?" I asked.
"The Chinese have spies in North Korea. They want to know what you told the Beloved Chairman; they wanted to try to intercept the money before North Korea could get it," Wishbone said. "Maybe they just want the code, so they can analyze it. If they can crack the algorithm, it could mean billions to them next time."
"Could you make this a little simpler? I just had my brains rattled around in the Ministry of Truth," I said.
"How's this for simple? You can't let the Chinese get a hold of you, we'd probably never see you again," Wishbone said. "We have some Chinese nationals we kidnapped. They're involved in internet piracy. We're holding them in a black location. Maybe the Chinese want to use you as a bargaining chip to get their guys back. But we don't bargain with them."
"What do I do now?" I asked.
"You can't let the plane take off. The simplest solution is you have to kill MacKenzie and the pilots. Then you have to get to Hawaii. I can't get you home from Guam." Wishbone said.
"Why can't you get me home from Guam?"
"Guam has been compromised. The Chinese have assets there. We suspect Colonel Li as being a double agent, a Chinese spy. You gotta get to Hawaii. But first, you've got to kill those guys. If the plane takes off, you're dead, or least in the hands of the Chinese forever," Wishbone said.

327

For some reason I was calm, probably because this situation was so bizarre that I wasn't processing it. "Okay. How do you propose I do that?" I asked.

"MacKenzie is a trained CIA agent. You've got to have the element of surprise. Go back to the galley of the plane. There must be knives, or something heavy. Don't fuck around, kill him dead, then take his gun and go up and shoot the pilots before they can start to taxi," Wishbone said.

"Just like that?"

"If you don't, you won't get to spend the $52 million that has just been deposited in your account," Wishbone said.

"Hey, it worked! That's a good incentive," I said. "Where did the extra $2 million come from?"

"I'll explain later. How about this for an incentive? Do you really want the Chinese to get their hands on you? What they'd do to you would make Pyongyang look like a picnic," Wishbone said.

"So how do I get to Hawaii?" I asked.

"Remember improvise? You'll figure something out. But you have to kill the guys first," he said. "I'm hanging up now. Get to work before MacKenzie gets back."

"How do you know…" the phone went dead. I was talking to nobody.

Chapter One Hundred Forty One
Guam Airport

There wasn't time to do anything but getting into the galley and finding a weapon that would kill MacKenzie. That had to be my focus.

But what if Wishbone was wrong. And I killed these three guys? I rejected that thought, what if Wishbone was right and I didn't?

I hurried to the back of the plane. A plaque in the galley identified the plane I was on as a Gulfstream G500. Beneath the galley counter were four drawers. I rummaged through from top to bottom. I was hoping for something heavy like a hammer, the only lethal weapons I could find were steak knives. I took one and put it in my right pants pocket. Then I took two more. Why not?

I considered waiting in the galley for MacKenzie to return, but thought better of that, because it was not where he'd expect to see me, and it might make him suspicious. No, it would be best if I returned to my seat. I hurried back to the front row.

I could hear the fuel sloshing as it was being pumped into the wings of the G500. Then the noise stopped. There was a clunk, which I guessed to be a fuel hose nozzle being disconnected.

On the screen in front of my seat the entertainment system came to life. I took this as a sign we were preparing for departure.

Moments later MacKenzie entered the plane, looked back at me, then turned and opened the cockpit door. I got out of my seat and walked as close to the cockpit as I dared; I wanted to hear what MacKenzie was saying.

There was some extended conversation between him and the two pilots. I couldn't make out all the words, but it sounded like a negotiation about money, and voices were raised before finally one of the pilots said, "For that kind of money who cares what the Chinese do to the guy." They all laughed. I could hear MacKenzie say, "It's settled, you each get two million. I'll pay you the extra out of my share."

One of the pilots said, "Alright, but right now we're programmed to fly to Hawaii. This autopilot system is complex.

329

It's going to take a while to flush out this destination and put in the new one. I've got to get final clearance from the tower first. It might take a few minutes."

I hurried back to my seat.

MacKenzie closed the door to the cockpit and started back toward me.

I had to kill him now. Right now. There was no time to be Hamlet, To Be or Not To Be. If I was going To Be, I had to kill him, then kill the pilots.

Chapter One Hundred Forty Two
Guam Airport

MacKenzie walked back and stopped by my seat. He paused, as if gathering his thoughts.

I pointed at the window on the other side of the cabin and yelled, "Holy Shit, there's a plane headed right for us!"

It worked. He turned.

This guy's a CIA agent?

I jumped to my feet and stabbed him in the neck with an overhand motion. The knife stuck solidly into the left side of his neck but did not produce the spurting of blood I hoped for and expected.

MacKenzie staggered back, his eyes wide open, but he kept his feet. A loud gurgling sound emerged from his mouth. It's unsettling to have someone you just stabbed look you right in the eyes.

I grabbed the second knife and stabbed again, this time with an underhand motion, deep into MacKenzie's gut. He bent and clutched the knife with both hands, like he was trying to pull it out.

This creep had two knives in him, he was still standing, and not bleeding enough! Maybe my sister Bitsy was right. If I had gone to Medical School, at least I'd be a more effective stabber.

MacKenzie let go of the knife in his gut and with his right hand tried to reach inside the left side of his suit jacket.

I picked up my last knife. This time I slashed sideways with both hands on the right side of his neck, starting just below the ear, only stopping when it hit his windpipe.

Blood gushed out of his neck, more blood than I thought possible. MacKenzie reflexively put his hands to his neck, then fell over backward. He gave out an inhuman bellow, then seemed to stop breathing.

I knelt, opened his suit coat, and felt for what MacKenzie had been reaching for, his weapon in a shoulder holster. I grabbed it and stood. It was a Sig Sauer 9mm. I took off the safety and slammed back the action, chambering a round.

I heard the cockpit door open. One of the pilots came out, "What the hell is going on here? he asked.

331

Without hesitation I shot him in the face. His body slammed backward against a bulkhead, and he collapsed to the floor.

The second pilot came out of the cockpit, He had a small snub-nosed pistol in his right hand. His hand was shaking. He more or less pointed the gun at me. "Drop your gun, or I'll shoot you," he said, without much conviction.

This guy must have had all his weapons training from movies. Instead of dropping my gun, I shot him with my Sig Sauer. His snub-nosed revolver slipped out of his hand as he flew backward, his head landing just inside the cockpit door. What a dope! I hoped that every bad person I ran into was as stupid as this guy.

I was cautious as I approached him. My shot had gotten him in the chest, maybe his heart, he was dead.

Chapter One Hundred Forty Three
Guam Airport

It had been an eventful couple of minutes. I sat back in my seat, and the adrenaline slammed into my bloodstream. My heart raced, and the pulsing caused every bruised area of my body to throb. I took some deep breaths.

Time to evaluate the situation. I was calm as I went through my status:

I had just murdered three guys. Maybe not murder, let's call it self-defense. They were laying in the aisle of this top-of-the-line Gulfstream G500. One of them, CIA agent turned traitor Alan MacKenzie had spewed more blood than I thought was in a human body, and still had two knives sticking out of him, one in his throat, one in his abdomen. The third bloody knife was lying in the aisle. MacKenzie was prone, toward the back of the plane, to my left. I had shot the first pilot in the face, the second in the heart, both at close range, and they were to my right, between me and the cockpit.

They say that when a person dies, especially in sudden violent circumstances, the victim releases anything stored in their bladder and digestive system. I knew this was true firsthand, having been there in New York when Gabrielle killed Robert Stanton Banks. Then, I had been pleased when the dead, Mr. Perfect, custom tailored, hotshot murdering bastard hedge fund manager had poo-pooed in his pants right after he croaked. This time, in the closed in space of the plane the experience was not so rewarding, because the nasty aromas were coming from all three stiffs, and that smell combined with coagulating blood, piss, and other fluids and bits and pieces I had violently separated from their bodies. It smelled worse than the torture room at the Ministry of Truth. But the plane did have a first-class ventilation system.

The pungent smell of gunpowder lingered in the air. It reminded me to check out the Sig Sauer 9mm. To my surprise it was still in my right hand. I flipped the safety on, then thought better of it, because if anybody stormed on to the plane, I'd have to shoot them too.

333

I was at the airport in Guam. I needed to get to Hawaii. Wishbone had warned me that if I went in the terminal, I'd be hijacked to China. It was time to improvise.

I'd just have to fly the plane from Guam to Hawaii. One drawback. I had never flown a plane.

How hard could it be? It couldn't be as bad as being tortured at the Ministry of Truth.

I thought for a second: I'd just use autopilot. These new planes had all kinds of fancy avionics. I'd just have to figure out how to engage the autopilot.

Would there be some manual in the cockpit? Then I had a flash.

I bet it's on YouTube. How-to-do-anything is on YouTube.

I used the touch screen on my Entertainment System in front of my seat. I got on YouTube and typed: how to use autopilot on Gulfstream G500.

There were twelve videos that were listed in response to that particular inquiry, but they weren't all on target. The twelfth one was titled: How to Play *Fly Away* on acoustic guitar. The first video on the list was five minutes and nine seconds. I selected that one.

The video was produced by Gulfstream. It had cheesy music and featured a couple of third-rate actors with $300 haircuts pretending to be pilots. It became evident to me that this wasn't a training video, it was aimed at selling the $75 million jet to a corporate CEO.

I didn't want to buy the fuckin' plane! I just wanted to borrow it and fly it to Hawaii.

After the introduction, one actor said," Okay, now let's get you checked out on the Gulfstream G500 autopilot system. It's state of the art. It can be used to take off, in flight, and even used to land the plane."

Then the second actor chuckled. "Of course, it's crucial to program the autopilot correctly before the flight!" They looked at each other, then the camera and both chuckled. "The autopilot is a powerful tool but requires extensive training and practice before actual in-flight use."

Smug bastards. In real life, I bet they couldn't figure out the cruise control in their own cars. Well, Oops. I think they meant

334

that the five-minute YouTube video I was watching was not the extensive training I required.

I decided that I should stay seated where I was and learn as much as possible from the YouTube videos. Then I'd go up to the pilot's seat and check things out.

I was racing through videos trying to learn, but programming the autopilot was just too complicated. Then I stumbled on one video that said: the advanced Gulfstream G500 autopilot system has a new prototype, that uses the AUTONOMOUS MODE and can even taxi when properly programmed. AUTONOMOUS MODE is displayed on the screen right next to: PROGRAM AUTOPILOT.

I just had to see if the plane was equipped with AUTONOMOUS MODE and if it was properly programmed. If not, I had to come up with something else. But right now, there was no Plan B.

I walked up the aisle, stepping over the bodies of the pilots. I felt no remorse. These pricks had been willing to sell me to the Chinese. It was me or them who were going to die, and I made sure it was them.

I sat in the pilot's seat on the right side and put on the headset. Seemed like a good idea.

A voice came over the radio. "Gulfstream flight Delta Alpha, what is your status? We're going to need your slot in 15 minutes."

That was a good question. What was my status?

I hit the button that said TALK. "Roger tower. Running final systems check," I said. *I think I heard that line in a movie.*

"Roger Delta Alpha. Call for final clearance for takeoff," the tower said.

The line worked! If I only knew how to do a systems check.

"Roger tower," I said.

Now if I can just figure out how to get the plane in the air, I'll be all set.

The control panel of a Gulfstream G500 is very high tech. There are multiple computer screens, and within each screen there are multiple displays. The vibe was more like a workstation of one of the network controllers at Cyber Command than what I had imagined as airplane controls. Any

335

actual gauges and dials were replaced by virtual computer avatars of these devices.

There was a display that read:
AUTONOMOUS MODE
PROGRAM AUTOPILOT.
Auto destination: 21.3186 N, 151.953 W. CONFIRM.

I touched the CONFIRM button on the touch screen. I was all set. I had AUTONOMOUS MODE!

The screen read: CONFIRM-Honolulu International Airport-HNL

The pilots hadn't had time to reprogram the autopilot before I, well, interrupted them. No need for Plan B.

A new electronic window came on the screen: ENGAGE

I was getting cocky now. This was easy. On the screen I hit: ENGAGE.

The engines revved up and the plane strained trying to lurch forward! It seemed to be stuck.

The tower voice screamed over my headphones. "What the hell are you doing?"

"Sorry, my finger slipped," I said. On the touch screen I hit: DISENGAGE. The engine rpms lowered to low idle, and the plane no longer tried to move forward.

"Do you require assistance Delta Alpha?"

"Negative." It would be a very bad idea to let someone come onboard and see the three stiffs. I decided to get pushy. "Tower, we're in a hurry. National security emergency. Let's get going."

"Roger Delta Alpha. We're clearing the wheel chocks now."

Oh, that's why the plane wouldn't move.

I saw a worker in orange coveralls back away from the plane and give me a thumbs up. I gave him a thumbs up back.

That gesture confirmed to me that I've never been more full of shit in my life. And this is from a guy who is full of it every day.

"Roger Delta Alpha, you have clearance for immediate takeoff, Runway One Whiskey."

"Roger that, tower." I said. I put on the seatbelt. Pilots get better seatbelts than passengers. I hit ENGAGE. The plane began to move. So far, so good.

336

The experience was just regular taxiing, straight ahead. When the plane got to the first runway it turned left. I debated with myself whether I should put my hands on the steering wheel. Then I decided that I wasn't sure the thing was actually called a steering wheel, and if the plane started to crash, any jerking from me on the wheel would just make me crash faster, so I went with hands-free piloting. I forced myself to fold my hands in front of me.

The tower came over my headphones. "You are clear for takeoff…." And some other stuff I didn't understand.

"Roger, tower," I said.

As the engine rpms revved up the brakes engaged. I knew that because a light came on a screen that read: BRAKES ENGAGED.

I had been operating under the assumption that Autopilot would just fly the plane without the manual controls moving; the computers would just take over. This was not the case. The controls moved as though there was an invisible pilot. The throttle lever moved itself forward as far as it goes.

A message displayed: FULL POWER.

A new message box came on the screen: CONFIRM TAKEOFF.

Why not?

I wanted to take off, so I hit CONFIRM TAKEOFF.

The BRAKES ENGAGED light went off. The plane began the shot-out-of-a-cannon, drag race mode that indicates takeoff is occurring.

The takeoff was bumpier than I expected. The wings on this multimillion-dollar flying toy of the overprivileged were shaking, flapping. I don't like it when the wings on a plane flap, in my amateur opinion they should be rigid. Lights on the edge of the runway were flashing by, faster and faster. A screen indicated the ground speed was: *150 kts.*

What were kts? Oh, knots. Knots are bigger than miles, so we must be going about 175 mph. That's a lot faster than even Barbara Jean's yellow Corvette roadster.

On a normal flight, as a passenger, I always experience a moment of panic when the plane goes through this period of wild acceleration. But then I calm myself by thinking that the pilots are experienced, well trained, probably Air Force Academy grads, or retired Navy carrier pilots, and I'm in

337

capable hands. This time *I* was sitting at the controls, with my hands not even on the steering wheel, and some robot was doing all the flying. I consoled myself by thinking that if I crashed, I wouldn't have to pay the property taxes on my compound in Austin.

I felt the front wheels leave the ground, then the back wheels. The ride continued to be bumpy. The engines screamed as the plane felt like it was going straight up. I heard a thump. A lighted box on one of the screens said: LANDING GEAR RETRACTED.

As the plane climbed the ride got smoother. It kept climbing, and I wondered if it was just stuck on "UP." At 42,000 feet the plane began to level off, and at 45,000 it stopped climbing and maintained that level. The computer indicated our speed was .85 Mach. I knew Mach was the Speed of Sound. Mach .85 is fast.

Funny, I thought of the flight as "We" or "Us", but it was just me and the three stiffs slowly decomposing in the aisle. I decided the other living being on the flight was the computer, which I christened "HAL" after the computer in *2001: A Space Odyssey.*

You may recall that the problems in that movie started when the astronauts tried to override HAL and take human command of the mission. That wasn't going to happen on our flight. HAL was in charge; I was just cargo. I'd be okay, as long as a computerized voice didn't wish me "Happy Birthday JR."

Chapter One Hundred Forty Four
In the air
Between Guam and Hawaii

At 45,000 feet and Mach .85 the flight was smooth. There was a bit of a bump every few minutes. The steering wheel would move a bit to compensate, and the throttle had adjusted itself to about 65 percent. There were two pedals on the floor, like in a car, and one pedal or another would lower itself occasionally, then slowly return to normal position. The experience reminded me of being in a sailboat in a gentle breeze on Chesapeake Bay when I was a kid.

The avionics computer screens showed that the flight was level; I understood that much. There was a lot of other data displayed and changing numbers that I didn't understand, had no idea what the numbers meant, and didn't care.

Maybe when all this was over, and after my face healed, I could make a promotional video for Gulfstream. I rehearsed my first line: "Say, Mr. or Ms., prospective buyer, it is not recommended, but if you ever have to steal a G500 with three dead bodies in the aisle and fly it to Hawaii..."

It's a strange feeling being on a flight with no pilots. I suspect a lot of other people feel like me; deep down man is not intended to fly, but it's better when you know that trained pilots are there to take care of any emergency.

With no one there except HAL, what would we do if there was a sudden problem?

It felt like it was wrong, but I decided it was okay to leave the pilot seat and walk around the plane. First objective: take a leak. Second objective: find something I could eat without chewing.

The lav was located toward the back of the plane. I stepped over the two dead pilots but paused at the body of Alan MacKenzie. I kicked at the knife sticking out of his gut. He didn't move. I'm not a forensic expert, but he was very dead. The pool of blood on the floor around his body was large and still sticky.

I entered the lav but didn't close the door until I realized that was how the lights were activated. The lav was luxurious, even

339

compared to first class on a commercial airline. There was enough space to make joining the Mile High Club almost comfortable.

My reverie was interrupted by glancing at the mirror. My face, bad enough when I had looked at it in Pyongyang, had turned into monster mode. It was tough to just look at myself.

Maybe it was the pulsing of blood, maybe the altitude, but my head was swollen beyond any size I thought possible. I'd have to wear a size 12 ½ baseball hat! My eyes were such narrow slits I was surprised I could see out of them, and the effect of the swelling was to blunt my features to unrecognizable. My nose looked small, almost hidden by the swelling, but my lips were huge and misshapen smears of purple and red. Seeing this horror film character staring back at me reminded me that my head and body hurt. I'd have to take some more Advil.

It hurt to unzip and get my pecker out. It was still the color of an eggplant, and the act of peeing burned, but was not as bad as I expected. I didn't understand the inner workings of a pecker, not having read the manual; I was just a user of this multi-functional device.

This mission completed, I went to the galley and searched the freezer. There were individual sized containers of ice cream, just what I wanted. I took a couple, and a spoon from the cupboard. Instead of returning to the pilot's seat I went back to the front row passenger seat. I wanted a tray, and to be able to surf the internet, not to look at all the avionics gobbledygook in the cockpit. I certainly wasn't flying the plane; HAL was doing that.

The ice cream felt great on my lips, and I needed some kind of nourishment. As I ate one container of ice cream after the other, I surfed Google, jumping from one topic to another. I learned: The thing I was calling a steering wheel in the cockpit was a *yoke*, it would take over six hours to fly from Guam to Honolulu, and I firmly established that I would not master, or even understand the fundamentals of flying a Gulfstream G500, or *any* plane during the six hours I had available before landing at HNL. That's how we aviators refer to the Daniel K. Inouye Honolulu International Airport.

340

The thought occurred to me that I might need money in Hawaii, and I had none in my pockets. Agent MacKenzie might have some in his wallet, and I'd check the pilots too.

MacKenzie, like any cool guy, had his wallet in his inside suit jacket pocket. I removed it. No blood had spilled on it, a random thing, because blood was all over his suit. I opened the wallet. It held $750 in cash, credit cards, other stuff, like a driver's license. But the big thing: right when you flipped it open behind a plastic sleeve was his CIA ID card. It was a photo ID, but nobody was going to compare the photo to my monster face, so I could use it in Hawaii if necessary. And nobody had notified Visa and American Express that he was lying dead in the aisle of the Gulfstream, so I could use his credit cards too. I pocketed the wallet.

A tip for would be spies: If you want to use somebody else's picture ID, just have the North Koreans chain you to a wall and beat you for several hours, and you can use anybody's ID.

Then I rifled through the wallets of the pilots. Cheapskates, less than $100 between them. After pocketing the cash, I searched their wallets. One of them had a Quick Pick Powerball ticket, that was the only other thing I took. Who says you can't win if you don't buy a ticket? You can always steal it off a pilot you just shot.

I sat back in my passenger seat. I was dog tired but remember thinking that I was too wired to go to sleep.

341

Chapter One Hundred Forty Five
Belarus, near the Polish border

Gabrielle and Manny sat without talking to each other for most of the flight from Minsk to the Polish border. The interior of the helicopter was very quiet, in keeping with its stealth design. Finally, Gabrielle said, "If we work together again, don't ever question me, or pull that insubordinate shit. I'll cut you some slack this time because you lost your---"

"It won't happen again. But not for the reason you think," Manny said. "I'm out."

"Alright. You did a good job, did what you had to do," Gabrielle said.

"I been taking chances for a long time," Manny said.

"Were you close to Moe?" Gabrielle asked.

"Nah," Manny laughed without humor. "I'm not close to anybody. Never have been."

Gabrielle got a bad sense from Manny's conversation. When someone was in the Army, they had discipline imposed upon them, but once they became an independent contractor those years of discipline abruptly stopped and some of the contractors became virtual soldiers of fortune who sold themselves to the highest bidder. She thought Manny might be leaning that way.

Jack yelled back from the pilot's chair. "We're crossing the Polish border right now. Only about three clicks from where we want to land."

Seconds later a tremendous whoosh filled the helicopter cabin. The chopper rocked hard to the right from the turbulence. A bright glow filled the windows but diminished. Jack yelled, "Did you see that!"

"Yeah Jack, it was hard not to see. What was it?' Gabrielle asked.

"At first, I thought it was a surface-to-air missile, but it was a fighter plane! One of ours, an F-22 I think. He can't see us on radar, we're in stealth mode," Jack said. "He must have missed us by 100 feet."

"How come we couldn't see him on radar?" Gabrielle asked reflexively, then she felt stupid. Before Jack could answer, she said, "Of course, we don't have our radar turned on, otherwise we wouldn't be in stealth mode."

"Yeah colonel," Jack said. "I'm surprised one of our fighters was that low."

"Should we light up the radar?" Gabrielle asked.

"Negative. We're almost at the LZ. I'll just dive down below where any fighters would be," Jack said. "We're this close, we don't want either side to see us land." He pushed the control stick forward and the helicopter went down with a purpose.

Within a minute the helicopter was hovering over a clearing in the forest. Jack pulled out of the dive and landed the stealth helicopter as softly as Marine One lands on the White House lawn. He shut down the engines. "Welcome to Poland."

Chapter One Hundred Forty Six
Forest near Bialystok, Poland

The main rotor of the helicopter seemed to take forever to stop spinning. Jack and Manny sat facing Gabrielle in the back of the chopper. The cargo door was open.

"It's time for you guys to scram," Gab said. "Disappear, per Ops plan. Give me your weapons."

Jack removed the side arm from his holster. "Here you go, Colonel." He was still wearing the uniform of an officer of the Russian General Staff. Jack took off the Russian jacket.

"Colonel, I'm getting out of here," Jack said. "I hope I can work with you again." Jack exited the cargo door.

Manny didn't move. "I might need to be armed. Some contingencies might come up," he said.

"That's not the plan," Gabrielle said. She was holding what had been Moe's assault rifle, her right forefinger on the trigger, the gun pointed at Manny.

Manny sat still then finally pushed his HK 416 with two hands toward Gabrielle. "Safety is on," he said.

"Give me your side arm too," Gabrielle said.

"What, you don't trust me?" Manny said.

"First, the plan is for you two to vanish, unarmed into Poland. If you want to get paid, you'll do that. Second, no I don't trust you," Gab said.

Manny sat still. Gabrielle pointed her HK at Manny. "Real careful now. Give me your side arm, or I'll shoot you."

"You won't shoot me, you bitch," Manny said. "But here's the gun. Ok?" Manny exaggerated the delicate motion of grabbing his side arm with just his thumb and forefinger. Gabrielle didn't take her two hands off the HK 416, still pointing it at Manny.

"Put the gun on the floor," she said. He did so. "Now get out of the chopper but stand 10 feet away. When Manny was ten feet away, Gabrielle got out onto the ground.

Pointing the assault rifle at Manny, Gabrielle said. "Now do what you're good at. Disappear. If I see you again today, *I will shoot you.*"

344

Manny started to say something, but caught himself, then jogged into the forest.

Gabrielle wondered how far Manny would go. She went back in the chopper only long enough to grab a duffel bag containing her combat uniform. She exited to stand in the clearing as she changed out of the black sweatsuit into her standard issue camo Lt. Colonel's outfit. She also stuffed what had been Jack's Russian officer's jacket into her bag. That done, she picked up the HK 416, stood in the clearing and slowly turned 360 degrees, scanning for Manny. She didn't put it past him to return, slit her throat, and somehow sell his information, and the stealth helicopter, back to the Russians. When Manny told her that he was never close to anybody, that set off an internal alarm.

The sun had come up. Gabrielle listened for any sound. There was nothing for over an hour until a squad of uniformed soldiers began shouting at her, in Dutch. Gabrielle put down her weapon and raised her hands. "Does anyone speak English?" she asked.

The Lieutenant leading the squad stepped forward, "We are capturing you as part of the war game," he said.

"Lieutenant, I am Lt. Colonel Gabrielle McHugh, U.S. Army. I need to talk to you privately. Have your men step back."

"They all speak English," the Lieutenant said.

"So have them stand back," Gabrielle said.

The Lieutenant knew an order when he heard one. He ordered his men to go back to the tree line.

"I am not part of the war game. I am on a covert mission. This is a Russian helicopter. I am ordering you to forget what I just told you, and I need your radio," Gabrielle said.

The Lieutenant was quiet. Finally, he said, "Yes Colonel."

345

Chapter One Hundred Forty Seven
Moscow
Office of the Lider

Very well, General Kusnetzov, you can go now," the Lider said. "I need to have a discussion with Colonel Nihisky."

Colonel Nihisky put his hand on the revolver strapped to his hip and looked questioningly at the Lider. The Lider shook his head.

General Kusnetzov nervously glanced between the two men.

"Go Kusnetzov. I'll call you when I need to speak to you," the Lider said. The General hurried out of the room.

"I didn't think it was time to shoot Kusnetzov. We can always do it later," The Lider said.

"Sir, may I make a suggestion? I should go to Minsk and investigate the situation. I'll bring my sidearm. It may be necessary to shoot a few people there," Nihisky said.

"That's a good idea, Nihisky. Use your own judgement regarding shooting someone," the Lider said. "Don't wait for my permission. And Colonel."

"Yes sir?"

"Take the HIP helicopter directly from here. It will be faster, and you can get around in Belarus if you need to. And try not to misplace this helicopter," the Lider said.

Chapter One Hundred Forty Eight
Minsk, Belarus
Military Airfield

Nihisky had taken the Lider's HIP from Moscow to Minsk. The HIP helicopter is a transport, this one modified to carry Russian officials in comfort.

"You haven't shot anybody yet?" Nihisky demanded of the base commander, a Belarusian General.

"No." the Belarusian had almost said 'sir' to Nihisky, who while only a colonel, in the real world outranked the Belarussian General, since Nihisky carried with him the authority of the Lider. Nihisky hadn't bothered addressing the Belarusian with any military courtesy.

"This situation seems stable. I want to see the offices of Network Designs. Can my helicopter fly me there?" Nihisky said.

The Belarusian told him yes, that Nihisky could fly there on his chopper.

"I'll be back," Nihisky said. "Continue vigorous interrogation of all the people involved. There must be a rat in the nest. It's hard to believe that some unknown party just walked in and stole the Kamov KA-53S without help."

The General nodded.

Chapter One Hundred Forty Nine
Minsk, Belarus
Victory Square

Colonel Nihisky's HIP helicopter landed in almost the same spot that Jack had landed the KA-53S. Nihisky was greeted by a Belarusian captain, the two of them walked across the street to the building where Network Designs had been.

The sidewalk was still littered with glass and the air smelled of fire and smoke. The building was cordoned off with temporary concrete barriers. Firemen in their heavy suits walked in and out of the building, and the diesel engines of the trucks droned. There were no gawkers. People in Belarus do not want to give the authorities any reason to question them.

"There is no one higher than a Captain to brief me?" Nihisky asked.

"Sir, I am an expert in these sorts of matters," the Byelorussian said.

"Is it possible to inspect the offices of Network Designs?" Nihisky asked.

"Yes sir. The fire department did an excellent job. Some evidence was preserved. If the fire had lasted another five minutes, there would be nothing worth looking at," the Belarusian captain said. "The fire was certainly set using incendiary devices. I'll show you."

The two men walked up the stairway to the second floor. The fire department had set up massive fans near the blown-out windows of Network Designs, so the air was breathable, but still made Nihisky cough.

Forensic technicians were outlining areas on the floor where the spent cartridges were strewn.

"Do you know what kind of weapons were used?" Nihisky asked.

"Almost certainly HK 416s," the Belarusian answered.

"That could be anybody," Nihisky said.

The Belarusian escorted Nihisky to the area where seven victims laid. Some were more burned than others, but they were all barely recognizable as people.

348

"We'll use dental records to identify them," the Belarusian said. He picked up a canister in a plastic bag. "This is one of the incendiary devices used to set the fire. It's standard issue NATO equipment."

"But it's available anywhere in the world on the black market," Nihisky said. "Doesn't prove anything."

"This should prove interesting to you," the Belarusian said, gesturing to Andrey's office. The two walked in.

What was barely recognizable as a corpse laid on the floor in front of them. It had no head, and all clothing was burned off. An incendiary canister was lying on the carpet, near where the head would have been.

"Where is this man's head?" Nihisky asked.

"Apparently vaporized," the Belarusian said. He walked around Andrey's desk. This body was the best-preserved corpse. A Marakov pistol was on the desk in a plastic evidence bag.

"We have been able to positively identify this man. It's Andrey Schmoltz, the new president of Network Designs. The pistol is still registered to Sergei Kravanesko, former president of Network Designs. Kravanesko is officially missing, whereabouts unknown."

Nihisky waited for a full minute. "Captain," Nihisky began, speaking to the Belarusian. "I am speaking off the record. I know the whereabouts of Kravanesko, at least part of him. His head is pickled, in a jar, and the jar resides in the Lider's office. The rest of his body, I don't know where it may be."

It was the Belarusian's turn to be quiet.

"The Lider enjoys adding to his collection of heads," Nihisky said. "Continue to do your excellent job, and I will continue doing mine, and maybe we can both avoid being part of the collection. Do not share your opinions regarding this evidence with anyone but me. Clear?"

"Yes, Sir."

"Now, in your opinion, could this atrocity have been perpetrated by an insider, someone in Network Designs, who then escaped in the Russian helicopter?" Nihisky asked.

The Belarusian was silent again.

"Captain do not feign ignorance of the Russian helicopter that landed in the square. It insults my intelligence. Now answer the question," Nihisky said.

349

"Sir, that possibility had not occurred to me. Why would someone from Network Designs do this?" the Belarusian asked.

'That's classified. It should go without saying that you should forget that I asked," Nihisky said.

A Belarusian enlisted man ran into the room. "Colonel Nihisky. An urgent call is coming in for you on your helicopter."

Nihisky said, "Run to the helicopter and tell them that I am on my way down."

The enlisted man turned and ran. "He's a much faster runner than me," Nihisky said to the Belarusian captain.

Chapter One Hundred Fifty
Minsk, Belarus
Victory Square

Nihisky strode to the helicopter. The pilot said, "Sir, it's the Lider for you."

"Yes sir," Nihisky said as he picked up the radio mouthpiece and put on the headset.

"You took your time, Nihisky!" the Lider said.

"I am here now sir."

"Colonel Nihisky, I have the Supreme Commander of NATO on the line. Also on the line is the U.S. General in charge of the war games currently being conducted in Poland, near the border of Belarus," the Lider said.

A tense conversation ensued. NATO informed the Russians that a prototype Russian helicopter had landed in Polish territory using some kind of advanced technology that made the flight undetected. NATO denied any prior knowledge of this operation and postulated that it was some kind of attempted defection. However, no defectors were at the scene, no one was on the helicopter. The Lider insisted on having a translator, which prolonged the discussion.

Nihisky stressed that he must inspect the helicopter in Poland before any further action was taken, because once the chopper was flown back to Belarus, NATO could deny taking any equipment off of the advanced prototype.

Eventually it was agreed that Nihisky could be landed by his Russian HIP helicopter at the site of the captured stealth chopper. Then the HIP would return to Belarus territory while Nihisky inspected the stealth unit. After both sides were satisfied, Nihisky's helicopter could return to the Polish site, carrying a pilot who could then fly the captured stealth helicopter back to Belarus.

Chapter One Hundred Fifty One
Near Bialystok, Poland

The Russian HIP helicopter carrying Colonel Nihisky crossed the border from Belarus into Polish airspace. Per mutual agreement only a Hummer vehicle and a U.S. Lt. Colonel with a driver waited by the captured Russian helicopter in the clearing. Nihisky's helicopter landed, Nihisky got out, and the Russian HIP returned to Belarus.

Nihisky shook hands with the American officer.

"I am Lt. Colonel Gabrielle McHugh. Welcome to the free world, Colonel Nihisky. I'll need you to give me your sidearm."

"Of course." Nihisky handed over his weapon. "Is it proper procedure to officially tell you that I am requesting Political Asylum?"

"Yes Colonel Nihisky," Gabrielle said.

Their driver waited in the Hummer. His arms were rigid, straight out. He was staring ahead, not daring a glance at the Russian officer.

"Before we get in the vehicle, let me tell you a few things, Colonel. First, General Goldstein asked me to give you his thanks for all the information you have provided for us over the years. It was time to get you out before your head ended up in a jar."

Nihisky looked surprised. "We know all about that," Gabrielle said. She went on.

"Second, I will be turning you over to the General in charge of the ongoing NATO exercises. By the time that you sit down to talk to him, I will have vanished into thin air. He knows nothing. Do not tell him anything, only that you are seeking Political Asylum, and that your instructions are to speak only to General Goldstein. The local commander will know not to ask any more questions. You will be fine. We take care of our friends. Understand?"

"Yes," Colonel Nihisky said.

352

Chapter One Hundred Fifty Two
In the air
Somewhere between Guam and Hawaii

I was lying in bed in Spicewood, my head propped up with a couple pillows. It was early morning. Barbara Jean stepped out of the master bath, wearing a nightie I had never seen before. She was backlit by the rising sun streaming through the window. She posed so she'd be in profile.

"You like it, sweetie?" she asked.

"You know Barb, I've read that the Mona Lisa, or the Grand Canyon, or the Taj Mahal is the most beautiful sight in the world, but the people who said that never saw you in that translucent---"

Barbara Jean said, "I would call it diaphanous."

"That's what I get for marrying an English major," I said.

The alarm clock went off.

That's strange, we don't have an alarm clock.

A piercing sound stirred me. Then another, different piercing sound. Then both sounds together. The sounds were loud, obnoxious. My bed rocked violently from left to right.

Damn! I was dreaming. I closed my eyes, but Barbara Jean did not reappear. And I wasn't laying down, I was sitting up.

The chair was tilting from side to side. My head slammed back in the chair, then was jerked forward. It was good that I had my seat belt on, because we were bouncing around so much that I might have been thrown into the aisle.

I began to wake up a bit.

Oh, I was on an airplane! And it wasn't flying very well right now.

Suddenly I was wide awake. I saw the three bodies in the aisle.

Oh yeah, them.

The plane must have hit an air pocket. Whatever that is. It felt like we sank a thousand feet in a second. All three stiffs rose into the air, as if they levitated, then hit the aisle again with thuds when the plane stabilized. I laughed.

Good. Fuck 'em. They deserve it. The knives were still sticking out of MacKenzie.

353

The alarms kept going off. Then a recorded voice started: DISENGAGE AUTOPILOT! ASSUME MANUAL CONTROL!

That wasn't going to happen.

I was cold. The Chicago Bulls hoodie was draped over the right arm of my seat. The act of putting it on was agony. When I pulled it down, it was hard to get my swollen head through the opening. But wearing the hoodie warmed me up.

Great. I'd be comfy as the plane plummeted into the uncharted depths of the Pacific Ocean.

The alarms kept bleating. I decided it was time to go sit in the pilot's seat.

I walked up the aisle. As I did, the plane shook. It pitched, yawed, and rolled. I forget which of those is which, but it means in all three axes, as I had recently learned on my YouTube crash course.

Perhaps that was poorly phrased.

The Gulfstream G500 felt like a kid's toy in the hands of a spoiled little creep who was bored with it and was testing to see how violently he could shake the model plane before he chucked it out of his bedroom window. Except this was real life, and it was about eight miles down to the Pacific Ocean.

One vicious pitch, yaw, or roll ricocheted me off the left wall of the plane's interior. I put my arm out to cushion the impact, a mistake. Electric pain shot through my shoulder and traveled down through my rib cage. The intense pain served to make me hyperalert as I made it to the pilot's seat and put on the seat belt.

The multiple control displays were rapidly giving new messages and flashing at what technical people might classify as 10.0 on the Apeshit Scale. The main thing that caught my attention was the flashing message: DISENGAGE AUTOPILOT- RESUME MANUAL CONTROL.

The only manual control I executed was to hit the button that said: DISABLE ALARMS. Crashing is one thing, but it's better than being annoyed to death.

For all the sophisticated avionics onboard, the computer did not have the judgement to verify the ability of the person sitting

354

in the pilot's seat. The wild violent buffeting continued. I decided to put on the headset.

"MAYDAY, MAYDAY, MAYDAY I transmitted. I've heard that in a lot of movies.

A voice came back to me. "This is Honolulu control. State call sign and location."

Good questions.

"Honolulu control, I've got a problem."

"Are you declaring an emergency?" Honolulu said.

"Yes, I *am* declaring an emergency." Saying that made me feel a little better.

"What kind of emergency?" Honolulu asked.

"What kinds do I have to choose from?"

"What is your call sign?" Honolulu asked.

"I'm in a Gulfstream G500. Where would I find the call sign?" I asked.

"It's right on top of the middle screen," Honolulu said.

I found it. "It's D-A00TD."

"That's Delta-Alpha Zero Zero Tango Delta?" he said.

"Yeah, that's it," I said.

"Are you a pilot?" Honolulu asked.

"No. Negative."

"Where are the pilot and co-pilot?" Honolulu asked.

I decided I should not say: I killed both of them, and they're lying in the aisle.

"Both pilots are unconscious. I am a...Federal Agent, and this is a National Security Emergency," I said.

"Identify yourself," Honolulu said.

"Negative. I cannot do that over an open circuit, due to the sensitive nature of the mission. There is a nuclear radiation leak aboard the plane. I need you to get me on the ground, and I will explain," I said.

Sounded good to me. I wasn't going to tell him I was CIA, because he could check with the CIA. There are a lot of Federal Agencies, ones that people never heard of. If pressed, I'd tell them I was on a mission authorized by General Goldstein of Cyber Command. They wouldn't know who to call. I was improvising. As I now understood it, improvising in this context means: Quickly manufactured bullshit combined with violence.

355

I'd had a lifetime of experience manufacturing the bullshit, and I began to admit to myself that I enjoyed the violence, if I was the one giving it out.

Chapter One Hundred Fifty Three
In the air
200 miles out from Honolulu

Do you have any experience flying a plane?" Honolulu control asked.

"Negative."

"Okay Delta-Alpha Zero Zero Tango Delta, here's the situation. A serious tropical storm has taken us by surprise. Near hurricane winds. We are diverting all inbound flights; all outbound flights have been cancelled," Honolulu said.

"Well, I gotta come in and land. I can't divert!"

"Roger that, Delta-Alpha Zero Zero Tango Delta," Honolulu said.

Geez, does he have to say that whole Delta-Alpha stuff every time?

"What now?" I asked.

"We're working on a plan, Delta-Alpha. Meanwhile, you are 200 miles out. And beginning descent. Current altitude 38,000 feet. This is normal. Stand by."

"Roger," I said.

What else was I going to do? Not stand by?

Okay, status check time: I was sitting in the pilot's seat of a two-engine jet plane, going just under 600 miles an hour at an altitude of 38,000 feet and in a controlled descent, as guided by the autopilot. The plane's autopilot had been programmed to land at Honolulu International Airport by the two now dead pilots who were lying in the aisle. I had shot them to death. Also aboard was the corpse of CIA agent Alan MacKenzie. I had stabbed and slashed him to death with three knives. The plane I was on was traveling through near hurricane winds and felt like it was out of control.

I had to get safely on the ground, off the plane, avoid being taken into custody, and get a burner phone to call Wishbone.

Since I had never flown a plane before, I needed Air Traffic Control's help to get the plane landed. I concocted a plan to take care of the other issues myself.

357

I was standing by, per instructions from Honolulu control. The radio crackled. Honolulu came back on.

"Delta-Alpha... do you read?"

"I read you, Honolulu."

"We have located an expert in the Gulfstream G500. He is sitting in the tower with me. We will both be on the radio with you. Do you copy?" Honolulu said.

"Yes, I copy."

Honolulu asked, "How many souls onboard?"

If only he knew.

I played dumb. "What?"

"How many people on the plane?" Honolulu asked.

"There are three besides me," I answered.

"Alright, what is your fuel status?" Honolulu said. "It is located---"

"I can see it," I said. "I have, uhhh, I'm 40 percent full."

"Ok, that's more than enough. To simplify communications, I will call myself HONOLULU, the other man in the tower will call himself GULFSTREAM. You refer to yourself as---"

"DELTA ALPHA," I said.

"Roger that, DELTA ALPHA. I am turning you over to GULFSTREAM," Honolulu said.

GULFSTREAM came on. "This is GULFSTREAM. Are you okay?"

I didn't know how to answer that. "I have a special situation. Do you and HONOLULU have Top Secret security clearances?" I asked, even though I suspected the answer was 'No.'

"Negative," GULFSTREAM said.

"Ok. I will give you a simplified version of the situation. I am on a highly classified mission. The plane has a nuclear device onboard. There is a critical problem with the device, a radiation leak. The two pilots are unconscious, as is the one other passenger. I was unconscious until being awoken by violent buffeting of the plane. Are you both with me so far?"

"Yes," both voices said.

That got their attention. Even over an airplane radio there's a certain timbre in people's voices when they think you are flying a plane that is carrying an unstable atomic bomb with the

358

intention of landing at their airport, you have no experience as a pilot, and you're arriving in the middle of a hurricane.

"Is there any chance the device could detonate?" It was HONOLULU talking.

I waited to answer. "A small possibility. What is certain is a radiation leak. I have been effected. My head is swollen to twice the normal size. The others, lying on the floor, look worse, they may be dead."

HONOLULU again, "You should not be landing here! And you should be talking to Joint Base Hickham, a military facility!"

"How far away is that from your tower?" I asked.

"We share the runways," HONOLULU said.

"It wouldn't make any difference then. Anybody within ten miles…" I let that statement hang. "But don't worry, it's probably not going to go off. But now you know the importance of not letting me crash. By the way, if the plane crashes in the ocean near you…well, you've heard of Fucushima, Japan?"

I was laying the improvising on thick. I wished I could see the looks on their faces.

"Do you copy that, HONOLULU?" I asked.

"Copy," HONOLULU said.

"When I get on the ground, do not have airport personnel enter the plane! Have me taxi to the farthest possible spot from the terminal. Send out two cars. Have the driver of one car get into the other vehicle, and that vehicle should leave the vicinity as soon as possible. I will drive the other car myself since I have been exposed to radioactivity. Have a new burner cell phone in my car. I will convert that to an encrypted phone. You got all that?" I said.

"Roger that DELTA ALPHA." Honolulu said.

"It is imperative that no one enter the plane. I will arrange with highly trained military personnel to handle that situation, including the three people currently lying on the floor," I said. "Now, let's get me on the ground."

Chapter One Hundred Fifty Four
In the air
100 miles out from Honolulu International Airport

GULFSTREAM spoke next. "The Gulfstream G500 has highly advanced avionics---"

"I saw that video," I said. "I don't want to buy one, just tell me what to do."

"You're about 100 miles out. Your airspeed should be 350, altitude 19,000 feet. Can you confirm?" GULFSTREAM said.

I looked at the screens. "Confirmed. Airspeed 350, altitude 19,000."

"The plane is very smart. There are only two things you have to do. One: when the airspeed hits 125, you are to lower the landing gear. I will tell you when. You will touch the part of the screen that says: GEAR DOWN. You will hear a thump that indicates the gear is down, and the control panel will display: GEAR LOCKED," GULFSTREAM said.

"Roger. You will tell me when to do that?" I asked.

"Affirmative," GULFSTREAM said.

"What's the second thing?" I asked.

"When the wheels touch down, you need to hit: REVERSE THRUSTERS. It will be displayed below the GEAR DOWN box." GULFSTREAM said. "You need to do that as soon as you hear the wheels hit. Otherwise, the plane will not stop on time, and you will slide into the ocean. Don't wait for me to tell you. You copy that?"

"I copy. Engage REVERSE THRUSTERS. Negative on slide into ocean. Roger," I said. "Anything else?"

"Good news and bad news. The good news: you will be landing at the furthest point from the terminal. No taxiing required," GULFSTREAM said.

"The bad news?" I asked.

"Winds are gusting up to 85 miles per hour. We wouldn't let even the most experienced pilot land in these conditions. Because of these conditions you could be tipped over or hit with a downdraft so that one second the plane is 100 feet up, and the next slammed into the runway. I just wanted to prepare you," GULFSTREAM said.

"Is there anything I can do about it?" I asked.

360

"No," GULFSTREAM said.

"Hey, I was in a worse jam yesterday," I said. "Did you guys ever see the movie *Airplane*?"

"Yes," and "Of course," I heard two voices say.

"Well, this is the part where Lloyd Bridges says, "I think I picked the wrong week to give up sniffing glue," I said.

Chapter One Hundred Fifty Five
In the Air
50 miles out from Honolulu International Airport

Fifty miles goes by fast when you're going 350 mph.
GULFSTREAM would update me with airspeeds and altitudes that I would confirm. Other than that, there was no chatter.

My speed was slowing, and the descent was gradual, but the wind buffeting the plane was more vicious than ever. Rather than a steady push, it kept changing direction and speed which produced vicious, loud slams. The noise was scarier than the movements, it sounded like the plane was being hit by slabs of concrete. On a random basis the bottom seemed to drop out and the plane felt like it just sank straight down. Then the plane would rise 100 feet at a gulp, but up wasn't as bad as down.

My one happy thought is that I had convinced HONOLULU and GULFSTREAM that I had an atomic weapon onboard, and if I crashed it would unleash a nuclear Armageddon. That made me smile. I knew that if I crashed it would just kill me. My three passengers could not get any deader.

"DELTA ALPHA, you should be touching down in two minutes," GULFSTREAM said. "What is your airspeed?"

"175," I said.

"Prepare to GEAR DOWN on my command," GULFSTREAM said.

As airspeed slowed and I descended, the wind had more command over the plane. Pitch, yaw, and roll all took their turns trying to make the plane crash. One moment the left wing lifted as though the plane was going to flip. HAL the autopilot was moving the yoke and pedals at frantic speed, trying to stabilize the plane. The wings leveled but a jolt of wind knocked the plane into what I was sure was a diagonal flight path.

"Airspeed 125. Gear down!" GULFSTREAM said.

I hit the gear down icon, and heard a mechanical sound, then a thump. GEAR LOCKED; the display announced.

"Gear Locked," I told GULFSTREAM.

362

Putting the gear down produced drag that slowed the plane. HAL had to increase throttle to keep the speed at 125. Altitude 200 feet.

"Prepare to engage reverse thrusters," GULFSTREAM said. "Altitude 100 feet."

The plane was over the runway. A downdraft hit, and the jet bounced off the runway, then rebounded into the air. I hit ENGAGE REVERSE THRUSTERS. The plane felt like it stopped, then bounced hard off the runway again.

A loud crashing sound came from outside and the nose went down hard. It was evident even to me that the front landing gear had collapsed, so the nose was skidding down the runway at 125 mph or so, throwing off sparks. Sparks are bad on an airplane that still has almost half its fuel in the tanks.

Rain from the tropical storm was pelting the runway. Even with no functional front landing gear the plane was still bouncing into the air when the unsteady wind gusts picked it up, then slammed down when the wind changed. When firmly on the runway the plane skidded on the wet pavement. Finally, the bouncing stopped.

There was a lot of noise. The engines screamed from what I presumed was the reverse thrusters, and a frightening metallic scraping emanated from the bottom of the nose. I wondered if the metal skin could get ripped right off the bottom of the plane. I lifted my feet off the floor of the cockpit, as though that would save me from injury.

The nose whipped from side to side on the pavement. We didn't seem to be slowing down. I could see a strip of bright lights in front of the plane, and behind the light strip was a fence. Behind that: the Pacific Ocean. The plane finally seemed to be losing speed, hit the bright light strip and knocked it down, then slid into the fence, still going what seemed like too fast.

The plane's nose knocked down a pole of the fence. The chain link fence stretched, then held. The very nose of the plane was suspended over the ocean, the rest on solid ground.

"Tower can you hear me?" I asked.

"Affirmative Delta Alpha. Shut down the engines." GULFSTREAM said.

"How do I shut off the engines?" I asked.

363

He told me.

"Engines shut down," Neither of us talked. I could hear the wind howling and rain pelting the windows. "That was fun. Can I go up and try it again?" I asked.

"The cars are on their way out to you," HONOLULU said.

"Good. Does my car have the burner phone?"

"Yes. You should get off the plane," HONOLULU said.

"Okay. Tell your men not to be shocked by my appearance. My head and face are grossly disfigured due to the exposure to the radiation." I figured this would get them to drop off my car and get the hell out of there without asking me anything, lest they be exposed to the nuclear mutant.

"Roger that," HONOLULU said.

I released the seatbelt. Because the front landing gear had collapsed it was an uphill walk, stepping over the corpses of the pilots on my way to the exit door. I stopped at my seat, picked up the Sig Sauer 9 mm, this time engaging the safety before shoving it down the front of my pants, careful to avoid hitting my swollen purple pecker. I pocketed the Advil. Agent MacKenzie still had the knives sticking out of him, but he was lying beyond where I turned to go to the exit, and I didn't bother giving him a goodbye kick. I figured out how to open the door. The built-in stairs extended, but were crooked because of the angle of the plane, so that the stairs didn't touch the ground.

I didn't have to wait long for the cars. It was easy to pick out which one was mine, even in the dim light I could see it was a thousand-year-old Ford Crown Victoria, that used to be blue but now was purple, the oldest piece of junk car they could find at the airport. I guessed they figured by sitting in it I would contaminate the car and it would have to be disposed of in a nuclear landfill.

The thought that my improvising was working pleased me. It was nice to be on the ground, not throwing off sparks, hurtling out of control down a runway in a heavily damaged piece of machinery at 125 mph, or chained to a wall at the Ministry of Truth.

Chapter One Hundred Fifty Six
On the ground
Honolulu International Airport

The strong unsteady winds made it hard to stand up. I would brace myself against a gust, then it would suddenly stop, and I'd almost fall over. The driving rain hurt as it hit my face. It was time for some more Advil.

The two cars sent out to greet me came closer. The old beater Crown Victoria pulled up maybe 50 feet from me. The driver was wearing a Hawaiian shirt; it was Hawaii.

He got out of the old car and stood looking at me. It was the kind of look of morbid curiosity mixed with pity that someone would give The Dogfaced Boy Freak at a carnival. As far as Mr. Hawaiian shirt knew, my head might pop any second from nuclear radiation overdose swelling.

I did my best to play the part of the Condemned Man and gave him a slow and grim thumbs up gesture. He returned it, then sprinted to the other car. If my head did pop the irradiated goo might spray all over his shirt!

The Crown Victoria was running, and I got in and picked up the burner phone. Wishbone picked up on the third ring.

"Hey Wishbone. I made it to Hawaii!" I said.

"JR, are you okay?" Wishbone asked.

"Short answer: Yes," I said. "No fifteen second stuff here, okay? I can't handle that right now. Let's just talk."

"Alright. Can you get to Joint Base Wickham? Wishbone asked.

"Where's that?" I asked.

"Right next to Honolulu Airport. Can you get there?" he asked.

"Yeah, I've got a car---"

"And you can go by yourself?" Wishbone asked.

"Affirmative," I said.

"It's easy. Go to Hickham. Just drive to the main gate and ask for Mr. Ed Sanchez. He's been briefed. He'll take care of everything," Wishbone said.

"Just like Agent MacKenzie?" I asked.

"Hang up now and go," Wishbone said.

365

I drove toward the terminal, looking for a gate to leave the runway area. There was no activity on any of the runways, but I stayed on what I thought of as service roads. Finally, I came to a gate in the chain link fence. There was a police car blocking the gate. I stopped my car.

I made some gestures with my hand, signifying that I wanted the cop to get out of his car and unlock and open the gate.

The cop must have been briefed on the radiation leak situation because he gave me the same look of pity as the last guy.

After he opened the gate and moved his car I drove through and stopped beside his vehicle. He was back behind the wheel of his cop car. I gestured for him to roll down his window. He didn't want to.

Some radiation might jump out my window and into his.

My Crown Victoria was so old I had to hand crank the window down, which was hard to do with my injured shoulder and ribs. I had to use both hands to accomplish the mission.

The things I had to do to get my $50 million back! It was a lot easier to come by the first time, all I had to do was inherit and invest the money.

Reluctantly the cop complied.

"How do I get to Joint Base Hickham?" I asked.

"We share the runways with them, but if you want to go to the base, drive around the right side of this big white building. It will take you out to the main drag. You can't miss the sign for Hickham," he said.

"Thanks for your help," I said.

Before I could roll up the window he shouted, "Hey are you... are you alright?"

"Look at me," I said. "What do you think?"

Chapter One Hundred Fifty Seven
Honolulu, Hawaii
Joint Base Hickham

I stopped at the main gate. The sentry asked me who I wanted to see. "Mr. Ed Sanchez," I said.

"Your name?" he asked.

I didn't answer right away. I thought about whipping out Alan MacKenzie's CIA creds but decided not to do that.

"Sir? Your name?"

"JR Johnson," I said.

He looked at a clipboard. "Mr. Sanchez is expecting you." He gave me directions.

Telling the truth is good policy sometimes. But not always.

I drove to a small plain building. As I got out a man walked out of the building and stood next to my door.

"I'm Ed Sanchez. You're JR Johnson?"

"Yeah," I said.

Ed Sanchez was maybe 5'8", trim, dark haired, neat, a sharp looking guy. "Have you looked at your face in a mirror lately?" he asked.

"Yup."

"That's some car they gave you at HNL. I'm surprised you made it over here. You're going to have to tell me what's going on so I can clean up this mess," Sanchez said.

"First of all, you're going to have to tell me who you are," I said.

"I'm a friend of Wishbone's," Sanchez said.

"CIA?" I asked.

Sanchez hesitated, then answered, "Yeah."

I reached in the pouch of my hoodie and flipped open the stolen wallet, displaying MacKenzie's CIA ID card. "You mean like him?" I asked.

"Where's MacKenzie?" Sanchez asked.

"He's still on the plane, but he ain't getting off. He's dead. I killed him."

Sanchez was quiet for a moment, then he said, "I never liked him anyhow. Look, it doesn't seem like you're comfortable telling me all the details---"

367

"Well, gee whiz, I'm a little paranoid right now," I said.

"Okay, okay. Why don't you call Wishbone? He'll tell you what to do," Sanchez said.

"Good idea," I said.

Still standing outside the building I called Wishbone on the burner. He picked right up. I explained the situation to Wishbone.

"Do I tell him everything?" I asked Wishbone.

"Look JR, do you trust me?" Wishbone asked.

"Yeah."

"I trust Ed Sanchez. You have to trust him like you trust me. You have to tell him everything. He's got to clean up the mess. And he's making arrangements to get you home," Wishbone explained.

"Home? You mean Spicewood, Texas home?" I asked.

"Yeah," Wishbone said.

"That sounds good," I said.

Chapter One Hundred Fifty Eight
Honolulu, Hawaii
Joint Base Hickham

I noticed a plaque on the building I was standing in front of. *Office of Experimental Physiology.*

"What is that? You're a Physiologist? "I asked Sanchez.

"Nope. The sign just scares people away. Especially pilots. They hate doctors. We like our privacy," Sanchez said. He opened the front door for me. In the foyer a nice-looking woman sat behind a desk. She wore a Hawaiian shirt. "This is Robin, she works with me."

"I suppose you're armed," I said to Robin.

"Hi," Robin said. She opened her middle desk drawer and got out a Glock. "We like to be prepared for any contingency."

I made a mock 'hands up' gesture as we walked past, into a larger office. Robin watched me without smiling.

"Have a seat," Sanchez said. He sat behind his desk. "Tell me the story."

"I don't know where to start," I said.

"I talked to Wishbone after he spoke to you in Guam. I know you were supposed to kill MacKenzie and the two pilots. Why don't you start there?" he suggested.

"Okay. I took three knives from the galley and stabbed MacKenzie to death. Then I took his gun and shot the two pilots," I said.

"Just like that?" Sanchez asked.

"What did you want me to do? Give 'em a Jury Trial? I overheard them in the cockpit, arguing about money with MacKenzie, how much they were going to get paid to sell me out to the Chinese."

"Do you have any training in field work?" Sanchez asked.

"No, but I've been told I'm a natural with improvising. In fact, the President of the United States told me that."

"No shit? You talked to the President of the United States?" Sanchez asked.

"Yeah," I said.

"I don't think I want to know any more about that. So, how did you get the plane from Guam to Hawaii?" he asked.

369

"Autopilot."

"You're a pilot?" Sanchez asked.

"No. The pilots had already programmed in the flight to Hawaii. They hadn't changed it yet. I just had to figure out how to engage the program," I said.

"So how did you do that?" he asked.

"I looked it up on YouTube," I said.

"I don't believe you,"

"I don't care. Look, I have to tell you the important part," I said.

"What's that?"

"I made up a story for the tower at Honolulu. I told them the plane was carrying a nuclear device on a highly classified mission, and that the other three people on the plane were overcome with radiation poisoning,"

"Why did you do that?" Sanchez asked.

"I couldn't have them coming on---"

"--the plane when you landed! That's brilliant," Sanchez said.

"It would have been hard to explain the three stiffs. MacKenzie still has two knives sticking out of him. I told the tower that my face looked like this due to exposure to radiation. You should have seen the look on the face of the guy who delivered the car to me!"

"That explains why they gave you that old car. Look, you're a real good bullshitter. Are you bullshitting me now?"

"No. I even told the tower that there was a chance the nuclear device would detonate if I crash landed," I said.

"Why did you do that?"

"I wanted them to focus on helping me. I told them that anyone within a ten-mile radius would be toast, so they wouldn't try to bail out on me," I said.

Sanchez sat at his desk. He twiddled his thumbs. "Wishbone knows some interesting people,"

"Wishbone is an interesting person himself," I said.

"You might have a future in this line of work," Sanchez said.

Chapter One Hundred Fifty Nine
Moscow
Office of the Lider

The Lider's secretary informed him that the Supreme Commander of NATO was calling him from Brussels.

The Lider waited until his translator could be located. The translator explained that he and the Lider were on the line.

The NATO Commander said, "I am calling to officially inform you that Colonel Nihisky, on his own free will, has requested Political Asylum, and that asylum has been granted."

The translator began to repeat the message in Russian, but the Lider interrupted, in English, "This is bullshit! I do not believe you!"

The NATO Commander said, "I see your language skills have improved, Mr. President."

"Go on," the Lider said. There was no longer any pretense of translation.

"I am calling for two reasons. First was to inform you regarding Nihisky. Second, we need to make new arrangements for you to recover the prototype helicopter, which is sitting untouched in Polish territory. My only other comment is that we had nothing to do with either of these situations."

"So?" the Lider asked.

The NATO Commander said, "Unless you want us to keep the prototype helicopter, I suggest your staff develop a new plan to get it back."

The Lider said, "Someone from our Army Staff will contact your staff to make arrangements. Any more pleasant news for me?"

"No, Mr. President," the NATO Commander said.

"Very well," the Lider said, then hung up. He jumped out of his seat and charged around his desk. The translator sat back in his chair, but the Lider's target was something else.

The Lider reached behind the drapes and picked up the jar containing the pickled head of Kravanesko, held it over his head with two hands, and smashed it down on the floor. The thick carpet cushioned the impact, and the jar remained in one piece. The Lider picked up one of the antique visitor's chairs and smashed down on the jar, this time breaking the glass

371

vessel and spilling the formaldehyde onto the carpet. Kravanesko's head rolled so that it rested face up.

The translator was sitting back in his chair, his hands clutching the arms. The formaldehyde stunk.

"Are you sure you want your job?" the Lider asked him.

The translator sat, frozen and silent.

"Never mind," the Lider said. "You can go now. Ask my secretary to come in, will you?"

The Lider's secretary came into the room. She was old, plain in appearance to the point of bordering on androgenous and betrayed no emotion. She had been the Lider's secretary since his days in the KGB.

"Just another day at the office," the Lider said, pointing to the head on the floor. "Get me Sierra Quinn's phone number, will you please?

Chapter One Hundred Sixty
Dallas
Omni Hotel

Sierra Quinn was watching True Crime TV in her hotel room. For Quinn it was like eating potato chips, she knew it was garbage, but she couldn't stop. None of the idiot criminals ever came close to getting away with their crimes. As a former cop this amused Quinn. Her iPhone rang.

"Yes sir," she answered.

"You recognize my voice?" the Lider asked.

Quinn said, "Yes."

"It's time for you to get to work. I need to send a message. You need to kill JR Johnson," the Lider said.

"Good," Quinn said.

"Go kill him where he lives. If anybody gets in the way, kill them too," the Lider said. "We don't need a clean-up crew this time. Leave a mess."

"Great" Quinn said.

Chapter One Hundred Sixty One
The White House

It's wonderful how this works Chan," the President said. "I tell you to get the story out, you whisper it to one person, who tells somebody else, and so on through 15 people. Then we get to watch it told, not accurately, on CNN, Fox, MSNBC, BBC, and so on."

In the aftermath of the Ransomware payments, and the subsequent restoration of the seized computer systems, a story was coming out of Belarus that several employees, including the CEO, of a sophisticated ransomware operation had been murdered, execution style. Commentators were asking whether this act was in some way a reprisal for the ransomware attacks.

The White House Press Secretary was asked during her daily briefing for a comment. She had truthfully stated that she had no knowledge of the incident.

Congressman Safi was waiting in a White House anteroom for the President. He had been summoned for an unexplained meeting. "Chan, go get Safi and bring him in, will you," the President said.

When Safi came into the Oval Office, the door to the private conference room was already open, and the President stood.

"I hope this is important. I have a very busy day scheduled," Safi told the President.

"You're going to want to reschedule," the President said.

No pleasantries, no handshakes were exchanged. The President indicated where Safi was to sit.

"Notice there are just three of us," the President said. "We will keep this whole thing quiet if you cooperate."

"What whole thing?" Safi said.

Without further explanation the President hit the button on a remote control. A panel opened and a video was displayed. The President froze the image.

It was slightly grainy footage of Safi and a woman on the top floor of a parking garage.

"The audio is excellent as well. The woman who you are meeting, who identifies herself as 'Patricia' is in fact named Sierra Quinn and is a former New York City detective turned

374

assassin. She's working for the Russians right now, as you know," the President said.

Safi watched the video without comment, until the moment that Quinn said, "The news I have for you is this: you will do everything we tell you, without deviation. If you follow your orders, you will be the next President of the United States. If you displease the Lider, I have permission to kill you---"

Then Safi said, "Alright, you've proved your point. What's to stop me from claiming that this is just one of those Deep—"

"Deep Fake videos? The public can't tell the difference, but that claim would hold up for maybe five minutes. Any expert can tell the difference. If you try that line, you'll just end up looking like a bigger lying sack of shit," the President said.

Safi said, "So what do you want? Me to pull out of the Presidential race? Alright, I'll do that."

"That's not enough. Before I tell you what you're going to do, let me share one other item of information we have," the President said.

"What?' Safi said.

"We have a source from inside the Kremlin. You knew it was this woman, who you call Patricia, not some robbers who murdered John Alteiri. You stood there and watched her shoot him, then lied about it to the Dallas police. All to protect your political campaign, and your corrupt deal with the Russians. Our source inside the Kremlin has defected and will testify against you if it comes to that. Lying to the police in a situation like that is a felony, and you will be prosecuted. You will be tried in State court in Texas, then brought up on Federal election charges," the President said.

Safi put his head in his hands. The President and Wheeler sat without talking. Finally, Safi said, "What do you want?"

The President said, "our non-negotiable demand: Today, within two hours of leaving here, you are to announce your retirement from public life. Effective immediately. Only reason: to spend more time with your family."

Safi sat silent.

Wheeler said," Look jerkoff, you have no cards to play. I advised the President not to cut you this deal. I want you to go to prison for the rest of your life. You better take the deal before he changes his mind."

The President said, "Let me reiterate. This is a one-time offer. Within two hours you will make an announcement to the press. You are leaving public life, effective immediately, the reason: to spend more time with your family. You are to take no questions. You are to never make a public appearance again. If you so much as attend a Rotary Club lunch in Bakersfield, or give an off-the-record interview to anybody, we will leak this story. If you live up to the terms of the offer, the story stays buried. Understand?"

"Yes," Safi said.

The President said, "Not that I care, but the Russians will be watching you. If you shoot your mouth off, they may decide it would be better for them if they kill you."

Safi said, "I...I didn't mean---"

"Get out of here. Don't let the door hit you in the ass," the President said. "We're watching. Two hours."

Wheeler called after the departing Safi, "Go work on your shitty golf game!"

When Safi was gone the President said, "That was fun. It's nice to have the power to rip a man's soul out in about 60 seconds."

Wheeler said, "He already sold his soul."

Chapter One Hundred Sixty Two
Honolulu
Joint Base Hickham

Ed Sanchez was writing on a yellow pad as I sat in his office. "This is going to work. First, we're getting you on an Air Force flight. It stops in LA then on to Lackland Air Force Base in San Antonio. Close enough to home for you?" he said.

I said, "Sure, about an hour and a half drive from home. When do I leave here?"

"Fifteen minutes. I have to get you out of here before anybody starts looking for you with a Geiger counter," Sanchez said. "I'll drive you out to your flight, but you might have to wait for hours for the weather to clear. Once you're on the plane, you're safe."

"Okay," I said. We walked out past Robin.

"You might meet this guy again, Robin," Sanchez said.

We got into his car, a standard issue government thing. "Left the keys in the Crown Victoria," I told him.

"I hope somebody steals it," Sanchez said. "It would save me having to explain how it got parked in front of my office."

We drove a confusing route to get to the plane, and Sanchez had to flash his ID to guards a couple times. He said, "You did a good job with your bullshit to Honolulu tower. They're not going to go near the plane. I'm going to arrange to have a team in Hazmat suits take the dead guys off in body bags, which I'm sure will be watched through binoculars from the tower."

"They're going to be watching to see if the body bags are glowing." I said.

"Well, it is their runway. It can't be used again until the Gulfstream is removed. I'll arrange for specially trained Air Force personnel to tow it away, then they'll foam down the runway with stuff used for chemical spills. The area will test okay for radiation levels, because there aren't any to begin with. Nobody will ever know that you just iced those guys," Sanchez said.

We arrived near a big Air Force transport. "What kind of plane is that?" I asked.

377

"It's a C-17 Globe Master. A big boy. This version has a couple bunks and a kitchen. You can sack out, get something to eat," Sanchez said.

"I'm not chewing too good right now," I said.

"There's only a crew of three on this flight. Don't bother them, they won't bother you." Sanchez said.

Sanchez got out of his car and talked to an Air Force officer. They laughed. Sanchez gestured for me to get out of the car. I walked up to the two of them.

"This is Major Terry," Sanchez said to me. Then to the major he said, "this is …your cargo."

I silently shook hands with the major, who looked at my face. "Are you going to be okay?" the major said.

I nodded. Sanchez took me aside. "I can't believe you made it this far. You look like shit."

"Yeah, but I'm alive," I said, "and the hard part is over."

Chapter One Hundred Sixty Three
The White House

Wheeler said to the President, "General Goldstein is on his way to Cyber Command."

"Good," the President said, "Now let's call our buddy Admiral Stockbridge."

Stockbridge came on the line.

"Admiral, this is the President."

"Yes sir?" Stockbridge said.

"Admiral, I am calling to personally notify you that you are fired. I will not accept your resignation. Get out of your building within five minutes if you want to keep your retirement benefits," The President said.

"Sir…I…can you explain---"

"You shouldn't have slept in the same bed as Safi. Now get out! The White House Press secretary will be announcing today that you got fired, period. General Goldstein is reassuming command. Understand? The President said.

"Yes sir."

"Have your ass in the parking lot in five minutes," the President said. "This will be the last free ride you get in a government limo."

Chapter One Hundred Sixty Four
Dallas

Sierra Quinn had to decide how to get into Barbara Jean Parker's ranch. It wasn't that simple. Quinn had to get in and still have the element of surprise, so she couldn't just bust down the gate.

The Lider had told her to kill JR Johnson and anybody else who got in the way. Quinn took that as carte blanche, and she wanted to kill Barbara Jean Parker first. Parker had ruined her operation in Spicewood the last time, and had killed her Russian assistant, Lev. Ideally Quinn would get to kill Barbara Jean Parker as her new husband JR watched, and then she'd kill him too.

Rather than fly to Austin, Quinn decided to drive a rental car from Dallas. She got an SUV, which Quinn thought would fit in as she drove around Spicewood, reconnoitering and looking for a weakness to exploit.

Chapter One Hundred Sixty Five
The White House

The President and Chan Wheeler met with Toni Anne Laudano in the small conference room.

"Okay, Toni Anne, we have the money, and we're using it as you suggested," the President said.

"Fifteen billion for your campaign, $50 million to JR Johnson, and the rest to the new operation?" Toni Anne asked.

"I decided to give Johnson a two million dollar tip. He got $52 million. To take care of the bogus mortgage the Russians took on his house. It's in his account," the President said.

"Good," Toni Anne said. "What are you going to call the new operation?"

Wheeler said, "In your honor, it's code-named Operation Baker Baker."

"B-B huh? Does that stand for what I think?" Toni Anne asked.

The President said, "Yes, Operation Ball Buster. It's perfect. You have around $150 billion to bust the balls of our enemies. The Lider is one problem. As you know it's really the Chinese we're worried about. And some of these internet near-trillionaires are starting to think they are above the law."

"Fantastic," Toni Anne said, "I've been a ball buster my whole life, but not with that kind of budget."

"With General Goldstein back at Cyber Command, you'll go back to work there. He knows about Baker Baker, but we've agreed that he's kept in the dark regarding any details. You're going to have to wear two hats," the President said.

"That's a big work load we're asking of you," Wheeler said.

"I need to work. I haven't got anything else to do," Toni Anne said.

The President said, "Well I do. I've got to get ready for an interview. Meanwhile, you start thinking of ways to bust the Chinese's balls, okay?"

381

Chapter One Hundred Sixty Six
The White House
Roosevelt Room

The President face was powdered, and Reporter Anne was very glammed up for this interview. All the equipment was in place.

"Mr. President, in light of the unprecedented events of the last several days, thank you for this opportunity," Anne started.

"Well Anne, thank you for this forum to explain some things to the American people," the President said.

"First, Mr. President, the nation is recovering from the effects of the biggest ransomware attack in history. What can the government do about stopping such attacks in the future?"

The President answered. "Anne, I need to be blunt. If the companies that were effected, had paid attention to directives sent to them by Cyber Command, this never would have happened. It turns out that Admiral Stockbridge, who had taken over Cyber Command, suspended, without our knowledge, any follow-up to get the laggard companies to comply. Admiral Stockbridge has been fired. General Goldstein has been reassigned back to Cyber Command."

Anne asked, "Are you implying that Admiral Stockbridge was somehow complicit in---"

The President interrupted, "No Anne. Admiral Stockbridge is a loyal officer with a long career of military service. What I'm saying is: He made an unacceptably poor and unilateral decision and deserves to lose his job. What he did, on his own, cost American companies untold billions of dollars."

Anne asked, "Admiral Stockbridge is said to be close with Congressman Safi. Does this situation have anything to do with Congressman Safi's announcement to so abruptly leave public office?"

"We have no comment on *former* Congressman Safi," the President said.

"Mr. President, it is being widely reported that the offices of a suspected ransomware perpetrator in Belarus were the site of an execution style slaughter of eight employees. This happened coincidentally when wargame exercises by NATO were taking

382

place nearby, over the Polish border from Belarus. Is there any connection to the killings and NATO?" Anne asked.

"Anne, let me say this: I categorically deny that the NATO forces participating in this regularly scheduled exercise had anything to do the killings in Belarus. But let me also make this point: The perpetrators of ransomware attacks have to get the message. When billions of dollars are stolen, the victims of the attacks may individually or collectively hire mercenaries to take reprisals. We are studying that possibility right now." The President said.

"Are you saying that mercenaries in the employ of U.S. companies carried out these executions?" Anne asked.

"We are studying the situation," the President said.

"Do you condemn this attack?" Anne asked.

"We are studying the situation," the President said.

Chapter One Hundred Sixty Seven
Austin, Texas

Sierra Quinn had checked into the Austin Proper Hotel, the most expensive in town. She dressed in more sensible clothes. Her work clothes in Spicewood would not be an expensive gown, but lace up boots, jeans, and plain blouse topped by a tan canvas jacket. Same gun, though, but no silencer needed this time. Quinn spent a moment admiring herself in the mirror.

Damn, I look good in a pair of jeans, she thought.

Quinn didn't want to leave anything behind, so carrying her oversized bag which contained all her clothes, she walked into the hallway.

She hoped she could go out to the ranch and get her killing done. If that was accomplished, Quinn wouldn't go back to the Austin Proper Hotel, she'd head for the San Antonio airport and eventually Bali, Indonesia.

If for some reason she couldn't get the job done today, Quinn would go back to the hotel, and try again in Spicewood tomorrow.

Chapter One Hundred Sixty Eight
Spicewood, Texas

Sierra Quinn was driving toward Barbara Jean's ranch, when she saw a farm truck pulled up in front of the ranch gate. Quinn decided to pull in behind the truck.

The driver, an enormous redneck in bib overalls was standing in front of the box that was used to call the house. He looked back at Quinn as she got out of her SUV and approached him.

"Help you ma'am" he asked.

"Go ahead with what you're doing. I don't want to interrupt. Then I have a question for you," Quinn said.

The redneck hit the call button. Barbara Jean answered. "Miss Barbara Jean, it's Homer. I just wanted to remind you that I'm coming by tomorrow morning to pick up the two head of cattle for the auction. About 9 a.m., okay?"

A tinny voice came back. "Yes Homer, see you then," Barbara Jean said. "I'll meet you out by the barn."

Homer turned back to face Quinn. "What is it you need help with, ma'am?"

Quinn asked for directions to Fredericksburg. Even in this day of GPS technology, people loved to give strangers directions.

Quinn had her plan. She'd be back at 9 a.m. tomorrow.

Chapter One Hundred Sixty Nine
Edwards Air Force Base, California

I slept the whole flight from Hawaii to California, only the descent of the plane woke me up. Before we landed Major Terry came to talk to me in the cubicle that held the two bunks. I was in the bottom one, the other was unoccupied.

"I'm gonna suggest that you just stay here in the bunk while we're on the ground, We are loading some cargo for Lackland, and it is unnecessary for the enlisted men to see you. Don't want to start any gossip," he said. He looked at my face. "Are you sure you feel okay?"

"I've been assured that I'm going to be fine, from someone with experience in this kind of injury" I told him. I didn't mention that the assurance came directly from the Beloved Chairman in North Korea.

"We'll be on the ground here for about an hour, then it's about three more hours to Texas," the Major said.

I said, "I've been through a lot of time zones. What time are---"

"Let me make it simple for you. We'll be landing about 7 a.m. Texas time," Major Terry said.

I thought about calling Barbara Jean and telling her, but I decided to surprise her with the good news.

386

Chapter One Hundred Seventy
Today
San Antonio Texas
Lackland Air Force Base

The landing was smooth. It's nice landing without 85 mile per hour crosswinds, and with a couple of Air Force pilots at the controls. When we stopped taxiing Major Terry came to see me.

"We've got a car here to pick you up. Hey, it looks like you've been through a lot, in the service of your country. So, thank you for your service," he said, as he extended his hand.

I shook with him. "It's not something I can talk about."

A lot of people are serving the country, but I'm the one who got $52 million for it. Life's not fair.

"You might want to put your hood up," Major Terry suggested.

"If you think my face looks bad, you should see my pecker," He looked surprised.

"Not that I'm meaning to show it to you," I said.

"I'll take your word for it," the major said.

Chapter One Hundred Seventy One
San Antonio, TX

An enlisted man who looked about 14 years old gave me a ride to a car rental agency that was just off the base. He didn't say a word to me and tried not to get caught staring at my gigantic black and blue head.

When I walked in the lobby of the car rental place there were only a few customers in there, and they all gave me the same slack jawed look that Lola used to get when people realized they were in the presence of a Movie Star. In my own way, I was a star, the star of my very own freak show.

As I stood in front of the rental agent, I remembered that I didn't have my wallet, but I did have Alan MacKenzie's wallet, and his IDs and credit cards. I hoped my buddy Alan had not been reported dead yet.

"Sir, are you okay to drive?" the agent said to me.

I chuckled. "It looks worse than it is. The doctor has given me clearance," I said. I flipped open MacKenzie's wallet to display his CIA ID. "I'm on official government business," I said in a low voice.

"Yes sir," the agent came back to me in the same quiet tone. "Of course, you get the government rate."

"I'm going to be needing a large vehicle," I said.

So my head will fit.

We completed the transaction to put me in a GMC Yukon. I handed the agent Alan MacKenzie's American Express card. I tried not to look nervous. With the state of my face, it wasn't hard to hide my emotions.

The rental agent told me where I could find the Yukon. I turned from the counter. The people in the lobby gave me a very wide berth on the way to the door.

I walked out the door. A hand grabbed my shoulder.

The rental agent said, "Sir there's a problem."

Oh-oh.

"I can explain," I said, but no explanation was coming to me just yet.

"Huh? he said. "Well, I slipped up. I forgot to give you the government discount."

388

"I'm on a time critical mission," I said. "It's okay, we'll take care of everything later. When I return the vehicle."

"Okay sir. When you fill out the online customer satisfaction survey, please don't mention this," the rental agent said.

"Your secret is safe with me," I said.

I was sure Alan MacKenzie wouldn't be complaining. American Express would have to work it out with his estate.

I went to the lot and found my maroon GMC Yukon. It was about an hour and a half drive to Barbara Jean's ranch. I didn't want to speed and get pulled over with MacKenzie's driver's license, but in Texas if you do the speed limit it makes the cops suspicious because you are driving too slowly, so I went with five miles an hour over the posted speed.

The Yukon's entertainment system featured satellite radio which was tuned to a station featuring Novelty Hits. Before I could turn it off, the 1976 abomination "Disco Duck" came on. I figured that must be an omen. The song has a good beat, and was fun for about a minute and a half, but unfortunately is four minutes long.

Chapter One Hundred Seventy Two
Spicewood, Texas

Sierra Quinn was in Spicewood at 8:30, cruising her SUV on the road near Barbara Jean's ranch. She had a plan for using Homer to get her inside the gate.

It seemed like forever until she saw Homer's truck approaching Barbara Jean's gate. She waited until Homer spoke on the intercom system and the electric gate began to open. Quinn sped her SUV right up behind Homer's truck and slammed on the brakes. She got out and ran to the driver's side of the truck. The window was open, and Quinn jumped up on the running board.

Quinn aimed her Glock at Homer's head and said, "Drive!"

Homer looked at Quinn, "Didn't I give you directions yesterday? What---"

"Shut up and drive inside the gate!" Quinn demanded. "Then stop."

Homer put both hands on the wheel and slowly drove about fifteen feet into the property. "Put it in park," Quinn ordered.

"Huh?" Homer said.

"Put the truck in park!"

Homer did so. Quinn raised her gun to shoot him. Homer ducked and threw up his hand with amazing quickness for a man so big. Quinn fired, but the bullet struck Homer's huge left bicep and deflected into his chest. He was wounded, but not dead.

"Damn," Quinn said.

Homer was leaning toward the passenger side.

Quinn said, "Well, Homer, I've got to make a decision. I'm not sure I brought enough ammo." She paused for a moment.

"I'm going to throw you out here in the ditch. You won't be going anywhere. When I'm done in there, I'll come back and kill you if I have any bullets left," Quinn said. She grabbed Homer by the collar.

The guy had to weigh 300 pounds.

Quinn pulled him out onto the ground of the gravel driveway. Then she used her feet to roll him off into the ditch running along the side of the long drive. He was still visible, but less so.

390

"Where's your cell phone," she asked, but Homer was delirious. Blood was running out of his mouth, but he was breathing. She checked and found an old flip phone in a holster on Homer's belt. "What, do you think you're Batman?" Quinn pocketed Homer's phone. "Don't go anywhere, I'll be back."

The electric gate was closing. Homer hadn't pulled the truck up far enough, so the gate hit the truck. Quinn got in the truck and pulled up, but the gate didn't close all the way. The two sides of the gate left a gap in the middle of maybe four feet.

Quinn decided to leave her SUV right where it was and to drive the truck out to the barn. Her Glock model carried the standard 17 rounds in a clip, she had used one. That would probably be enough to have one left over for Homer on the way out. He was the lowest priority target, and he might just die before she got back anyhow.

Quinn drove past the house without seeing anyone. She pulled the truck near the big front sliding doors of the barn, grabbed her Glock, and got out of the truck. She was ready to start shooting, if necessary.

Barbara Jean was fussing with a latch on one of the horse stalls and didn't look up when she heard someone enter.

"Homer, I'll be right with you," Barbara Jean said.

Sierra Quinn hit her in the temple with the butt of her gun. Barbara Jean went down in the aisle of the barn. When she came to, her hands were tied together above her head, the rope slung tight over the beam at the far end of the barn, and her feet were bound.

Chapter One Hundred Seventy Three
Spicewood, TX

We've met before," Sierra Quinn said. Then she slapped Barbara Jean hard across the face. Barb spat some blood but remained silent.

"Where's your husband?" Quinn asked.

"What?" Barbara Jean asked.

"Your husband, JR Johnson. Where is he?" Quinn asked.

Barbara Jean looked at her hands, then her feet. "You're pretty good at tying knots. Have any experience in 4-H?" she asked.

Quinn slapped her in the face again. "Where's Johnson?"

"I don't know," Barbara Jean said. "He's not here."

"When is he going to be back?" Quinn asked.

"I don't have any idea," Barbara Jean answered.

Quinn pressed her Glock up to Barbara Jean's left temple. "You better start giving me better answers, or I'm going to start shooting the horses. How many of them do I have to kill before you start telling me the truth?"

Barbara Jean said nothing.

Quinn walked to the first stall. "Oh, isn't this precious! All the horse's stalls have little name plates. Well, *Molly* is going to be the first horse to get shot unless you cooperate."

Quinn aimed her Glock at Molly. The horse stood still. At the last possible second Quinn raised the gun to the ceiling before she pulled the trigger. The loud sound of the gunshot filled the barn. Molly whinnied but remained calm.

"Damn. I can't get myself to shoot a horse. I've got nothing against horses. But I have no problem shooting people. That fatso Homer is laying out there in a ditch. He was alive when I left him. If I have any ammo left, I'll kill him on the way out," Quinn said.

"You sick bitch!" Barbara Jean said.

"You ain't seen nothin' yet," Quinn smiled. She punched Barbara Jean in the stomach.

"Ouch, my hand," Quinn said. "If I won't shoot the horses, and there's no other people around, I'll just have to torture you until you talk. You got any power tools around here, electric drills or anything? I don't want to hurt my hands."

"Why don't you cut me down? Give me a gun. We could have a gunfight. What are you afraid of? C'mon. Why not a fair fight?" Barbara Jean asked.

"A fair fight? Life is not a fair fight," Quinn said.

Chapter One Hundred Seventy Four
Spicewood, TX

As I approached the gate to Barbara Jean's ranch everything looked wrong. There was an SUV parked maybe 20 feet in front of the gate. The gate was half open. There were no people around.

I pulled up my GMC beside the SUV and got out. I went and tried to push the gates open enough so that I could drive through, but the gates were stuck.

Screw it, I'm ramming the gates.

I drove the GMC fast into the opening and with a crash the gates sprung apart. I saw what looked like a man's body sticking out of the ditch on the left side of the driveway and walked over to check him out. I found a guy unconscious but breathing. Blood covered the left side of his overalls.

I called 911. I prepared myself for a Texas country slow talker, but I got a very efficient operator on the other end and gave her the situation and the address. "There's a shooter out here. Send the cops too," I said. When she pressed me for more information I said, "I gotta go. Send help now!"

It's a long way, at least ten minutes, to Barbara Jean's ranch from the volunteer fire department where the ambulance waits. I was on my own.

I hopped back in the GMC and spun the tires as I headed for the house. I ran in the front door and called out, "Barb. Barbara Jean. Are you here?"

No response. I looked out the kitchen window and could see the light was on in the barn. I went out the back door, running as fast as I could. It was 300 feet to the barn.

Chapter One Hundred Seventy Five

I could hear Quinn yelling as I approached the barn.
"Life isn't a fair fight, you rich whore! Look at this. What did you do to deserve to have this ranch, this mansion, all your money? The history of the world, all the wars. They're supposedly about religion, ideology. They're about money! And people, when it comes down to it, are willing to kill other people to get the money. So what, I kill people? That's what all the armies are for. Money for the rich people. Everybody I killed deserved to die."

I walked to the opening of the barn door. "Lola didn't deserve to die," I shouted.

Quinn spun around. I used that second to aim my Sig Sauer with both hands, and squared up my body, just like I learned in the shooting lessons. Quinn's face was maybe a foot away from Barbara Jean's. When Quinn turned and made eye contact with me, I shot.

One shot and I was sure she was dead. Quinn's blood splattered onto Barbara Jean's face and blouse. I walked up to Quinn's body and shot her again. I suppressed the urge to empty the whole clip in her. Just to be safe I kicked away her Glock.

Barbara Jean was quiet. When I got closer, she said, "JR what happened to your head?"

"You should see the other guys," I said.

"What?" Barb asked.

"A couple North Koreans. I kept hitting them in their hands with my face," I said.

"Untie me, will you?" Barbara Jean said.

I couldn't untie the knots, so I found a big, serrated knife and cut through the rope. "Where are Tommy and Alice?" I asked.

"They're at the county horseshoe championships. Tommy made the finals," Barbara Jean said.

I looked down at the dead Sierra Quinn. She was lying on her back; her eyes were wide open.

"I'm back. I got the money. One drawback, though," I said.

"What's that?" Barb asked.

395

"My pecker. It looks worse than my face. I don't think I'm going to be able to use it for any…marital purposes for at least a few days," I said.

"Well, I don't think you going to be needing to use it until we get some things worked out," Barbara Jean said. She rubbed her wrists where the ropes had been.

I said, 'What do you mean? I fulfilled my side of the bargain---"

Barb backed away from me, "First of all, you told me that there wouldn't be any danger at the ranch, that all the action would take place thousands of miles from here. She said she shot Homer?---"

"I saw him on the way in. He's alive. I called the ambulance," I said.

She pointed down at Quinn. "Just before you shot her, you mentioned *Lola*! You didn't mention me? You're still in love with Lola?"

That had been a tactical error.

I stammered, "hey, I did save—"

The sounds of sirens were in the distance, getting closer.

"We've got to work things out," Barbara Jean shook her head. "More important. Who do you think… JR, was it you who robbed my father?" Barbara Jean asked.

Trillion is the New Billion Series

Book One: Losing Lola

JR is suspicious…
        …A Wall Street hotshot who's number are
Too good to be true

JR needs to talk to his client, movie star Lola Madison.
She wants to move her money to the hotshot.

Lola is JR's sometime lover. It's complicated.
        …and more dangerous than JR can imagine

Five star review:
I was hooked on Jim Flynn's style after reading his first book "Be Sincere Even When You Don't Mean It," which is written as a fictional memoir. I've just finished his novel "Losing Lola," and it's a compelling, page-turner. His signature humor and economy of words moves the story along at record pace. Flynn's work always offers the bonus of educating us as well. We are not just entertained—we learn things! His characters are well-defined and the story line is well-crafted. "Leaving Lola" is an insightful look into the dubious machinations of the corporate and financial world revolving around a Madoff-like character who develops an ingenious Ponzi scheme. But will he be clever enough to outwit the protagonist J.R. Johnson? Read "Losing Lola" and find out—you won't be sorry!

Amazon.com
Keyword: losing lola jim flynn

Trillion is the New Billion Series

Book Two: The Bitcoin Gambit

Two killers think JR knows…
    …who is really behind Bitcoin

And the killers will do anything to JR to find out

The Government told JR this wouldn't be dangerous

Five star review:
Jim Flynn's latest book, The Bitcoin Gambit, picks up on the further adventures of his intelligent, hilarious protagonist JR Johnson. The mysterious and very current topic of bitcoin is the focus of this action-packed adventure. Once again, Flynn educates us as much as he entertains us. There's a continuity from his previous book, Losing Lola, but JR Johnson fills us in well. Still, I highly recommend reading both. There's a third one in the works as well, and we'll look forward to that. Flynn's style is engaging, fast-paced, and each book is a real page-turner. There's nothing trite or repetitious about the subjects he takes on. His sense of humor and smart analyses are the components of a well-oiled engine that propel the vehicle of his storyline forward. Flynn's gift as a writer is combining humor and savvy in innovative and original ways that distinguish his voice and style. Treat yourself and indulge in an informative and enjoyable journey.

Amazon.com
Keyword: the bitcoin gambit jim flynn

Made in United States
North Haven, CT
29 March 2022

17645090R00238